And The Rain Came Down

TERRIE B. CAMBRIDGE

ISBN: 0615622585
ISBN 13: 9780615622583

Dedications

This book is dedicated to all those who survived Hurricane Katrina and those who didn't. You are not forgotten!

II Corinthians 4: 8

"We are hard-pressed on every side, yet not crushed; we are perplexed, but not in despair; persecuted, but not forsaken, struck down, but not destroyed...."

Acknowledgements

Holy Spirit - Thank you for guiding me daily on this journey of life; I am madly in love with you. Thank you for your kindness, patience, grace, protection and the provision you have dispensed upon me throughout my years on this earth.

Lois and William Barney – My wonderful parents, who sacrificed to give me the best of everything; *Alma Alexis* - My grandmother, who loved me unconditionally, I miss your presence in this realm so very much. *Little Harold* – My cousin; you left us way too soon, but we'll always have fond memories of you. I know one day we will see you all again, on the other side at the appointed time.

Bob Cambridge - My husband, thank you for taking such good care of me during this process. I love the fact that I learn something new from you everyday and I am fascinated by your wisdom. I appreciate you for being the awesome, loving, patient man that you are.

Amanda – My daughter, remember that your past is not your present and your future is fueled by the words you speak and the choices you make. Always let peace guide you; never make a major decision without it.

Julie - My sister, you are the strongest woman I know; thank you for believing in me. Your prayers and your love have gotten me through many hurtles in this race called life.

Michael - My brother; ***Roman and Evan*** - My nephews and ***Ashley*** - My niece; I will always love you unconditionally.

Sharon – My sister, thank you for encouraging me, your words have given me wings to fly beyond what I could have ever imagined and the tenacity to soar beyond my expectations. Love Sunshine!

Special thanks to ***K. Roland Williams***. You gave me the courage to dream and then act on it. You pushed me gently into a realm of creativity without even knowing it. None of this would have been possible without you. Thank you for your friendship and always handling me with extraordinary kindness.

Thank you ***Lamont Gant***, for making my trailer and book cover so spectacular, your patience and professionalism was fleur-delicious!

Lorraine Elzia - My editor, thanks for asking the hard questions that forced me to fill in the blanks. One day we will meet face to face.

Sheryl Wright and Lauren Spalding – Thank you for believing in me from the very beginning. You were officially my first editors. I will never forget your thoughtfulness and positive feedback. Muah!

Catrina - My dear friend, thank you for all your love and support; how interesting, they named a ferocious hurricane after you. Meow.

Dr. Clarence E. McClendon, thank you for your prayers and encouragement. But most of all, thank you for the abundance of extraordinary revelation you've given me over the years. Your willingness to sacrifice your life has changed mine for eternity.

Much love to those of you that have encouraged and supported me during the process of penning this novel. Thank you for the feedback and insight. You know who you are!

And The Rain Came Down

TERRIE B. CAMBRIDGE

Prologue

Edmond Bordeaux had always dreamed of being a doctor, but med school was much different from undergrad, where he had excelled. Tulane University was more than he could handle. He found himself drowning under the rigorous demands of his course load. He'd always been an A student, but now he was hanging on by a thread. Anxiety overtook his senses as he became torn about disappointing his family and giving up on his dream.

The demons of his past had gotten the best of him and the torment had become a distraction. Edmond craved a forbidden temptation that would cause his father great despair, not to mention, an anger that would result in dire consequences. The constant longing for what had been considered taboo in his household, brought a profound sense of guilt for his unacceptable desire.

It all came crashing down on him with the stress of his pending exams that week. Dreams of piercing dark eyes, observing his young naked body haunted him nightly as he slept. He was failing miserably on all fronts, because of the limitation of self-control over his lusts, coupled with sleep deprivation. He was no longer able to focus. His depression became a heavy cloak of protection, against most who tried to befriend him.

Unable to bear the weight of his unrighteous appetites, he pressed his right foot down hard on the gas peddle, closed his eyes and whispered, "God forgive me." He turned the wheel sharply. Suddenly, there was a jarring crash and a calming sensation came over him as a suffocating wind blew swiftly across his face. He was flying, his eyes opened as he went over the Huey P. Long bridge.

Chards of glass swirled about him as the blood gushed from his head. A large piece from the windshield gouged his face during impact and was now deeply imbedded in his frontal lobe; but he felt no pain. The soothing numbness he felt in his body was the result of the bottle of *Vicodin* he had swallowed in the last hour.

He observed the overwhelming sight of the spectacular dark body of water, as his car dropped one hundred thirty-five feet. His midsection was crushed instantaneously by the steering wheel as he hit the water. Amazingly, he was still alive. His brand new convertible that he'd gotten for his graduation was slowly being swallowed up by the murky waters of the Mississippi. Edmond disappointed by the miracle that he was still alive, stretched his trembling bloody hand into the glove compartment and quickly wrapped his fingers around the cold hard steel. There was more than one way to achieve his goal, and since the crash hadn't relieved him of his life as he had hoped. He cocked the gun, put it up to his temple and pulled the trigger. His pain, shame, guilt and confusion, were now over. Finally, all of his unanswered questions would be answered, as it was his plan to confront God face to face.

Approaching Turbulence

*M*ajestic blue skies surrounded us as we began our descent into New Orleans. No matter how good the weather appeared to be, there was always turbulence approaching the Big Easy. YaYa used to say, "It's all those demonic spirits in the atmosphere down here…you know, because of the constant influx of sin and voodoo in these parts." I had lots of memories, some good and some really bad. But I was still madly in love with the tastes, the sounds, the culture and the people of the mysterious town that I grew up in.

I looked forward to diving into that big, lofty, silver pot, with the wooden handles, filled with file' gumbo and French bread drenched with butter. YaYa always made me feel special whenever I came home. She took the time and energy in the kitchen every-day, preparing all of my favorite Creole dishes. My mouth waters just thinking about red beans and rice with hot sausage; crawfish bisque and New Orleans' style barbeque shrimp. And of course, we have to make sure our schedules allow for visits to some of New Orleans' finest restaurants. *Drago's* has charbroiled oysters that are to die for, while *K-Paul's* has the best turtle soup in town, and *Mr. B's* has a hot buttered pecan pie that will knock your socks….

"Please put your seat belts on and place your tray tables and seats in an upright position, as we prepare to land at Louis Armstrong International Airport. Flight Attendants, prepare for landing. Thank you for flying our airline and enjoy your stay."

"Girl, you sound like Bubba Gump. It seems like you eat like a pig, when you come home." Slone said with a smirk. She's been one of my best friends for a long time and is more than eager to accompany me home for a family wedding.

"Yep, in New Orleans we talk about what we are going to have for lunch during breakfast, then plan our dinner menu as we *eat* lunch; and as our dinner is digesting, we're mapping out a course of action for our midnight snack."

"Oh yeah, speaking of pigs, wait until you taste the pig's feet."

"Pig's Feet?"

"Yes, they are simply divine and the pig lips are great too. We'll go a few doors down from my Grandpa's house to the old Gee-chee lady's house. She sells Roman candy, wine candy, huck-a-bucks and just about every part of the pig that can be pickled. Her pig's feet are so juicy, that when you drop one inside a nice bag of *Lays*, plain potato chips, with a shot of hot sauce, you've got your-self the snack of all snacks."

"I'm not going to be eating any pig's feet, while I'm down here!"

"Good, more for me."

We laughed as the plane touched down. When the doors of the plane opened, the heat and humidity rolled through the cabin like a hostile take over. As we deplaned into the terminal, it felt as if we had stepped into a sauna.

"So, what the hell is a – huck-a-buck?" Slone asked as she instinc-tively brushed her long bangs from her eyes. As if on key, Roman pulled up in his brand new *GMC Denali*. His SUV looked like it could be a part of a secret service motorcade. It had a coal black paint job, dark tinted windows, shiny chrome rims and a sound sys-tem so impressive, it could blow your hair backwards while sitting still with the windows rolled up.

Slone stopped in her tracks when she saw him get out of the truck. Roman was six four with a muscular build, that he had

2

obtained from his days playing football at St. Augustine High School. His light butterscotch complexion, wavy sandy brown hair and stunning blue eyes, were accentuated by a smile that forced most women's knees to buckle when his lips parted.

He grabbed me around my waist and lifted me off my feet. "Hey Sister, it's good to see you." I know it's weird, but the boys sometimes called me 'Sister' because YaYa would always say, "Go get your sister" or "Ask your sister." So for a long time I think my brothers just thought that was my name.

"Hey man, how've you been?" I said.

"You know, I've been down here running this town so Mayor Ray Nagin can take all the credit. It's been a long time Sister. I miss hanging out with you."

"Yeah, I guess that's why in all these years, you never came to visit me once in California, right?"

He chuckled as he opened the trunk to put our luggage in. I looked up, and finally there was Slone, just standing with her mouth open.

"Oh, close your mouth and hand Roman your bags would you."

She smiled so hard, that I swore I saw all thirty-two of her teeth, as well as her new fillings, as she handed him her bags.

"Hi, I'm Jenna's friend, Slone."

Roman looked up at her with a big smile. "Hey, I'm Jenna's brother Roman."

"I've heard a lot about you over the years." Slone said.

Roman casually glanced at her, as he turned to get back into the truck, "Okay, ladies let's roll out."

"I heard YaYa had to be put in the hospital last month."

"Yep." They say she was having some problems with her heart. She's all good now; at home cooking fo' y'all right now. When she was in the hospital, we knew she would be alright, because she always had the strength to get herself together to eat whenever she smelled them coming with the food. You know YaYa ain't 'bout to miss no meals."

Before I knew it we were pulling up to the house. As I opened the car door and swung my feet onto the ground, I exhaled. Strangely, I always felt a false sense of security when I was home.

Living in a big city like Los Angeles, offers mounds of stress on a regular basis. The first of the month in California seems to come at a more accelerated pace, than it does for the rest of the country. I didn't worry as much when I was home; as long as I didn't stay longer than four or five days. Any time my visit lasted passed that, my illusion of tranquility would dissipate and turn into a melting pot of regret.

"Wow, this is nice. I didn't realize that you guys lived on a golf course." Slone said.

"Welcome to Pontchartrain Park. We call it, "Pontilly" because Pontchartrain Park and Gentilly Woods are virtually merged together. They're so close to one another that we sort of a combined the two. This was the first black subdivision built during the Jim Crow era, right after World War II. A black man named Joseph Bartholomew designed most of the golf courses in New Orleans, but he was never allowed to play on them, so he built this one back in nineteen fifty two. It was the only golf course opened to black people in the country back then.

This was a very special place to grow up. It was like a beautifully manicured village, where all the families looked out for each other. The close knit community that developed was a blessing and a curse, because if you got caught doing anything you weren't supposed to be doing, your parents heard about it instantly from one of the neighbors. We were especially well-known because Grandpa delivered everyone's mail. So we had to be on our best behavior.

The screen door flew open and out came Grandpa. "Is that my baby girl, Jenna?"

"Yep, in the flesh Grandpa." A smile came across my face the moment I saw him. He stood on the front porch. Two rocking chairs that looked relatively new were on one side of him; and a swing that looked like it had been there since the signing of *The Emancipation Proclamation* was on the other. He grabbed me and hugged me tightly. His scent was almost as comforting as my memories.

"I missed you baby girl."

"I missed you too Grandpa. How is YaYa?"

"She's feeling much better now. She's in the kitchen cooking."

"Grandpa, this is my friend Slone."

"Hey, Baaay-Bay." Holding the A for a three second count was tradition, when Grandpa was happy to meet someone.

Slone extended her hand to shake his. "Pull my finger!"

"Pardon me sir?"

"Pull my finger girl!" His arm was stretched toward her with his index finger in the wind. She innocently pulled his finger, and he let out a thunderous fart. Roman stepped onto the porch with our luggage in tow.

"You're officially part of the family now."

We laughed as Slone flushed with embarrassment said, "Uh, nice to meet you Grandpa."

Slone was one of my best friends. She and I met at a mutual friend's baby shower seven years ago, in Cheviot Hills. We had heard so much about each other, that by the time we met it was if we had been friends for decades. We made an instant connection.

Slone was delightful. Her personality was as optimistic as they come. She saw the world through rainbow-colored eyes. She wore her golden brown hair in a sassy, short haircut which was accentuated by chunks of blonde streaks. She had big green eyes with naturally long lashes that looked as if they had been drenched in *Maybelline* mascara. Her skin was olive and considered dark in the circles she ran in. She was five seven, lean but shapely, firm bodied and gorgeous. She was of Italian decent; her family was from Sicily. She loved to cook whenever she was in town. She was happiest when in the kitchen with an apron on, while a secret pot of ingredients bubbled from one of her newly-found recipes.

Slone was a designer *whore.* She followed the trends of the fashion world with precision. Her closet was filled with the finest of *Norma Kamali, Dolce Gabbana, Issy Miyake, Versace* and *Chanel.* She owned several nice pieces of jewelry from *Harry Winston* and *Tiffany's* that she showed off on occasion. But one of the things I loved most about her was that she wore her material possessions, as well as her subtle beauty, very loosely.

YaYa was in her usual spot; in the kitchen and in front of the stove.

"YaYa!"

"Hey Bay-Bay, how y'all doing?"

She never stopped stirring the contents inside her gigantic gumbo pot, as she turned to look at me. "It's so good to have you home. The gumbo is almost ready." I ran and gave her a big kiss on the cheek, while she gave me a one armed hug. "I want you to meet my friend Slone."

I motioned in the direction of Slone. "This is my Grandmother."

"Just call me YaYa."

"Hello, it's so nice to meet you."

"Pull up a chair and have a seat."

We sat down at the large rectangular kitchen table. It had a tinted glass top that peeked through a pea green laced tablecloth, surrounded by six ugly yellow leather chairs with chrome trim that my grandparents had since I was a kid. Strategically placed on the table was a glass bowl with crawfish painted on it, filled with fruit. There were figs, two pears, an apple and green grapes cascading down the sides, all of them plastic of course, and next to them was a small wooden bowl of pecans, longing to be cracked and eaten.

"How come y'all have a new kitchen and didn't manage to get a new dinette set? You've got new, beautiful oak cabinets, a stainless steel stove, a microwave oven and matching refrigerator; while this old, awful, raggedy table and chairs sits smack dab in the middle."

"I wanted to wait for you. I want you to help me pick one out. You've had many a meal at that old table. Anyway, I know you've got good taste."

"Thanks YaYa, I would love to take you shopping for a new table. That should be fun. Maybe, on Monday, after all the wedding festivities are over. Speaking of wedding festivities, where is Gabriel?"

"He and Sidney went to pick out a few more things for their registry."

Gabriel and Sidney were the reason I was home. They were getting married this weekend. Gabriel is the baby boy of the family. He's caramel colored like me with light brown eyes, thick eye brows and long, dark, perfectly curled eyelashes. He's tall like our dad with huge dimples, a bright smile and a playful personality. Gabriel was a good kid growing up, always eager to help with projects around the house. He always helped Grandpa cut grass, pull weeds in the yard and work on the cars. He also worked four days a week at *McKenzie's Bakery* and still managed to graduate valedictorian from St. Augustine all boys' high school, commonly known as St. Aug.

Gabriel and Sidney started dating when they were juniors in high school. She came from a good upper middle class family. Sidney had straight coal black hair that cascaded down her back and big dark brown eyes that were warm and inviting. Short and stacked is how the boys described her; including Gabriel. She was the kind of girl that most Louisiana men wanted; beautiful, smart, a great cook and her demeanor was sweet and quiet. She graduated from St. Mary's Academy, then went on to Southern University in Baton Rouge and studied Education. Gabriel went to LSU and majored in Architecture. They both graduated and were able to find pretty good jobs in their respective fields. They had been inseparable throughout the years and now having built a solid foundation, they looked forward to starting their family together. Sidney was pregnant with twins and due in October. We were all very excited and happy about both the wedding and the babies. I could hardly wait to become an auntie for the first time. I'd already done way too much shopping for the little ones, at just about every baby store in Los Angeles.

Roman came in, grabbed a piece of French bread and sunk his teeth into it. "So how much longer you gonna stir that pot? When is the food going to be ready? I'm hungry."

"You need to watch your tone, yeah." YaYa said.

"Aw, you know I'm just messing with you. But really YaYa, when is the food going to be ready?"

"Sit down boy. I'll fix you and your Grandpa a plate. Don't forget, you promised to make groceries for me today."

"I didn't forget. I'll get after it when I'm done eating."

"You girls...can fix your plate after I get your brother and Grandpa settled."

"Okay, we're going to wash up and get comfortable first."

Slone and I walked down the hallway, between the walls of pictures that hung on each side of us. Each picture had a different frame–metal, wooden, or plastic–and most of them were older than me. Slone attempted to get a full glimpse of as many family photos as she could.

"We can look at those later." I said, as she kept her stride close behind mine.

Slone remarked as we dragged our suitcases upstairs, "I'm starving, that food on the plane sucked."

"This is your room and bathroom."

"Oh, I didn't know I would have my own room. How many bed rooms are in this house anyway?"

"Five."

"Wow. This is a pretty big house."

"Yep, I'll meet you in the kitchen in a few minutes."

I went to my room and hung a few things in the closet. I loved that all the bedrooms had their own connecting bathroom. It was great not having to share a bathroom with my brothers, while growing up here. I washed up, put on my comfortable sweat suit with my flip flops and headed back to the kitchen. YaYa, Roman and Grandpa were quiet with their heads down concentrating on shrimp po boy sandwiches and bowls of gumbo, each with a small scoop of potato salad right in the middle.

I was preparing some food for me and Slone, when she walked in with a long-flowing, aqua blue, *Bloomingdale's* sundress on, and white sandals with tiny clear rhinestones on them. Roman looked up at her, laughed and said, "Girl where you think you at?"

"Slone, don't pay him any attention. His wardrobe is navy blue; his NOPD uniform or blue jeans."

"You're a New Orleans police officer?" Slone asked.

"Yes, and I'm proud of it."

"Oh."

"What does that mean?"

"I've always heard they were corrupt."

"You mean like those Los Angeles cops that kicked the snot out of Rodney King?"

"Uh, yeah, I guess so."

Slone carefully sat down next to Roman, as he glaringly looked her over. I placed half of a dressed shrimp po boy sandwich and a bowl of gumbo down in front of Slone.

"Thank you. This smells wonderful." She replied, barely looking in my direction.

I sat down with my food and dug into it without hesitation.

Grandpa lifted his head and said, "It's alright if you crack your knuckles at the table, just as long as you don't put your knuckles in your crack." He laughed at himself and went back to eating his gumbo. Slone chuckled nervously. We were used to him, but Slone was a bit taken aback by Grandpa's humor.

Roman finished his food and began to question Slone. "So Slone, what do you do for a living?"

"I am a flight attendant."

"Oh really, where you been to?"

"I've been lots of places."

"Like?"

"Well, I've been to Argentina, Italy, China, Spain and a few others places."

"Did you know that YaYa's been to Italy?"

"Really, how did you like it?"

"That was a very long time ago Cher. My grandfather took me to several countries in Europe when I was a young girl, if I can remember correctly, it was, "Magnifique!"

"So, you learned a little French while you were there, huh?"

"I learned to speak French fluently as a child. My grandfather was actually born in France and my grandmother was Creole."

"Slone, can you speak French?" Roman said.

"Vous avez de beaux yeux."

Roman responded immediately and said, "Merci, your eyes are beautiful too."

"Slone blushed and asked, "Does everyone in the family speak French?"

"Just about Cher." YaYa said.

"Roman let Slone eat her food before it gets cold. You can pick her brain another time."

Roman pushed his chair back, stood to his feet and rubbed his belly.

"So are y'all up to going out tonight?"

"Sure, what do you have in mind?" I said.

"I was thinking *Tipitina's*."

"Great, I love that place."

"Can you hang Slone?" Roman said while still rubbing his belly.

"Yes, I would love to go, thank you for inviting me."

"Girl you need to relax, you're in the Big Easy now."

Grandpa moved into the den, Roman ran off with the grocery list, and YaYa started the water for the dishes, while Slone and I finished our dinner.

"This food is delicious YaYa. Could you could teach me how to make some of your recipes?" Slone said.

"Of course Dawlin, I'll give you as many as you like. I have them all in a book that was hand written by my mother and grandmother. How 'bout you start learning in the morning, for breakfast."

"Oh, thank you so much. I'll look forward to it."

I got up from the table and began to help YaYa clean the kitchen.

"Do you ladies need any help?" Slone asked.

"No, we're good. Maybe you could go in the den and keep Grandpa company for a little while. I'm sure he would like that."

Slone made her way into the den. We could hear Grandpa excitedly invite her to sit down.

"Okay, YaYa, you wash and I'll dry." Staring at the kitchen walls and all of the knickknacks that sat in the same cozy corners that they had for years, everything seemed like old times to me and I was instantly taken back to when I lived here. YaYa and I would have deep conversations, while washing dishes after dinner. She seemed to have a knack for getting the inside track on everyone's business, and I loved to hear her describe all the gossip from the neighborhood. Lots of people trusted her and shared their personal affairs with her. Often when people had problems, they would call her for counseling and prayer. She never denied anyone her time and was always available to share her wisdom.

One night when I was a young girl, she told me a story about my dad, who worked as a seaman. "When the seamen would come into port, they would deposit their semen into any young woman they could find." She said. Well, it was obvious that he had made several deposits into my mother, at least four that I knew of. That's how my brothers and I were born. My parents met one night at a juke joint on Louisiana Avenue called *Jennie's,* whom I was named after. Yes, my parents named me after the neighborhood juke joint. I am Jenna Alexis Bordeaux. I was the second of four children born to Lupanare and Michael Bordeaux.

I live in Los Angeles California. I am an attorney for McBeth & Hastie, one of the largest law firms in the United States, an international firm with offices in Beijing, Munich, Hong Kong, Riyadh and Dubai. I specialize in Intellectual Property Law; patents, trademarks and copyrights.

I'm a mixture of all the attractive qualities of my mother and father. I have light brown eyes and honey colored skin like my dad. My mother's genes gave way to my keen nose, almond shaped eyes, full breasts, shapely long legs and I even have a trace of her long, wavy hair.

I have my dad's wit and sense of humor, but unfortunately I inherited a lesser dimension of my mother's naïveté and paranoia. My brothers and I are products of both of their unresolved issues.

"YaYa, I heard you were in the hospital, how are you doing?"

"Oh, I'm good."

"Roman said you had something wrong with your heart. What did the doctor say?"

"He told me I should rest and try to stay calm. He said it's not a good idea for me to get upset. He put me on a diet too. No red meat, no shrimp, crab or crawfish and low salt. What's there left to eat? Guess his plan is to starve me back to good health."

"Make sure you do what he tells you, your heart is nothing to play with YaYa."

"He told me I need to walk every day for forty five minutes. You know I never been one much for exercise."

"I'll get you a treadmill while I'm here then."

"That would be nice baby, thank you."

"So, you heard anything from Lupanare?"

"No, not for a while now, I think that Dorothy Laveau put some kind of hex on her. She hasn't been right in years. Whenever she would come in town, she was always at that witch's house, sitting there letting her fill her head, year after year, with all dem stories about the Catholic Church and teaching her that silly voodoo mess. After she dropped out of school, I couldn't tell her nothing; she changed Cher. When she met your daddy and had you kids, I thought she would be okay. She was fine for a while, and then all of a sudden, she went awry. Can't nobody control her, she still runs away for long periods of time, and then she shows up months later and dares anyone to ask her 'bout where she's been. We stopped worrying about her and just asked the good Lord to protect her. She's been gone now for ova a year. Last I heard from one of her friends, she was in Europe, roaming around Rome.

You know Miss Dot had the nerve to come ring my bell last week. I ran her off of my porch with my broom. She got so mad with me that I think she tried to put some kinda curse on this family. I told her that Gris-Gris crap don't work on us. She threw some funny looking plastic cards inside the doorway, with the word 'DEATH' written on them, before I could close the door on her. The next morning when I opened the door to get the newspaper, I found a bloody chicken head and feet tied together with some string and pitted olives wrapped in aluminum foil. I threw it in the trash before your Grandpa saw it. I knew he would try and go over there and give her a piece of his mind, and end up with her trying to give him a piece of her–you know what.

Miss Dot is a bit like *Oscar Mayer*, she never met a wiener she didn't like. She had a thing for your grandfather from the first time she laid eyes on him. He ignored her advances and she wasn't happy when he and I got married. Your grandfather was so fine back in the day, that whenever he walked in a room, all the women paused, even the men took notice, the dogs stopped barking and the cats stopped meowing."

"YaYa, I see your funny bone is still working."

"Well, you know what they say, first they put the umbrella in and next thing you know, dey tryin to open it."

Throw Me Somethin Mister

S o, young lady, is this your first time in New Orleans? Grandpa said as he took a bite of a lemon-flavoured *Hubig's pie.*

"Yes sir, it is."

"Well, if you have any questions about our lovely city just let me know. I'm sort of the historian of the family."

"Sure, I have lots of questions for you." Slone said to Grandpa.

"Hit me."

"Well, this is a bit off the subject, and not to be rude, but why does YaYa keep calling me Cher?"

Grandpa laughed and said, "She don't mean no harm child, New Orleans folks call everyone Bay-Bay, Dawlin', or Cher; it's a term of endearment for people we like or want to make feel at home. That's all."

"Oh, thank you for clearing that up for me. I didn't think she remembered my name. So why do they call New Orleans the Crescent City?"

"Well, it's called that because the Mississippi River is in the shape of a crescent, as it bends around the city."

"And the Big Easy, where did that name come from?"

"Well Dawlin, musicians came to New Orleans from some of the upper Mississippi River cities like St. Louis, Memphis and Nashville. When musicians arrived in New Orleans, it was easy for them to score a "*gig*" with bands that played in many of the night-clubs and riverboats that docked along the river. It was easy for them to make a buck; it was easier than any other city around. The "*gigs*" were plentiful and the tips were even better. So as time passed and the name caught on, New Orleans was often referred to, as *The Big Easy*. It fit the personality of our town, and somehow, it just stuck."

"Please Grandpa, tell me more."

"We'll, we've always done things a little bit differently than the rest of the country down here in New Orleans, Louisiana. You can tell that when you cross the Louisiana State line. There's a sign that reads, "Bienvenue a Louisiane" which means, "Welcome to Louisiana" that's the first sign you see when you step foot in the state, and it lets you know that we're somewhat unique. We even operate under a legal system slightly different from the rest of the country, the *Napoleonic Code*. We can walk the streets drinking alcohol. We have a real estate law called "forced heirs" so we don't need a will for our property, because we're automatically forced to give it to our children, even if they treat us like crap. Our politicians and police get away with extortion, stealing government issued funds and infiltrating the poorest areas of the city with drugs and guns. They've even been known to get away with murder on occasion. But whatever you do, be careful not to tie an alligator to a fire hydrant, 'cause they will sho-nuff give you a ticket." Grandpa chuckled and Slone laughed with delight, as he continued.

"Louisiana is the only US state that has "Parishes," a local government equivalent to counties. Louisiana was named after the King of France, Louis XIV. De La Salle claimed the territory for France and he named it La Louisiane meaning, "Land of Louis.""

Louisiana is called by many names, the *Bayou State, Creole State, Pelican State* and the *Sugar State*. New Orleans is known by many names too. *The Big Easy, The Crescent City, NOLA, Nawlins* and *The City That Care Forgot*. Our festivities are decadent and passionate. We dance with umbrellas when it's not raining. We have a day called Mardi Gras where we get to dress up and be somebody other than ourselves for a day, while we eat and drink ourselves into a stupor.

We have what we call *Krewes* that ride on floats in the parades, and if you raise your hands and scream out, "Throw Me Somethin', Mista" they'll throw you some colorful Mardi Gras beads, a cup or some doubloons. And if you go to the Zulu parade, you might just get yo 'self a decorated coconut. You can also partake in one of the *tableau balls*; that's when we celebrate by choosing a king and queen, and dress up in our best formal attire as we become their loyal subjects for an evening.

We have a cake called, *"King Cake,"* that we hide a small, plastic baby inside; if the person that finds it is lucky enough not to swallow the baby and choke to death, then it's their turn to buy the next cake. On Fat Tuesday, or any day for that matter, loose women will expose their naked breasts to you, if you yell "Show your tits" for a pair of plastic Mardi Gras beads. Then the next day we begin the Lenten season on Ash Wednesday, confess our deliberate sins to our parish priest, who probably has a hangover himself; then we receive ashes on our foreheads and spend the next forty days atoning for our debauchery.

Hell, we even created our own music called Jazz, Zydeco and Blues. We have catfish and crabs that are blue. We have mud-bugs that we eat called crayfish. When you go out to our restaurants, they usually give you a little something extra with your meal; it's a small complimentary gift which we call "Lagniappe." Then, to stay cool when it gets hot, we stand in line for a styrofoam cup filled with thinly shaved ice with lots of heavy syrup topped with condensed milk, which we call a *Snowball.* But when we're too broke or too lazy to go to the snowball stand, we go to one of the neighbor's houses, and for fifty cents you can get a good old fashioned *huck-a-buck*, which is flavored syrup and *Kool-Aid* in a frozen *Dixie* cup.

We call our Godparents, *"Parain"* and *"Nanan,"* and we don't 'shop' *for* groceries; we '*make*' groceries.' And we don't just have normal roaches like everybody else; we have super hero roaches, dey fly, dey hard to catch and difficult to kill. If anyone tells you dey put a Gris-Gris on you, then dey put a voodoo spell on you.

Which nobody really believes in anymore, most people just do it for fun nowadays.

The older folks speak French in front of their kids so they don't understand when they're gossipin' or cussin'. And we celebrate any and everything; a graduation, a birthday, a wedding, a retirement, a new baby, a new job, a good day, a bad day, or even when Pookey comes home from jail. We make sure that every celebration has excessive amounts of food, alcohol, music, loud talking and a good card game.

By the way, did you know that Jenna was the queen at the *Beau Brummel Mardi Gras* ball when she was a senior in high school?"

"Really, she never told me that."

"Oh, yes Cher, she was simply beautiful. She had on a big white fluffy dress with sequins and fine embroidery on it. The huge crown she wore was filled with jewels that looked like diamonds and a scepter to match. We were her humble servants for one spectacular night. I will never forget how stunning she was that night. Then afterwards we had a big catered breakfast at one o'clock in the morning, with the best grits and grillades this side of the bayou. Let me go check and see if I can find the pictures for you."

"Okay Grandpa, that's enough history for one night."

"No, I'm enjoying this. I want to see the pictures from the ball, Queen Jenna."

"We can look at those tomorrow. Slone you need to change so we can get out of here."

"What's wrong with what I have on?"

"Nothing, you look fine. YaYa, we're leaving now." I yelled."

"Okay, y'all pass a good time."

"Goodnight Grandpa."

"Night Cher; y'all be careful out there in dem streets."

Who Dat?

I grabbed my *Birkin* bag that Slone bought me for my birthday, then, Roman, Slone and I headed out. As we drove up Napoleon Avenue and turned the corner, Slone asked, "How do you pronounce the name of this street?"

"Tchoupitoulas (Chop-a- two- les)"

"So where are we going?"

"We're going to check out one of Crescent City's favorite sons; James Rivers. Have you ever seen a black man play the bag pipes?" Roman said.

"No, I can't say that I have. Does he wear a kilt?"

"I don't know about the kilt Slone, but trust, you'll enjoy this set. We walked up to the entrance of *Tipitina's*, "Five Dollars" the man at the door said.

"Oh, I'll get it. In LA, clubs cost a small fortune to get into." Slone said.

"No, I got this, go on in with Jenna."

As we walked in, the smell of Creole and Cajun cuisine mingled with alcohol and cigarette smoke instantly filled our nostrils. The crowded uptown jazz club seemed bigger than I'd remembered. As we canvassed the dimly lit room for a table, I looked forward to seeing the James Rivers Movement. I had fond memories of hanging out with his daughters after school and spending time with him and his family. Mr. Rivers slept by day and played music by night. The soothing sounds I heard floating through his house during my adolescent years, became the origin for my love for good music.

"Hey Jenna, get us a table upstairs and I'll order some drinks and oysters on the half shell." Roman said. "What y'all drinking?"

"I'll take a *Corona* with lime."

"What's your poison Slone?"

"Can I get one of those Hurricane drinks please?" Slone's glance was fixated on Roman as she made her drink request.

We spotted the last open table upstairs and moved in quickly to snatch it up.

"Roman seems really nice, he's good looking too." She shifted in her seat avoiding eye contact as she spoke.

"Not a good idea Slone." The look I gave her emphasized my point.

"What? I just said he was nice that's all."

I saw Roman walking toward us, as he motioned for us to come.

"Hey, y'all come on back downstairs; you'll never guess who I ran into."

"Who?"

"Just come on and you'll see." When we got downstairs, I looked around to see who he could be talking about. As we approached the table, I saw Chase jump up from his seat. "Hey girl, come over here and give me a hug."

"Is everyone in this town beautiful or what?" Slone said under her breath.

Chase wrapped his arms around me and kissed me lightly on the curve of my neck. Then he turned to Slone and said, "Hi, I'm Chase."

Roman came to the table with drinks in hand from the bar. "The food is coming."

"Food? We just ate dinner with your family." Slone said.

"I just ordered some oysters on the half shell."

"So Jenna, how's life in Los Angeles?" Chase said.

"Oh, it's good. How've you been?"

"Everything is cool with me."

"How's your family?"

"Mom is hanging in there, she's been sick. She is diabetic now and my sister Ashley is married with two kids."

"Tell them hello for me."

"Why don't you come by the house and tell them yourself? My mom would love to see you."

"I doubt that." Chase didn't respond, he picked up his drink and took a long, uncomfortable sip. Chase had been my first boyfriend, but he was also a part of our family. He grew up three blocks away from us and was at our house almost every day. His home was not a happy one. His parents fought all the time, his dad wasn't the ideal husband or father. He was like Houdini; he would disappear for weeks at a time and then reappear like he'd been present the entire time. His mom eventually became nothing but an emergency contact person.

Chase spent lots of time with my brothers and my grandfather. Guess he loved grandpa's old stories as much as we did. They spent countless hours outside, cutting grass, fixing cars, cleaning out the garage and whatever men folk do. Back in the day, Chase was the love of my life. He didn't take my moving to California very well, I'd heard that he was so dispirited that he walked around for months looking like a dirty *Q-tip*, gaunt and emaciated. It was still hard to imagine him that way. Needless to say, his mom didn't take kindly to me being the cause of her son's suffering.

Chase was charming, witty, funny and highly intelligent. Six one, bow legged, beautiful hazel eyes, a head full of curly hair and a *Colgate* smile that could make your heart skip a beat. He was something special and definitely a southern gentleman. We were so young to have developed such a bond back then, but it was sad when it ended with such unbridled sorrow. When I close my eyes, I can still smell the fragrance of the dark pink azaleas and white rose bushes that were in full bloom in YaYa's garden that day. I will never forget the sadness in his eyes. He had pools of tears mingled throughout his long eyelashes that hot summer day. With his heart in my hand, I cut the umbilical cord with one clean stroke. I was teary eyed too, but determined to leave New Orleans, the place that had ultimately become the source of so much pain and disappointment for me.

Roman turned to Slone as the waitress put down the large tray of oysters on the half shell with lemon slices and a bottle of *Tabasco* sauce on the table.

"Ever had raw oysters before, Slone?"

"No, I don't like the look of them."

"Try one."

"No, thank you."

"Please, just one." Roman squeezed lemon juice across a few and doused them with hot sauce. "Let me show you how it's done." He threw back one, two, and then a third one down his throat really fast and swallowed. "Now the key is not to chew, just swallow. *You do swallow don't you?*" We laughed as Slone hesitantly picked one up. She had a scowl on her face; she pinched her nose and put one in her mouth but had a hard time swallowing.

"Put your head back and let it go down your throat smoothly." Roman coaxed her through the motions. She did exactly as she was told and came up with her eyes wide open.

"Yuck." She sipped some of her Hurricane and blinked her eyes and smiled. "Okay, I did it. What about you Jenna, why don't you have one?"

"Oh no, I like my oysters fried."

"That's not fair."

Roman stood up behind Slone and said, "Let's do another. This time I'll help you."

"Okay, one more."

Roman stood over her as she held her head back. She opened her mouth, he slid one off the shell and gently moved his hand across her throat. "How was that?"

"Not so bad this time," she uttered as she gagged.

"I knew the first time I laid eyes on you girl, that with a little encouragement and proper instruction, you had the potential to *swallow*." A wicked grin crept across his face and it was evident that he was amused by his own statement.

"Roman, please! Sit down and leave Slone alone." He sat down like a little mischievous boy grinning from ear to ear.

The crowd began to cheer and clap as James Rivers took the stage. I swayed as he played so many of my favorite songs. *Southern Comfort, Ball of Funk, Baby What You Want Me To Do* and *Smokey, The Funky Soprano* all flowed melodiously out into the crowd. We were captivated by the sexy sounds of New Orleans jazz, that we all loved. He switched his instruments from saxophone, to flute... flute to harmonica and then to his glorious bagpipes. As he played the bagpipes, Slone's mouth dropped as she marveled at one of only three known artists in the history of jazz to play the bagpipes. I sipped on my drink as I took in the hypnotic sounds and intoxicating aromas of the city of my youth. I enjoyed the feeling of being totally submerged within the intensity and passion of the people of New Orleans.

James Rivers began playing the sultry song, *Summertime.* My eyes searched across the table for Chase. Our eyes met, and without a word we both went back in our minds to the time we first heard this song. One night after picking up muffulattas at the Central Grocery Store, we strolled along the Moon Walk, as a street musician played a *provocative* rendition of this song on his saxophone. It was the first time I realized how romantic New Orleans could be.

Chase stood to his feet and gently took my hand and led me onto the dance floor. We made our way through the other couples who felt the same gravitational pull toward the dance floor as we did. He pulled me towards him, his cheek touching mine. I closed my eyes and held him tightly. He felt so good. I could feel the shape of his well-chiseled body. Not an ounce of body fat. Before I could allow myself the satisfaction of reminiscing fully, the song changed and the popular song *Mr. Magic* brought a flood of people to the dance floor. Suddenly, it was an immediate shift into the old school bus stop. Chase and I laughed as we fell in line with the familiar moves. Step forward, then back, side to side, tap, tap; dip turn and begin again. The dance floor was jam packed, as everyone moved harmoniously. I realized that there are just some things you never forget, no matter how much time has passed.

Then, the first blow of the horn of the second line lit up the entire place. We dashed back to our tables to reach for our napkins. Everyone in the place knew that the song being played was traditionally the signal that the set was coming to an end. Roman seized the moment and grabbed Slone into the single-file line that formed and we danced around the room.

"The rhythm of the music is so intoxicating." Slone said as she fell ungracefully back into her seat.

"Maybe it's those Hurricanes you been sucking down. You need to slow it down, this isn't one of those Mexican margaritas you get at *El Torito's* in LA you know."

"I can hold my liquor; don't worry about me, I've got this."

"Okay, don't say I didn't try to stop you." The crowd was beginning to thin out. "I think I'm ready to call it a night guys."

"Me too." Roman said. "Gabriel and I have to get up early to get fitted for our tux."

"That's right man, so do I; I totally forgot." Chase took one last sip from his drink.

"Chase are you in the wedding too?"

"Yes indeed, you know that's my brother from another mother."

"So I guess that would make me your sister now, wouldn't it?"

"Please Jenna, spare me."

Sure enough, as soon as we were getting ourselves together to leave, Slone stood up with a peculiar look on her face. Then, without much warning she projectile vomited on just about everyone within range. Everything she had eaten was now on the table and some even went as far as the dance floor. We all ran for cover and the people around us scattered like cock roaches on a hot summer's night. The contents of her stomach now laid in full view for all to see. YaYa's file' gumbo, shrimp po boy, and oysters on the half shell now mixed together and smelled like rotten eggs. Not to mention the three hurricanes she'd drank like it was *Kool Aid*, which turned it all a shade that I don't think exists on the color wheel. The grotesque stench made us gag. I saw several people, searching desperately for napkins to wipe the putrid regurgitation from various parts of their bodies and clothing. Slone sat down at the table, wiped her mouth with a napkin, picked up a half full glass of water, swished it around in her mouth, spit, then let out a really loud belch. She popped up out of her seat and said, "Okay, I feel great, what's next?" We all burst into laughter and shook our heads as we cleaned ourselves off. "I think it's time to go home now. You've had enough fun on your first day in the *city that care forgot.*

We walked silently and briskly to the car, our clothes clung to our bodies. The humidity was so thick it felt as if you needed a chain saw to cut it. I wondered as we walked, "*How in the hell could it still be ninety degrees at three o'clock in the morning? I guess I've been gone for far too long.*"

As we were getting into the car Slone yelled, "Oh, no. Not yet. When do I get to show my tits? I thought that was a New Orleans' tradition."

"Not ever. Now get yo' behind in this car, now! Nobody wants to see those mosquito bites anyway."

"Oh, I wouldn't mind seeing them." Roman said.

"Oh, you hush, don't encourage her. No one's showing any tits tonight."

"It was good to see you again, Chase." I said.

"What are you guys doing tomorrow?"

"We have a full day. I promised Grandpa I would go with him to visit my Parain, doing some shopping with YaYa, and showing my company around town."

"Can you make some time for me?"

"Let me get back to you on that."

"Alright, but all I have to do after I get fitted for my tux is go ova by my mama n em."

"Good night Chase." I blurted out.

The next morning I got up and went to the kitchen for some juice. YaYa and Slone were ready to make breakfast. I sat down at the table and picked up *The Times-Picayune* newspaper.

"So Slone, we're gonna make some salmon and shrimp croquettes, cheesy garlic, shrimp and grits, with homemade biscuits this morning, okay? Here is the recipe book. Read me the ingredients and afterward we'll do this together." YaYa said.

Salmon and Shrimp Croquettes
    Ingredients:
    Salmon
    ½ pound Shrimp
    1 small onion minced
    1 egg
    ½ cup bread crumbs
    1/8 teaspoon hot pepper sauce
    2 tablespoons all purpose four
    2 tablespoons chopped parsley
    ¼ teaspoon black pepper
    ¼ cup butter
    3 tablespoons olive oil

Combine salmon, chopped shrimp, onion, egg, bread crumbs, hot pepper sauce, black pepper, parsley. Mix. Shape into patties and dust with flour. Chill in ice box for 20 minutes. Then in a large skillet, heat butter and olive oil over medium to high heat. Cook patties until nice and brown.

Slone was beaming like a kindergartener who was ecstatic about learning from her favorite teacher at a Creole cooking school. It was refreshing to see her happy. She had gone through so much in the past few years. She was a breast cancer survivor; she'd gone through chemo, loss her hair and had been on strong meds for a couple of years.

She had survived one of the nastiest divorces ever in the history of divorces. She was married for five years to one of California's most successful premier real estate tycoons. He was older and had two daughters, which Slone helped him raise. She took care of those girls as if she had given birth to them. She took them shopping, helped them with home work, and even took them on trips.

Once she became Mrs. Ethan Beck, she retired from the airlines and became a stay-at-home wife. He was rich and away from home often. They lived in a beautiful three story glass house in Malibu. Life was wonderful and Ethan seemed as if he really loved her. They appeared to have the perfect family situation, until Slone became ill. He was no longer affectionate and was always too busy to go with her on doctor visits.

I took her when she was too exhausted and nauseous to drive. It was the least I could do for my friend. She was like a sister to me. We talked every day and spent time on the weekends going out or just hanging out at the malls shopping and eating out. We'd get our hair and nails done every other week on Saturday mornings, then to breakfast at the *Rose Café* in Venice. Every now and then we would make sandwiches, get a couple of bottles of *Chardonnay*, go to the news stand, pick up the latest tabloid and fashion magazines and head for the beach. We would laugh and talk like two high school girls for hours at a time. When she married Ethan, those times, for us, became few and far between.

When she was no longer able to take care of his girls the way he had become accustomed to, he became pensive. Their love affair came to an abrupt end as he announced that she was of no value to him any more. This hurt Slone to the core. She tried at first to convince him to hire a live-in nanny until she recovered. But he stood firm on the fact that he didn't believe in wasting his money on that kind of foolishness, because that's what his wife was for.

On her last day of chemo, she was served divorce papers before she'd left the house. She was almost destroyed, but somehow she managed to handle it with dignity and grace. Slone ended up with an enormous settlement that included the house they lived in and everything in it. His car collection, a beach house at *Martha's Vineyard*, two other properties, a strip mall and alimony payments that would make the average person's head spin. But their divorce settlement meant nothing to Ethan. He had so much property and money that he never missed a beat because of what he had to give Slone.

Slone kept her head up high and continued on her journey to recovery. She's been in remission for two years now, her hair has grown back and she looks great. She didn't allow herself the luxury of becoming bitter, angry or resentful and never let what happened to define her.

Southern Biscuits
Ingredients
2 cups flour
4 teaspoons baking powder
1/4 teaspoon baking soda
¾ teaspoon salt
2 tablespoon butter
2 tablespoons shortening
1 cup chilled buttermilk
Preheat oven to 450 degrees

In a large mixing bowl, combine flour, baking powder, baking soda, and salt. Use your fingers and rub butter and shortening into dry ingredients until mixture looks like crumbs. Make a well in the center, and pour in the chilled buttermilk. Stir just until the dough comes together. The dough will be sticky.

Turn dough onto floured surface, dust top with flour and gently fold dough over on itself a few times. Press into a 1 inch thick round. Cut out biscuits with a 2 inch cutter; be sure to push down through the dough. Place biscuits on baking sheet. Place in oven for 15 to 20 minutes or until golden brown.

YaYa of course could make these dishes in her sleep. She wanted Slone to feel like she was helping, but most of all, that Slone was learning to cook some of our beloved family recipes. She was wonderful that way. Cooking was something I had never really been interested in. I figured, *why bother when everything was always prepared by the time I got home anyway.*

"Okay Cher, now that we know that you can read, it's time for you to get your hands dirty and get to cooking."

"Okay, YaYa, what do you want me to do?"

"Take the shrimp out the ice box and start peeling and deveining them for the grits."

Slone was happier than a pig in slop. She was really getting into the idea of learning how to cook some traditional Creole food. I was proud of her. We rarely cooked at home in LA, we dined at the hottest new restaurants in town as often as we could, unless Slone begged me to come over and try one of her new dishes.

"After you get done with the shrimp Slone, you can chop up the seasoning, while I check on the biscuits."

"Okay, YaYa."

Slone yelped when she opened the refrigerator. YaYa and I laughed knowing that she must have spotted Grandpa's extra set of teeth. "Oh Cher, don't mind that, those are just Grandpa's dentures. Don't worry dey not gonna bite you." YaYa said as she giggled. "Jenna, can you get off your butt and put the chicken broth on the stove please?"

"I didn't ask anybody to teach me how to cook."

"Just do what I asked you. You know I'm not too old to put you ova my knee no."

"Okay, okay. I'll get it, YaYa."

"When you're done, show Miss Slone over here that you can read too. Read the recipe for the shrimp and grits out loud so she understands what she's doing."

I put down the newspaper, slowly got up from my comfortable chair, took out a large skillet, poured the chicken broth in and turned the fire on high so it could come to a boil. I never said I didn't know what to do, I just choose not to. I've watched YaYa all of my life, slave over a hot stove. I was determined that it would not be me in the future. It was way too time consuming. "Alright Slone, listen up."

Spicy Garlic Shrimp and Cheese Grits
Ingredients:
4 cups chicken broth
1 teaspoon salt
1 cup quick grits
2 tablespoons margarine
1 bunch green onions
1 green bell pepper
2 cloves garlic
1 pound peeled and deveined shrimp
1 cup shredded cheddar cheese
½ teaspoon black pepper
Pinch of cayenne pepper
Preheat oven to 350 degrees
Grease baking dish

Bring chicken broth and salt to a boil in a saucepan. Stir in grits, return to simmer, stir. Cook 20 minutes. Melt butter in saucepan, stir in green onions and garlic for 10 minutes. Stir in shrimp, cheese, black and cayenne pepper. Pour sautéed ingredients into grits and stir. Place in baking dish and sprinkle more cheese on top. Bake 30 minutes or until cheese is melted.

Chinese Laundry

aYa was sitting in the den. She had a pile of freshly washed and dried clothes on the sofa next to her. She was folding them while watching a rerun of *The Jeffersons*. Every now and then she'd let out a slight chuckle in response to something George Jefferson said that tickled her; it was her idea of relaxing. I decided to join her and pushed the fragrant bundle of clothes closer to her as I made room for me to sit down. She turned toward me and smiled, then went back to enjoying her show. We sat together folding and glancing at the television screen and giggling. These were the moments that I missed. The small, seemingly insignificant times I'd spent with YaYa means so much to me now. I smiled on the inside with pure joy. I was glad to see her sitting for a change. She was always cooking, washing, changing bed sheets, gardening or out making groceries to cook for some event. When YaYa retired from nursing, she started her own catering business, successfully I might add. But even during her so-called time of relaxation, it still involved keeping things in order around the house.

Roman had taken off for the week, he and Slone went sightseeing. Grandpa was at one of his friend's houses playing Tonk and

Bid Whist. Gabriel and Sidney were at the doctor's office and I was finally getting some much needed rest.

The show ended and the clothes were folded as neat and tight as Chinese laundry. YaYa had taught me very young how to fold everything neatly. That became one of my pet peeves. Sometimes when I go over to a friend's house and see their linen closets in disarray, I refold and rearrange everything in it until I'm satisfied. They love it when I say I need to use the bathroom, because they know I'll always sneak a peek into their linen closets.

"I sure wish that Edmond could have been here for the wedding." I said.

YaYa was very quiet.

"I miss him. I remember when he'd take me by the hand while we'd run down to the corner to catch the Roman Candy man in the horse and buggy when I was a little girl. Why doesn't anybody talk about him anymore? You guys act as if he never existed."

"Your Grandfather was so happy when he was born. Your parents gave him the honor of naming him, and he took one look at him and said, 'This one is strong and smart, he's going to be a doctor.' So he named him after Edmond Doc Souchon, a jazz guitarist who recorded some of the first jazz albums ever made, before eventually becoming a successful doctor. Edmond was everything that your grandfather said he'd be and more. He was strong, brilliant, and the happiest child we'd ever seen until..."

"Until what, YaYa?"

She stood to her feet, picked up as many of the folded clothes as she could carry and walked away into the bedroom. When she came back to get the rest of the clothes, I said, "So YaYa, you never answered me, what happened?"

"I'm done with this conversation Cher. I'm going to put the rest of these clothes away and start my dinner."

"How about you just sit down and put your feet up for a change. You need to get some rest, you just got out of the hospital two weeks ago, remember? I'll take care of it. As a matter of fact, I'll cook dinner too." As much as I hated cooking, I would do anything to get YaYa off her feet.

"Oh, thank you Bay-Bay; I sure do miss having my girl at home. You know these men act like their hands are broken; if it doesn't have anything to do with fixing something or breaking something they're not good for nothing.

I knew not to push YaYa when she was done speaking on a particular subject, so I let her be. As I walked back towards the kitchen, I stopped to look at the family photos that lined the walls of the hallway. There was a beautiful black and white, eight by ten, picture of YaYa and Grandpa. The faded print gave me a warm and cozy feeling as if I were stepping back in time. She was stunning and he was very handsome. I stared at generations of graduation, baby and holiday photos. She even had a picture of Chase and me at our prom. My hair was a hot mess, but my dress was fabulous. There was a really cute photo of Roman and Gabriel, both of them with their two front teeth missing, posing on their big wheels.

I was so proud of my brothers; Gabriel graduating from LSU with his degree in architecture and Roman a New Orleans' police officer. Unfortunately, there were no pictures of Edmond, YaYa kept the pictures of him hidden and tucked away in a safe place. She said it was just too painful for Grandpa to see him every day after he died. I didn't agree; but it was her house—her rules.

It was sad that Lupanare and Daddy were absent from the majority of the years displayed on YaYa and grandpa's walls. There was only her high school graduation picture and one with Lupanare as a baby sitting on YaYa's lap. There was also a wedding picture of her and daddy cutting their wedding cake and one with the two of them jumping the broom. None of the pictures depicted my parents with their kids, probably an omen of their absence throughout our lives as we were growing up.

I sort of understood Daddy Bordeaux's situation; I guess. He lived on a ship nine months out of the year. He always came home and brought lots of presents from places from all over the world for us. One time he brought each one of us kids these beautiful, 18-carat gold, handmade, Egyptian cartouche pendants that we all still wear to this day. He also gave Lupanare and YaYa, beautiful glass perfume bottles with intricate hand-painted flowers on them. He told us intriguing tales about foreign places and how people were generally the same everywhere and the only differences were their customs.

One night Daddy Bordeaux took us to the drive-in movie theater. It was so much fun, we rolled down the windows and the waitress would come and take our orders. He'd hook the speaker onto the window so we could hear the sound in the car. Going to the -drive-in became the foundation of some of the best memories that we all shared together. The worst thing about trying to enjoy a movie outdoors was the mosquitoes. They tore into us as we laughed, cried, and closed our eyes tightly during the scary parts. The aftermath of bites always resulted in the constant scratching of our arms and legs all the way home.

When we got home from the movies that night I distinctly remember that although he had given everyone their presents earlier that day, Daddy Bordeaux called Roman into the bedroom.

"Hey little man," he said. "Let me holla at you for a minute."

He handed Roman a small wooden box with a shiny gold lock with his name written in hieroglyphics on the top of it.

"If anybody ever fucks with you on a grand scale, give them a dose of this."

He opened the box and it was filled with some exotic looking dried leaves, that when boiled became deadly.

"These were created by the hands of the devil himself. Now make sure you use the good sense that God gave you when choosing to use this, because it is a decision you will have to live with for the rest of your life. A few sips of this and they'll be dead in minutes. Now I'm not talking about someone just irritating you, making fun of you, calling you out of your name or getting on your nerves. If you decide to use this, make sure that the cause is something so profound, that it touches you deep down in the pit of your stomach. I pray you never have to use this in your life, but I want you to have it just in case you need it. Treasure it and keep this in a safe place at all times. Never, as long as you live, tell a living soul about this. Do you understand me son?"

"Yes, Daddy Bordeaux, I do."

"That's my boy" he said as they went to find a hiding place for Roman's special gift.

The next day Daddy Bordeaux took us to Pontchartrain beach. He let us ride all the rides as many times as we wanted and let us eat all the junk food our little tummies could digest. I remember Lupanare came with us. I was so happy. She sat on a bench and watched us ride. She smiled, clapped and worried all at the same time. My dad, brothers and I rode the Zephyr, the tea cups and the Ferris wheel with glee. Lupanare didn't like the way the rides made her feel. She said they made her dizzy and nauseous. I didn't mind that she wouldn't ride. I was just happy that we were all together.

We all cried when it was time for Daddy Bordeaux to leave. It was almost unbearable to watch Lupanare during the day's right before his departure. She would follow him around the house, hugging and kissing him so much that it got on his nerves. She prepared all his favorite dishes and even made extras for him to take with him. I know it had to be hard for her not to have her husband around while raising four kids, but he always made sure that the house-note, gas and lights were paid every month on time.

Lupanare was a bookkeeper at Rhodes Funeral Home, so she made more than enough money for clothes, food and some savings. She must have gotten a raise or something because all of a sudden she had extra money to shop for some nice things for herself. I remember her coming home with shopping bags from *Gus Mayer, Maison Blanche, Godchaux's* and she began buying her makeup from *Katz* and *Besthoff* drug stores. She eventually accumulated lots of jewelry and clothes. All her friends envied her exquisite taste.

Then she started going out with her girlfriends every Friday and Saturday nights. That's when the tide seemed to change. All of us kids began spending weekends with either Uncle Harold and Auntie Sharon, or YaYa and Grandpa. That was always fun. We played games like *Scrabble, Monopoly,* and *Operation,* blind man's bluff and hide and seek. My cousins always tricked me though. When it was my turn to hide, they would leave me hiding and go outside and play while I was still in the closet somewhere counting. Children can be so cruel. One time I had been hiding for so long that Auntie Sharon had to come and find me. I cried with embarrassment because everyone made fun of me. They teased me a lot growing up because I was so gullible. I have to admit I began to enjoy the attention a little.

We were too young and so well insulated by our extended family to realize that our father had abandoned us and eventually our mother would follow suit. Sometimes you don't realize until you're an adult that the family you grew up in was dysfunctional. At the time, you don't know anything else, so your world seems normal. That's how we viewed our upbringing – normal

I went into the kitchen and put a big pot of water on to boil, then turned the oven on three hundred seventy-five degrees. I decided to make a Creole eggplant casserole and some Cajun fried green tomatoes. I rinsed the eggplant real good and peeled five eggplants. I took out all of my ingredients.

1 onion chopped fine
½ cup chopped bell pepper
1 stalk celery chopped
1 tablespoon minced garlic
½ stick butter
½ cup green onions chopped
½ teaspoon black pepper
A dash of cayenne pepper
Cajun seasoning to taste
1 pound shrimp peeled and deveined
½ pound crabmeat
2 cups Italian bread crumbs

While I boiled the eggplant until it was very tender, almost mushy, I cut up my seasonings, melted the butter on medium heat then put in my onions, bell pepper, garlic and sautéed for about five minutes. Then I added my eggplant, shrimp and crabmeat and cooked for twenty-five minutes, stirring it occasionally, gradually adding bread crumbs until all of the liquid was absorbed. Then I added cayenne pepper, black pepper and seasoning salt to taste. I placed the mixture into a rectangular, glass baking dish and spread more bread crumbs over the top and put it in the oven until the bread crumbs on top where nice and brown.

I was slicing my tomatoes when the phone rang.

"Oh, hi Auntie Bristol, yes, let me get a pen so I can take down the information. Okay, yes, yes. I'll let her know. I'll see you guys soon. Bye, bye."

"Who was that on the phone?" YaYa yelled.

"That was Auntie Bristol; she said they would be in on Friday morning."

"Why is that girl so hard headed? I told her I needed her to get here to help me with some last minute things for the wedding."

"Lennox has a school project she needs to finish on Thursday. But don't worry, I'll help you with whatever you need."

"But I asked *her* to do it."

"Okay, YaYa whatever."

"You be careful girl…"

"Sorry YaYa."

I went to the bed room and grabbed my Ipod. I needed some entertainment while I cooked. On my return to the kitchen, I popped in my ear plugs and pressed play on my *iPod shuffle* and snapped it onto my shirt. I gathered my ingredients to make my fried green tomatoes.

4 large green tomatoes
2 eggs
1/2 cup milk
1 cup flour
½ cup bread crumbs
½ cup cornmeal
2 teaspoons seasoning salt
¼ cayenne pepper
Vegetable oil

I finished slicing my tomatoes, then poured the vegetable oil into a deep skillet on medium to high heat, then put the milk and eggs in a bowl and whisked. I put flour in a bag, then on a plate I mixed the bread crumbs, cornmeal, seasoning salt and cayenne pepper. I put the tomatoes in the bag of flour and shook them until they were completely coated; then one by one I dipped them into the egg and milk mixture. I dredged them in the breadcrumb and cornmeal mix and placed them in the vegetable oil, fried up several batches until they were crispy and brown on both sides and then started on my tangy tarter sauce for dipping.

Cities Of The Dead

*R*oman and Slone playfully brushed against each other periodically as they walked the tiny streets of the cemetery, while he gave her a brief Crescent City history lesson.

"Folks used to try and put coffins six feet under, until one day they realized that the water level during the rainy season made them pop up out of the ground. So to keep the coffins under ground, they'd drill holes in the top to let the air escape. Then they weighted them down with rocks and sand. That didn't work and the soggy corpses didn't decompose the right way. Eventually that practice lead to some nasty and really unsanitary conditions. The only solution was for them to bury the dead above ground." Roman said with an air of drama in his words before he continued.

"They usually put the bodies inside the walls of the tombs because it gets so hot and humid that the tombs become like an oven and the high heat causes the bodies to decompose faster than normal; sort of like a slow cremation. Then within about a year they're nothing but bones left. Then, they sweep the bones into a hole in the floor of the tomb, and get ready for the next occupant. It's common practice to bury all the members of a family or even multiple families in the same tomb. They just add names and the dates to the headstone that's already there."

"I love how the family tombs look like miniature houses complete with iron fences and the rows of tombs look like real streets, with street signs and everything." Slone showed her fascination for her surroundings with a gleeful innocence.

"That's why it's called the "Cities of the Dead.""

"Oh my God, what is that?" Slone said.

"Don't be afraid."

Roman took Slone by the hand and led her to the tomb of Marie Laveau the voodoo queen. They both stared with curiosity at the sight of the items that adorned her tomb. People had left all sorts of offerings; flowers, Mardi Gras beads, some Canadian coins, a dusty discolored skull, a bottle of whiskey, something unidentifiable in a small jar and even a pair of old high heeled shoes.

"She must have been popular. Who was she?"

"Marie Laveau, but most people don't know that her legend was actually that of two people; the first was the mother and the second, her daughter. The mother was born in New Orleans and was a free woman of color. She was mixed with black, white and Indian blood and considered mulatto. She was a hairdresser that catered to wealthy white and Creole women who divulged their most intimate stories about their husbands, lovers, business dealings, and even about the other women their husbands slept around with. She eventually gave up the hairdressing business and spent her time becoming the voodoo queen of New Orleans.

People used to tell stories about secret rituals they had in the bayous with wild orgies, drinkin' and dancin'. A lot the folks were white women who wanted to find a man, get rid of an aggravating business partner, or just wanted something horrible to happen to someone they just didn't like. Whenever they got together, the white masters were afraid that the coloreds would plan an uprising and come against them. So the *New Orleans Municipal Council* passed a law forbidding black people to gather for dancing or any other purpose, except on Sundays. The meeting place was Congo Square on North Rampart Street, which is now in Louis Armstrong Park. White folks used to call it the "place of the negro." Marie

Laveau managed to gain control of the Congo Square dances by getting there before the other dancers and charming people with her snake.

Marie Laveau became one of the most powerful women in New Orleans. Her charisma and ability to cast spells, along with knowing the secrets of many whites and Creoles, helped her to organize secret orgies for wealthy white men that wanted beautiful black and mulatto women for their mistresses. White politicians paid her lots of money to help them win elections. Other folks shelled out up to ten dollars for love powder, curses and getting a reading from her became the in thing to do. Most colored people saw her as their leader. By the beginning of World War II, most every New Orleanian had a story about Marie Laveau.

After she died, her daughter Marie Laveau Clapion followed in her mother's footsteps. Rumor has it that the pupils of her eyes were half-moon shaped and if the devil was a woman, she woulda been it. She started off as a hairdresser too, and then continued to run the business at the *Maison Blanche*, the house that her mother had built for secret voodoo meetings and liaisons between white men and black women. For a hefty price, she would make any man's sexual fantasy come true.

She threw parties with the finest wines, the best Creole food in town, with black girls dancing for white men and high ranking officials. Her place was never raided by the police. They were scared that if they crossed her she'd put a curse on 'em.

People told so many stories about this mother and daughter over the years that they became know as one person, Marie Laveau, the voodoo queen of New Orleans."

"Have you, or anyone you know, ever seen a ghost or any vampires out here?"

"No, but I've seen some crack heads and muggers though. We've run across a few people out here at night having sex on Marie Laveau's grave and sometimes performing rituals with chicken blood, garlic beads and some strange looking gadgets. Some folks have become permanent residents fooling around out here in these cemeteries. Most people don't have a clue, as to how dangerous it is around here, especially at night."

Roman wrapped his arms gently around Slone's waist. Pulling her seductively toward him, he whispered, "I'm really diggin' you right about now White Meat."

Slone blushed as he leaned in and kissed her passionately. She felt a tingling surge right beneath her lower abdomen, unlike she had ever felt before. Roman firmly pressed her body against the wall of the tomb of the famous voodoo queen, held her tightly and whispered into her ear, "Voulez vous coucher avec moi ce soir?"

Slone's body shuddered, as if the temperature were ten below zero instead of ninety- eight degrees. Roman's words tap danced happily around her head, as she began to anticipate being his *Lady Marmalade* for the night. She blushed; unable to articulate a proper response to Roman's sultry French question. "*Would you like to sleep with me tonight?*" Moisture converged on Slone's body so abruptly that she suddenly felt lightheaded. She couldn't tell if it was because Roman was so sexy, or because of the balmy heat and humidity of the Deep South.

Supper Time

I was getting hungry. I bobbed my head and sang along with the *Black Eyed Peas*. They are my favorite group to date. I thought to myself as I washed my dishes. "*Why did my favorite musical group have to be named after food?*"

Someone tapped me on the shoulder and scared the heck out of me. I turned quickly to see Slone standing behind me with a really big smile on her face.

"Sorry" she said, "I didn't mean to startle you. Smells like a five-star Creole restaurant in here."

Roman came in behind her and said, "Damn, smells like a hot, sweaty vagina up in here. Oh Lawd, Jenna, you cooked? Slone hand me the phone so I can call and make some reservations at *Commanders Palace* 'cause I don't want you to take the risk of getting no food poisoning from whatever yo' girl here has conjured up."

"Oh, you got jokes huh? Everyone can start fixing their plates, but you Roman."

"I'm just kidding Sister. What did you attempt to...I mean, what did you cook?"

"I made a seafood eggplant casserole and some fried green tomatoes."

"No problem, I'm starved."

"What else is new? Oh, crap I forgot to fix the potato salad."

YaYa came into the kitchen. "Smells pretty good in here Cher, I hope it tastes as good as it smells. And don't worry about the potato salad I have some already made in the ice box."

"These are a lot of carbohydrates for one meal." Slone said.

"Girl, you're in the Crescent City, we don't count carbs or diet, we eat whatever we want, when we want, and then we take a nap before the next meal is served. You look like you could stand to eat a few more carbs anyway."

"What are you trying to say Roman?"

"I'm saying you're fine as wine Snowflake. Now, do you mind fixing me a plate?"

"Sure, I would love to."

"Slone, you don't have to fix him a plate, he can get his own food." I said.

"Oh no, it's okay, I don't mind."

I turned and looked at Roman and made an ugly face at him.

"Whatever; your face is gonna get stuck like that and your fancy clients won't recognize you when you get back to work."

Where is Grandpa?" Roman asked.

"He went to play cards with Marshall Steptoe and 'em."

"Oh, I need to go over there and show 'em how it's done."

"Really, the last time you went over there to teach them a lesson, you came back short two hundred dollars, if I remember correctly."

"YaYa, you better get your story right; I came home with more than I left with."

"That's not what I heard." YaYa said with a smirk across her face.

Roman sucked his teeth and put his head down and ate his food without another word. YaYa humbled him real good, in front of Slone. We laughed at him and he gave us a dirty look before he finally took his plate into the den and finished his dinner in front of the television.

Slone looked as if she was about to get up from the table too.

I said, "Where do you think your going little miss? You sit right here with us. Don't worry about him, he's got tough skin. If he can't take the heat in the kitchen, then move it on into the den." I said loud enough for Roman to hear me.

"I heard that Jenna, I'm gonna get you back when you least expect it."

Slone, YaYa and I giggled like three amused little girls, as we finished our meal.

"That was good Jenna. You should cook more often." Slone said.

"I wanted to give YaYa a break, that's all."

YaYa got up from the table and went to start the dishes.

"You go watch TV with Roman. Slone and I can clean up."

"Thank you Cher."

She leaned over and gave me a kiss on the forehead. "I'm going to my room now. See y'all in the morning."

"Night, night YaYa!" Slone yelled.

Roman stuck his head in the kitchen and said, "Since Angela's in Lake Charles for the night, I'm going uptown to hang out with Logan at his crib. Check y'all later."

"So Slone how was your trip to the cemetery?"

"It was awesome. I'd never seen any thing like it in my life. The rustic ironwork on the gates and the sun bleached tombs had so much character. The above ground graves were eerie but intriguing. It was different from any grave site I've ever been to. Not that I make it a habit of visiting grave sites, but it was really interesting.

"Which cemetery did you guys go to?"

"St. Louis Cemetery… number one, I think."

"You and Roman look like you guys made a connection."

Slone said, "Yes we did" with a smile that stretched from her ears, to her vagina.

"What's that look about?"

"Nothing, he was a wonderful tour guide; that's all."

"Where else did you guys go?"

"We took a trolley along St. Charles Avenue. There was such beautiful architecture on each of the houses. Then we went to a snow cone stand that had such an abundance of amazing flavors that it was hard to choose just one. I think it was called *Pandora's*, near a beautiful park."

"City Park, and it's not called a *trolley* down here, we call it a *street car.* And it's a *snowball* not a *snow cone.* Girl, I thought Grandpa already schooled you."

"Jenna, something else happened at the cemetery today, but I'm not sure if I should tell you."

"What? Don't tell me you got bit by a vampire?"

"Well, sort of."

I raised one eyebrow and stared intensely at her.

"Slone if you don't mind me saying, I don't think Roman is your type."

"Why? Is it because I'm not black?"

"No Slone, of course not, it's just his state of mind. I don't think he's refined enough for you. This is not the kind of man you want to take to the country club for brunch before playing doubles on the tennis court."

"Jenna, that's just lack of exposure."

"Okay, when one of your associates looks at him the wrong way, and he puts them in a head lock before you can call his name, don't call me crying because he's embarrassed you out in the street.

But let me make something clear; he attended one of the finest private schools in New Orleans. So yes, he has been to the symphony, plays, and museums as a child, but not as an adult. Living as a black person in America is not about a lack of exposure, it's a constant state of living in a society where you have to work harder than everyone else to prove that you are just as intelligent, witty and clever as the next person. We have to fight stereotypes on a daily basis. No other nationality in the state of the union has to function that way. When you speak proper English it's not a big deal. When one of us can string more than one sentence together and hold an articulate conversation, they say, *oh,* she speaks *so well.*' What the hell does that mean anyway?"

"Jenna, not to cut you off but are we still talking about Roman and me, or are we talking about you now? Stop making everything about you all the time. I had a wonderful time with your brother today. I haven't laughed or felt this good in ages. I came here with you to enjoy myself and forget about all the pain and suffering I've endured over the last couple of years. I'm not going to apologize to you for allowing myself the opportunity to live my life to the fullest. I'm not going to waste my time on being afraid of what other people's opinions are of me, or allow the potential possibility of failure to stop me from trying new things. I am going to enjoy the second chance at life that God has given me, whether it's with Roman, or someone else. Jenna, you need to lighten up and learn not to take yourself so seriously; life is too short."

"There's a lot that you don't know about him Slone. I love you like a sister and I don't want to see you disappointed. I just know my brother. Roman used to stay out in the streets sometimes for days at a time. Hanging out in dem bricks."

"Bricks?"

"That's what we call the projects down here. He even tried to join a gang once, but Grandpa put a stop to that.

That's why we were so proud when he went to the police academy. He developed a slight problem submitting to authority figures during his teenage years, so he decided to become one. Even the dirty politicians in New Orleans quiver when Roman walks into a room. He's got the *dirty* on all the power players in this town. He caught the chief of police with his pants down in an ally in the Quarter and a respectable judge giving him *head*. Not to mention seeing the DA with a woman, other than his wife, going into a dingy motel at two o'clock in the morning. Nobody's gonna mess with Roman Bordeaux in this town or any other town in the Tri-State area, that's for sure. He's got judges, lawyers, lieutenants, the police chief and even the Mayor in the pocket. So if he were to ever get himself in any kind of trouble he could just make a call and it would *go away*."

"So you're saying he's a bad cop?"

"No, I'm just saying, "Be careful." He's a real sweetheart; but he's been known to have a bit of a temper. I don't know Slone, maybe it makes me uncomfortable. If one of you gets hurt, I'll feel as if it was my fault, but y'all are grown. Just know that you've been sufficiently warned."

Sweet Tea

*L*ogan and Roman played dominos, drank Tequila shots and beer all night, while listening to old school rap music. They talked about the days when they used to play marbles and dodge the ball barefoot in the middle of the street and afterward drink sweet tea, sitting on the curb.

"Man we used to have some fun, back in the day." Roman said.

"Remember that time your dad caught you kissing that cock-eyed, bowlegged, nappy-headed girl, Wanda, on the side of the house?"

Logan laughed. "I sure do. My dad snuck up on us and said, "What y'all doing out here? And when she turned around he said, "Damn boy, you can't do any better than *that?*"

"He told her that she had better get her ugly ass from around here and never come back. Wanda started crying and ran home. He looked at me and asked me, 'So how was it?' I said, 'Well, it was my first kiss and it felt really good as long as I kept my eyes closed.' My dad laughed so hard, he had tears rolling down his face."

"What ever happened to that girl that your grandmother caught you eating for lunch in the garage that day?"

Roman shook his head and said, "Man she was sweet as hell, I used to see her at the St. Aug dances all the time. YaYa shamed her so bad that she wouldn't even talk to me anymore. That girl was moaning and jerking around so loud, that YaYa came running outside to see what all the noise was about. I didn't realize that she was in the back kitchen. YaYa came in with her broom and ran her outta there so fast, she left her panties. YaYa called herself telling Grandpa on me, thinking he would punish me. He laughed when she told him and she was mad with both of us for the rest of the day. Years later, she had to laugh at that one herself. She said she had no idea what she was going to do with that broom, but it scared the mess out of that girl, that's for sure. Guess she was planning to sweep her off the property."

"Not to change the subject, but I ran into that ass hole Father Timothy the other day."

"I thought that was yo' boy?" Roman said.

"Hell no, that was yo' deal not mine. I remember when Father Timothy was sniffin' little black altar boys asses and yours was one of them."

"Logan, after all these years you still sticking by that lame ass story that Father Timothy never touched you."

"Yep, just because the rest of you dummies let him do wicked shit to y'all, doesn't mean I let him get after me. But we need to talk about what happened out there at Honey Island the other night. I've never seen you that angry before, man. It was like you were possessed or something." Logan said.

"Don't you ever mention that situation to me again; or to anyone else for that matter."

"I'm just saying you can't let what happened to you as a boy, affect who you are as a man. You need to get some help or maybe counseling would be good for you. You know what I mean?"

Roman looked across the table at him and shouted, "Man, I am telling you...you need to take that *effing* shit to the grave!"

"Alright Bruh; calm down. I got you, okay? I won't speak on it again."

"And anyway Logan, you know some of the same stuff that happened to me, happened to you up at that rectory, just admit it man. You've been in denial about that bullshit for years."

"I told you man, that was your circumstance, not mine. Nobody did anything to me."

"Yeah, a'ight. If that's how you want to play it, that's fine with me. But just so you know, you need to face your own demons and get yo 'self some help too."

Roman pushed back his chair and stood to his feet and said, "I need to use the bathroom."

Logan yawned and said, "Go ahead Bruh, you know where it is."

Roman peeked into all the rooms as he walked down the narrow hallway of the shotgun house as he strolled to the restroom. On his way back he spotted Logan's gun sitting on top of the dresser in his bedroom. He went into the room and pulled a standard revolver from the small of his back and switched it with Logan's. When Roman returned to the front of the house he conveniently found Logan passed out in the lazy boy. Roman grabbed an oatmeal raisin cookie out of the big red cookie jar that was slightly hidden behind a silver mixing bowl on the counter top. He went into his pocket and decided to leave a little something wicked in the cookie jar for Logan, to insure they would never have this conversation again. He took one more glance at Logan, shook his head, grabbed his keys and took a drive back out to Honey Island.

Shadows Of Dysfunction

he smell of fresh mint mixed with lavender, seeped into their nostrils from the candles that flickered in the room. Only the vague buzzing sound of blades turning from the ceiling fan could be heard. Roman gazed into Slone's radiant, green eyes, as he gently ran the back of his hand across the curve of her high cheek bone. Not a word was spoken between them as they lay in each other's arms, depleted, yet thoroughly fulfilled. Sunlight crept across their naked bodies as they accidentally slept into the morning, only to be awakened by the sound of YaYa's voice, "Slone, time for breakfast."

Roman jumped up out of bed, disoriented. "Damn!" He said, as he tripped on one of Slone's shoes.

"Slone, are you alright in there?" YaYa said through the door.

"Yes, Miss Ya, I'll be out soon." They looked at each other and laughed as quietly as they could. Slone whispered exuberantly, "How the hell are you going to get out of here without anyone seeing you?" Roman was putting on his clothes, then, they heard a knock at the door.

"Slone, it's Jen, can I come in?"

"Ugh, give me a minute."

"Girl, what are you doing in there, I've seen you naked a million times. I need to talk to you about last night. I'm coming in now sleepy head."

Roman didn't have a shirt on, but he had at least gotten into his pants. Slone waved her hands frantically for him to go in the bathroom. Before he realized what she was doing, Slone pushed him into the bathroom as the door to the bedroom opened.

"I thought I heard some strange noises coming out of here when I came home last night. It sounded like you were moving furniture around the room or something. I was too tired to come in and check on you. Did you sleep well?"

Roman burst through the bathroom door smiled at Slone, then looked me directly in the eyes and said, "You heard something alright. Thanks for introducing me to your friend. She really is something special and tasty too. So delicious in fact, I wanted to get my gun and hold that puunani hostage. But I need to get to the station for a couple of hours. Paperwork trumps puunani."

"What happened to the buttons on your shirt?" I said.

"Slone ate 'em last night. Let's just say it was a part of her Creole epicurean experience."

Roman grabbed his gun and holster and walked out of the room. I turned and looked at Slone with disgust and walked out behind him.

"Roman, what are you doing?"

"I'm going to get in the shower, get some breakfast, and go to work. Why?"

"No, what the hell are you doing with Slone?"

"Jenna look, just mind your own business."

"She is *my* business." I said, as I grabbed his arm when he turned and attempted to walk away from me.

"Look girl, chill out. Don't try to booty block because of what ever happened to you with 'dem nuns up at that school. It seems like it made you frigid."

"Frigid? You don't know anything about me."

"I might not know that much about you these days, but a man knows when he feels ice cold air coming off a woman. Trust, we can sense it as soon as you walk into a room. Anyway, I talked to

Wolverine yesterday and he said you never called him back. So you need to handle that and stay out of my business."

"Wolverine?"

"Yeah, one of your X men, Chase."

"Listen, I'm not one of those women that need a man to complete me; nor do I need one to define who I am as an individual. I complete myself."

"And you're a complete idiot if you really believe that dumb shit. You need to lay off that *Lifetime* channel and come back to reality. No man or woman is complete within themselves Jenna. Look around you, none of us would exist if that were true. Yes, women are the entrance for mankind into this world, but nothing can enter this realm without a seed. They have yet to figure out how to create sperm in a laboratory, so let's just say that we just might need each other. So do yourself a favor and go get yo 'self some sperm the old fashioned way, so you can relax."

"Don't worry about me. What you need to do is learn to handle your real business."

"And what exactly is my real business Jenna?"

"I heard about that insolent behavior of yours that put you on desk duty for losing your temper Roman."

"Who told you that bullshit?"

"Don't try to play that good cop, bad cop, mess with me. I heard it from a reliable source; trust. I heard you lost your temper at some house party ova in Gert Town. We were all so proud of you when you worked so hard to become a police officer. You have a job with great benefits. Don't let that temper of yours make you lose your job. What are you going to do if that happens? What, you gonna trade your gun in for a whistle and a baton and work at the strip mall?"

Roman closed his eyes, breathed in deeply as his body tightened.

"Shut your mouth!" His voice was so loud that not only did my heart skip a beat, but I think my hair stood up on my head. Clearly I had struck a nerve. It was as if I had just unleashed a dragon that had been hiding inside him that had been waiting for the perfect opportunity to come out.

"You need to get your facts right Jenna, and learn to watch that mouth of yours or one day somebody's going to tap that ass because of it."

As I heard the venom in his voice and studied the scowl on his face, I hoped that today was not the day that he planned to fulfill that prophecy. He stared at me so hard with those piercing blue eyes, that the fear I was feeling on the inside of me began to manifest itself on the outside. Tears streamed down my face, and I began to tremble. I was angry and my feelings were hurt. He had never talked to me that way before. He hardly ever called me Jenna. I guess I had really gone too far with him for him to call me by my name, instead of Sister.

YaYa came into the hallway and said, "What's going on in here?"

Roman put his head down and strolled past her and into the kitchen.

YaYa said to me, "Come in this room and let me talk to you Cher." I followed YaYa into her room as if I was a little girl again. I sat down on the bed. She stood over me and said, "I know nobody can't tell you nothing since you moved to California; but I'm telling you child, let him be. He has been having a bit of a hard time lately. He's been walking around here looking real sad for the last couple of months. He's just now getting some joy back since you've been home. You need to take yourself in that kitchen and apologize to your brother."

"Yes ma'am." I looked up at her, my eyes filled with tears. Maybe I had over reacted; maybe I did have some unresolved issues of my own that needed to be dealt with. Guess it's just easier for me to shine the light on other people's baggage, while I hide in the shadows of my own dysfunctions.

Crawfish Boil

*G*randpa, Roman and Gabriel boiled crawfish and crabs, along with corn and red potatoes in the back kitchen. Slone, YaYa, Sidney and I, covered the tables with tablecloths decorated with wedding bells and doves. The centerpieces were vases in the shape of a bride and groom, filled with flowers from YaYa's garden. We placed white and silver balloons strategically around the yard, and tied satin bows on every wooden white folding chair. Grandpa strung tiny white lights along the gates, throughout rose bushes, trees and the around the tent that he and the boys had set up this morning. It was absolutely grand when we were done.

Slone was so excited to be a part of the New Orleans style festivities. She was bubbly and energetic, and made herself available to help in any capacity she could, now that she had recovered from Roman chasing her around the yard with a live crab, as she laughed and screamed like a six year old girl. She fit in effortlessly with our family, just like I knew she would. Everyone welcomed her and treated her as if she had grown up in New Orleans with us.

The table tops were filled with huge mounds of boiled crawfish and crabs. We sucked heads, pinched tails, cracked crabs, talked trash and sipped on ice cold *Coronas.*

"Slone you had better quit trying to be cute out here and get your hands dirty or you're going to starve to death girl." My Uncle Harold said.

Slone held up one of the crawfish, scrunched up her face and said, "I'm not quite sure how to eat this."

Roman began cracking and peeling shells. He placed crawfish tails and crab meat onto Slone's plate, as quickly as he could. Uncle Harold laughed with a deep raspy voice and said, "Boy, you better go on and teach her how to suck those heads and pinch those tails now. You'll regret it later if you don't."

Auntie Sharon hit him on the arm and said, "Stop picking on those kids Harold. She'll figure it out in her own good time. With a little practice one day she'll be as good at it as me."

"Sharon you done already sucked down five pounds all by yourself in record time. You need to learn how to pace yourself before you hurt somebody. I mean hurt yourself. Oh damn, I'm confused what are we talking about again?"

"Auntie Sharon you look like you gained some weight since I saw you last time." I said.

"Girl that's just baby weight you know."

"Baby weight; McKenzie is ten years old. Damn, how long does it take these days?" Roman said.

"Boy, don't make me spank you like I used to when you were little. I'm not scared of that badge and that gun you got no."

"Alright Auntie Sharon, you can come work out with me next week then."

Uncle Harold put his two cents in and said, "Please, you have a better chance of the *Saints* winning the Super Bowl and we all know that ain't never gonna happen in our life time."

YaYa walked past Grandpa's table and he looked at her and said, "Must be jelly, 'cause jam don't shake like that." He pulled her down onto his lap and kissed her on the cheek.

"You betta stop yeah, don't make me embarrass you out here in front of family Jaquet." YaYa said with a huge smile as she playfully returned a kiss that she planted on his lips.

"So who is this fine quadroon you got here?" Uncle Harold said.

"This is my friend Slone; she lives in Los Angeles too."

"She sure is good looking."

"Roman, don't sleep on this one man. I know quality when I see it. Slone if he drops the ball, I have a younger brother that would love to holla at you. He's got a good job and makes good money working out at *Michoud*."

"Yeah Slone, he's also three hundred and fifty pounds with a mouth full of gold teeth. But we promise, you'll live in a really nice house." Roman said as he laughed.

Slone smiled graciously as she glanced at Roman. She wasn't sure what to make of all the banter. She had a hard time figuring out if they were serious or not.

"Don't be scared girl, you can laugh; you're part of the family now. So with that said, can you go get me another beer?" Uncle Harold said.

"Your wife can get you a beer Uncle Harold." Slone answered with sarcasm.

"Damn girl, you're a fast learner."

Chase finally arrived. He made his rounds shaking hands with the men and giving hugs to all the kids and women. He was so handsome and charismatic that everyone was always happy to see him. Everyone at our table adjusted their seats so he could sit next to me.

"Hi Jenna, you look pretty tonight." All the men at the table chuckled.

"What's so funny?" I said.

"Oh, it's a man thing, you wouldn't understand." Roman said.

Chase looked at my little cousin Lincoln and said, "I like that ink you got there boy."

Young Lincoln had a tattoo of a *Fleur de lis* on the inside of his wrist.

"When did you get that man?"

"Last month, my pops let me get it when we won our last basketball tournament. We have another one coming up this weekend in Atlanta. Chase, you wanna come watch me and my team slaughter those losers?"

"Sorry man, I can't. But let me know when your next local game is and I'll be there fo' sho'."

Uncle Harold pulled out a blade guillotine to cut his cigar. He sat there puffing and watching Chase and me.

"What?" I said.

"When y'all two gon' stop playin' games and go on and get married. You two have been on this merry go round for years, just jump off and do the damn thing already. You young folk get on my nerves with that cat and mouse shit. The two of you been in love since you were kids. Quit being a punk man and show her who the big dog is. Woof, woof!"

"Stop barking at them kids Harold and break out the Gran." Auntie Sharon yelled.

Uncle Harold placed a gorgeous, black walnut box on the table in front of Gabriel and Sidney. Uncle Harold opened the velvet lined box and inside was a beautiful crystal bottle with an embellished crystal stopper. It was a *Patron Gran Burdeos Anejo Tequila Bordeaux Cask.*

"Oh my God man!" Gabriel said as he held up the bottle. "If I ever doubted you man, I recant!"

"What is it baby?" Sidney said.

"This is an extremely, limited, aged, ultra-premium, tequila sourced from Bordeaux barrels from *Chateau Margaux* wine cellars in France.

"Thanks man, you did us good."

Uncle Harold stood up on his chair and said, "I'd like to make a toast to the bride and groom. May your love continue to grow as you embark on this special journey together; I hope that the two of you have a lifetime of happiness, beautiful children, great success, and every now and then have a few disagreements, so that y'all can have the best belly slappin' make up sex ever. To the bride and groom!"

We shouted joyfully, as we splashed our pallets with the taste of almond champagne, mixed with a hint of orange liquor, sipped from miniature chocolate cups. We tingled with excitement as the fusion of flavors and the celebration for Sidney and Gabriel intoxicated us.

Gabriel stood up and said, "I have something to add to that."

We all gazed at him with anticipation. "Sidney and I are now the proud owners of our own home on Valence Street. I'm an uptown ruler now Y'all!"

We clapped and cheered, while Uncle Harold and Chase whistled loudly as we had something else wonderful to celebrate. The DJ turned up the music and the real party started. We danced the night away. Most of the guests went home by five a.m., but the die-hard folks washed up and stayed for breakfast. We didn't get to sleep until noon. Thank goodness we decided to have the rehearsal dinner a few days before the wedding.

We relaxed the next day. I slept, read and talked on the phone with some old friends. I didn't come out of my room until six o'clock that evening.

"Well, look who decided to come out of their cage."

"Hi Grandpa, how are you today?"

"I'm still a little tired from yesterday too, but I'll be alright. I'm making plans for a nap soon as I'm done with my dinner."

"You're making plans in advance for the *Itis*?"

"Yes, indeed young lady. I need to get my rest so I can keep my *sexy* together, you know what I mean?"

"You're really funny Grandpa." I said as I laughed and poured myself a tall glass of sweet tea.

Roman dragged himself into the kitchen. He fixed himself a big plate of Jambalaya, grabbed a cold drink from the fridge, a *Delaware Punch* to be exact and sat down at the kitchen table. I quickly said before he started to eat, "I was thinking maybe we could take Slone out to dinner tonight?"

"Okay, where do you want to take her?"

"Well, I was thinking one of three places, *Drago's, Dookey Chase* or *Ralph & Kacoos.*"

"Let's take her to *Ralph's*. Then afterwards we can go walk on Bourbon Street and stop by Pat O' Brien's for drinks."

"Sounds like the plan." I said.

"You know you need to go over and see Leah. She hasn't seen you in ages Jenna."

"I know Grandpa. We might stop by there on our way to the Quarter and see if she's at the restaurant tonight. I remember when we were little, y'all used to take us over there and get stuffed shrimp and po boy sandwiches and they served them through a window. Do you and YaYa still go over there on Holy Thursday for the gumbo z'herbs?"

"Yes, indeed, we never miss it. YaYa used to love going to and look at all the fine artwork that she had in her first restaurant. She used to make a mean rabbit gumbo back in the day when we used to have meetings ova there during the civil rights movement. You know she and my sister Grace went to St. Mary's Academy together."

"Yes, Grandpa, you've told me that story a million times already."

"What's gumbo z'herbs?" Slone asked.

"It's made with the same roux we use for file' and okra gumbo, but with nine kinds of greens. Collard greens, mustard greens, spinach, turnips, cabbage, lettuce, chard, parsley and scallions. She only serves it on Holy Thursday and Good Friday during the Lenten season. "Grandpa responded.

We invited Chase to come hang out with us. We were sitting in Pat O' Brien's and ordered a huge punch bowl filled with hurricanes that came with four big straws. We were quickly becoming intoxicated and enjoying every minute of it. Prior to leaving for the bar, I'd called Angela and asked her to meet us since Logan was on duty that night. It had been a while since I had seen her and I knew she would enjoy a night out with all of us. In the midst of ordering another punch bowl, Angela walked into the courtyard. At first it was hard to make out who was with her since the lighting was so dim, but as they came closer, I realized it was Juliann Pavageau.

Juliann was Roman's ex-girlfriend. She loved her some Roman. They started dating in their senior year of high school and during the first three years she attended Dillard University. She was in the nursing program there and graduated with honors. I heard she was working on her Masters in Psychology and working full time at Memorial Hospital.

Juliann was the perfect combination of *class* and *trash*. She had light skin, shoulder length, dark brown, naturally spiraled curly hair, a tiny waistline and a rear end that you could serve a seven-course meal and a few drinks off of. She always wore high-heeled shoes and short dresses with as much cleavage showing as humanly possible, without one of her breasts peeking out to greet you. Men always stared and yelled out cat calls whenever she arrived on the scene of any event.

"What's up y'all?" Angela said as she motioned for the waiter to come take their orders. Roman got two chairs from another table so they could sit with us.

"Hey Roman" Juliann said as she gave him an inappropriate seductive hug and kiss on the cheek.

"Hi Juliann, this is my friend Slone." I said. They exchanged hellos, but Slone was oblivious to the situation at hand and continued sucking down her enormous alcoholic beverage.

So Roman, Angela said. "How did you manage to get off tonight while my man is out fighting crime?"

"I'm officially on vacation for the next two weeks. I had to go in the other day to finish up some paperwork. I wanted to hang out with my girl Jenna and spend some time helping Gabriel with his wedding stuff. But anyway Angela, what I want to know is does Logan know you're out here in the street with dem tight ass jeans on?"

"Yes, he knows I'm out; but he had already left for work when I slid into these jeans." She gave Roman a wink and started to look around the room.

"Slid? More like 'struggled' you mean; right? It looks like you needed a giant shoe horn to get your big behind in them coochie cutters."

"Don't start with me Roman, I'm grown" Angela said.

"Damn girl, I'm just kidding with you, lighten up already."

"So Jenna," Juliann said, "how's California treating you?"

"Oh, it's nothing but sunshine, celebrities and paparazzi."

"I guess that's good right?" Juliann said with a dumb look on her face.

"Yeah, it's going pretty well for me in Los Angeles. We do all the same things you guys do here like go to work every day, shop, take in a movie or go to a club every now and then. Except, you guys do it with better food and to-go cups filled with alcoholic beverages, that you can walk down the street with while you drink them. I can't believe that y'all have drive through Daiquiri shops since I was here last. The only thing that stands between people and driving is a tiny piece of paper they leave on the top of the straw."

"Girl, I guess it has been a while since you've been home 'cause that's old news around here." Juliann said.

Slone whispered to me that she was going to find the restroom.

"I'll come with you." I said.

Slone smiled at Roman as she got up from her chair. After we both used the bathroom, we were washing our hands and Slone said, "That Juliann lady is beautiful, she could be on the cover of a magazine. Did she grow up with you guys too?"

"Well, sort of, she and Roman dated for a long time after high school.

"Oh really, like how long?"

"Three or four years I guess." Slone wiped her hands and the smile that was previously on her face melted away.

"That's a long time. Did she break up with him?"

"No, in fact he broke it off with her right before she graduated from college."

"Why?"

"He was just bored I guess. He started acting like his shit didn't stink after he got his badge. Women started to really take notice of him after that. I guess there's some truth that women have a thing for a man in uniform."

Slone didn't seem to find my joke funny at all. She put on a fresh coat of lipstick and left the bathroom.

Slone and I arrived back at the table only to find that Juliann had taken Slone's seat which was right next to Roman. She had the nerve to have her lips wrapped around Slone's straw drinking out of our hurricane punch bowl. It seemed as if Juliann and Roman were engaged in an intense conversation.

Slone's posture changed immediately, she hunched her back and let out a big sigh. Then suddenly she confidently pulled up another chair and sat on the other side of Roman.

She quickly vetoed Juliann's advances toward Roman, as she placed her hand on the small of his back. I braced myself for the backlash that was sure to ensue. Juliann kept talking, putting her face closer and closer to Roman's, pretending that she couldn't hear what he was saying over the music.

Angela, Chase and I sat with our straws in our mouths watching to see how the whole scene would play out. I had never seen Slone in a predicament like this one before, so I was anxious to see how she would handle it.

Juliann pulled out a pen and a small spiral notebook from her purse and started writing her phone number down. I was wondering, *who does that any more, doesn't she have a cell phone or a business card like everyone else.*

Slone was damn near rubbing the black off of Roman's back. Roman sat up straight, which forced her to remove her hand. Juliann then playfully said that Roman had something on his face. She swept her hair to one side, exposing the tramp stamp that was on her neck which was a dragonfly with some dude's name tattooed under it. Juliann began to stroke Roman's face as if the two of them were alone in a hotel room. Roman was so cool. With one hand, he took hold of Slone's hand and with his other hand pushed Juliann's away.

"Daaammn!" Angela blurted out as we laughed. Slone grinned with pride as she sat proudly next to her new man.

Chase sat quietly observing with his arm propped comfortably around my shoulder and shaking his head in amazement.

Juliann jumped up and said, "I'm ready to go now Angela."

Angela being a little tipsy said, "I bet you are girl, I would be too if I were you."

Juliann stormed off and said, "I'll meet you out front."

Slone yelled after her and said, "It was nice meeting you!"

We sat there drinking and talking for another two hours. We took pictures and got a hurricane glass packaged in a nice to-go box for Slone. We headed up Bourbon Street drunk as hell. We stopped in one of the gift shops along the way, Slone and I tried on masks, hats and boas. I did a sexy dance for Chase; he had been really, touchy feely with me during the evening, but I had consumed so much alcohol that I was actually turned on by it. At one point, we started to salsa dance in the store and he cupped my derrière with such sexual bravado that I felt like I would crescendo in my panties.

Slone and Roman were hugged up as we walked down Bourbon Street. She was snapping pictures of everything she could. Slone stopped in her tracks when she saw the lady swinging in the window of *Big Daddy's* strip club.

"Wow, now that's really cool." She said.

Roman turned around to Chase, pointed and said, "Hey Bruh, those chicks are tryin to holla at you man."

We all turned in the direction of Roman's stare, as we did, there were three half-naked women with tons of make up on, beckoning for us to come into their den of decadence. Roman looked at Slone and said, "Are you game?"

"What? What do you mean?"

"I got a pocket full of one dollar bills, let's go in."

"I've never been in a strip club before."

"Girl this ain't just any strip club, you're on Bourbon Street; you might as well get the total experience."

"I thought I got the total experience the other night." Slone blurted out, then put her hand over her mouth as if she had told us a secret we didn't know.

Roman called to Chase and me and said, "Don't be scared. Come on, let's have some fun."

I was drunk but I wasn't *that* drunk. Chase looked down at me and saw the look of 'hell no' across my face. I wasn't about to go up in that seedy place with those transvestites.

"No way in hell." I said to Chase.

"Y'all go on and have a good time. We're going down to the jazz spot up the street; we'll wait for you guys in there." Chase said.

Chase and I sat enjoying a phenomenal local jazz band for about twenty minutes or so when Slone and Roman finally came in.

"So, how was the parasitic, disease-infested strip club Slone?"

"Oh, it was fun. Several of the women were really tall and they had really big hands but they were nice. Roman gave me a bunch of one dollar bills and let me *make rain*."

"You mean, 'make it rain' right baby?" Roman said.

"Oh yeah, there were ladies in there with big feather head pieces on, with rhinestone bikinis and really sparkly platform shoes. Roman lifted me up onto one of the tables and I danced while he put his head under my skirt. He said that I tasted just like the cotton candy you guys used to eat at Pontchartrain Beach when you were kids."

"Uh, Slone, that's a little too much information sweetie." Chase said.

Roman gave Chase a low five and they snickered like two sixth-grade boys.

We went over to Café Du Monde. We were all throwing back one Café Au Lait after another, trying to sober up. The beignets came out nice and hot. Slone must have been really hungry because she wolfed down two orders all by herself. She started licking her fingers.

"Mmmm, these taste so good, I want to take some home with me." Roman finished his order while Chase and I were still working on ours. He flung a handful of powdered sugar onto the side of my face.

"Oh, no you did not." I said.

"You've been in California way too long Sister. You sound like a valley girl."

Slone was laughing so much that she became his next victim. We were in an all out powdered sugar fight. Chase ran me all around the tables hurling sugar on me. Slone had turned over a plate of sugar onto Roman's head when he wasn't looking. It was war. He emptied two plates full into his hands and smashed it in Slone's face. Roman laughed and said, "Now you're really white."

Slone laughed so hard that she almost peed on herself. She was hopping around in a circle, white as a sheet from all the powdered sugar we had thrown on her. It was all over her face, her clothes and throughout her hair. She had gotten it the worst since its custom to blow powdered sugar on a person that visits for the first time and to make a wish while doing it. Guess we got a little carried away. We settled down and tried to get as much of the white sugar off of us with the thin napkins that were on the table.

Slone and I hurried to the restroom to release the enormous amounts of alcohol and *Café Au Lait's* that we had consumed. When we returned, Roman and Chase stopped their conversation abruptly.

Chase turned to Slone and said, "Would you be interested in a horse and carriage ride?"

"Oh, yes, I would love to." Slone responded.

We crossed the street and boarded the first available horse and carriage we saw.

The carriage driver asked, "Where y'all from?"

"We from Pontchartrain Park, but these two young ladies are visiting from Los Angeles. We're playing tourist with them tonight, so we need the deluxe tour man." Chase said.

Chase put his arm around me and gave me his signature kiss on the neck. Slone and Roman held hands as she enthusiastically waited for the driver to begin the Vieux Carre' tour.

"To da right is Jackson Square formerly called Place d' Armes, but after the Battle of New Orleans it was renamed after General Andrew Jackson. Dat's a statue of him in the center.

Right behind his statue are three eighteen century buildings. In the center is St. Louis Cathedral which was once a Basilica for Pope Paul VI. To the left of it is the Cabildo, that's where dey signed the Louisiana Purchase and that building used to be City Hall. To the right of the Cathedral is the Presbyter which was originally intended to house Roman Catholic priests. But first dey turned it into a courthouse and now it's a museum."

"Oh, you mean like a rectory?" Slone said.

"Yes ma'am. But much larger."

66

With a bit of silly sarcasm, Chase said, "I always wondered why they called the place where the Priest's live, the rectory. That's probably where the priest's play with little boy's rectums in their free time."

Everyone laughed but Roman, he didn't seem amused. He started sweating so much that Slone reached over and wiped his forehead with a napkin she had brought with her to finish cleaning herself up.

Chase said, "Man, are you okay?"

"Yeah, I'm cool. Let's just get on with it."

"On the other sides of the square are the Pontalba Buildings built in the 1840's. The ground floors are shops and restaurants and the top floors are the oldest continuously rented apartments in America. Across da way is Jax Brewery, dat was the original home of a local beer and after it was shut down, dey put shops, restaurants and some of the space has been converted into some really nice riverfront condominiums and behind it is the Toulouse Street Wharf, the port of the steamboat *Natchez*."

Now dis area ova here is da riverfront dat was once filled with old wharfs and warehouses for da shipping industry. During Mayor Moon Landrieu's administration, dey was demolished and he built the scenic board walk dat we call the "Moon Walk" named in his honor.

Laissez les bon temps rouler –Let the good times roll." The driver said loudly as he pulled the reins of the horse moving us down Decatur Street.

Click, clack, click, clack, click, click, clack was the sound of the shoes of our dusty white horse who was dressed up with a yellow straw hat with a red feather and a pair of Mardi Gras beads around its neck.

The driver pointed to a small grassy area near the French Market, "This is called *Place du France*. Dat's the statue of Joan of Arc dat da people of France gave to New Orleans as a gift in nineteen fifty-eight. She is known as da 'Maid of Orleans.'

Adrian de Pauger did da layout of the city of New Orleans and named the streets after the royal houses of France and Catholic saints. Like Rue Bourbon was named after the *Royal House of*

Bourbon, and if you look at da wrought ironed fences, balconies and courtyards, you can see evidence of da Spanish influence especially in the French Quarter. In seventeen sixty-two, the colony was given to Spain. America bought New Orleans in eighteen o-three through the *Louisiana Purchase* from the French, for fifteen million dollars.

The uppity French and Spanish Creoles thought dat the Americans was beneath dem, so they built Canal Street on the edge of Rue Bourbon to keep 'em out. They used to call it the 'neutral ground' and we locals use that term for medians still to dis day.

Canal Street was intended to be an actual canal but dey never finished it.

Da Americans changed all da 'rues' into streets on dere side. That's why deys no longer called Rue Bourbon, Rue Decatur or Rue Royal fo' example but 'streets' now and so it is with all da streets of New Orleans.

Okay, now we're comin' up on Royal Street, home to some of the most expensive shopping in da world. You can buy some of the best antiques, fine jewelry and art dat yo' money can buy. This is the *Royal Sonesta Hotel* and dis location back in seventeen twenty-one had actual stables and even its own private brewery. Now the *Court of Two Sisters* is right up here; dey have one of the cities best brunches served seven days a week. I'll take y'all pass the *Old Maringy Plantation* too, it's around da corner. Rite ova here is the *Napoleon House* on Charters Street, Nicholas Girod was mayor of New Orleans from eighteen-twelve to eighteen-fifteen and offered dis house to Napoleon Bonaparte as a refuge to him during his exile." The driver belched out a hardy laugh and said, "Napoleon never made it dere."

As we turned onto Iberville Street I began to yawn as we approached the oyster house. I laid my head on Chase's shoulder and decided to relax and let my guard down for a moment. Hell, it had been a long time since I had been that comfortable with any man and I needed a little TLC.

The *Acme Oyster House* used to be on Royal Street, till a big ol' fire destroyed it in nineteen twenty-four. Acme shucked oysters throughout the great depression and dey made prices so damn low, things didn't seem dat depressing. Y'all should come on back in April during da French Quarter Festival and join the oyster eating contest. Last time a woman dey call the 'black widow' ate forty-six dozen in ten minutes, that's fifty-five oysters a minute, an oyster almost every second.

"Slone, I know you can dethrone her." Chase said. "I saw you slurping down those oysters the other night at *Tipitina's*. We gotta make sure you get back here in April so you can win the Acme oyster eating contest championship belt. You have eight months to practice."

"No way, I could hardly get those few I had that night down my throat and I'm not ever planning on eating any more raw oysters in the future. But I'm really enjoying this carriage ride, I'm glad we decided to do this. This is great."

"Have you all been down to Bourbon Street yet?"

"Yeah man, we were ova there earlier." Roman said.

"Well, lemme tell y'all a lil' sum tin 'bout a few of de famous spots. *Lafitte's Blacksmith Shop* right here on Bourbon and *St. Phillip* is now a popular restaurant and bar. It was built before seventeen seventy-two. This is where Pirate Jean Lafitte and his brothers opened up a blacksmith as a front to cover for sum of dere piracy and questionable activities. Legend has it that Lafitte's treasure is hidden in the basement in the fireplace and his ghost is there protecting the gold for eternity. Some folks ova da years said dey seen his ghost. Dey say he gotta a mean scowl on his face, standing in da dark in a corner twistin' and curlin' his mustache with his famous hand wit da glove. As soon as he realizes somebody can see him, he disappears into thin air.

If you walked down Bourbon Street back in the forties and fifties, the red-light district was the place to be. Dey called it *Storyville*. Dis was the place where carnality gave birth to decadence and sin twenty four seven. Neon lights, prostitutes and strippers, drew tourists and local folk into the *500 Club*, the *So Bar* and the *Casino Royale*. The burlesque shows brought out a bunch of people, dressed in their best *duds*. *Storyville* was the birthplace of jazz in America, til dey shut it down. But the girls that worked down there made a whole lot of money. Dey had fancy costumes, had dere own hairdressers, makeup artists, and some of dem even had their pictures on postcards and glasses. A few of dem even owned property and had maids.

Colored women were in demand back then too. Dem white boy politicians and lawyers paid big dough to have relations with pretty young quadroon and octoroon girls.

Now *Big Daddy's* is the longest operating strip club on Bourbon Street. That's the one famous for the swinging mannequin in the window. It kinda looks like a haunted house inside, but dey used to have a sign outside a long time ago that said, "Wash the Girl of Your Choice." Dere used to be a shower stall by the stage where the men paid five dollars to spray water on half-naked women. Da patio between *Big Daddy's* and *Unisex Love Acts* next door used to have female wrestlers, male strippers, dancers, magicians, contortionist, escape artist, fire eaters and live bands in the seventies."

"Sounds like a real circus man." Roman said.

Roman moved closer to Slone. Putting his arm around her waist he whispered in her ear, "So French Fry, when you gonna break me off another piece of that *Kit Kat* bar?"

"Hush, Roman I'm trying to listen."

Slone was multitasking, listening to the historical facts of this romantic city, while thinking of how she was going to wrap her legs around him later on that night.

"The old *Absinthe House* on Bourbon and Bienville has been here since eighteen o-six. A mixologist in eighteen seventy-four named Cayetano Ferrer opened the *Absinthe House Frappe*."

"Excuse me sir, but what is Absinthe?" Slone said.

"Absinthe, is a green-colored liquor often called the 'Green Fairy or Green Devil.' Marble fountains was used to drip water over perforated spoons with sugar cubes into the glasses of Absinthe.

Absinthe was very popular among intellectuals, poets, writers and artists in France and across Europe. Dis drink is known to have some strange powers. Some folks say dat da herbs in that alcoholic beverage gives a person da ability to unlock dere creative powers, enhances their senses and makes dem really hyper and alert.

70

Vincent van Gogh, Ernest Hemmingway and French poet, Arthur Rimbaud, drank it for its extraordinary effects, claiming that it gave them clarity of mind. Other folks claimed dat it's a powerful aphrodisiac and could take your sexual experiences to another dimension."

"Hey man, pull this horse and buggy over. We need to get a hold of some of that shit right now!" Roman shouted.

"Sorry man, *a*bsinthe is illegal in the US and ain't been served in no bars or restaurants for at least a hundred years. But I hear it's the new drug of choice for some of the celebrities dese days."

To your left is *Café Lafitte*, the oldest gay club in the United States. Further up the street is the *Bourbon Street Pub* and *Oz* these are the two largest gay clubs in New Orleans. Down here is packed on Labor Day weekend for the Southern Decadence Festival known around these parts as the gay Mardi Gras. St. Ann Street is called the 'Lavender Line' and with that said, this is the end of the line for you good folks."

I think I dozed off, right after we passed the *Old Absinthe House*. I was so glad when he dropped us off right next to our car. When we got home we all crashed right in the den. Chase slept in YaYa's rocking chair all night, with Slone and Roman on the big sofa, and I slept on the love seat.

We were awakened by the smell of French Market coffee and chicory, boudin balls with remoulade sauce, spicy Creole mustard and fig preserves on the side. Omelets filled with shrimp, pepper jack cheese, bell pepper and onions, along with a batch of crispy fried French bread, sprinkled with cinnamon and brown sugar. YaYa stuck her head in the door and said, "Alright y'all, it's eleven o' clock. Grandpa and I waited long enough for breakfast. Now get yo' behinds up and come and eat with us."

"Alright YaYa, we're comin." Roman slurred.

We each dragged ourselves one at a time to the table.

"So, what did y'all do last night that's got y'all so tired?" Grandpa asked.

"We had a wonderful time touring the French Quarter. I had the time of my life. I loved it so much that I might just move down here one day." Slone said.

"Wow, you musta drank a gallon of hurricanes if you're thinking of leaving paradise to move down here girl." Grandpa said.

"Well, I must admit, I did have my share of hurricanes, but the robust character, mixed with the strong elixir of drinks that I had last night, made me consider it. I've traveled all over the world and I have never been to a place with so much charm and appeal. It's simply magical."

Grandpa chuckled and said. "Well Dawlin, if you ever decide to move, just let me and YaYa know. You're welcome to stay with us as long as you like."

Slone turned toward Roman and said, "And by the way I'm not white, I'm Italian. My parents and their parents and their parents, and so, on were all born in Sicily for your information. You thought I was so drunk that I didn't hear you huh?"

Roman and I laughed and Grandpa said, "Oh, Slone you're just probably feeling the gravitational pull from your ancestors.

"What do you mean by that?"

"The Italians have a rich history in New Orleans. The French Quarter used to be called 'Little Italy.' In the late eighteen hundreds, there were more Italians in New Orleans than any city in the United States. By nineteen-ten, the French Quarter was eighty percent Italian. The immigrants from Naples went to New York, but the Sicilians ended up down here. There's still a good size Italian population still here today. I'd say maybe about two hundred thousand or so.

We eat red beans and rice on Mondays but spaghetti and meatballs on Tuesdays. I'll take you down to the *Central Grocery* store and get you a Muffuletta and a wop salad before you leave."

"Did you say wop salad?"

Grandpa laughed, he knew he would get a rise out of Slone with that one.

"Yes, ma'am, we used to be able to find it on the menu at some restaurants around the city. It's a Creole Italian dish with lettuce, tomatoes, anchovies, shrimp, asparagus, Romano cheese, and of course the famous olive salad mix."

"So no one had a problem with how politically incorrect that was?" There was more curiosity than anger in her words.

"Oddly enough Cher, nobody, including the Italians seemed to mind. It was the out-of-town folks that complained so much about the ethnic slur on the menu that they discontinued the name in most places; but I guess they're calling it something else these days."

The *Monteleone Hotel* was opened by an Italian shoemaker and is still run by the *Monteleone* family to this day. The Sicilians brought the tradition of St. Joseph's Day Altars and it's been said that *Henri de Tonti* explored Louisiana before it existed. There's a street named after him not far from here.

"Wow Grandpa, I think I've learned more from you in the last few days than I learned back in grade school. I had no idea of all the Italian history in New Orleans, it's amazing. I can't wait to call my mom and tell her about this great city."

Grandpa chuckled and stuck out his chest.

"Why thank you young lady. Anytime you have a question about this wicked, wonderful city you let me know, alright?"

"Okay, thanks Grandpa." Slone had known both of those dishes very well; heck, she was Italian. But she didn't want to bruise Grandpa's ego, he is such a proud man, but in a good way. Slone was falling in love with YaYa and Grandpa and they felt the same way about her.

White Magnolias

ennox and Auntie Bristol were waiting when I arrived at the airport. Lennox looked so pretty with her lavender sun dress and silver sandals. Her hands were freshly manicured, while her toe nails matched her dress with tiny little colourful dots.

"Hi Jenna," she said as she gave me a really tight hug.

"Hi Honey, how was your flight?"

"It was fun at first. But right before we landed, it got a little scary and bumpy, but other than that it was great."

I gave Auntie Bristol a hug.

"How are you?"

"I'm hungry and I hope I can get in a nap before the wedding."

"Well, we have to go and pick up the dresses at Canal Place and then we can go on to the house.

"I can't wait to see my sister; I haven't seen her since she came to LA to see Lennox when she was a baby. I know, nowadays we can hardly get her to cross the bridge ova to the West Bank." Auntie Bristol said with a chuckle.

Auntie Bristol was YaYa's baby sister. They'd talked on the phone almost every other day, since she'd moved to California for medical school. Although she is very busy working at the hospital and taking care of Lennox, she always made time to talk to YaYa.

I remember how I wanted to graduate from the high school that all the women in my family had attended- *Xavier Prep*. When YaYa, Auntie Bristol and Auntie Sharon had gone to the school, it was co-ed. But by the time I arrived, it had been changed to an all-girls school. Just looking at all the pictures of how much fun they'd had made me want to go there so badly. Finally I had the chance, but only for a brief time.

When we arrived at the house, there was organized chaos taking place everywhere. YaYa and her staff were putting the finishing touches on the food for the wedding and packing up the van. She had a private kitchen built in back of the house that she ran her popular catering business from.

"Hey you guys, where's YaYa?" I said.

"She's in the back kitchen. You can leave your bags here and I'll carry them inside for you. YaYa's been waitin' for y'all." One of the male workers said.

I let Bristol and Lennox go in front of me. I could see the pleasure in YaYa's face when she laid eyes on her sister and niece that she'd not see in years. She took off her oven mittens and threw them onto the counter top.

"Hey, Bay-Bay; How y'all doing?"

She hugged Bristol then looked at Lennox and said, "God did some of his best work when he made you child. Look how tall you've gotten. Come on and give your Auntie YaYa a hug." Lennox was beaming as she gave her a big bear hug.

"Hi Auntie...YaYa...ma'am, I'm so glad to finally meet you." We all burst into laughter. She was so cute.

"I met you when you were just a baby. You know I have all your school and dance recital pictures; your mom has been sending them to me over the years. But I must say those pictures did you no justice; you are absolutely beautiful."

I took several pictures of them with my camera phone. Then YaYa said,

"Y'all go on in the house and wash up and get yourselves something to eat. There's some stuffed mirliton, glazed ham, dirty rice, greens and jalapeno and cheese hot-water cornbread on the stove. I need to get back to work." Auntie Bristol offered to help, but YaYa insisted that she get some rest before it was time for us to get dressed for the wedding.

The day was beautiful, but hot. We all lined up in front of St. Louis Cathedral. There were only about thirty close friends and family. Sidney had three bridesmaids: Lennox, her best friend Kirsten and me. The groomsmen were Roman, Chase and Evan.

As I walked up I saw that the priest from our old grammar school was going to perform the ceremony. I was shocked to see him standing there with a big stupid wide grin on his face. He was the last person I wanted to see. I noticed that Roman had an ugly scowl on his face as he watched Father Timothy prepare to perform the ceremony. He didn't realize that just about everyone in the wedding party heard his horrible version of a whisper when he asked abruptly before Sidney came down the magnolia pedaled walkway, "What is that 'son of a bitch' doing here?"

After the brief ceremony, we all did a mini-second line up to Decatur Street where the wedding party stepped into beautifully decorated horse and carriages. Ours was adorned with white and silver tulle. Gabriel and Sidney's carriage was breathtaking. It was outlined with magnificent white magnolias, sage colored ribbons, white balloons and feathers.

I noticed Roman standing in front of the Andrew Jackson statue smoking a cigarette. He had an intense look on his face that reminded me of when he was a little boy. He looked like he was about to erupt like a volcano.

When we were growing up, it appeared that Gabriel would be the sensitive one because he was so quiet. But Roman wore his emotions on his sleeve. His reactions to the smallest disruption in his day always turned into a mountain of anger, and sometimes even evolved into tears and rage. He would turn red in the face and sweat so profusely that YaYa would have to get him a change of clothes. Grandpa used to have to drag him kicking and scream-ing into another room to get him to calm down before he could reprimand him for his behavior. He was the worst when we would sometimes tell lies on him and say he did something that he didn't do. Eventually that's how YaYa and Grandpa could tell if he was innocent or not. If he was guilty, he would try to play it cool and say that one of us broke the lamp, ate the last piece of cake or messed with the TV or whatever the crime was; but if he was innocent, it was hell to pay.

Grandpa had gone to Xavier University for three years and was a pre-med major before he was drafted. He had pledged *Sigma*. He had a thick blue paddle that was relatively long, with holes in it. He called it 'Blue Boy.' He would whip the boys with it when they had done something really bad. YaYa wouldn't allow him to whip me and never let him use it on Lupanare when she was growing up either. She said girls just needed to be threatened, not beaten.

Although Grandpa rarely had to use 'Blue Boy' on Gabriel, Roman became acquainted with it on a regular basis. Grandpa used to tell them that he was whipping them, so the police wouldn't. He was determined to make responsible men out of them, and that if he had anything to do with it, neither one of them would ever see the back of a police car. It must have worked because now Roman drives in the front seat of one; and Gabriel had become a college graduate and a responsible man.

Chase whistled and then called out to him, "Hey man, are you coming with us or what?"

He waved us on and yelled, "I'm good, I'll catch up with y'all later."

Chase and I looked at each other with confusion, shrugged our shoulders, and wondered what could be wrong with him. Roman had been so excited about the wedding and all, so we couldn't understand his mood.

When we arrived at *Gallier Hall* there were at least another eighty-five people waiting outside; clapping, cheering and whistling with streamers. Bubbles galore floated in the air as we stepped out of the carriages; we all turned and joined in the celebration as the bride and groom pulled up and sat smiling and waving taking it all in before they walked through the crowd of well wishers. Kisses, hugs and hand shakes of congratulations overtook them as they walked up the stairs of the three-story marble structure with rows of fluted columns draped in white peonies and pink roses.

Pompeii

aYa and Grandpa glided onto the dance floor as Gato Barbieri's *Europa* played in the background. Grandpa grabbed my hand and switched partners with Chase. As he motioned to him to dance with YaYa, he leaned in close to me and said, "Guess who's here?"

"Who?"

"Lupanare"

I stopped dancing abruptly. "Where is she?" I asked. My heart began to race, my head and hands started to sweat uncontrollably.

"Stay calm Jenna, and whatever you do, don't make a scene. This is Gabriel and Sidney's day. Let's not forget that." Grandpa said.

"Okay. Just let me get a drink."

I hurried off the dance floor, Grandpa on my heels. I walked so fast that I lost him in the crowd. I canvassed every chandeliered room. I searched for the bar. I didn't want Lupanare to catch me off guard. I hadn't seen my mother in years. Nobody had.

As I went from room to room, I remembered this one time when Lupanare was admitted to the third floor at *Charity Hospital*. She'd had a nervous breakdown of some kind. We heard that someone called the police, because she was found running butt naked through the *Calliope* projects screaming, "Repent, repent of your sins, for the day of the Lord is near. The world will end soon. Repent or you will burn in hell for eternity."

She was strong as an ox and as fast as an African marathon runner. It took three policeman and two paramedics to catch her. They finally took her down with a jolt of electricity from an experimental stun gun. Paramedics then brought her to *Charity Hospital.* It was a running joke where we lived about somebody going to the third floor at Charity. That meant the person had gone crazy, was psychotic, or had completely lost their mind. It was always a funny joke until it happened to *our mother.* They initially thought she was on drugs, but come to find out she had just gone plum mad, for no apparent reason.

When we arrived at the hospital, she had been sedated. They only allowed us to stay for an hour. She was on 72-hour lockdown. While YaYa and Grandpa took care of business, I sat with her watching her closely as she slept. I brushed her long beautiful hair and sang hymns to her. I didn't fully understand at that age what was happening to her; I was only nine years old then. I thought she was just sick. I whispered in her ear. "God will make everything alright Mother, and I promise you'll be okay."

Grandpa came back to the room and said, 'Time to go now Cher.' I rose from my chair, kissed my mother on the forehead and went home with my Grandparents.

Three days had passed, and my dad, Michael Bordeaux, whom we affectionately called Daddy Bordeaux, took us to see our Mother. They took us to a room that they called the Day Room. She was sitting at a long table, like the lunch tables at our school. Edmond, Roman, Gabriel and I sat down across from her. Daddy Bordeaux stood with his arms crossed tightly over his chest.

Her hair was uncombed; she was dressed in a hospital gown and wore white tube socks. Her eyes were glazed, piercing and frightful. Daddy Bordeaux said, "Lupanare, do you know who this is?"

"I know dem my kids Bordeaux."

The women in our family commonly called their men by their last names. I guess it was some odd tradition. I've never heard her call him Michael, ever.

Gabriel asked Lupanare with the sweetest voice, "Are you feeling better Mommy?"

She grunted and put her head down.

"I miss you." He said. "When are you coming home?"

Gabriel got up from the table and tried to give her a hug. She threw her hands up in the air like a referee, as if someone had made a touchdown. She startled him and Daddy Bordeaux pulled him back.

"Sit down son. Your mother is not feeling well."

I could see he had a pocket full of tears that were not going to be released until he and his feelings were tucked safely in his bed that night. He was only five at the time and already learning how to manage his emotions. I remember him crying himself to sleep that night.

Lupanare ran her hands roughly through her hair. She jumped up onto the long table and began to scream frantically, then squatted and urinated right there in front of us, never taking her eyes off Daddy Bordeaux. She laughed as if something or someone invisible was tickling her on the inside. When she was done, her hair was standing up all over her head. She kicked, scratched and cursed as the workers rushed in and pulled her from the table, and out of the room.

It was difficult for us to see her that way. She was usually so poised and proper. She was a beautiful Creole woman. She had light brown, wavy long hair, light skin, with deep-set, hazel colored, almond shaped eyes, a beautiful smile and a body that would make most men, stop in their tracks. The essence of her elegance could change the atmosphere in any room she entered. I had no idea who the person was that I'd sat across from; she was someone other than the Mother I had known and loved.

Lupanare had gone to high school at *Xavier Prep*. After four years of nearly perfect grades, she went on to *Xavier University*.

One summer she was walking home from a friend's house and took a wrong turn into the neighborhood voodoo lady's domain.

Miss Dorothy Laveau was of the lineage of Marie Laveau, the voo-doo queen of New Orleans.

Lupanare was unaware, of the legend of Miss Dorothy Laveau. She often lured people into her house, and looked like a typical nice little old lady. But it was said that she would cast spells on peo-ple, as she sat in an old rocking chair, looking off in the distance with her one good eye, while rubbing a rosary, as she gave them a glimpse into their future. Her life vaguely mirrored her ancestors; but her fame never reached beyond our neighborhood.

One day Lupanare was walking passed her house.

"Come now Cher, come and help me get inside."

Lupanare ran to help her without hesitation.

"My name is Dorothy Laveau, everybody 'round these parts calls me Miss Dot. What's yo' name girl?"

"Lupanare"

"What an exotic name. Do you know what it means?"

"*Love*, I think."

"Who gave you that name?"

"My mama, Lois Jaquet; but her maiden name was Coubillon."

"I shoulda known; you look just like she did when she was a young woman."

Once inside Miss Dot sat down and pulled out her rosary beads and began to rock back and fourth.

"Yo' mama and I spent a lot of time together; we were friends, once upon a time. We worked together and made some decent money back in the day."

"Where did y'all work?"

"Down in the French Quarter, Cher."

"What kind of work did you all do, Miss Dot?"

Miss Dot smiled a devilish grin and said, "We was prostitutes Cher." Lupanare stood frozen.

"Your great grandfather was pure French. He took your mama to Italy for a few months when she was a young girl. While they were there, she was raped near the Lupanare by two Italian boys.

The Lupanare was known as the "Pleasure Palace" and were found with erotic art, frescoes, with symbols and inscriptions and images that were extremely pornographic in nature. Your freaky ass great grandfather thought it was a good idea to take her with him to the unveiling of this new found art exhibit. This art was said to be so offensive, that they opened it and closed it many times over in a hundred years. Children were only allowed in with a guardian. Your mama had mistakenly wandered away when the boys got her. Pompeii officials warned that not only was the exhibit very offensive, but that the spirits surrounding the Lupanare sometimes provoked people to act lustfully.

The Italian government investigated the rape and concluded that her grandfather should leave the country at once and take his black granddaughter with him. I guess she could pass for white until those boys took her panties off. So you see, your real father is one of two Italian thugs living in Italy. Ask your mama, she'll tell you. They found out their names after the police caught the two boys and released them because of her blackness. I'll bet you they still have them on file.

She gave birth to you and your grandparents took care of you while she ran away, went wild on the streets of the Quarter and worked in a secret underground bordello. Boy, we had some fun. Dancing, drinking, smoking and…well, you get the picture. She said she was going to make enough money to go to nursing school. One day she decided she'd had enough and Lois enrolled in nursing school and then became very religious. She met the man that you call daddy at church and turned her life around. She never looked back, but I'm sure she had her own personal demons to live with, just like us all."

"So sit down girl, tell me somethin' about yo' self."

Lupanare was confused and unable to string a sentence together, as she tried to process what the old voodoo lady had just said.

"Do you go to school?"

"Yes ma'am."

"Where?"

"*Xavier University*, I'm going to be a junior in the fall."

"What's your major?"

"Uh, Religious Studies"

Lupanare sat up straight with her shoulders back and proudly announced, "I'm going to be a nun."

Miss Dot laughed so hard that she dropped her rosary beads.

"Are you kiddin' me Cher, a nun? Well, why don't you come back here tomorrow and I'll tell you what you *really* gonna be when you grow up. I'll tell you about dem devils that live in those rectories down at that church y'all at every Sunday too. Oh, and by the way, your name, 'Lupanare' is from the Latin word, 'Lupa' which means *prostitute*."

Lupanare hung her head down low, bent down and picked up Miss Dot's rosary and handed it to her.

"Good day Miss Dot."

"Hold your head up girl, you about to be free. The truth will make you free."

She could still hear the sinister laugh of Miss Dot, as she walked out of the house and wandered the neighborhood in a daze till dark. Grandpa drove around until he found her and brought her home.

Miss Dot was supposed to tell Lupanare her future. But instead she told her YaYa's past.

As I stood by the bar sipping diligently on my Kettle One and cranberry juice, my eyes darted across the room franticly, searching for Lupanare. I loved her and hated her at the same time. I stood, frozen with emotion remembering her caring touch. I remembered how she would lovingly take hold of my hand as we walked across the street; on days when I was sad, she would fix me a huge bowl of *Blue Bell* ice cream, just so I would feel better. Once I had Scarlet Fever, and she gave me ice cold alcohol baths everyday to break the fever and she rocked me most nights, until I'd fall asleep. More nights than I could count, I missed the smell of her freshly bathed body splashed with *Jean Nate'*, as she brushed my hair away from my face before kissing me good night.

When she lost her mind, I lost my mother. She was often tempestuous for no apparent reason and when she wasn't, she was quiescent and aloof. She appeared to have it all; a loving husband, four beautiful children and a nice home. But nothing seemed to quench the demon of discontentment inside of her. Satisfaction seemed to continually evade her. My life became a marinade for her constant dissatisfaction. It opened a door for my own rejection and failure in relationship to my own self worth.

I was deep in thought and deeply entrenched in my drink. Someone tapped me on the shoulder.

"Hi Jenna, how you been girl?"

"Logan Honore' how have you been?" We hugged.

"I heard you were the big baller, shot caller in LA these days. Roman told me you finished law school and doing very well at some big time law firm. He said you were living in *Niggarly Hills* these days. I'm proud of you girl and I must say you still look great Jenna."

"Thank you. So I heard congratulations are in order. Where is the soon to be Mrs. Angela Honore'?"

"She's around here somewhere."

"When is the wedding man?"

"We gonna do it sometime around Christmas time. And you'd better be back here or we gon' have a problem, you hear me?"

"Don't worry, I'll be there. It took y'all so long; I gotta see it go down with my own eyes."

"I know das right." Logan said as he laughed.

"I know you must be a Lieutenant or Chief of Police by now."

"I could have been much further along if your asinine brother would just straighten up and fly right."

"What do you mean by that? Is he in some kind of trouble?"

"That's an understatement." He looked hesitant.

"Come on Logan, what's going on with Roman?"

"Promise me that you won't say anything to him about this Jenna."

"Just tell me what's going on."

"Well, it's a long story anyway, and this is not the time or the place. How long you in town for?"

"I'm here until……"

"Here's my card. Let me put my cell on the back."

As Logan turned and leaned down on the bar to write down his number. I looked up and there she was, standing right in front of me. Lupanare was in a white long flowing dress and her makeup looked like she had tripped and fell on a powder puff, pasty, and dry as a cotton ball.

"Hello Jenna." She said.

"Hello Lupanare."

"You mean, 'Mother' don't you?"

"You stopped being a mother to me a long time ago."

"Remember Cher, I'm still your mother and you *will* respect me."

Logan slipped the card to me and mouthed, "Call me."

"I will. It was good seeing you."

I turned back to Lupanare, and as she was about to speak again, YaYa, Grandpa and Roman walked up behind her. "Hey Bay-Bay, how you been?" YaYa said.

"I've been great Mama. Hey daddy."

"Roman, look how fine and handsome you are; come give me a hug."

Roman stepped forward looked at her and said, "Where the hell have you been? Why are you here?"

"I came to support my baby boy on his wedding day. I thought it would be fitting for me to be here. I *am* his mother you know."

"Yeah, I know. But don't you think it would have been *fitting* for you to have been at his PTA meetings, and it would have been *fitting* for you to have been at the hospital, when he fell out the damn tree and broke his leg; it would have been *fitting* for you to show up at his high school and college graduation, it would have been…"

Grandpa stepped in and said, "Okay Roman, that's enough. You've made your point man. You kids go on back and dance now. I have some business to discuss with your mother."

Roman took two steps backward, looked Lupanare up and down and said, "You come up in here looking like *Casper* the unfriendly ghost, in that pathetic white dress, with your hair looking all thirsty and shit. But I guess that would be appropriate since ain't nobody seen or heard from you in years."

We were interrupted by the sound of a tambourine. Gabriel stepped through the double doors dressed in his illustrious Indian costume. As the doors were shut behind him, everyone gasped at the splendid coronation of white feathers and incandescent crystals that adorned him. As he began to chant, the room was silent and still. He danced to a rhythm of his own. His movements so precise, so calculating, while the crystals that were intricately placed on his headpiece reflected in the light, shined like diamonds; he looked like an angel that was about to take flight. He posed sharply, the doors opened again.

Big Chief Bordeaux entered the room with an even more elaborate arrangement of feathers, the color of a beautifully teal colored ocean, with ornate jewels placed intricately across the back. His skin was honey brown with red under tones. His dark wavy hair perfectly braided in two. He stood sternly with his arms folded across his chest for a moment, commanding the undivided attention of an audience in awe of his magnificence. He stomped his foot three times, and Gabriel joined him, as they stretched out their arms like the wings of an eagle; they began to spin in opposite directions to the beat of the bamboulas. The dance of celebration was captivating.

I could see the absolute delight and excitement on the faces of Slone and Lennox. Their eyes partaking of something they had never seen before. Sidney was proud, teary eyed and joyful as she watched Gabriel dance with his father. I also noticed that Father Timothy had his eyes fixed on me, but I ignored him and focused on the splendor that was before me. Next thing I knew, he had found his way over to Lennox.

"Hi young lady my name is Father Timothy. What's your name?"

"Hello, I'm Lennox."

"Oh my goodness, you are simply beautiful. This might sound strange to you, but you have such a strong resemblance to my younger sister when she was your age." Father Timothy had tears in his eyes as he extended his hand to shake hers.

"Excuse me, but we have to go. I jerked Lennox away from him by her arm so hard, that I didn't realize I was hurting her.

"Ouch Jenna, what's the matter, did I do something wrong?"

"No sweetie, I'm sorry. Just stay away from him."

"Why, he seemed nice." I took her firmly by the shoulders, leaned down and looked into her eyes.

"Promise me, that you won't talk to him anymore and if he tries to touch you or even looks at you funny, run away!"

"Uh, okay."

Auntie Sharon motioned for us to come to the center of the room as she held a microphone in her hand.

"We will now have something we call, 'Toast Quotes'; famous author's quotes on marriage, to the bride and groom."

Auntie Sharon handed the microphone to Grandpa. He held up his glass while looking at Sidney and Gabriel, and said. "*You don't marry one person, you marry three; the person you think they are, the person they are, and the person they are going to become as a result of being married to you. Richard Needham.*"

I took the mic next and said, "*Marriage is like a pair of shears, so joined together that they cannot be separated; often moving in opposite directions, yet always punishing anyone who comes between them. Sydney Smith.*"

Gabriel was shaking his head and yelling, "That's right!"

Then, YaYa came next. "*Love talked about can be easily turned aside, but love demonstrated is irresistible. W. Stanley Mooneyham. A successful marriage requires falling in love many times, always with the same person. Mignon McLaughlin.*"

Chase came from the other side of the room and took the mic and said, "*Married life will teach you a valuable lesson; to think of things far enough ahead not to say them. Jefferson Machamer. Nobody will ever win the battle of the sexes. There's too much fraternizing with the enemy. Henry Kissinger.*"

Roman snatched the mic from him, as everyone had a hard time quieting down from laughing so much. He waited patiently until he had everyone's undivided attention and finally he said, "I love you both and I am very proud of you brother. Sidney, *it isn't tying himself to one woman that a man dreads when he thinks of marrying; it's separating himself from all the others. Helen Rowland. Whoever thinks marriage is a fifty-fifty proposition doesn't know the half of it. Franklin P. Jones. And last but not least. "Love, honor and negotiate. Allen Loy McGinnis.*"

Everyone lifted their glasses filled with champagne, as some of the men turned to one another and pounded each other's fist, as Roman finished his last quote.

We could hear the sound of the tuba, the trumpet and the trombone in the distance, the music became louder and louder as they approached the room. Then, the doors flew open and in came a brass band, playing the second line. The crowd roared, while white napkins went up into the air, delicately scripted in silver, Sidney & Gabriel August 27, 2005, with a tiny rhinestone fleur de lis on the bottom. The umbrellas opened all over the room. Green ones, purple ones, black ones, yellow ones; small, medium and large ones, all ostentatiously decorated for the traditional New Orleans dance. Sidney's umbrella was gorgeous, white and silver topped high with feathers and fringe. Gabriel's was black, trimmed with black feathers and a black and white tuxedo stacked bow on top.

We danced the night away to *Hey Pokey Way; They All Asked for You; When the Saints Go Marching In,* as well as many other great and familiar traditional New Orleans tunes. As the reception was winding down, Chase walked up to me, placed his hands around my waist and whispered in my ear.

"Can I steal you away for a while?"

"What did you have in mind?"

"Let me surprise you. I promise you'll like it."

"Okay." I said.

I made my way to the little girl's room, and as I was coming out I saw Roman and Daddy Bordeaux in what looked like a deep conversation. I noticed he handed Roman something that looked like test tubes. They both seemed startled, as I interrupted to embrace my father whom I had not seen in years. He took one look at me and smiled, flashing a perfect set of white teeth and extraordinary dimples. His skin was smooth and brown, his hair wavy dark and sprinkled with strands of gray, while his goatee was trimmed to perfection. He looked distinguished, dressed in a dashing dark grey *Armani* suit with a light green tie. His light brown eyes sparkled as he lifted me off my feet and swung me around like I was still his little girl.

"Jenna, you look so beautiful. You're all grown up now. How are you?"

"I'm good." I said with a big smile.

"I get to see the boys every year when I come home for Carnival. I know I haven't kept in touch with you the way that I should, but I promise that is all about to change. I'm going to take a trip to Los Angeles and come and visit with you soon. Okay Jen?"

"Sure dad, whatever you say."

"It was good seeing you Jenna. I need to get back to the hotel to my wife."

Roman looked at him and said, "Your wife?"

"Oh, I thought YaYa told you guys, I got married last year to a lovely Portuguese lady. I wished I could have brought her with me, but I didn't want to upset the family, you know."

Roman said, "Oh man, don't worry about it. You upset the family a long time ago when you abandoned us. And now you didn't even have the common decency to tell us you were getting married. Man I'm cool on you."

Roman walked away and I was left standing there looking at my father that still didn't have a clue as to just how deeply he had hurt us over the years. I got up on my tippy toes and kissed him on the cheek and said, "Congratulations Daddy Bordeaux, I hope she makes you very happy."

I walked away with a clear resolve, that my father was the most self-absorbed man I had ever known.

We all gathered together to say goodbye to Auntie Bristol and Lennox. They were taking a flight back to Los Angeles that night. Grandpa was hyped up and ready to drive them to the airport, so he could get back as soon as possible, to his sofa and big screen TV. We made sure all of the presents, flowers, food, and left over alcohol were packed in the cars. Good thing Roman brought his truck. The bride and groom were off to the exquisite *Windsor Court Hotel* for the night. They weren't able to plan a honeymoon, because the doctor wouldn't release Sidney to fly until after the babies arrived.

Sensual Gumbo

*J*enna, can we go now? Chase said.

He opened the door of his midnight blue convertible *Lexus*. It had cream colored, smooth as butter leather seats, beautiful wood grain and a *Bose* sound system that made the music sound as if you were sitting on the front row at a live concert. I sat quietly, as we rode to the romantic sounds of Aaron Neville's, "Just To Be With You." I listened to the words; it was absolutely, one of the most beautiful songs I'd ever heard. I rejected the idea of allowing myself to romanticize about Chase.

"Where are we going?" I said.

"Not far, just around the corner."

"We've already had a full day Chase. Can we do this another time?"

"When Jenna? Before I know it you'll be gone again."

Chase turned the corner onto Decatur Street into the *Jack's Brewery* parking lot. He turned off the ignition, turned toward me and looked into my eyes. The depth of his gorgeous eyes, were still just as mesmerizing as they were years ago.

"I just wanted to spend a little time alone with you. Can you stop trying to control everything just for about an hour, Jenna Bordeaux?"

"I think I can manage that."

We walked hand in hand up Decatur Street, then onto St. Peters near the illustrious *St. Louis Cathedral.* I was still in my *Vera Wang,* A-lined, chocolate bridesmaid dress. It had sage green ribbons that wrapped around my waist and flapped in the air as we walked. We slowed our pace, so we could peek into the windows of antique and gift shops. Chase with his slightly bowed legs, was dressed in *Hugo Boss* brown tuxedo pants, no tie, no jacket, two buttons opened on his lettuce green shirt with a brown paisley vest, now completely open — looked so sexy; a vision of masculinity that I knew would eventually be hard to resist. I could feel the moisture in the palm of his hand from the dense humidity. I sensed the contentment in his stride, as we strolled down the quaint streets of the French Quarter.

"So Jenna, are you dating anyone in LA? I'm sure you get a lot of attention; you're beautiful, intelligent, successful and sexy as hell."

"No Chase, not at the present. Haven't you heard? The ratio in the West is twenty to one these days? And the white girls found out that everything tastes better with chocolate."

Chase raised his eye brows and opened his eyes widely as he laughed out loud. "Haven't you figured it out by now Jenna, I'm the only man that can handle you."

"Oh Chase, that ship has sailed."

That's the thing about ship's Jenna; they always have the ability to sail back into port."

We reminisced about old times and continued our walk along the river, enjoying each other's company.

"Can we sit for a moment?" I asked Chase as we approached a wooden bench on the Moon Walk. I kicked off my shoes, as soon as I sat down.

"Put your feet up here."

I slid one foot at a time onto his lap. He began to slowly massage my feet. I was beginning to relax way too much. I was aware of how vulnerable I was at that moment. It had been quite some time since I allowed myself the luxury of letting my guard down with any man; and it was becoming so exhausting trying to stay in control, that I'd resigned myself to taking a break from dating. I realized a long time ago, that I have enormous trust issues with men. But Chase was not just any man, he was a gentleman; he was my first love. But I still felt, deep down inside of me, that I needed to continue to guard my heart with all diligence. I have too much on my plate to start a long-distance relationship. Those rarely seem to have any longevity anyway.

"That feels wonderful Chase. Thank you. I'm good now."

I moved my feet back on to the oak planked walk way. There was a warm breeze blowing on the Mississippi that night. And as if in sync with my needs, Chase wrapped his muscular arm around my shoulders. We sat silently watching a huge barge, with an unusual configuration of lights flashing as it floated past us.

"I've never seen this much movement in the river before, have you?" I said.

"No, not this time of year, not unless there's a storm brewing. But there is a hurricane in the gulf that just hit Florida; it's on the way here. It's supposed to be a category three or four."

"Maybe that's why there aren't as many people out tonight."

"Probably, it was all over the news today." Chase said.

"We've been so busy with the wedding festivities the last few days that I didn't really focus on the details. Maybe we should go."

Chase turned toward me, looked into my eyes and said softly, "I miss you Jenna."

I looked at him not knowing how to respond. Before I could really process how I felt about what he'd said, he slid his hand behind my neck and gently pulled me in toward him. Our lips met, our mouths opened slowly and our tongues greeted each other with a passionate salutation. A surge instantaneously shot through every part of my body. He began to run his fingers through my tousled hair. We held each other closely, as if time had never come between us. His lips found themselves giving soft kisses to the curve of my neck. My off-the-shoulder dress was now an exposed breast dress. He gave great recognition to my full breast; as he nursed one, the other he gave a gentle caress. Our eyes locked, as his hands moved up my dress, reaching for my wetness, I was fully engaged with every venture of his touch. He carefully navigated me and my designer dress to sit on top of him. Our tongues playfully found each other again. A warm breeze swirled around us, as he flicked his tongue strategically across my nipples. My legs were wrapped around his waist, as he carefully leaned me back, licking my belly. My eyes opened to the dark sky, and beheld the stars that attempted to hide behind black clouds filled with tenacious anticipation.

He entered me slowly, inch by inch. I was as wet as the Mississippi. We found our rhythm simultaneously, as we became a pot of sensual gumbo. Our juices gradually mixed, creating a delectable roux. His hands clawed my body like a blue crab, his throbbing member standing at attention, like one of Louisiana's finest brands of hot sausage. As he dipped his ladle deep into my pot, I began to simmer, longing to be eaten. I hungered for more, as our sensuality brought me to an overwhelming boil. I moaned loudly, burying my face into his shoulder. Tears streamed down my face as he held me tightly. I turned my face toward the river, as I watched the reflection of the moon dance across the muddy waters of the Mississippi. His thrusts synchronized with the cadence of the colossal drops of rain that had begun to fall as they hit the boardwalk. Light and unhurried, then stronger and faster. My dress was cozily wrapped around my waist as he placed his face between my breasts while he gently licked the drops of rain from my chest. He held my face between his hands and looked into my eyes as he penetrated me so deeply; it felt as if he'd touched my soul. "I miss you... I want you.... I need you." He whispered.

I was breathless, as the lightning flickered and the thunder clapped. We had an audience of absolute nature, as he released a warm decadent cream, filling my insides and spilling over like a half-eaten Creole desert.

Abomination

I was curious to hear what Logan had to say about Roman. If he was in trouble on his job, I wanted to do everything I could to help. After the way I treated him the other day, I felt like I owed him that much. I called Logan the next morning and we met for coffee at a local coffee house. When I pulled up, I could see them boarding up the windows preparing for the hurricane. We ordered, then sat and sipped caramel cream lattes, Logan still had a look of hesitancy on his face.

"So Logan, what's the deal with Roman?"

"This is hard for me to explain, but I don't know who else I can trust with this. I thought I would have to take this one to the grave, but it's affecting every aspect of my life. My job performance, my relationship with Angela and I haven' been able to sleep at night because I've been having really bad nightmares. One night we stopped at *Snug Harbor* for a minute. There were two gay guys outside when we were leaving. One of them turned and looked at Roman and said, "Hey sweetheart, come and get some of this. I can take one look at you and see that you'd like a taste of my anaconda."

He unzipped his pants and pulled out his fully erect penis.

"Come arrest this, officer!" He laughed and said to his friend that was standing next to him. "I know the type when I see them. I have *gaydar!*"

"You know you want it pretty boy, come and get it."

As he waved it towards Roman, I could see a distinct embarrassment and boiling anger creep across his face. Roman stood there paralyzed for a moment, then turned and got behind the wheel of the squad car.

I said to them, "Just move it along ladies."

As I got in the car I could see them getting into a black *Jaguar.* Roman watched as they pulled off and then he started to follow them. We drove behind them for about ten minutes.

"What you doing man? It's time to clock out. Angela is waiting for me."

He was silent, still following them tenaciously. He put the flashing lights on and quickly hit the siren twice. They pulled over and Roman flung the door open and stepped out of the vehicle, yelling to me at the same time.

"Come on man!"

"Let's not do this tonight, let it go." I said. "They're drunk, just having a good time, Bruh."

"I'll be right back." He said.

He forced them out of the car at gunpoint. I got out of the car. He had them assume the position; you know, legs spread, hands on the car. He did a quick search, and of course, the one that agitated him in the first place started running his big mouth again.

"I knew you would come back and check on some of this. I told you I could pick 'em baby."

Roman was focused and unemotional.

"Let's get them in the car."

I saw him take the car keys out of the Jaguar and put them in his pocket. We put them both in the back seat. We got back in the police car. Roman put the siren on full throttle and drove off like a bat out of hell.

"What the hell are you doing man? Where are we going? I told you I need to get to the house."

He never said a word. We drove for forty-five minutes going east. It was pitch black dark as we were coming up on what looked to me like Honey Island Swamp out, by Pearl River. It seemed as if Roman was very familiar with the area, because he drove with an eerie confidence.

"Hey man, what you planning, just let me know what's going down."

No response.

We pulled over to a marsh area, as he turned off the ignition and exhaled. He turned to me and said, "Let's do this."

"Let's do what?" I replied.

Roman got out the car and yelled to me.

"Get them out here Logan!"

He went into the trunk and came out with a big red ax with a silver edge across the blade.

"What the…" was all I managed to get out of my mouth before he started swinging this thing between the two of them; over their heads, taunting them with it. I figured he just wanted to teach them a lesson, you know. I leaned back against the car to watch the show. They were screaming like two lil' bitches and Roman and I laughed. He leaned the ax onto the side of the car and took off his shirt. I could see the sweat pouring off of him as he stood in front of the head lights. He lit up a cigarette and gave me one. After a few drags he looked at me and said, "So, what you think we should do with these ladies?"

"Whatever man, just do it fast so I can get home." I figured I would go along with his attempts to scare them.

Before I could blow the smoke from my mouth, he had thrown down his cigarette and grabbed the ax again.

"So which one of you bitches was trying to holla at me outside the club earlier?"

He walked around them slowly as they knelt on the soggy marsh land.

"Let him go, it was me. I'm sorry Mister Officer. My mouth gets me in trouble every time I drink too much."

"So what's your name boy?"

"My name is Rodger but most people call me Dizzy, like Dizzy Gillespie, 'cause I can blow really well.

"Blow what?"

"Uh well, you know, I give the best blow jobs." He said, with a big smirk on his face. Roman looked at his friend and asked him the same question.

"What's your name?"

"Conrad sir" He said nervously.

"So Mr. Conrad, what's your specialty?" Conrad stood still, afraid and unable to speak. Roman chuckled, shook his head, walked to the trunk again and came out with a whip. He had a trunk full of deadly toys that I knew nothing about. That Negro came back snapping a whip like he was *Indiana Jones.*

"Did you know that Jesus was whipped before he went to the cross to die for your sins?"

"Uh, no sir...officer, I didn't know that." Dizzy said.

"Do you realize that what you do with your friend Conrad here is an abomination according to *Leviticus 18:20*."

Everyone was silent and I was trying to figure out where he was going with his statements. He was beginning to take a turn that made me uncomfortable. He started whipping dem two white boys like they were slaves.

"Okay dude, can we wrap this up now." I said.

Roman took the cuffs off of them and said, "Take off your clothes."

They took off their clothes and tried to cover their private parts with them. I thought how ironic, seeing that exposing themselves is what got them in this mess in the first place.

"Oh no, I don't think so, let's see those anacondas you were telling me about earlier. Throw those clothes over there." Conrad refused to take his underwear off.

"Take those off I said!"

Roman's eyes intensified with a chilling stare. He looked up to the sky and mouthed what seemed to be a prayer

"Put your hands on your head." He said. Then, as if in a trance, Roman pulled out one of the biggest *Bowie* knives I had ever seen in my life, out of his back pocket. He stepped toward the one named Dizzy, that was talking shit to him outside the club, grabbed his penis real hard, and chopped it clean off. My eyes almost popped out of my head. He dangled it in his face and said, "Riddle me this, bitch!"

He stuffed it in his mouth, and blood was all over his face as he fell to his knees, naked with his own penis in his mouth. His friend Conrad collapsed onto the ground and started trembling and crying hysterically by that point "Jesus shed his blood for your sins and you don't even appreciate it. Next time, you had better recognize who you talking to before you open up your nasty ass mouth."

Conrad started screaming uncontrollably, it seemed, until Roman walked over to him and he quieted down immediately.

"Yeah, that's what I thought." Roman said.

By now, of course, the other dude Dizzy was still on the ground, clearly in excruciating pain, covered in blood, with his *johnson*, in his mouth. Roman continued and said as he was walking back and forth, "The bible says, according to *Matthew 5:28*, "*If you're right eye causes you to sin, pluck it out and cast it from you, for it is more profitable for you that one of your members perish, than for your whole body to be cast into hell*".

He then gouged Dizzy's eye right out of its socket. Roman stood up grabbed the ax, as he swung upward.

I yelled, "Please man, stop this!"

He came down hard and then cut Dizzy's hand off.

"The Bible says in *Matthew 5: 30*, "*If your right hand causes you to sin, cut it off and cast it from you; for it is more profitable for you that one of your members perish, than for your whole body to be cast into hell.*" And I can tell you've been doing some foul shit with this hand."

Roman wiped the sweat from his forehead with his undershirt. He turned and looked at me and smiled. Then with two hands, he wielded that ax high in the air and came down ferociously on his neck. He decapitated that dude Dizzy, right there in front of me Jenna. He cut his head off without blinking. What I was looking at was not my friend and partner; he was a man seemingly possessed by something foreign to me. As if he was haunted by some weird religious experience from his past.

Conrad was vomiting; Roman just walked up to him, pulled out his revolver and executed him in cold blood. One shot to the head, and once in the chest. I have to say, I was overcome with a fear I had never known before. I thought he was going to kill me next, so I pulled my gun and pointed it at him. I couldn't talk, my hands were unsteady and I, a grown ass man, peed in my pants. Roman walked past me, got a towel and a bottle of water from the car. It was like he had plans on killing someone that night, because he had all the tools and cleaning supplies necessary for a premeditated vicious act. He attempted to clean himself off, watching me as I held the gun in my hands.

He laughed and said, "Man put that thing away. You making me nervous, like you gonna shoot me or something. I'm tired and thirsty as hell. Help me dump these punks in the swamp and give the alligators a little midnight snack, then I'll get you back to the house."

We stood on the swamp shore, our feet slowly sinking into the marsh, as we carefully threw them along with their body parts into the swamp. We watched as the bodies began to sink, but right before they disappeared from the surface of the water, we saw the alligators come for their prey. They must have smelled the blood, because we stood holding flashlights for less than five minutes and watched them aggressively consume, what was left of the bodies. We witnessed them perform the infamous death roll and Dizzy and Conrad vanished. He threw the gun into the swamp behind them, and casually turned to me and said, "Sorry, this took a little longer than I thought. I just needed to blow off a little steam. I'll make it up to you later man."

He acted like we just came from a football game or something. The dude was crazy, we had been involved in a lot of shady things in the past, but that night was way over the top. We left and went and picked up some *Popeye's* chicken, and ate it in the squad car.

A few weeks ago, we were at a party in Gert Town and he got into it with some chick; she called him a punk and before I knew it he had cracked her in the face with a beer mug. I still can't figure out how he got out of that one, but they only gave him a slap on the wrist and desk duty.

"Jenna, Jenna." Logan called my name to gauge how I was feeling about his story.

I sat there with tears running down my face. The front of my blouse was soaked in tears. I had used every napkin on the table. I couldn't talk.

"You see why I have no idea what to do with this. I watched him do this and I did nothing to stop him. I never even called it in. I helped my life-long friend that I grew up with—played marbles, touch football, and went on double dates with—throw two dead homosexuals into the swamp; then I went home and went to bed."

"Sir, we are closing now. We just opened up until noon today. We have to pack up so we can evacuate. Didn't y'all know? There's a ferocious storm coming."

Logan and I walked silently to the car. The rain began to fall so hard that it was a clear indication of what was ahead. Unfortunately, there was not enough rain to wash away the ache I felt in my chest. Logan hugged me tightly, and then opened my car door for me. I looked up at him; his left eye leaked one tear that spoke a volume of words, without him ever parting his lips. He turned and walked away solemnly, as the rain came down.

I sat in the car unable to move. The rain was pounding the roof so hard, it sounded like a thousand rocks being hurled at me. I struggled to see, not only through the windshield, but beyond the shock of the monster my brother had become. My entire body trembled as tears welled in my eyes, but never fell. I was numb. I couldn't think straight. I had difficulty digesting the information just revealed to me. As I drove out of the brief patch of torrential rain, I took a deep breath trying to get home as fast as I could.

When I made it back to the house, I knew I had to keep my composure. As I pulled into the driveway, I could see Grandpa frantically covering the windows with plywood. He had nails in his mouth and a hammer in his hand, banging away.

YaYa was teaching Slone, her mother Josephine's Eggs in Purgatory recipe.

"First we're gonna chop half a bell pepper, an onion, a couple of sun dried tomatoes, a clove of garlic, and a medium sized tomato. Now let's pull out the cast iron skillet from the bottom cabinet, and fry up some bacon. Make sure you pull it apart into small pieces, before you put it in the skillet. Then when the bacon is almost done, drain some of the grease but not all of it, you always want a little for flavor. Throw in the onions, bell pepper and garlic, then after a few minutes add the chopped tomato, a teaspoon of dried oregano, a pinch of salt, black pepper, red pepper, a small can of tomato paste and a can of tomato sauce, then let it all simmer for about twenty minutes, or till the sauce gets a little thick. Oh, and look in the ice box and get out some basil and break a couple of leaves in small pieces and toss it in the pot too. I've already got a batch of cheese grits cooking. Turn the oven on three, fifty and I'll pass a spoon through the tomato and bacon sauce." Slone moved around the kitchen, cheerfully doing as she was told.

"Now take the spoon and make five wells in the sauce, while I get the eggs."

Slone carefully made the spoon sized wells in the sauce, while YaYa cracked an egg inside each one, and then sprinkled salt, pepper and parmesan cheese on top of the eggs. YaYa grabbed her crawfish shaped pot holders and took hold of the cast iron skillet and placed it in the oven, until the eggs were just right. Then, she spread lots of shredded cheddar cheese over the top and put it back in the oven, until the cheese melted. "Okay Cher, hand me your plate. YaYa spooned some cheese grits onto the plate then scooped out an egg along with some of the sauce, tossed a few sliced jalapenos on top, and placed two fluffy biscuits on the side and handed Slone the plate.

"Now taste that young lady." Slone slid her fork onto the plate, making sure she had an equal amount of all the ingredients to get the full taste.

"Oh YaYa, this is so delicious. I could sit here and eat the entire skillet, all by myself. But the sauce is so spicy they should have called it 'Eggs in Hell'."

She and YaYa were laughing and having a good time, when I walked into the house. I was greeted by the smell of the Eggs in Purgatory and homemade biscuits. Any other day this would have smelled delicious to me, but today the smell of food made me nauseous.

YaYa called out, "Jen, is that you? Come fix yourself a plate."

"I'll be there in a minute."

I didn't want to hurt her feelings, so I went into my room, threw some cold water on my face, took a deep breath, and went back into the kitchen. Slone and YaYa were still giggling and chatting. I picked up a biscuit, some eggs and grits and put it on an antique 18 carat, gold-trimmed saucer that my great grandmother had left when she passed. I poured myself a half glass of fresh squeezed orange juice, went into the den and pulled out a bottle of *Montaudon*, from one of the left over cases from the wedding; I unwrapped the foil from one of the shapely bottles, grabbed a towel and popped the top.

"Perfect."

"Are you having champagne with breakfast?" YaYa said.

"Yes, it's called a Mimosa." I held up the bottle.

"Slone?" I motioned the bottle in her direction.

"Yes, I'll have some."

"YaYa?"

"No child, I had enough to drink yesterday at the wedding. But can you get me some ice and a *TAB* outta the ice box please? So, what kind of meeting did you have this morning anyway? What was so important?"

"Oh, just met with an old friend before I head back to LA."

"Well, you look like you saw a ghost. And why are your hands trembling?"

"So, are we evacuating soon or what?" I said, ignoring YaYa's question.

Grandpa answers the question as he walks into the kitchen, grabs a biscuit and sits down. YaYa jumps up and begins to make him a plate.

"I have lived in this town all of my life. I built this house and have lived in it for over forty-five years. This house has withstood Hurricane Betsy in 1965, Camille in 1969 and Andrew in 1992 and all the ones in between. Surely it can handle this heifer Katrina. I don't care what that nagging Nagin says, I am not leaving my house. We are all going to stay here and ride it out, just like we always have. Roman went to move the cars onto the neutral ground. Auntie Sharon, Uncle Harold, and their bad ass kids are coming later."

"Oh no, the news said we must evacuate; it's too dangerous. This is supposed to be a category four hurricane." Slone, blurted out nervously.

Grandpa laughed, "Don't worry girl, everything is going to be alright. We gonna have a good old fashioned, New Orleans hurricane party. We've got lots of food, liquor, dominoes, cards, candles and the best of Erma Thomas and Al Green. Yes indeed; it's gonna be one of the best times you ever had in your life, and I promise you'll never forget it. Anyway, three weeks ago we evacuated for Hurricane Dennis. We drove all the way to Baton Rouge for nothing. He took one look at us and went in the other direction. We wasted our time and our money. They not gonna get us this time."

Slone looked at me wide eyed. I guess she was expecting me to convince him otherwise. She had no idea, that when Grandpa made up *his* mind, there was no way to change it.

"Did you call the airline?" I asked Slone.

"Yes, I checked and all the flights are overbooked. Even with my seniority, we wouldn't be able to get on a flight. Maybe we could rent a car and drive to Houston. I have a cousin that lives there. I'm more than sure, that she wouldn't mind taking us in until the storm blows over."

"I think if Grandpa says it's alright to stay, maybe we should just ride it out. It'll be over before you know it."

We could hear the news blaring from the other room.

All inbound and outbound flights are cancelled as of six o' clock this evening.

Slone exhaled, her shoulders dropped. She grabbed the bottle of champagne and began to pour.

"Well... bottoms up then."

Crystal Rosary

*Y*aYa and Slone were in the kitchen preparing BBQ shrimp and Crawfish Pie's for the hurricane party. Grandpa was outside moving everything up high and trying to hook up the generator. I was busy gathering candles and putting kerosene in the hurricane lamps. The news broadcast had been on all day.

In the back of my mind as I listened to the warnings of the great possibility of a catastrophic category four or five hurricane, I began to feel like instead of preparing to ride it out this time, maybe we should get out of here. The city was virtually empty already, people and cars were jammed packed on the streets and freeways clamoring to get to the surrounding cities of Baton Rouge, Houston, Atlanta and any place else where Katrina couldn't get them.

Maybe I would try and talk to Grandpa once more in private. But I knew in my gut, it would be like talking to a brick wall. I couldn't bring myself to leave him and YaYa alone. What if something happened to them and they couldn't get help. I would never forgive myself. With that resolve, I made peace with the idea that this house had withstood many floods, tropical storms, and hurricanes before; I hoped it would be able to stand up against Katrina.

I went back into my room to straighten up and watch the news. I could hear a familiar voice coming from the kitchen. It was Lupanare; I guess she'd spent the night after all. I was putting away my bridesmaid dress and shoes from the wedding that I'd thrown on the ottoman last night. I turned and got a glimpse of Katrina. She was huge and looked like she nearly covered the entire Gulf.

Oh my God, we have got to get the hell out of here. I've got to convince Grandpa to leave somehow before it's too late.

I thought I heard someone arguing. The noise came from the front of the house. I quickly threw myself across the bed and reached to turn down the television. Slone burst through the door and shouted, "Jenna, come quickly something is wrong with YaYa!"

I literally leaped off the bed, pushed passed her anxiously and ran into the kitchen. There was YaYa on the kitchen floor, clutching her chest. Lupanare was standing over her, with an asinine look on her face. I pushed her out of the way and bent down close to YaYa. I put my hand on hers and said, "It's going to be alright, just hold on." "Did you guys dial nine, one, one?" I yelled out.

"Yes, I just hung up, they're on the way." Slone said.

"Slone, please run and get a pillow off the sofa, in the den!" She moved expeditiously, while Lupanare stood frozen, staring at YaYa with tear-filled eyes.

"Go get Grandpa; he's out in the garage!" I said to Lupanare.

When Grandpa came in, there was a strong redolence of turpentine and Hennessey that clung to him like sweat on a homeless dog.

"Lois, are you okay? What happened? Oh my God, she looks like she's having a heart attack. Let me move her to the sofa and get her off this hard floor."

Grandpa, as gently as he could, picked up YaYa, carried her into the living room and placed her on the sofa. Grandpa said, "Jenna, go and get her rosary off the dresser."

I ran up the hallway with tears running down my face. I snatched the *Swarovski* crystal rosary and a few of her prayer cards off the dresser.

When I returned to the living room, Roman was sitting with her trying to take her blood pressure and attempting to check her heart rate, as she gasped for breath. I carefully put the rosary in her hand, and laid one of the prayer cards on her lap. The doorbell rang. Grandpa rose up quickly and let the paramedics in. Roman stood up to give them room to work. Slone held my hand to try and comfort me as we stood, almost holding our breath, not knowing if they could save her.

Roman said, "Go get yo 'selves together, so we can follow the ambulance to the hospital."

It was hard watching them take my most precious YaYa away on a stretcher. She was much more than a grandmother to me. She was a mother, a friend, a loyal confidant, and I didn't want to think about having to live in this world without her. I never loved another human being in my entire life, as much as I loved her. She was the most important person in the world to me. I didn't want to get married unless she would be there; I didn't want children unless she would be around to help me raise them. YaYa had given me enough discipline that I wasn't spoiled, and more than enough attention to let me know that I was loved unconditionally. She was my rock, my support, my comforter. She was the evidence of my affirmation. If she was gone, who would pray for me when I didn't have the sense to pray for myself? If she was gone, there would be no one to say to me, "Job well done, Cher." We still had stories, gossip and mounds of laughter to share with one another; not to mention we still had to shop for a new dinette set.

Roman was driving his truck like it was his police car, close behind the ambulance.

"You better slow down, yeah. You're about to slam into the back of the ambulance." I said.

He reached behind the seat and pulled out a flashing red and blue light of his own, and slapped it on the dash board of the truck. We saw them wheeling YaYa into the emergency room, as we pulled up. We tried to go in behind them, but the security guard threw his arm up in front of us before we could enter the double doors. Roman flinched, as if he was going to punch him. The guard blinked his eyes really fast and took a step backward.

"I'm sorry" he said, "You guys have to wait outside. Someone will come out soon and let you know how she's doing."

Slone took Roman by the arm and led him into the waiting room and I followed. We sat down across from the television. We watched the news updates on the hurricane silently for three hours before anyone would come.

Grandpa finally came out. He sat down next to us and said calmly, "She's going to be alright. The doctor said she had a mild heart attack. They've stabilized her, and she's resting now. They're going to transport her to a nursing home, not far from here in a few hours. She will be safe there with the nuns, you remember, a couple of them came over to the house for dinner when you guys were younger. They took excellent care of her the last time she was sick, and I trust them to make sure she gets through the hurricane safely. I want y'all to go home, and I'll stay with YaYa until they get her settled."

"But we want to stay too Grandpa." Roman said.

"No buts. Go home, and when I'm ready, I'll take a cab home."

"No, Roman said, I'll come pick you up. Most people are evacuating, there's no cabs out tonight anyway."

"Okay son, now go on and get these ladies home."

We all gave Grandpa a big hug. Lupanare, when she hugged him goodbye, whispered in his ear, "I'm sorry Daddy."

Roman said, "Come on let's go."

Our hearts were heavy, as we headed back to the car. We were all saddened by the event and it was clear that none of us were going anywhere, now that YaYa had taken sick. This was going to be a long night.

Slone and I decided we would make the BBQ shrimp. The Crawfish Pie was done before we went to the hospital, and thank God, she remembered to turn off the oven before we left the house. Slone took out the cookbook, to read the ingredients I would need. I remember that this was a relatively easy recipe, but I needed a little reminder of exactly how it was prepared. I'd watched YaYa make this one many times before, it was one of my favorites.

"Okay Slone, talk to me."

Ingredients:
6 pounds medium to large shrimp
2 pounds butter
1 onion chopped fine
6 cloves garlic, minced
2 stalks celery, diced
¼ cup chopped parsley
2 tablespoons Creole seasoning
2 tablespoons dried rosemary
Ground black pepper to taste
½ cup Worcestershire sauce
3 lemons

"Okay, finish reading the directions to me and then come over here and help me cut up the seasoning."

"YaYa and I already did that earlier. The seasoning is in the fridge, inside the rectangular *Tupperware* with the blue top."

"Oh, that sounds like music to my ears, I sure didn't feel like cutting up any seasoning. I know Roman and Grandpa were looking forward to having the shrimp, although I'm not sure if they're going to still want to eat after the day we've had. I just want it to be ready if they decide they want it."

Directions

Preheat oven to 350 degrees

Arrange shrimp in a large roaster and set aside

Melt ½ stick of butter in large skillet over medium heat. Add onion, garlic, celery, parsley, Creole seasoning and rosemary. Stir until onions are tender, then add the rest of the butter and cook until melted over low heat. Stir in pepper, Worcestershire sauce.

Pour the mixture over shrimp so that it is completely covered. Squeeze lemon juice and put the lemon in with the shrimp. Bake in the preheated oven for twenty minutes.

The **BBQ** shrimp were done and in the oven. We had tons of champagne left, hurricane daiquiris, and *Sazerac* for Grandpa. I'm sure he would need a drink, by the time he came home from the nursing home, but it wouldn't surprise me a bit, if he decided to stay there with her until the hurricane passed. We had two new decks of cards, *Backgammon* and *Dominoes,* ready to be played at a moment's notice.

Category Four

*I*took my shower, put on some comfortable yoga pants, and a clean tee shirt. I was brushing my hair up into a high pony tail, when my cell phone rang. I looked at the caller ID, it was Chase.

"Where are you?"

"I'm at home."

"Where are you?"

"I'm in Baton Rouge with my mom, my sister and her family. When are you guys planning to leave?"

"Chase, I have some bad news, YaYa had a heart attack this afternoon. She's in the hospital, so were going to stay here and ride it out."

"I am really sorry to hear about YaYa, she's always so sweet to me. But I have one question for you. Are you insane? Look, I can come back and get you, although it took me four hours to get here, but I am more than willing to drive back. The traffic was gridlocked, but we still made it here."

"Chase they have already closed the freeway coming inbound. They're not letting anyone even come into the city. All the lanes are going out. Listen, we have lots of food, candles and a case of *Kentwood* water. We'll be fine, don't worry."

"How in the hell can Roman let you guys stay there, he knows better than anyone how dangerous this is. Do you all understand the magnitude of this hurricane? It's building momentum, and by the time it touches down in New Orleans it will be moving at speeds of over one hundred seventy-five miles per hour. Please Jenna, just get in the car and start driving away from there in any direction, so I know y'all are safe. You can come back after the storm and get YaYa."

"We can't leave town without YaYa, and you know as well as any of us, that Grandpa is not leaving his house."

"If you were as intelligent as I thought you were, you would check YaYa out of the hospital and get her out of there. Have you seen the news?"

"Yes Chase, we've been watching it all day."

"I see I'm not going to convince you, but please think about it Jenna. I'll call and check on y'all later."

Before I could hang up the phone, he said, "Jenna, I love you."

"Okay, thanks Chase, be safe and tell your mom I said hello."

I hung up the phone and went back to combing my hair, and with every stroke, anxiety began to build up inside me. I had a bad feeling about Katrina and the infamous possibility of her wrath, way deep down in the pit of my stomach.

Grandpa stood waiting at the tall, egg-shell colored desk. He was deep in thought, when a homely looking nun suddenly appeared behind the desk.

"Hello, may I help you?"

"Yes, my wife was just transported from the hospital and…"

"Oh yes, is her name Lois Coubillon Jacquet?"

"Yes, yes, that's her."

"The hospital called about an hour ago. Her room is almost ready. Mr. Jacquet, please fill out these forms."

As Grandpa sat filling out the forms, another nun approached him, "Hello, Mr. Jacquet, I'm Sister Alma Elizabeth the home administrator."

Grandpa rose to his feet and shook her hand eagerly.

"Do you have any questions?"

"Is it safe for me to leave her in this facility during the hurricane?"

"Oh yes, of course it is. We have all the medical equipment, medication and nursing staff to accommodate her recovery, and we have special buses being prepared for evacuation, that should be here in a few hours."

"Is there a doctor on staff?"

"Yes, we do have two doctors that will be with us until the storm passes. Mr. Jacquet, I assure you that we have weathered many hurricanes over the years, including Betsy and Camille; two of the worst hurricanes this city has ever experienced. We run a tight ship around here, and I promise you, she will receive the best of care. God is with us."

"Will I be able to stay with her?"

"Sure. I'll make sure you're comfortable until the buses arrive. We can order a meal for you too. If that is all, I must get back to work; let me get one of my business cards for you from the desk. You can contact me anytime, if you have any other concerns." Grandpa walked with Sister Alma Elizabeth to the desk. He noticed a prayer taped to the wall behind the desk.

Heavenly Father, through the powerful intercession of Lady of Prompt Succor, please make haste to help us in all our necessities, that in this fleeting life you may be our succor. As you once saved our beloved city from ravaging flames and our country from an invading army, have pity on us and obtain for us, protection from hurricanes, and all other disasters. Be to us truly, Our Lady of Prompt Succor now, and especially at the hour of our death. Hasten to help us!

Somehow the prayer brought comfort to Grandpa, although he didn't quite understand why the prayer mentioned death, if she was supposed to protect them.

"How are you feeling Lois?"

"I feel much better now, since they shot me up with something that felt like cold silver flowing through my veins and then to my heart. The excruciating pain that felt like an elephant sitting on my chest, stopped immediately after that injection. I'm just really tired."

"Can I get you anything?"

"I'd love to have a *TAB* right about now"

"I don't think the doctor would take kindly to you having caffeine, but how about a nice ice cold cup of water?"

YaYa smiled and shook her head *yes.*

"The nuns seem like they run this place pretty good. They're going to send someone down to bring me a meal. I'm staying here with you."

"Oh no Cher, you need to get back to the house. The sisters promised me they would take real good care of me and they have everything I need. You do best, if you go home and finish getting the house ready for the storm and check on the kids."

"They're grown and the house is already boarded and taped up."

"Please Jaquet; go home, I'll be fine. I wish I could go with you, but they got me hooked up to all these damn machines."

"Aren't you afraid of being alone?"

"I've been through many hurricanes, and God willing, I'll make it through this one too. Anyway I have all these praying nuns and the drugs they gave me before we left the hospital; I'll probably sleep right through it. Someone is going to check on me every hour, and anyway the buses are coming to transport us downtown to one of the high rise hotels. Jacquet, get on outta here before it's too late. The Lord is gonna take care of me. I'm not leaving this earth until it's my time and if it is my time, there ain't nothing no one can do about it anyway. To be absent from the body is to be present with the Lord. Go on now. I need to get some rest."

Grandpa took her hand and kissed it softly.

"Okay, boss. I'm telling you, I'm going to let them know before I leave that if anything happens to you, that I'm coming back up here and kick these nun's asses. Especially that Sister Mother Alma what's her name."

"Alright Jacquet, that's enough talk for now."

Grandpa ran his hand through her salt and pepper hair, kissed her on the cheek and said, "Je t'aime beaucoup."

YaYa whispered. "I love you more."

Slone came into the room and plopped down onto the big, over-sized chair and put her feet up on the ottoman.

"How are you doing?"

"I'm just worried about YaYa that's all. I wonder what could have triggered her heart attack. She was doing everything the doctors told her to do. She changed her diet, she stayed calm, I had filled her room and bathroom with lavender potpourri and candles, and we've even gone for a walk twice since we got here."

"Well Jenna, that's what I wanted to talk with you about." Slone got up from her chair and closed the door.

"I need to tell you something, but I need you to stay calm until I'm done."

"What's up?" I sat comfortably on the bed and gave her my undivided attention.

"YaYa and I were cutting up the seasoning for the crawfish pie. We were having a nice talk about Italy. I was telling her about my Sicilian grandmother and she was sharing stories about a trip to

Europe, that her grandfather had taken her on when she was a young girl. I thought I'd heard someone come to the door, but I ignored it. I didn't realize that Lupanare was eavesdropping on our conversation. She came in and sat down at the table, and YaYa looked up and saw that it was her, and abruptly stopped talking. I tried to continue the conversation, but she shook her head and gave me the look that mothers usually give their children, when they're talking too much at the wrong time and needed to zip their lips. I got the message immediately. Then Lupanare started talking really disrespectful to YaYa. She asked me if YaYa had told me how she had been raped when she was in Italy, how she used to be a street walker, and for me not to be fooled by all this religious crap. She said YaYa was hiding who she really was, behind the cross. She said that YaYa had abandoned her and left her with her parents when she was a baby, to go sell her body for money and gifts."

In the midst of Slone's commentary, I rolled off the bed, stood up and started to pace back and forth, while she finished her story. I was livid; I could hardly believe what I was hearing.

"YaYa said, 'That's enough girl, you'd better shut your mouth.' Lupanare became belligerent; saying the most awful things, cursing and swearing at her. YaYa raised one hand and slapped her across the face, still holding the knife in the other. I could see that they were both beyond upset. YaYa lifted the knife, and just as I was about to grab her hand, YaYa dropped the knife, grabbed her chest, and fell to the floor. That's when I came to get you. Jenna it all happened so fast. If YaYa hadn't passed out on the floor I believe she would have cut Lupanare with that knife. That's how upset she was."

I bolted out of the room, stomping up and down the hallway going from room to room screaming, "Lupanare, Lupanare, where the hell are you?"

I went into the den yelling so loudly that I woke Roman up from his nap. He had fallen asleep in YaYa's rocking chair. His eyes popped open and were blood-shot red.

"Girl, what is wrong with you? Don't be screaming like that in this house, no."

"Have you seen Lupanare?"

"I think she walked around the corner to go check on that creepy lady Miss Dot. I heard she went over there yesterday before she came to the wedding and Miss Dot told her some foolishness about how there's going to be a bunch of deaths in our family. She came over here a few weeks ago to warn YaYa but she wouldn't even let her in the house. Supposedly, YaYa closed the door in her face. She told me Miss Dot came over here shaking some funny looking beads, speaking some strange version of patois and threw some cards in the doorway right before she closed the door on her. Those weird lookin cards had the word death written all over them. Go check them out, there in the desk in her bedroom."

"Whatever, ain't nobody thinking about Miss Dot with all her silly superstitions. You just tell Lupanare to come see me when she gets back."

"Oh Lawd, what has her crazy ass done this time? Just let me know if you need me to put her in a head lock fo' you. I've been looking for a reason to legally whip her behind for years."

"This is serious Roman, quit making jokes."

"Who said I was joking?"

Recipe For Disaster

One day when we were kids. Lupanare had gone over to Miss Dot's house. They were having idle chit chat and Lupanare blurted out, "I know he's cheating on me when he goes out on that ship for months at a time to all those different places all over the world. He's always talking about how much he loved it in Brazil and how he would love to live there one day."

"Only thing that would make a man wanna move that far away from his family is another woman child." Miss Dot said.

"That's what I wanted to talk to you about Miss Dot. Can you give me something to make my husband stop cheating on me and stay home with me?"

"I got a recipe that will make him straighten up and fly right, but I would need something from you."

"What is it? I'll do what ever you say."

The next time Lupanare went back over to Miss Dot's house she had with her, her monthly feminine discharge in a small jelly jar. Miss Dot took the jar and went to the refrigerator and pulled out a bottle of Italian dressing, opened it and with a dropper began to transfer Lupanare's red bodily fluid into the bottle. She was chanting a weird, incoherent lyrical patois over it, and then waved some black feathers around it.

"Geaux ova dere and reach me sum black peppa gurl." Miss Dot said.

She made a funny clicking sound with her mouth over and over. This ritual went on for about three minutes or so. Then she took the salad bottle, wrapped it in aluminum foil, shook it three times. She then told Lupanare to put it in the refrigerator for twenty four hours and she sent her home.

I have no idea why the people in New Orleans love wrapping everything in aluminum foil. I remember one time Lupanare wrapped some raw chicken gizzards, a piece of burnt liver with one of those tiny baby dolls you get out of a *"King Cake"* and a sweet pickle in aluminum foil and left it on the porch of the lady next door's house. I think she thought Daddy Bordeaux was sneaking out going over there after she went to sleep. The next thing we knew she and her two kids had moved out of the neighborhood. Lupanare said she'd cast a spell on her, but if you ask me, it sounded more like lunch. I never told her that I'd seen that lady bringing in boxes for weeks preparing to move out, long before she had the idea of putting one of those silly, so called hexes on her that she'd learned from Miss Dot. This was a clear indication to me, how ridiculous all this Gris- Gris crap I grew up around actually was.

Lupanare began pouring the period salad dressing on Daddy Bordeaux's salad, days before he was to leave. It was not an easy task to get him to eat it because salad was not really a staple in our house. Rice and bread were the two things that had to be on the dinner table at all times in our home, and most households in New Orleans. Nevertheless she managed to get him to eat it, so she thought. He was hiding it in his napkin whenever she put her head down to eat her own dinner. Not to mention, Daddy Bordeaux recognized that he was the only person with salad on their plate at the dinner table.

A few days later Daddy Bordeaux ran into Miss Dot at the *Winn Dixie* and she asked him, "How'd you like the salad dressing Bordeaux? I made some up special just for you."

She laughed with her own brand of creepy cynicism as she walked passed him down the frozen isle section.

Lupanare's plan to keep Daddy Bordeaux home was a disaster. Three months later, he presented her with divorce papers and moved to Brazil. She never found out that Miss Dot had sold her out.

A few days later, the boys and I came in from school only to find Lupanare on the bathroom floor comatose. There was a tinted plastic medicine bottle lying next to her and a half empty bottle of *Jack Daniel's* turned on its side on the floor. She had white foam coming from her mouth. We tried to wake her, but she wouldn't move or talk to us. Roman was shaking her uncontrollably screaming and crying.

"Mommy, Mommy, please wake up, we need you, don't leave us please."

I ran and called YaYa, and she and Grandpa came right over. YaYa must have called for an ambulance because the paramedics arrived right before they did. Lupanare almost died that day. The doctors said she was psychologically unstable and shouldn't be left alone. That weekend we moved from our house in Gert Town on Telemachus Street to Pontchartrain Park to live with our grandparents. Grandpa and YaYa sat all four of us down and explained to us that we would not be returning home and that the boys and I would be going to different schools. They would take turns driving me uptown because I would be transitioning to *Xavier Prep* at some point and they didn't want to disrupt the flow of my education.

I wondered if it had ever occurred to them that our father had not only divorced our mother, but he had also divorced his four children; and the fact that our mother just tried to take her own life minutes before we arrived home from school, had already disrupted the flow of our lives.

After that, Daddy Bordeaux only came home once a year, two days before Fat Tuesday. He came to parade the streets of New Orleans with his Black Mardi Gras Indian tribe on Carnival day. He was still referred to as, "Big Chief Bordeaux" and was well respected amongst the locals. He spent the first days of carnival in Brazil. He felt a strong kinship to the Brazilians. He said they were our cousins. The culture, cuisine and the music almost mirrored ours. But he loved the beaches and the simplicity of the lifestyle and said he would take us there one day, but he never did.

I went back into the kitchen and Slone was taking the BBQ shrimp out of the oven.

"Maybe we should go on and eat."

"I've lost my appetite. I'm going outside and get a couple of those gallons of frozen hurricane daiquiris, that Roman bought the other night from the *Daiquiri Shop*."

"So we're going to drink *hurricanes* during the hurricane?"

"That's right, that's how we get down in da Big Easy." I said with a smirk.

"Anyway that's not a good idea; you haven't eaten anything since breakfast. Let's eat first and then I'll have one with you."

"Okay, I'll be right back."

I went outside to the other kitchen and opened the huge freezer and pulled out the daiquiris. I brought two just in case we couldn't get back out there before the hard rain started. Slone had already fixed three bowls of BBQ shrimp and placed the crawfish pie on the table with the French bread for dipping. Roman came out of the den yawning and rubbing his eyes vigorously. He eventually spotted me coming in with the daiquiris and said, "Now that's what I'm talking bout, pour me some of that. I need a good stiff drink after all the junk that's happened today. Have you heard anything from Grandpa yet?"

"No, he hasn't called yet."

The three of us sat quietly and ate our dinner. Roman got up from the table and went to the den. He came back with the domino set.

"Do we have any takers in here?"

"Yep, I'm in." I said.

"What about you Slone?"

"You guys go ahead. I'm going to clean the kitchen."

"Alright, but when I get done whipping Jenna, I got something for you too."

We could hear the rain; it was coming down harder with each drop. The phone rang, it was Grandpa, and he was ready to come home. Roman said, "I'll be right back, don't cheat Sister."

As Roman reached for his keys and headed towards the back door, Gabriel and Sidney came in.

"What are you guys doing here?" Roman asked.

"We just left the hotel. I thought you guys were going to evacuate or at least stay at the hotel with us until the hurricane passed. We thought we would stock up on some food and drinks and take y'all back over there with us. Grandpa called me earlier and told me about YaYa so I wanted to come by and check on him and see if I could get him out of this house before the hurricane hit."

"I'm on my way to pick him up now. Come ride with me man."

As Roman and Gabriel went out, Sidney came in and Slone and I gave her a hug.

"The wedding was beautiful." Slone said.

"Thank you, I hope you had a good time. Slone was our wedding your first New Orleans wedding?"

"Yes and it was so much fun. I liked that dance that you guys did with the umbrellas and the handkerchiefs."

"Oh, you mean the second line."

"Yes. I was wondering why you guys dance with the umbrellas and handkerchiefs. And why is it called the second line?"

"Well…" Sidney said, as she and her oversized belly sat down, "this is the story that has been passed down in my family for generations. It started as a sort of tribute at funerals. The family members of the deceased person were the First Line mourners, the jazz band, and the Second Line was the non-family members who came to pay their respects. They would also be the rear guard to chase away any evil spirits that might want to take the soul of the loved one.

Traditionally the Second Line mourners were identified by their accessories, like fans, handkerchiefs, and umbrellas. These things were necessary for the long procession to the cemetery in the hot sun. On the way to the grave site, the mourners would quietly walk to the slow dirge played by the band. But once the deceased had been buried, the sound of trumpets would move the mourners to celebrate the life of the deceased and help them to release their soul into eternity.

The handkerchiefs were carried and waved in the air to show that their tears did not hit the ground. They say that if your tears fall and hit the ground at a funeral in New Orleans, you are the next to die.

Over the years the Second Line umbrellas and handkerchiefs had become so popular that we use them to celebrate just about everything from weddings, Mardi Gras, funerals, showers, birthdays or any other reason we can conjure up to have a celebration."

"Wow, that's interesting, thanks for sharing Sidney. I guess I'll think long and hard before I cry at another funeral." Slone said.

"That's a good idea. And on that note I'm going to take myself to bed. The babies have been moving around a lot today, maybe they can sense that the big storm is coming."

The house had emptiness about it. Without YaYa at home, her presence was tangibly absent. Slone and I took our drinks into the den, but not before we had both grabbed a few pieces of fudge that YaYa had made that morning.

"This fudge should be sold in stores it's so good. What's that yummy flavor in the center?"

"I know, it's her own special recipe—chocolate fudge with a praline pecan center. It's the only recipe that she vowed she would never share with anyone. She said she was taking this one with her to the grave, but I plan on getting it out of her as soon as she comes home. She said there was a secret ingredient that she learned about when she was in Paris. Her grandfather knew a family that owned a charming little candy shop called *Fouquet* and it's actually still one of the oldest candy shops in Paris today. They took a liking to her and let her spend the day with them in their store. She said she had the most delightful time learning about French pastries and candy. That's when she fell in love with the idea of one day cooking for a living."

She always said, "Don't leave this earth until you can make a living doing what you love to do or your life will be wasted."

She had earned enough money as a nurse to start her catering business and became one of the most highly sought after caterers in these parts. She's prepared dinners for dignitaries at the governor's mansion several times, catered parties for mayors and a few judges. When Mayor Dutch Morial was alive, he and his wife loved her cooking. Even a few of the local celebrities have called on her for her culinary skills. She does everything with excellence."

"So now I understand why you're such a perfectionist and a control freak. And by the way when are you coming over to my house to straighten out my linen closet again?"

"Please girl, you have a maid to do that for you, remember."

We laughed nervously as we watched the news. It was unnerving knowing in our hearts that we should have evacuated. But there was no way we were leaving without YaYa.

Slone changed the subject to break the odd silence that was between us.

"The dance with Gabriel and his father was phenomenal. I've never heard of a black Indian before. Is that real or was that just another type of show that you guys put on down here? Those costumes were amazing."

"Grandpa once told us that the Native American Indians were taken as slaves before they came and kidnapped us. But the Indians loved their freedom so much that they ran to the bayous and disappeared. The French and Spanish soldiers were scared to go into the swamps, because the Indians knew the land better than they did and were experts in silent warfare. Grandpa said an Indian could overtake you so fast that you wouldn't have time enough to scream. The slaves began escaping into the bayou too and became allies with the Indians. The slaves learned from them how to survive off the land in the forest camps outside the city which became known as *Maroon Camps*. These camps were more like freedom camps, very different from the camps that the slaves that were not sold were held in. They were kept in pens like animals along what is now called Camp Street.

The Indians and the slaves got together so the Indians wouldn't get their land taken away from them by the French for tobacco farms. Hundreds of slaves joined with the Natchez Indians and fought in what was called the Natchez Revolt. The revolt was so brutal and savage that a lot of slaves were beheaded, and their heads were mounted on pikes and displayed on the levee as a warning to the others that might have had any ideas of rebelling.

The costumes that the Black Mardi Gras Indians wear are a cross between the Native American symbolic accouterments, and the African ritual costumes. To honor the Native American Indians that helped them in their struggle as well as their own ancestors. Some of the slaves married and had children with the Native American Indians. They began to form their own tribes and incorporated celebrations with St. Joseph's Day and Mardi Gras and now Super Sunday. We used to see them parading down Magnolia Street when we were kids."

"I had no idea how rich the history was in this city. All I've ever heard about New Orleans was the food and the Mardi Gras celebrations. Slone had the look of pure intrigue on her face as she changed the subject.

"Anyway I was watching YaYa and Grandpa at the wedding yesterday and they seem like they're still very much in love after all these years, the way he looks at her and how attentive he is had a profound impact on me. If I ever got married again, I would hope to have a marriage like theirs. So how did they meet? I could tell that they must have an extraordinary story." Slone said.

"Well, YaYa has always been hard working and dedicated to her family and business. When she was growing up, her mother always told her that you could never be successful in this world without a good work ethic, being on time, and honoring your word. She said that was how you could ensure a good life. But YaYa also believed that a good life also meant having someone you loved, that loved you back; to share your life with was just as important. She was one of those rare women that actually married the man of her dreams and he didn't turn into a nightmare.

Lois Coubillon and William Jaquet met after mass at Corpus Christ Church. YaYa was waiting for Auntie Sharon to pick her up. She was dressed in a pair of black slacks, a silk flowered blouse and a light weight, black maxi coat. Her coal black, long wavy hair blew in the fall wind as she stood rehearsing in her mind how she would go about finishing her chores and her homework before it was time for bed.

Then a tall, handsome, neatly dressed young man approached her and said, "Hello, my name is William Jacquet."

YaYa looked up slightly irritated until she saw his kind face and warm eyes. She cleared her throat and said, extending her hand, "I'm Lois Coubillon."

They talked briefly until Auntie Sharon drove up to take her home.

"It was nice to have met you William."

"I hope to see you again next week at service." Grandpa said.

YaYa never missed another Sunday service again. She started wearing nice dresses, shoes and sometimes even fancy hats to church after that day. They used to sneak out of service and meet on the back steps to talk and hold hands. YaYa was nervous about bringing William home to meet her family. Her grandmother, Mama Beulah, was the worst kind of quadroon and hated being around anyone that was darker than a brown paper bag. She was a mulatto woman in a left-handed marriage and confused about her identity. You see, YaYa's grandfather was a wealthy white French Creole, that's who Roman inherited his blue eyes from. But anyway he had two families, one with his white wife and children and in a *Placage* with Mama Beulah. Back then marriage between the races was forbidden according to the *Code Noir*, but the *Placage* system was a common law marriage usually between a white man and a Creole woman that was part of an extra-legal methodology that was embraced by the culture.

Mama Beulah forbade YaYa and her sisters from spending time out in the sun, and if they did, they would be punished. Anytime they would, she would say they looked *too black* as she called it. They would have to stay inside for the next two days until any hint of tan from the sun left their skin. She even kept them out of school until she was satisfied with the shade of their skin color.

But Grandpa was the nicest, smartest, most handsome guy YaYa had ever met. The first time she saw him, she said her heart raced and her belly felt like it did the first time she had seen a scary movie. She was in love with everything about him, every time he told her a story, that love became stronger and she adored him even more. She knew she wanted to spend the rest of her life with him no matter what the consequences.

She finally got the courage to invite him over for Monday night red beans and rice. It was odd because it was like the movie with Sidney Poitier, *Guess Who's Coming to Dinner*. But everyone was Creole. Strange that light-skinned blacks and regular-looking black folks often separated themselves and kept the slavery tradition of house nigger and field nigger going long after the slaves had been freed. Nobody had to use a whip to help them continue this ritual of separatism. They enjoyed the intangible perks of a nullified cast system amongst each other.

Grandpa and YaYa entered the dining room. They knew she was bringing home a guest for dinner and they looked forward to meeting him. YaYa had spoken very highly of him and had told them stories of how smart, witty and charming he was. Somehow they assumed he was light-skinned Creole like them. When they entered the dining room, Mama Beulah dropped a big silver serving spoon and splashed the red beans and rice on her freshly laundered blouse. She fumbled angrily trying to clean up the mess with a napkin while periodically glaring up at Grandpa, mumbling words like: coon, monkey and black nigger over and over underneath her breath. YaYa said those words haunted her for the rest of her life.

YaYa's father, Robert Coubillon was a wise man. His mannerisms let you know that he understood many things without saying them. He politely invited Grandpa to sit down and eat. Mama Beulah took her food to her bedroom mumbling racial slurs the entire time. Her father and Grandpa talked for hours about the war, prohibition, slavery, education, politics and even the best way to train a dog.

Auntie Sharon and Auntie Bristol, YaYa's younger sisters, giggled as the three of them cleaned the kitchen listening to every word. Grandpa finally said goodnight and thank you to everyone.

"Come back anytime young man. As a matter of fact, why don't you come by on Sunday and have dinner with us? Don't worry we'll lock Mama Beulah in her bedroom until you finish your dinner." Great Grandpa Coubillon said. They laughed, shook hands and Grandpa headed out the door.

YaYa stood on the front porch and watched Grandpa leave that night. She felt relieved and happy that other than Mama Beulah, everyone else, including her mother Josephine, who could pass for white as well if she ever chose to, was delighted with his visit. She just wanted her girls to be happy.

As time went on, they dated for a year and Grandpa was drafted into the Army. They wrote each other love letters and YaYa sent him packages of fudge and creamy pralines every month. Everyone tried to encourage her to date other guys, but the love she had for Grandpa never allowed room in her heart for another man. Right after Grandpa came home from the Army, Mama Beulah died from a horrible bout of pneumonia. Three months after she died, they were married.

Grandpa couldn't afford medical school, so one of the best jobs to have at that time for blacks was to work at the Post Office. He worked as a mail carrier for over a decade; then landed a job with *Equal Employment Opportunity for Colored People.* He told us stories of how he used to drive into different towns around the country and the police would escort him back to the city limits. He would drive a few miles and hide out for a while and then turn around and go back. It was his job to make sure that blacks were actually being hired and working at various companies, small businesses and being treated fairly and equitably. He worked that job for ten years and then went back to the Post Office and worked there until his retirement.

YaYa finished nursing school and took a job at *Charity Hospital.* She was a nurse for many years. She comforted many patients, as she dispensed medication, changed bed pans, gave shots and cleaned bed sores. She said it was the most humbling job anyone could have. Having to wipe someone's behind after they crapped was not an easy thing to do. Seeing people in their most vulnerable state and trying to handle them with compassion, no matter how ugly, nasty and depressing the situation became, was no easy task. After twenty-five years, YaYa retired from nursing and opened

YaYa's Catering. She said the only ass she was going to wipe after that was her own.

Grandpa and the boys came home. "How is YaYa?" I asked.

"She is brave." Grandpa said. "She wouldn't take '*no*' for an answer when I tried staying the night with her. The nuns assured me that they would take good care of her and they have a fail-proof evacuation plan prepared. I hated leaving my YaYa there in that place all alone. She was so worried about you kids that I had to come home just to shut her up. She was a little groggy from all the medicine they gave her, so I'm hoping she can sleep right through this one, you know. Jenna, you mind fixing me a plate? Roman said you and Slone cooked up a pretty good batch of BBQ shrimp."

"Of course Grandpa, what would you like to drink?"

"I'll have my usual, *Sazerac,* baby girl."

"Gabriel, are you going to eat something?"

"You go on and take care of Grandpa, I'll get something after I check on Sidney." Roman came into the room chomping on a praline and said, "Damn, these pralines are sum good yeah."

After Grandpa and Gabriel were done eating, we were playing cards and listening to Al Green and Erma Thomas records when we heard someone come in the back door. It was Lupanare.

"Where you been in all this chaos girl?" Grandpa said. She came into the den and stood in front of us, soaking wet, dripping water all over the floor.

"You betta go and dry yourself off. If YaYa was here, you'd be in a heap of trouble." Gabriel said.

Lupanare sat down on the sofa.

"Well, she's not here right now is she?"

It was as if I had levitated off my chair and was standing over her before I knew it. "You are walking a thin line Lupanare. If it wasn't for the hurricane I would have Grandpa, make you leave."

"This is my mama's house and nobody can make me leave if I don't want to. If Grandpa wasn't here, I would slap the taste out of your mouth."

"Let's see you try. It's your fault that YaYa is in the hospital in the first place. Slone told me how you disrespected her and provoked her so much that she had a heart attack."

Our voices carried well over the music, banter, strong winds and rain. Grandpa stopped dealing the cards, as he turned in his chair to listen more intently. Gabriel put down his beer and sat up straight and Slone looked like a deer caught in head lights.

"It's not my fault!" Lupanare said.

"Yes, it is! You knew how vulnerable she was and you were determined to make a point, no matter what the cost. You're still trying to make a pathetic attempt to fix what ever happened between you two when you were a little girl. Get over it and stop making everyone around you miserable. You tried to deliberately hurt her."

As the thunder rumbled and the lightning flickered brightly throughout the house, Lupanare screamed over the bellicose sounds of the hurricane.

"That's not true. I knew that dirty white bitch was going to open her mouth and tell lies about me!"

"Now that's enough. You all fighting and calling each other names is not going to change anything. Lupanare, you know I don't allow that kind of talk in my house. I don't want to hear another word about it. Do you understand me?" Grandpa said.

"Yes sir." We both said as we locked eyes.

"Lupanare, you need to apologize to Slone for your offensive language and Jenna, calm yourself down and let's finish playing our game."

I was fuming as I said to Grandpa, "How are you going to let her get away with doing that to YaYa?"

"Hush now Cher, let it go, come on, it's your move."

Slone flinched every time she heard a noise. "Baby you need to try and relax, it'll all be over soon. I promise we're going to make it through this one just like all the others." Grandpa said.

"Oh, Grandpa I forgot to tell you, Auntie Sharon called." I said.

"Yeah, I thought they were coming ova here."

"No, they just decided that it would be better to take the girls to the Convention Center. The girls got so upset watching the news and begged them to go to the Superdome. She said there were too many people there, so they decided to go to the Convention Center instead."

When B. B. King's, *Down Home Blues* came on the record player, Roman came over and pulled Slone out of her chair and began twirling her around. He tried to teach her the old school hand dance. Then *Grazing in the Grass* came on. Lupanare and Roman started cuttin' a rug, doing the cha, cha, cha. The rest of us joined in and we were having a good, old fashioned hurricane party. As the rain came down and the fierce winds blew, we tried to forget our problems, and the reality of the threat of a category four hurricane.

Then we heard a loud crash. We jumped to attention as our brief moment of merriment was interrupted by a huge oak tree that had fallen onto the side of the house. Roman and Gabriel ran outside to access the damage, while Grandpa followed after them, grabbing his galoshes along the way. I foolishly grabbed an umbrella and went out behind them leaving Slone and Lupanare alone. I didn't consider the possibility of the danger of not only leaving the two of them together, but Katrina's wrath was more vicious than I'd realized. Her wind savagely snatched the umbrella from my hand and sent it flying down the street. I pressed myself as hard as I could against the swirling air, but with regret, I attempted to get myself to where the men were as the rain pounded me mercilessly. I was blinded by Katrina's rain as her fierce wind feverously blew clusters of drops into my eyes. I was knocked to the ground as I fought with all my strength to rise from the wet concrete. I tumbled down the street while my head bounced on the side walk and I ended up in the bushes. I felt a pair of big strong hands pick me up and carry me back into the house. The arms that had rescued me without hesitation that dark night belonged to Grandpa.

Lupanare and Slone had gotten some towels to dry us off. I was soaked and shaking. The first of Katrina's rain had just assaulted me. My head was bruised and the skin from my knees had been left on the sidewalk. I sat on the sofa with throbbing, bloody knees and an excruciating headache. As my family tended to my wounds, I felt a sting that snapped me out of my state of oblivion.

"Ouch, that hurts!"

There was Grandpa putting *Mercurochrome* on my knee just like when I was a little girl. Lupanare wrapped gauze and taped both of my knees. I was glad she took some initiative to participate in the process of my healing.

Gabriel stood behind me drying my hair with a towel. Sidney had awakened from the noise of the storm and was by my side encouraging me to change my wet muddy clothes and lie down. Slone was calm and had gotten me a glass of ice water and two *Tylenol*. I hobbled to my bed, and they graciously moved the party to my room. Roman brought in a card table, some chairs and a deck of cards. Sidney and Slone got on the big, king-sized bed with me, while Lupanare sat in the over-sized, fluffy chair that sat in the corner of the room. Roman wanted to play the *Remember When* game. It was appropriate since it had been years since we were all together like this. Too bad YaYa couldn't be with us, she always enjoyed this game because she and Grandpa got to hear about all the stuff we did growing up that they knew nothing about.

"Okay Roman, you go first." I said, as I fluffed up my pillows and put them behind me so I could sit up comfortably. I was feeling better just being surrounded by my family. I had missed them so much over the years.

"Jenna, remember when Gabriel and I had about six of our guy friends over? We were all sitting in the back yard and you and Natasha were parading around trying to get some attention. He looked at Slone and said, 'Natasha is our first cousin.' Anyway, Jenna was out there trying to be cute in her jean booty shorts and a bright red tube top. Natasha ran up and pulled it down exposing her flat ass chest. She was all nipples back then. They started slapping, pulling hair, punching and scratching each other. Then Grandpa came out of the back kitchen because all of us were laughing making bets and throwing dollar bills on the ground waiting to see who would win the fight. Jenna went so buck wild mad, that she snatched her earrings out and Natasha had blood running down her ears and neck. Grandpa had to come pull Jenna off that girl. She even popped him in the mouth when he tried to break them apart. Jenna was on punishment for a month after that."

We were laughing so hard that we forgot there was a hurricane going on outside of our walls.

"Okay, okay." I said. "I remember when we were at the Audubon Park Zoo. Roman and Gabriel started playing and running around so much from all the sugar they'd had from eating too much cotton candy and ice cream. Roman was so hyped up, that he ran himself right into a big pole. He knocked his two front teeth out and busted his lip so badly he had to get thirteen stitches. We spent the rest of the day at the emergency room."

"I still have that scar on my lip to this day." Roman said, as he wiped the tears from his face from laughing so much.

"I remember when Grandpa thought he heard somebody trying to break into the house. He ran into the bedroom closet, grabbed his gun and started running down the hallway in nothing by his underwear. He tripped, fell and broke his nose. It was in the middle of the night so we all had to get up out of bed and go to the hospital because YaYa said we were too young to stay home alone. I wondered who she thought was going to come to our house at three o'clock in the morning and steal four bad ass black kids out their beds. That shit only happens to white kids. Black folks should know by now that since slavery ended, don't nobody want us any more."

"Grandpa you could have shot yourself in the foot man." Gabriel said.

"Yeah, that was a good one. I remember that like it happened yesterday, I went flying into the air and I just couldn't stop myself from falling. I fell flat on my face."

"Okay Lupanare, your turn." I said.

"I can't think of anything."

"Sure you can."

"Well, I remember one time when I was about twelve, I was sassing YaYa and she got so mad at me that day that she ran me all over the house with her broom, and forced me into the bathroom and washed my mouth out with *Ivory* soap. She said, 'I'm the *HPIC* in this house and I'm gonna make sure you never forget it.' It took me years to figure out what that meant. I was too afraid to ask at the time. Then she took me into the kitchen got some uncooked rice out of the cabinet and made me kneel in it for hours while I watched her cook dinner and fold clothes. My knees had the indentation of hard rice for two days. I never sassed her again after that."

"Slone do you have an, 'I remember when' story?" I asked.

"None of them quite as funny as you guy's stories. I'll pass."

"Remember that time YaYa sat up all night licking dem *Green Stamps* from the *Piggly Wiggly*? She was too hard headed to use a sponge. She got so sick that she couldn't get up out the bed the next day to go redeem the gifts. We used to get some nice stuff with those *Green Stamps*. I liked helping YaYa get the books together. I just used a sponge though." Roman said, wishing she was there.

"Lawd, I can remember the welts as clear as day." Grandpa said. "One night YaYa told Edmond to clean the dishes. But Edmond had it in his mind to go off and play with his *Hot Wheels* racing cars instead. He was smiling and laughing as his cars went round and round the track. YaYa came in and took one look at the unclean kitchen and I thought she was going to blow a gasket that night. She went into his room, snatched the car and threw it across the room, grabbed the hard plastic track and whooped his behind wit that race car track. She ran that child all over the house with that thing til she was good and tired. I sure do miss that boy. He was a good child, I swear to God.

"Who's Edmond" Slone asked innocently.

There was an uncomfortable silence that hung in the air for a moment before Grandpa finally said, "Edmond was my first grandson, these kids' older brother."

"Jenna, you never told me you had an older brother, where is he?

"He died in a car accident on the *Huey P. Long Bridge*. He had just started medical school." Grandpa said, with tears in his eyes.

Slone could tell it was a sensitive subject and didn't want to spoil the fun, so she broke the mood by asking.

"Anybody want some fudge?"

"Yes." I said.

"Me too." Gabriel said.

"Me three." Lupanare yelled.

Slone got up and went into the kitchen and Roman followed her.

"What's up with those two?"

"Nothing Lupanare, they're just friends."

"Hmm. Looks like more than friends to me."

Roman wrapped his arms around Slone's waist as she put the chocolate fudge in a napkin. He kissed her on the back of her neck. "So, when you gonna let me make that kitty cat of yours purr again *Wonder* bread?"

Slone turned toward him and said, "You can have it whenever you want it."

Roman licked his lips and tried to kiss her, but before he could, she grabbed the fudge and ran back into the bedroom. He followed behind her like an untrained puppy.

"Alright Jenna, get yourself on over here and shuffle me a good hand." Grandpa said.

Suddenly, the electricity went out. We lit three of the hurricane lamps and Grandpa, Roman and Gabriel played cards all night while the rest of us tried to get some sleep. The invisible winds of Katrina treacherously wrapped themselves around sign posts, street lights, houses, cars and buildings; threatening our way of life for hours on end. It was as if she had a whip that she snapped methodically, bringing with her boisterous sounds of thunder, while blinking her ferocious eye with flashes of lightning that rode on her lashes, above us every time she swirled buoyantly up and down the streets of our vulnerable town.

Hail Mary

Early the next morning, I got up to see if I could find something to eat for breakfast. I was starving for some reason. I was fumbling around in the kitchen, checking the refrigerator for anything that might still be edible before it all went bad. I was minding my own business when Lupanare came in and asked me, "Jenna why were you acting so strange at the wedding? You were so rude to Father Timothy. He was looking forward to seeing you this trip."

"I don't want to talk about Father Timothy, okay."

"Why not? He was the only person that took up for you when all that mess happened up at the school. He had Sister Francis sent to another parish. Did you know that? He would even light a candle for you every week and pray for your protection and emotional healing after you left for California."

"A candle, huh."

"I think you should give him a call and apologize to him for being so ugly with him the other day."

"I don't have anything to say to that hypocrite!"

"Wait one minute girl, you are on the verge of blasphemy."

"Blasphemy? He's not God Lupanare."

"He is the representative for God on earth, so don't ever disrespect the man of the cloth again in this house."

She came so close to me; that I could smell just about every ingredient in YaYa's chocolate fudge recipe that lingered on her breath from the night before.

"Leave me alone Lupanare!"

"What?"

"You heard me. I said leave me alone."

"You think you're better than us now that you moved to California and got yourself a job making some money? It was my hard work and those nuns and priests that educated you. You had the finest parochial and college education that money could buy, so you could get a good job and make something of yourself. You ungrateful bitch! All that was sacrificed for you and this is the attitude you come here with."

By this time our voices had carried throughout the house. It was morning and all was quiet. The hurricane had passed but it was clear another one was about to begin. I could see out of my peripheral vision, Grandpa and Gabriel come into the room. I thought Grandpa would intervene, but I guess he knew it had to come to a head someday.

"Fine then, let's talk about your precious Father Timothy, whom *you* say, represents God. Remember when Sister Frances asked you if I could work after school in the rectory three days out of the week? Well, at first it was sort of *cool* to work in the rectory. It made me feel special, important, you know. Sister Francis and Father Timothy were so nice and accommodating. I even had dinner with them sometimes when we had lots of paperwork to get done. Then one Friday afternoon, I worked while the other kids had gone home early after a half day of school. I was in the office filing, when Sister Francis came in with her usual bubbly self. She was babbling going on and on about the parent-teacher conference next month. She went on to say how we had a lot to do to prepare for the conference. She walked around the desk and reached over me to get something out of the bottom drawer, when it was obvious it would have been more appropriate to walk around. As usual I ignored her subtle maneuvers. She always found a reason to brush up against me or put her hand on my shoulder or leg when she was giving me instruction. I never really thought anything of it, but I do remember one time, she leaned so close to me that I could damn near feel her breath on my eyeballs. But this particular day, Sister Francis was a bit jumpy. I figured she was just glad to be out of the classroom early. She asked, "Jenna would you mind staying for lunch? Father and I would like to go over some details about next week's report cards."

How could I say, 'no'? It would be disrespectful right?

"Yes ma'am. Just let me call YaYa and let her know."

I let YaYa know that I would be home before dark, and *of course* before the Friday night family and friends, fish fry. About an hour had passed when I heard a knock on the door.

"Yes, come in."

"Just wanted to let you know we will be having lunch in the den today."

"Oh, Hi Father, I'll be in soon." I said.

I organized the desk all nice and neat for the next person that would work on Monday. There were a few different kids that came in and helped in the rectory, but never on the same day as me. The other kids worked in pairs. I knew because I made out the schedules quarterly. I figured it was because I was so efficient, that I never had a work partner like the other kids.

I went into the dining room, sat down and ate my lunch quietly as we listened to soft classical hymns in the background. I was always quiet around Father Timothy, he was intimidating. He often had a glare that made you think he could read your mind. As if he wore *judgment* on his shoulders. You could sometimes brush up against it as you passed him; it was so intense it was almost palpable.

"So Jenna, how are things at home?" Father Timothy asked.

"Good."

"And how is Lupanare?"

"She's good."

"By the way, can you help me upstairs after lunch? We need to take the drapes down for cleaning this weekend. We can get them down faster with an extra pair of hands." He said.

I finished my plate quickly. Sister Francis began to gather up our plates from the table soon after Father Timothy went upstairs. I had never been upstairs in the rectory. Somehow I always thought it was off limits to civilians. I wasn't sure what to do next, but Sister Francis interrupted my thoughts and read my mind, "You can help me with the dishes and then we'll go up together."

As we finished the dishes, I folded the towels neatly and yawned. I followed her out of the kitchen, then down the long hallway and up the stairs. She was humming along with *Great is Thy Faithfulness* as the sounds of another hymn met us as we approached the top of the stairs. We walked past several closed doors, then into the modestly decorated bedroom where Father Timothy stood looking up at the gaudy, dust-filled drapes. He turned abruptly toward me, and said.

"Please sit down for a moment. It'll be good for you to take a break before we get started."

I looked around the room for a place to sit other than the bed. Sister Francis had sat in the only chair that was in the room.

"It's alright dear, sit down." Sister Francis said.

As I sat down I noticed that she had closed the door behind her. The bed felt so firm and comfortable; I wished I could have dismissed them both, so I could have taken a nap. The headboard was a dark mahogany wood with deep nonfigurative carvings that matched the nearby chest of drawers and vanity. I observed on the bedside table, a beautiful crystal amethyst rosary and a really cute square box, outlined with little white pearls surrounding a picture of the Virgin Mary. I looked at the clock hanging on the eggshell painted walls. It was almost four o'clock and getting close to time for me to get home. I was uncomfortable sitting on the bed. I jumped to my feet and said, "Can we get started on the curtains now? I need to get home before dark."

"Don't worry. I'll take you home when we're done."

Father Timothy sat down on the bed. He took my hand and pulled me back onto the bed. I couldn't look at him, I was so frightened, so confused. Why weren't we taking down the curtains? Why did he have me sitting on what I assumed was his bed? Wasn't it forbidden somewhere in the bible, *thou shall not sit on the bed of a priest?*

"Jenna, I want you to relax, lie down." He said.

"No thank you sir, I don't want to lie down right now."

"Lie down girl!"

My eyes watered with tears, as I obeyed. Sister Francis sat quietly in her chair, watching, as he began to slide his hand under my navy blue pleated skirt. His eyes wide with excitement, he began to fondle my private parts. His eyes gazed upon my face as if he were judging my inability to comprehend what was happening. Sister Francis reached for the cute, small, square metal container. She removed the pearl trimmed top and stretched her arm out offering him the container and its contents to him. He dipped his fingers in it and proceeded to put one finger inside me, then two with difficulty, and then he attempted three. Sister Francis covered my mouth with her freshly dish-washed hand, and put her other hand over my chest to keep me from moving. The tears streamed down my face. Father had his five o'clock shadow now nestled into my neck, scratching me with his every movement. I was dizzy with confusion as his fingers penetrated my tiny virgin vagina. My eyes caught Sister Francis, as they begged for help through the river of tears that flowed rapidly beyond the moans of pain and the manifestation of shame that they knew would surely come.

I closed my eyes and began to focus on the rhythm of the violation. Then he stopped. I tightened my eyes, afraid of what I would see if I opened them. Sister Francis removed her hand from my mouth and said, "Shhh, its okay; God has chosen you to be a blessing to his servant. God wants you to please Father Timothy, it's an honor."

I opened my eyes, because I couldn't believe what she was telling me. I looked out of the corner of my eye only to see Father Timothy taking off his belt, then his pants and underwear. I tried to get up and run, but she grabbed me and held me down. I was old enough to know, that what was happening to me was a violation of epic proportions. I would not go down without a fight. I tried kicking her but my foot wouldn't reach. As I wrestled with her, I heard a loud pop, then, I felt a terrible sting across my legs.

"Move out of the way Francis, now!" Anger dictated Father Timothy's words.

When she moved, all I saw was a big black piece of leather coming toward me. Kapow! Kapow! She was holding my hands up over my head, trying to tie me to the bed which she did successfully.

"No, he said, turn her over."

He put down the belt as she untied me and he aggressively turned my body onto my stomach. Sister Francis explained the meanings of the colors of the scarves as she tightly tied my wrists and ankles to the bed posts. She said the white scarf was for purity, vermillion for lust and sin, and the grey scarf was for weakness, then she whispered in my ear that the black represented the sorrow I would feel after this was over, but that it would pass and God would reward me for my sacrifice.

Father Timothy began to whip me. I had never been whipped with a belt before. YaYa would not allow the girls to get whippings. So everything was very surreal for me—painful and humiliating. Now, I knew how the boys in my family felt when grandpa said he was going to make men outta them with the belt. Father Timothy had beaten the innocence and naivety out of me with every stroke.

"Hail Mary full of grace the Lord is with thee, blessed art thou amongst women and blessed be the fruit of thy womb…" I prayed to the Mother Mary that was on the top of the tin pearl trimmed box to help me, but she never did.

While Father Timothy and his big black belt made sure that I was physically and emotionally prepared to submit without resistance, the sun was going down rapidly, and I would be in trouble if I didn't get home before dark.

"Father, I have to get home, my YaYa will be looking for me."

"Shut your mouth, I'll tell you when you can go home. You're not done being punished for your sins."

He climbed on top of me and thrust his hard penis inside me. I screamed as loud as I could, before Sister Francis stuffed the crimson colored scarf in my mouth. She watched quietly and lustfully as he ravaged me from the chair in the corner of the room.

I wondered during his brutality, shrouded by religion, *Where was my God?* I could only think, *God please help me, please Lord, I need you now. Help me!* I had prayed every night before I went to sleep from the time I began kindergarten, *Now I lay me down to sleep, I pray the Lord my soul to keep and if I die before I wake...* I had been betrayed by the very people that had taught me to pray.

I was only thirteen years old, what sin had I committed that made me deserve such punishment? I had done everything I was told to do. I made good grades in school, I went to mass every Sunday, I always put money in the offering basket, I went to confession, and said all of my *Hail Mary's, Our Fathers* and *Glory be to the Fathers.* Never missed catechism, I even lit candles for the poor and less fortunate. I did every ritualistic exercise I needed to do for God's love and acceptance. Maybe I'd missed a *Hail Mary* or two while doing my penance. But the atrocity performed on me was in no way equal to the lack of focus in my counting during my prayer time.

"Needless to say, I have carried this secret down in my belly for long enough... Lupanare! Father Timothy might have stolen my *innocence*, but he can't have my *mind* and I won't let him have my *life*."

My arms dropped to my sides, the room was eerily silent aside from the sound of the dripping rain water running out of the gutters that lined the top of the house.

Lupanare said, "I went to the Archdiocese and filed a complaint. They made a deal with me that if we would let this go, all you kids could go to any Catholic school for free. You know I wanted the *best* for y'all, so I did what any good mother would have done. Look at y'all, successful because you had a good foundation. You should be thanking me girl."

There I was standing in the middle of the floor in front of my family, ashamed, incensed and resentful.

"Why didn't you tell someone he did this to you? Why did you blame Sister Francis? I don't understand how you kept this all these years Jenna." Gabriel said.

"I was afraid of him, but I hated her because she wouldn't help me. I thought she was my friend. Lupanare, you didn't even believe me when I told you that Sister Francis had done something to me. You *never* defended me, you let those hypocrites use me and throw me away like I was a piece of trash. You said God would handle it and to keep quiet. That every family in the dirty south has secrets, and you just have to take them with you to your grave."

"Quit crying over spilled milk. I know it's hard, but you'll be alright child. Take some of that hard-earned money and get yourself a psychiatrist and *get over it already*. That was years ago, and you shoulda told me the whole truth, back then. Why are you bringing all this up now?"

"Is this *how* you comfort me Mother? This is why I didn't tell you in the first place. If you weren't so dammed self-absorbed, you would have noticed that when I came back from Los Angeles, that I had gained twenty pounds.

"What does that have to do with anything?"

"Why do you think I lobbied so hard to go and stay with Auntie Bristol after what happened?"

"I thought you just needed to get away from all of the tension and drama after all that happened. I figured you needed a change of scenery. I don't know Jenna; tell me, why did you leave then?"

"I WAS PREGNANT!"

"I knew something was going on with you and that little boy Chase. I told YaYa and your Grandfather to keep a close eye on you kids and they had that boy up in this house almost everyday. Now I find out that you and he were screwing."

"No, Lupanare, the baby I gave birth to is Lennox! I know Auntie Bristol told you she went through an adoption agency but *that's* why I went away."

"So has Chase been notified that he has a daughter?"

"No, the baby was Father Timothy's!"

"WHAT? You're a god damn liar Jenna!"

"That's why I was so nasty with him at the wedding. He was the vile man that stole my innocence while hiding behind a lying cloak of chastity and holiness. Y'all knew what he'd done to me and still let him officiate the wedding. How sick is that? He even noticed the resemblance Lennox had to his own family when he saw her at the wedding. He had the nerve to start tearin' up and shit."

"Well, for your information, I overheard YaYa telling your Grandfather that the priest that was scheduled to do the ceremony opted out. He took off as soon as he heard the first report about the hurricane. He wanted to evacuate his elderly mother before the freeway backed up. So they just sent Father Timothy. Nobody knew he was the replacement until he'd gotten there and by then it was too late. But let's get back to these lies you tellin'. Who else knows about this?"

"YaYa and Auntie Bristol are the only ones that know."

"I don't believe any of this mess. It's just too far fetched to me. How can this be? Father Timothy is one of the nicest Priests in the parish. He's going to become a Cardinal soon you know."

There was a generational curse raging through the women in our family. YaYa and I were so close because we had something in common. We had both been raped. But Lupanare had yet to realize that she had been raped too. She had been raped by life, and it had thrown her away like a dirty dish rag just like Father Timothy had done to me and those boys in Pompeii had done to YaYa.

"Do you realize all I had to go through at such a young age to have to live with the fact that I was viciously raped by a priest, and then had his baby? Why do you think he made sure that the Archdiocese paid for us to go to the best schools that money could buy? I'm sure they paid for me to go to USC too. I know none of y'all around here could afford to pay for me to go to an expensive school like that."

When I got there, everything had been taken care of. My books, tuition, room and board and even food paid in full for four years. I knew you had nothing to do with it, because by then, you were long gone. Auntie Bristol was finishing her residency and I knew the money couldn't have come from her. YaYa would deposit obscene amounts of money every year in my bank account on my birthday and she still does. I guess YaYa went down there and made an *even better deal* than you ever could. Y'all must really think somebody is stupid. I figured it out when I told YaYa that I needed a car and a week later parked in Auntie Bristol's driveway waiting for me, was a brand new convertible BMW with all the bells and whistles."

I looked up only to see Roman standing in the doorway listening, his face bathed in tears. It was clear that he had heard the entire story. We all turned our attention toward him as he walked toward me. I watched him closely as he approached me; he was always so unpredictable. He grabbed me and held me tightly. He put his head on my shoulder and sobbed uncontrollably. Everyone in the room stopped breathing. *I know I did.* I gently ran my hands over his sandy brown, wavy hair, trying to comfort him.

We all waited patiently in shock of the sight of this proud man that allowed himself to expose his emotions openly before his family without shame. His cry sounded as if it had been held in captivity for years, masked behind his anger and false bravado. Roman leaned on me so heavily that we both went down to the floor. He put his head in my lap and continued to sob ever so lightly. One by one, each member of our family came to comfort him. Lupanare came first; she sat next to him and began to rub his back like she did when he was a baby. Grandpa held his hand and Gabriel sat in front of us both. He put one hand on my shoulder and the other on Roman's head. None of us understood the cause of his pain. We had all suffered to some degree at the hand of organized religion. Yet, we loved each other and God immensely.

Our own personal brand of hurricane had washed up the secrets of our past. Rains of relinquished responsibility, waves of frustration and winds of disappointment were constantly bellowing over us.

Gabriel our angel began to pray…

Father we come humbly before you. We honor you and worship you, for we acknowledge that you are worthy of all praise. We thank you for this opportunity that has come to us disguised as an insurmountable circumstance. We thank you that when we are our weakest, you become strong within us. You are more than able to make what is crooked straight.

Lord, we ask that you bring healing to this family. Use our tears to wash away the pain, the hurt, and the disappointment that we have endured over the years. Give us the courage and the faith to forgive those that have betrayed us. Please allow your powerful presence to restore our hearts, minds and emotions. Move us into a place of perfect peace as we release the wrongs that have been perpetrated upon us. Forgive us for our sins as we make a conscious decision to forgive those that have attempted to trample over us and take us for granted. Lord, we know that we can not do these things without you. We trust that you hear our cry and that you would move swiftly to answer our prayer. We thank you for this time of purging, and that only good things will come from it and not evil. We know that you have a great future prepared for us. Thank you that no matter how difficult things may appear all things work together for our good in the end. We love you Lord. Amen

Each of us wept for different reasons. Lupanare from Catholic guilt, Grandpa from the shame brought on our family name, Gabriel because of his compassion and I assumed that Roman needed to acknowledge his own indiscretions and whatever led him into such a phenomenal state of darkness.

I cried because I had felt for years each one of those emotions to the fullest. I tried to anesthetize the pain, only to find my emotional demons operated in every dimension imaginable. I couldn't drink them away, smoke them away, or sex them away. They had yet to make a pill to help me forget the pain and humiliation I'd suffered. I knew I had to make a conscious decision to resist the demented tormenting voices that spoke to me in the night.

No one could do it for me, not YaYa, not Grandpa or Lupanare. No religion, no therapist, no counselor, no priest or preacher, not even God would override my will. Only I had the power to choose to be free with God's help. But I choose to be free today and I have finally decided not to allow the treacherous demons of my past to control my future. I had to take full responsibility for the quality of life that I deserved to live. I continually resist the temptation of blaming God, Father Timothy or Sister Francis for the fact that I couldn't connect emotionally with any man. I always found a reason to end the short-lived relationships I've had over the years. Either they were too egocentric, not smart enough, not attentive enough, or didn't speak the King's English well enough. The sex was bad, his teeth weren't nice enough or I couldn't imagine bringing them around my friends for some reason or another. No one ever stood a chance of actually having a long-term meaningful relationship with me because they had to compete with the insurmountable dysfunction of my past.

We sat huddled on the floor, everyone captured by their own thoughts. We wiped our tears and basked in the lingering elements of Gabriel's beautiful prayer. I sat with Roman's head, still nestled in my lap. My intellectual process was being challenged from every direction. Questions too numerable to count, pushed through the cobwebs of my clouded past. I wondered if the same God that allowed those calamites to come upon us from the most formidable religious institution in the world, would somehow care about us now. How could any good come from so much pain? I admit, I never stopped loving God, but I so longed to understand his ways.

We each sat silently, paralyzed by our thoughts on the den floor. Oddly enough the generator kicked in and the electricity came back on and Al Green's, *How Can You Mend a Broken Heart* was playing. Al talked about an inability to envision another tomorrow. Know one ever prepared us for the sorrows of life and as we listened to the lyrics, we wondered how the broken places in our own hearts could *ever* be mended. The sun shines on the just and the unjust, and those that attempted to devour my youth and infiltrate my family with hypocrisy were clearly broken themselves. How could we be fixed, when disgrace and dishonor had penetrated the very essence of who we once were? Were we so broken that we could not be fixed? Maybe after the storm that had pillaged our hearts, we *really could* begin to live again.

The Rooftop

We were oblivious to the magnitude of what was approaching. We heard a rumbling noise that mimicked the sound of an earthquake. At first it seemed faint and far, then louder and closer. Our attention shifted instantly, toward the profound interruption.

Grandpa, Roman and Gabriel stood hastily to their feet. Grandpa walked into the living room towards the door. Gabriel went to check on Sidney. We could hear something coming, like the sound of a hundred *Clydesdale* horses running toward us at full speed. An enormous raging wave of water burst through the front door so rapidly, that there wasn't time enough to think that this occasion was surreal. The flood of water hit us so hard that it stung like a million bees.

The glass from the windows was blown out, the heavy antique furniture began to tumble and float like children's bathtub toys and Grandpa had disappeared under the wave of terror.

"Sidney! Oh my God, Sidney where are you?" Gabriel's eyes had a look of sheer determination and horror at the same time. He looked frantically for Sidney as the waters rose rapidly, fighting him with every step. Gabriel cried with a loud voice, "Lord, please, help me find the wife you just gave to me. Please!" His voice cracked with a level of desperation, I had ever heard come out of *any* man. "God, my babies, please don't let anything happen to our babies. Jesus, I am begging you. Help us!"

The water was pouring in so fast, that we knew we had to get to higher ground. Lupanare was so frightened, that her face was contorted and her head was bleeding. Everything was happening so fast and the debris was hitting us from every side, "Oh my God… Slone! Roman we have to get to Slone!"

"Where is she?"

"She was in the back bedroom asleep."

Roman pushed through the water like a mad man.

"Slone, Slone! Baby where are you?" By the time he reached her, she had been knocked unconscious and her body was lodged between the dresser and the heavy brass bed that had been a family heirloom for nearly a century. The water was up to her chest and her face was turning a peculiar color of blue. Roman toiled with every ounce of strength he had, to pry her from between the heavy furniture.

Gabriel made it upstairs to the room where his new wife was. The water was so violent that it had thrown Sidney from the bed into the wall, then against the edge of an old marble topped wooden desk. Her mouth oozed red with blood. She held her stomach in excruciating pain. Gabriel managed to get to her, but not before her water had broken, which was now mingled with the filthy waters of Katrina. He picked her up and pushed through the water with every movement more difficult than the last.

"Baby, I have to put you down, okay." He leaned her up against a random piece of furniture. Then he went to the back of the house attempting to open the door to the attic. He yelled, "Grandpa, Grandpa are you all right?" There was no answer. It was a hard decision, whether to get the attic opened and get Sidney to higher ground or go look for Grandpa. He wrestled fervently to get the door to the attic opened. He knew he needed help but he didn't have time to figure out where Roman or Grandpa was at that moment. He pulled and pulled; nothing happened, the door was stuck. He tried again and again, to no avail. Then, he breathed in deeply and pulled with all *his might* and the door opened.

"Slone, please talk to me." Roman said, as he splashed some of the dirty hurricane water in Slone's face. "Come on girl, I know you stronger than that. You looked cancer in the eye and beat it. I damn sure know you're not going to let this bitch Katrina take you out." He worked diligently to remove her lifeless body from between the furniture. He kept talking to her as he continued to fight the water that was now gradually rising toward his own chest. Finally he was able to make enough room to pull her out. He held her head back into the muggy brown water and gave her the kiss of life. She came up coughing water and fighting. "Open your eyes Slone. Open your eyes, it's okay, I got you."

As her eyes opened, she felt a hard sting on her leg. She screamed so loud, that it made Roman's heart skip a beat.

"What, what is it?"

"Oh my God, something just bit my leg."

Roman moved his hand through the water, "Don't move Slone."

He quickly removed a pair of pliers from his back pocket, remembering he'd used them earlier to tighten the locks on the windows. He grabbed the snake by its neck and squeezed its head until it popped. Slone was in excruciating pain, while an unfamiliar feeling of nausea crept into her throat.

"Let's try and get you out of here."

Roman carried Slone out of the room, pushing past drenched clothing, furniture and toiletries that had floated onto the surface of the dirty water. Slone wrapped her arms around his neck with the vague amount of energy she had left. Then they heard a chilling loud shriek, undoubtedly, coming from Sidney.

Lupanare and I were so frightened that we held on to each other tightly. She had a nice size piece of glass stuck in the side of her head. It was difficult to stop and take it out, because the water was rising quickly, constantly forcing us to pay attention to it, not to mention, trying to dodge the uninvited trash and vermin. We needed to find Grandpa. We slowly moved toward the living room, using our hands and feet to get through the water without hurting ourselves. My right leg was throbbing, but I knew we had to keep moving. As we waded through the filthy water, our arms were in pain from pushing what was left of the surge of debris and furniture out of our path.

There was a heavy antique mirror that had fallen across the doorway, leaving only a small space for us to climb through before it would completely collapse. Lupanare was trembling with fear. Her long wavy hair floated on top the water, trailing behind her. I stayed as close to her as I could, every now and then taking hold of her hand and guiding her as safely as I could. The touch of her hand brought a sense of comfort to me. As difficult as the relationship between my mother and I was, experiencing the possibility of losing her in the midst of a storm like this was unfathomable. She had just come back into our lives, we still had so much to sort out, more fights to have and a lot more making up to do. I didn't want to lose her again. In that moment, I didn't care what she had or had not done. I wanted to protect her. I wanted to tell her that I loved her and how much I had missed her over the years. I couldn't find it in myself to form the words. I'd hoped that by the simple gesture of reaching for her hand, she would detect what was truly in my heart.

I dreaded having to stick my head in the nasty water, but I had to see if there was a large enough opening for us to pass through.

"Lupanare, I'm going to check to see if we can get out by swimming underneath the mirror."

"No, just wait for Grandpa or one of the boys to come back."

I ignored her, held my breath and went under the grimy water anyway. I opened my eyes, it was difficult to see, but as I moved through the water I could vaguely see a picture frame, a lamp and a big pillow that used to sit on the sofa in the den. I came up out of the water and realized it was now up to my chest. I wiped my eyes trying to find Lupanare. She was not there and I became frantic.

My words were terribly muffled; the water was going into my mouth. I turned my body in every direction I could, trying to find the woman that I'd not called *Mother* in years. "Mother! Where are you? Oh, my God, Mother."

Gabriel had managed to get Sidney up to the damp attic. She cried out in pain, she was in labor. There were some old dusty blankets and comforters up there, mostly spotted with paint and the faint smell of turpentine. They would have to do. He rolled up one of the smaller ones and propped it under Sidney's head, the other he was able to get just underneath her hips. She grabbed his arm with her nails and embedded them into his skin with such force that it made him cringe.

"Let me take a look, okay honey."

He removed her panties as gently as he could. To his amazement one of the babies had begun to crown.

"Oh my God, the babies are coming. Breathe Sid, just breathe. I have to get Roman."

She attempted to take hold of his hand, without success, as she moaned with pain. She shook her head '*no*', but he was already half way out of the stuffy damp attic.

Gabriel spotted Roman coming out into the hallway carrying Slone.

"Hey man, come this way. I need you to help me with Sidney, she's having the babies."

In the background, Roman and Slone could hear Sidney's screams more intensely.

"Roman, I know you've done this before. Give me Slone and get up there."

Gabriel took Slone and Roman moved as rapidly as he could toward the attic. As he came closer, all of a sudden, there was silence. Roman climbed into the attic and found Sidney passed out and hemorrhaging.

"Sidney, you gotta wake up." He said. Clearly something had gone wrong.

As I struggled to wade through the rising water, my heart was racing at a pace foreign to my body. The fear was overwhelming. I needed to find Lupanare as fast as I could. I moved slowly through the water feeling around for her. I could feel the shape of a statue of the Virgin Mary that YaYa used to have perched on the mantle. God only knows how one of Gabriel's track meet trophies got into the living room, but I could feel the shape of the tiny little man on top, with legs in a huddled position. Sofa cushions and pillows floated past me as I waded through the water towards the kitchen. I came to an abrupt stop when I felt something that I was unable to push past. I felt around to check what it was. It was much too big to be Lupanare. I felt an arm that was three times the size of hers and a broad torso that seemed to be partially stuck between the refrigerator and stove.

"Grandpa!" I quickly grabbed his face and gently lifted his head from the water.

"Oh my God, Grandpa!"

Out of the corner of my eye I saw something black and eerie floating on of top the water. It was Lupanare. I jumped with my legs like a frog, frantically trying to get to her. As I reached for her, my foot came down on something with a sharp edge. It was painful, but I didn't allow it to hinder me from getting to her. I pulled her up and brushed her hair from her face. She was unconscious. I had no place to put her down to pump her chest.

"Jenna!" Thank God, it was Gabriel.

"I'm here!" I yelled. "Help, Lupanare is unconscious and Grandpa is stuck in the kitchen!"

It was a difficult choice to make. Do we save our mother, that had been vacant from our lives for so long, or the man that sacrificed everything to help raise us? I could see Gabriel coming towards me.

"No, go help Grandpa. As he went to take care of Grandpa, I tried giving CPR to Lupanare. I checked her mouth for any obstruction, held her nose and blew.

"One, two, three…"

I blew again and counted, to no avail. I knew somehow I had to get the water out of her lungs. I subconsciously probably always wanted to do this to her anyway. I punched her in her chest really hard once, twice and the third time, she coughed up the water.

"Are you all right?" I said, as I patted her on the back. "Hold on to this cushion. I'll be back." She was still coughing, but I had to see what was happening with Grandpa.

Gabriel had a horrified look on his face. "I can't get him, his legs are pinned and the refrigerator is jammed. Help me Jenna."

Gabriel went under water and began to push the refrigerator while I pulled Grandpa as hard as I could. Gabriel came up for air and went under again. He must have released something because I was able to suddenly and effortlessly pull Grandpa toward me. Gabriel came up, panting. He wiped his eyes.

"You get Lupanare and I'll take Grandpa."

Gabriel moved the mirror to the side and I pushed Lupanare carefully through the opening on her cushion. The water chased us up the stairs as it continued to rise and with much difficulty, we managed to get Grandpa, Lupanare and ourselves into the attic.

We were a sight to see. Grandpa was on the floor barely breathing. Lupanare was weak, sopping wet and curled up in a fetal position next to her father. Slone was sitting in a corner trembling and in what appeared to be shock, but grateful that the snake that had bitten her was not poisonous. I'm not sure how Roman knew that, but I guess sometimes men just know things like that.

Sidney was in pain, her clothes completely absorbed by the water that gushed into the attic. I was doing my best to clean up some of the blood off the baby, as Roman had just cut the umbilical cord with his pocket knife. He tenaciously used every technique he could to revive the baby. After several attempts, he looked toward Gabriel who was tending to his wife.

"Man, I'm sorry, I did everything I could, he's not responding."

Roman wrapped the baby in an old dusty towel and handed him to his Father. He looked as if he were asleep. Gabriel looked at the baby and smiled, rocking him and humming a nursery rhyme as he turned to Sidney and said, "Look honey, isn't he beautiful? He looks just like you." He stroked his silky thick black hair, counted his little toes and fingers and then laid the baby on Sidney's chest. But she was unresponsive. It appeared that she had passed out for the time being and she was still breathing. But there were still no signs of the other baby.

Roman stood to his feet and said, "We can't stay in here much longer, the water is still rising. We have to get to higher ground."

"Where do you suggest we go?" I said.

"To the rooftop!"

Roman checked on Grandpa. He seemed to be breathing better. He went to Slone and ran his hand through her wet hair and said, "You're gonna to be fine." As Roman snatched his revolver from his holster, he made an abrupt announcement.

"Back away and put your heads down!" He unloaded the bullets from his gun into the ceiling, exposing the roof. He then reached for an axe and finished the job, making an opening for us to climb through.

"Gabriel I need your help man."

He was dazed as he watched his family disintegrate before his very eyes.

"Gabriel, I need you to snap out of it for a moment and come over here and help me get up to the roof!"

Gabriel handed the baby to me and got up slowly, never taking his eyes off Sidney. His face stoic as he obeyed his older brother. The boys helped each one of us onto the roof, then, Gabriel returned for Sidney. As he lifted her out of several inches of water—her legs dangled, garnished with blood and placenta—he carefully maneuvered her body toward the opening and handed his new bride to Roman, his face covered with tears and the dirty residue of the aftermath of Katrina.

A Way Of Escape

*Y*aYa cringed at the sound of the fierce winds and hard rain. It was so loud, it sounded as if a freight train had driven right through the front door. The room was bright as the lightning flickered every few minutes through her window. She held on tightly to her rosary as she prayed, *Our Father who art in heaven, hollowed it be thy name, thy kingdom come thy will be done...* Boom! The thunder had invited itself without a formal invitation during YaYa's anxiety and prayers. *Someone should have come and moved me upstairs by now.* She thought to herself. YaYa could hear sounds of commotion coming from outside the tightly shut door.

She continued patiently waiting and praying, although deep down inside, she felt a sense of abandonment from the nuns she respected and trusted so much. Her intellect superseded her intuition, as she closed her eyes and tried to rest during the loudness of what now sounded like clanging cymbals at her window.

There was a frightening symphony of wind, rain, lightning and boisterous thunder, all harmoniously pounding the city. No one would rest tonight without a strong drink or drugs. Only fear abounded with the hope that we would all live to make it through another tumultuous hurricane.

YaYa awoke, hours later to the sensation of water seeping into her nostrils. She pulled herself up, holding on to the side railing of the bed. She felt around and snatched the needle from her arm and the oxygen mask from her face. It was pitch black dark and the only light in the room was from the frequent flicker of lighting. She attempted to get herself onto one of the machines that were designed to keep her alive. She gasped for breath, her heart racing, vehemently palpitating far beyond what was considered normal. She fumbled, as she noticed things floating passed her. She finally managed to climb atop the heavy machinery. The water rushed in from underneath the door, which was half blocked by an old EKG machine.

She tried to calm herself, as she positioned her frail body on top the equipment. She knew she couldn't stay there for long, because at any moment her seat would give. She watched as bandages, syringes, her tray table and even the big ugly grey chair that sat next to her bed, floated effortlessly past her as the current continuously moved throughout the room. As she sat trembling, her chest felt as if it was closing up. If she didn't get to higher ground, her lungs would be consumed by the toxic flood waters. Her arteries hardened as they filled with an intense concern for her life. But she was not going to allow the pain in her chest, to take away her desire to live.

YaYa looked around the room, to see what the best strategy was in order for her to escape; it seemed there was no way out other than heaven. A sense of complete peace seemingly wrapped itself around her as she prayed yet another prayer.

Nevertheless, not my will Lord, but your will be done. Heavenly Father, take care of my husband and our children. Please do not let anyone of them succumb to this savage storm. I believe that my heart is right before you, but I ask you to forgive me for any secret sins that I unknowingly have hidden in my heart.

Her mattress was afloat in the aggressive water. She hurled herself onto it using her arms to control it. The water continued to rise as she lay on the mattress calling for help with a strained voice.

"Help me please! Somebody, anybody come and help me!"

She cried out, but no one answered. She was an old woman, sick and alone in a nursing home run by God's servants, whose promises were becoming more of an illusion of grandeur, coupled with an emptiness that the hurricane water was about to fill.

Maybe they just forgot I was here and evacuated without me. She thought, as fear began to evade her mind.

She heard voices, and then heard someone screaming, but that had been quite some time ago.

Maybe everyone else is dead.

Entertaining the thoughts that she was alone in this room became all the more dark, lonely and dismal.

Her heart rate had finally slowed down, but *that* had no bearing on the rising of the water. She was trapped lying on her mattress. Her face was parallel to what was left of the water stained ceiling. She lay still with her eyes closed and began to have a conversation with her creator.

Thank you Lord for the wonderful life you allowed me to have on this earth. Thank you for my wonderful husband, beautiful daughter, and grandchildren. I am grateful for the love, laughter and memories we shared all these many years. Forgive me for speaking against your servants. I know that they did the best that they knew to do and that they are only human. God bless them and keep them safe. Amen. Jesus, I'm ready to see your glorious face.

YaYa laid there quietly for a moment, watching as the water continued to rise. She closed her eyes and pondered the grim reality that she had probably uttered the last prayer she would ever pray. Then, her eyes popped opened and she decided that she refused to go out in that manner. She was not going to let Miss Katrina turn her into a wuss. She was not going to give up that easily. She was once a good swimmer.

Why not just try and swim outta here, it's only water; right? She thought.

YaYa turned over onto her stomach and used all of her strength to move the mattress, as close to the door as she could. The current had pushed the furniture far enough away, that she might be able to maneuver the door open enough for her to get herself through to safety. She figured the water couldn't be more than six feet deep. She took a deep breath, slowly slid her body off the mattress, and into the water. Her feet landed on top of one of the bedside tables, as she fumbled to move the rubble from in front of the door.

Finally, YaYa was able to pry the door open. But once she did, the water came in on her with brute force and the powerful surge broke most of the bones in her body. The door that was meant to be an *exit* became an *entrance* to her death. YaYa drowned that night with her crystal rosary beads securely wrapped around her neck.

Roman and Gabriel managed to get each one of us on to the rooftop. It was at least a hundred degrees and humid once we reached the light of day. As I looked out, there was a sea of water all around us and most houses were completely covered in Katrina's excretions. It was desolate as far as we could see. There were no other signs of life. We were miserable, confused, hot and thirsty. I hoped someone would come soon to rescue us from our living nightmare. I was heartbroken that the city that we loved so much was now under water. We should have left. Our current reality was no one's fault but our own. The day had become the most tragic day in any of our lives and clearly in the lives of thousands of residents, of the humbled region.

I laid out the blankets so that we could put Grandpa and Sidney down on the steamy, wet rooftop. As I arranged them as best I could, I watched as my friend Slone, tattered and bruised, limped toward me saying, "If I don't make it, will you please tell my family that I love them?"

"Slone, I'm so sorry that I didn't listen to you, I should have gotten you out of here. And the answer to your question is, 'no'. You can tell them yourself. We are going to make it out of here alive, I promise you."

Slone sighed and walked away looking for a place to sit down and rest. We were all tired and saddened by the events of the day. We'd a wonderful visit until Katrina showed up. I grew up with hurricanes; every year for all of our lives and the lives of our parents and grandparents. We always turned it into a reason to have a party and we always survived with maybe only a few shingles off the roof or an uprooted tree. But this time things were different. This was a catastrophic situation that touched us deep down in a place within each one of us that we hadn't realized existed.

Sidney's body began to convulse as they laid her down. Roman checked for the other baby, it was coming. Sweat was pouring off of his face, as he attempted to deliver yet another baby, in a matter of minutes. We prayed for the best, although under the current conditions it wasn't likely that the second baby would make it out alive either. Even if he or she did come out alive, they would need medical attention and soon. Sidney was lying on mildewed, germ-filled rags, on the roof of our old house, with a busted lip and dried blood all over her legs and feet, still unresponsive. Her heart rate was faint, but still pumping.

"Jenna, I need you to manipulate her stomach for me, do it gently, you don't want to hurt the baby, but it needs some help to get through the canal and Sidney can't push."

I gently put my hands on her stomach and rubbed downward in small circular motions.

"That's good Jenna, keep that up."

I did that for about three minutes before Roman said, "Stop Jenna; the umbilical cord is wrapped around the baby's neck."

I stopped immediately and watched as Roman strategically held the baby's head in one hand and tried to remove the cord from around the neck with the other. I quickly and carefully took hold of the baby's head, while Roman used his two hands to unwrap the cord. Once the baby was out, he cleared the air passages, slapped its bottom, the baby cried and so did we.

"Yes, it's a girl!" Roman declared.

Gabriel's face lit up like the sky with fireworks on a Fourth of July evening. We all had a temporary moment of delight. Roman wrapped her in an old damp pillow case that he had gotten from the attic. He passed the beautiful new life to his brother. He took one look at her and said, "Your name is Zoë' Arabella Bordeaux; Zoë' means life and Arabella means, "Answered prayer."

Sidney was hemorrhaging badly. Roman was doing everything he could to stop it. He was not a doctor and even if he was, we had no access to any medical supplies. Sidney opened her eyes. Gabriel showed Zoë' Arabella to her and she smiled. He kissed Sidney tenderly on her cheek as he gazed into her eyes lovingly.

Roman was mumbling something I couldn't quite understand. I went to him and whispered, "What's wrong?"

"If she continues to bleed like this, she's not going to make it."

I watched with teary eyes as every piece of cloth he used to stop the fountain of blood was being consumed by the dark colored liquid flowing out of her womb. It wasn't long before Roman was sitting in a puddle of red clotted after birth, with his hands covered in blood.

Slone screamed and Lupanare gagged. I turned to see what all the commotion was about. A dead swollen corpse of what appeared to be a man floating face down covered in mud and bloated beyond recognition paraded passed us. Rats and snakes mounted on it, having a feeding frenzy on its arms and buttocks.

I wondered, "*Who was this man? Was he a father? Was he a husband that once shared a gentle touch and the smile of his wife, who was probably unknowingly a widow now? Was he a bus driver, a teacher, a waiter? What kind of music did he like: rock, rap, jazz, R&B?*" This was a life that had been snatched away with only memories to be kept alive in the hearts and minds of those who loved him. Every memento that would have helped remind his family of him, pictures of him growing up, a token that had been past down through generations or a favorite shirt, all most likely drowned with him, this was more than just a dead body, just a few hours ago, this was a human being with hopes, dreams and loved ones. I'm sure they were searching for him. His kids were probably crying out for their father with no answer; his wife praying, hoping and longing for his presence that would never be felt again. Would he be identifiable when they found his body? How would they contact his wife, his mother, or his siblings to inform them that he had been swallowed up, by the monstrous mouth of Katrina?

The mosquitoes converged with a vengeance onto our musty damp skin. I saw bugs I had never seen before. We were all itching, scratching and drained; waiting, watching, listening, for any glimmer of hope that might arrive on the horizon. But in the meantime, we were surrounded by water and trapped in a frightening hell that we could have never imagined.

Roman dipped a rag into the muddy water and attempted to clean some of the blood off of his hands. I loved my brother with everything in me, but I couldn't help but wonder if this was all too familiar to him. Was the gun and ax that he used to save his family, the same as those that he'd used to slaughter those men down by the Pearl River? From the moment that the storm hit, he had jumped into hero mode. God knows we could not have survived without him. But I worked desperately trying not to believe the terrible things Logan said he'd done. Yet, stranger things have happened down in these parts. Maybe the magnitude of the hurricane was forceful enough to have washed away all the corruption, gluttony, promiscuity, lasciviousness and witchcraft the city had freely offered to millions over centuries, under the guise of *Napoleonic Law.*

I had taken out much of the glass from Lupanare's head. She was still in a ball on a funky wet blanket. My leg was still throbbing and my foot had a nice big gash in it and was tied with a tourniquet, made from a sleeve from one of Grandpa's shirts. I realized that I needed to get some rest. I didn't dare ask Roman to take a look at my wounds. I knew that although well trained, he had to be even more exhausted than any of us.

Roman made his way over to check on Grandpa. He was still alive, his pulse a little stronger, his legs so black and blue he looked like he had been hit multiple times with a baseball bat. Roman made himself comfortable next to Grandpa. He secretly held his hand as he fell asleep. His tank was now on empty.

"Sidney, Sidney!"

Gabriel shook her over and over again with absolutely no response from her. Gabriel let out a grief stricken wail from the deepest part of his diaphragm. Roman and I jumped to our feet and Lupanare and Slone looked on with sheer anxiety. We all watched in horror as Sidney took her last breath.

In the midst of mournful shrieks and hysterical tears, Gabriel sat holding a dead baby in one hand, another one barely alive in the other. His eyes were fixed on his new wife, lying hemorrhaged to death on a hot blistering summer day, on the roof of a home that had always been a safe haven for us.

Gabriel handed the babies to Roman. He leaned down over Sidney and kissed her softy on the lips and said to her in French, "Je ne peux pas imaginer en train de mener ma vie sans toi." *I can't imagine living my life without you.* "Je taime" *I love you.* "Je te manquerai pour toujours." *I will miss you forever.*

Having said his final goodbye to his new bride, he laid his head on her chest and wept.

We all walked to the other side of the roof to give him some semblance of privacy. Roman handed Zoë Arabella to Lupanare. He took the other baby and wrapped him snug in the towel and placed him gingerly in the corner. Tears flowed from each of our faces, as fluid as water being pumped from a well. *How could God let this happen?* Once again, He was absent in a time when we needed Him most.

I wiped my tears on my damp clothes and took a deep breath. I had allowed myself the privilege of becoming desensitized to the pain and sorrow that had become so familiar in the last several hours. I was devoid of any human ability to feel emotion. I was completely shut down. I had nothing left to give and I needed a moment to think. I found a place away from the others and slowly lowered myself onto the hot, wet roof. My mind had become barren and all the fear had left me. I had no more questions for God or anyone else for that matter. Any desire, I once had to reason, had escaped me. I pulled my legs up to my chest and wrapped my arms around my knees. I sat there waiting, wondering if the analytical voices that usually spoke to me would have anything important to say. I heard nothing.

Suddenly, a profound sense of gratitude crept into my heart, as my mind went back to the extraordinary day, I gave birth to Lennox. She was the most beautiful baby I'd ever seen. I can almost hear the sound of her cooing, which always brought a smile to my face. She had come into this world as a result of one of the worst experiences of my life. Yet, her arrival brought me so much joy. Father Timothy had stolen my youth, but God had replaced it with something far more valuable. Lennox would be the evidence, that I was once part of a vast universe that could swallow me up at any moment. While I sat in two inches of dirty hurricane water in hundred degree temperatures, I was so grateful that Lennox was safe.

I remember how difficult it was for me to leave her when I left Los Angeles to come back to New Orleans and finish high school. We had an indescribable bond. She cried and reached out for me the day I left. Tears ran down my face as I turned and walked away from her at the airport. After boarding the plane, I covered my face with one of those creepy navy blue airline blankets and cried for the duration of the flight back home.

The day after I graduated, I packed everything that was mine, kissed Grandpa, YaYa and my brothers goodbye. Then I boarded another plane and moved to Los Angeles, just so I could watch her grow up. I was determined to be a part of her life. She doesn't know me as Mom yet, but one day I will have the courage to reveal to her that I am her mother. I'll tell her that the man that I snatched her away from at Gabriel's wedding was really her father, a small parish priest who violated me. Yet through that violation, he gave me the best thing that ever happened to me.

Would this life altering event compel me with the courage to speak the words I've wrestled with saying to her for twelve years? I imagine that I would take a deep breath, then gently place my hands on her shoulders, look into her eyes and say, *"Lennox, I love you very much, I am your mother and I'm sorry that I abandoned you. I did what I thought was best for you."* But in this moment, I finally had come to the resolve that enough lies had been told and too much time had passed and it was time for me to be honest with Lennox, once and for all. I hope that she would be delighted to have me as her mom. Of course, I would have to have a talk with Auntie Bristol first. The very thought of it gave me an excruciating pain in my stomach. I know she loves her too and sacrificed a great deal for us both, but she must know in the back of her mind, that one day I would realize that life is too short and it can be snatched away without a moments notice.

More hours than I could count had passed and no one had come for us. We all sat quietly staring at the river of death and disease that surrounded us. Roman had gone back into the house and found a few bottles of unopened *Kentwood* water, a couple of sodas, and three pop open cans of *Campbell's* soup. We each took a few sips of water and a small gulp of the cold chicken and rice soup. We were not yet completely famished, but we had no idea what would take place next, that might require us to have some strength.

I stood up and stretched my legs, walked over to Roman and sat next to him. His eyes were red with dark circles and they had a sort of emptiness to them. His face was drawn and pure exhaustion had enveloped him.

"Hey sis, how are you doing?

"I'm worried about YaYa. Do you think she's alright?"

"I'm sure she's okay. I'm glad she wasn't here to have to go through this. I'm sure they evacuated everyone from the nursing home by now. Grandpa said they had buses coming to evacuate them, to one of the hotels downtown. As soon as we get out of here, we can go check on her."

"Do you think the entire city is under water?"

"Probably not, uptown usually can withstand the storms much better, since it's on higher ground. But this shit looks so bad, I really don't know for sure."

"Can I ask you something?" I said.

"Yeah, what's up?"

"What was going on with you this morning? Did Father Timothy try something weird with you too?"

"I was just feeling sad for you. I'm so pissed off with that bastard, Father Timothy, that I could kill him for putting his hands on you. I wish I had known then, what I know now. God only knows where he is by now with the hurricane and all. I shoulda clipped that punk's wings when I saw his ass at the wedding. He had some nerve, knowing what he'd done to this family. I hope Katrina drowned his funky ass already because if I ever run across him again, there's gonna be hell to pay. Do you think God has forgiven him?"

"I don't know what I think right now. All I want to do is get off this roof, get on a plane and go home."

"You are home girl. No matter how far you go or how long you stay away, you'll always have muddy water flowing through your veins. New Orleans will always be your home. You were born and raised here; it's a major part of who you are. That's just the way it is.

Jenna, I'm real sorry about what happened to you. I thought dem priest only liked little boys. I had no idea those bastards were driving in both lanes."

Roman put his arm around me and I cried for fifteen minutes. At that very moment, I realized a major hurricane had hit my family, long before Katrina had been conceived or given a name. We had never truly recovered, we walked around broken, hollow, and regretful for years. The same will probably hold true for the eclectic city of New Orleans. It will clearly take an obscene amount of years, to restore and reconstruct our city that had succumbed to so much devastation.

Grandpa was coughing and trying to sit up. That was a good sign. It was the most movement we had seen from him, since we'd pulled him from the kitchen. It must have been a traumatic experience for him to be fighting for his life, alone in his own kitchen. We almost lost him. Thank God he was going to be alright. We all got up to check on Grandpa, everyone except Gabriel, he and the baby were resting.

"Grandpa, are you okay?" Slone asked, as she patted him hard on his back.

"I'm alive, so I guess that means 'yes' Cher."

Roman was checking his pulse and gave him the last of the bottled water.

"What the hell happened?"

He looked around, only to realize he was on the roof of his home surrounded by water. He shook his head and said, "Lord have mercy. What did we do to deserve this? Where's YaYa?"

It was clear that he was a bit disoriented.

"Grandpa, remember we took her to the hospital and then to the nursing home earlier today." Lupanare said.

"Can you go get her for me? I needs my YaYa, now!"

"Daddy, YaYa is not here right now, she went to make her groceries; she'll be back soon. You just lie down and try to get some rest." Lupanare tried a different course of action to soothe him.

He looked at her and scrunched his face and said, "Where you been girl? You look like fifteen miles of bad road."

This was the first time we'd laughed all day. Grandpa almost drowned to death and was still making us laugh.

Roman said, "Come on man, chill out. You need to reserve your energy if we're going to get through this."

"Alright son, I love you."

"I love you too Grandpa."

He whispered in Roman's ear loudly enough for everyone to hear.

"So really, what is she doing here? Ain't nobody seen her in years."

"I know man. I'll bring you up to speed on that later, just lay back down dude."

"Okay son."

Roman sat with Slone and put his arms around her and kissed her gently on the lips. I was too exhausted to care. I'm glad she had him to comfort her. After all, he did save her life.

"How you holding up, Snowflake?" Roman asked.

"Like Grandpa said, I'm alive, thanks to you."

"Slone, you need to be thanking God that snake bite didn't take you on a trip you couldn't come back from. Let me take a look at your leg." No one had noticed, but it was swollen, fire red, and full of puss.

"It hurts really badly, but I can handle it. I'll be fine."

Roman sat for an hour, holding her close to him and running his hand through her grimy, smelly hair. He closed his eyes, his mind racing trying to figure out what to do next.

My skin crawled as I was being tormented by the idea that the sun was going down. There were roaches, flies, and mosquitoes everywhere, and I had seen way too many rats and snakes for one day. I must admit, I had not really taken the time to pray in years. But I guess the moment at hand was as good a time as any. Fear gripped us all. I prayed it wouldn't start to rain again. The air was muggy and moist, while the smell of mildew had blanketed itself around us as a constant fragrance. If we didn't die from hunger and thirst first, the mosquitoes would surely eat us alive.

My hope was dwindling rapidly. The atmosphere that surrounded us was bleak and void of substance. Our only motive was to stay alive. Our family was no longer divided, we had become a unit. A vast fusion of our minds, wills, and emotions had crept between our past disagreements, blame and shame. We needed each other more than ever. The love we had in the moments on the rooftop, had become thicker than the density of the humidity, that was present in the dimension that we dwelled in. It was tangible, selfless, and radiant. Our love for one another is what compelled us to continue in faith, hoping that we would make it out alive. I'd tried to get some sleep, but feared the rodents would devour me the moment I closed my eyes.

Roman's eyes opened abruptly, early the next morning.

"Paint, I saw a can of paint in the attic."

He stood to his feet and left Slone lying on the sticky roof alone, as he took his arm of comfort with him.

She was flustered, "*What is he going to do with paint?*" She thought.

He went back into the house. He was gone long enough for us to become uncomfortably worried. Slone stumbled, trying to get up onto her feet. She began to limp toward the hole in the roof, that Roman and Gabriel had torn open for us to get to safety.

"No, Slone, don't try going back in the house." I said. "You'll only make things worse. Your leg is already swollen and you can hardly walk."

"What if something happened to him? What if we can't hear him calling for us?"

She was right, but was in God's hands. The water was too dangerous and too high.

"Someone has to go in and check on him." Slone said emotionally.

Gabriel jumped to his feet and handed Lupanare the baby.

"I'll go and see about him, you guys stay put."

As Gabriel began to lower himself into the man-made hole, he was gone for the longest twenty minutes we had ever experienced. He finally returned with Roman behind him. Roman handed Gabriel a can of paint and some brushes, while he held a liter of *Barks Root Beer* in the bend of his arm and two cans of evaporated milk, in his hand. He was soaking wet and the stench that was on him was almost unbearable. He smelled like a dead fish. But nonetheless, he was prepared to use the paint for something that none of us had even thought about.

"Thank God." Slone said as she collapsed back onto the floor of the roof.

"Are you okay?" She asked Roman.

"Yeah, I'm good."

Gabriel grabbed a can of milk from Roman's hand and used the pliers he had earlier, to punch a hole in the top. He rushed to Zoë Arabella and attempted to feed her, by placing a bit of milk in his mouth and transferring it into hers.

Roman passed the root beer to me, then turned and opened the can of paint. He walked over to the far side of the roof. We all watched intently as he dipped the brush into the white paint that Grandpa used to do touchups around the house.

HELP US PLEASE, he spelled out in big, bold letters. It was as neat as any third grade school kid's penmanship, but legible. Then suddenly, Grandpa pulled himself up onto his elbows and shouted, "That's my boy!"

Then for no apparent reason, Lupanare rolled her eyes at Grandpa with disgust. I walked over to her after taking a swig of root beer and offered her some of it.

"No!" She said, as she slapped the bottle from my hand. It rolled toward the edge of the roof and the life saving liquid poured out. I ran to try and catch it before it went over the edge.

Gabriel yelled, "No, Jenna, don't run up here, it's too slippery." But it was too late. As I went down to catch the bottle, I slipped into the feces and urine filled hurricane water. The water was at least twenty feet deep since it was up to the roof and had already completely immersed many of the other houses in the area.

All I can say is, *Thank God, for all those swim lessons YaYa made us take at the YMCA, when we were kids.* She said, "You never know when you might need to save your own life or someone else's."

As usual she was right. The only problem was, up until the moment of slipping off the roof, fear had never been a factor in my ability to swim. There were horrible vile things in the water that wasn't in any YMCA pool I had ever been in, other than the urine of course. I panicked from the thought of how deep it was as I kicked my legs and moved my arms as fast as I could against the rapidly moving current.

The grotesque water raced into my mouth with every stroke. My eyes were stinging and my vision was impaired. I could faintly hear familiar voices calling my name. Then suddenly, everything went black. I anticipated seeing angels with wings and halos at any moment, with the sweet sound of an angelic choir singing and pure nirvana all around me. But there was nothing but consuming fear and panic that raged within me. I had never experienced a darkness of this magnitude before. Maybe what I was experiencing was the prelude to hell. All my life I had imagined my death with heaven marching close behind it. Maybe I should have prayed more, been a little kinder to others, less judgmental and not so selfish. But it was too late, my life was over. I was dying…along with all of my hopes, dreams and fantasies of a future I would never get the chance to live out. They would all drown in the river of destruction surrounding me.

I could feel my body beginning to surrender, to an unsuspecting stream of death. Then all of a sudden, I began to feel a distinct sense of peace come over me. I looked forward to resting and hoped there was a big pot of okra gumbo and a white chocolate,

Kettle One martini waiting in heaven for me. I was hungry as hell, and badly in need of a drink. I was being lulled to sleep, as the current of the muddy waters of Katrina filled my lungs, more eloquently than I'd imagined.

I felt an arm around my waist, dragging me away. *Was this the angel that I'd anticipated would always come for me and lay me safely in the bosom of Jesus?* If it was, then I was at peace with it. I prayed silently, hoping it was not the tentacles of the demons I had been running from most of my life. Maybe they had finally caught up to me during my most vulnerable appointment with death.

Suddenly, I could vaguely feel that my back was hot, almost burning, yet somehow air flowed through my water-filled lungs. I coughed within the depth of the thick darkness. I felt the sensation of water running down the sides of my mouth and pressure on my chest. Then, there was a hard slap across my face. I opened my eyes and there I saw my angel. It was Gabriel. He lifted my body upward from the hot rooftop and continued to slap me, now on the back, over and over again. I coughed up more water and anything else that had randomly taken advantage of me in the garbage-filled water.

"Jenna, Jenna, can you hear me?"

I frantically shook my head, 'yes'. I wasn't able to talk.

Gabriel wrapped his arms around me and cried, "Oh my God, I thought we had lost you too."

Every one of them, including Grandpa who was being held up by Roman and Slone, had surrounded me with a love I had never felt before. I saw the perfect combination of worry and relief on their faces as they gathered around me.

Grandpa said, "That was a close one Cher."

Then out of nowhere we heard the sound of a helicopter in the distance. Roman and Gabriel began to shout, "Help, help!"

They were waving their arms and jumping up and down. We could see them over ours heads and then, they were gone. Our hearts sank as we watched our only means of rescue, fly away. Roman was so upset that he kicked the air and blurted out a scroll of indignant profanity, that clearly intimidated Slone. I watched as a vulnerable uneasiness crept across her face, but I didn't have the energy to explain his crude and demonstrative method of revealing his frustration.

Gabriel went to him to try and calm him down. Slone, Lupanare, Grandpa and I sighed as we could all relate to the profound disappointment he was feeling. He was the only one left with enough energy, to fully express his keen disapproval of our beloved city officials, to dispatch help in a timely manner to those of us in dire need.

Gabriel said, "Don't worry, they saw us, they'll come back for us soon."

We were all holding on by a thread. Zoë Arabella didn't look good either. She was sucking on Lupanare's finger, which pacified her between naps for the moment. It was blazing hot and I wasn't sure how much longer we could endure it. It seemed as if time stood still.

The baby started crying so much, that Gabriel tried to see if he could get milk from Sidney's breast, because she had not responded as favorably to the evaporated milk as he'd thought she would. As he was about to attempt to lay the baby on her breast, he was shocked to see that Sidney had rapidly become almost unrecognizable. Surely it wasn't safe for the baby to nurse on the breast of a dead mother. The temperature was so hot, that within a few hours, decomposition had rendered Sidney's beautiful caramel skin to have a visually unpleasant color. Her face and body was already swollen and an unbearable stench began to draw flies and insects onto her body, like moths to a flame.

While we were all focused on Gabriel and the baby, no one was paying attention to Grandpa. Somehow he tried to stand up without any help. With nothing stable for him to grab a hold of, he lost his balance and fell into the deep water.

"Oh my God, Grandpa!" Slone cried out.

Roman responded with wisdom. He checked to see the area where he had fallen to get him faster. But there was no sign of him. The fast moving, swirling current had swept Grandpa away quickly. Lupanare was about to lose the last bit of mind that she had left. She was screaming at the top of her lungs. "Daddy, Daddy!"

Every part of me that I thought had gone numb was now awakened by a terror that had begun to circulate through every ounce of my body. I was suddenly alert, and was on my hands and knees trailing the water with precision, my eyes trying to find our beloved Grandpa.

"How could we have lost him that quickly? He had just fallen in!" I said.

We had no idea how deep the water really was. Suddenly I realized why it was so difficult for me to swim, when I had fallen in. This water had an aggressive circulating stream that moved rapidly. Surely Grandpa would have a hard time kicking his legs, since they were still recovering from his episode in the kitchen. We were petrified as we stood looking over trying not only to find Grandpa, but praying we didn't lose Roman too.

Gabriel handed me the baby, then jumped in the water after Roman. This was more than Lupanare could take. She walked aggressively toward the edge as if she was about to jump in after them. I grabbed her leg with my one free arm and held on to it with every bit of strength I had left.

"Slone, help me please." I said.

Slone came over and took hold of Lupanare. She fought her wildly. Lupanare was losing it and I wasn't sure how to deal with her. I screamed as loudly as my sore throat would allow me, "Mother, stop it, settle down! There is no one to save you if you choose to jump in that water. Let the boys handle this."

"My boys, my baby boys, please Jesus don't let them die out here in this mess. Have mercy on us, please!"

"Lupanare, please sit down, you are not helping the situation. I know you're upset, but I can't deal with the extra drama right now."

Roman's head came up out of the dirty water, but there was no sign of Gabriel. Our eyes searched desperately across the water for him, after what seemed like an eternity. There was no indication that he had not been swallowed up by the rapacious water as well. Roman took another deep breath and went under again. Our eyes were glued to the water for any signs of Grandpa, Gabriel or Roman. They were good swimmers, but under these conditions, what normally would come easily, became ten times more challenging and life threatening. Finally Gabriel and Roman's heads popped up out of the water and we exhaled. We waited with nail-biting anticipation as they searched and searched for what we used to call him when we were very little, Grandpa Jacquet.

The situation had become an ultimate challenge to the human spirit. We watched each other closely and vowed that not another member of our family would die on this rooftop. We sat huddled together with our eyes canvassing the water for any signs of Grandpa when we heard the sound of another helicopter. Slone helped me to my feet and we waved our hands frantically and called out to them with what little strength we had left. We were operating from pure adrenaline, we were desperate and traumatized. Lupanare seemed as if she was on the verge of having another nervous breakdown which none of us were in any condition to deal with.

As the *Black Hawk* helicopter hovered, circles formed in the contaminated water under the fast winding propeller. There was a ladder made of rope that came down from the helicopter, with a Coast Guard Sergeant strategically attached to it. But none of us wanted to leave without Grandpa. He had been the glue that held our family together.

He and YaYa had taken us to live with them after Daddy Bordeaux stopped paying the bills and Lupanare gave into her unruly demons that ultimately forced her to abandon us. He raised us and taught us things that most parents teach their children. Like how to hold a fork correctly, how to do a book report, how to mow the lawn, how to fix things, he'd even taught us to drive. The list goes on and on about the special man he was in our lives. He and YaYa scarified their own lives to care for us, as if we were their own children. We had to find him, and we just couldn't leave without him.

"I'm Sergeant Minor. I'm here to get you guys out of here!" He yelled over the loud noise coming from the helicopter.

"Sir!" He said to Roman. "I need to get you all into the helicopter now!"

"We have one that went into the water and we can't find him." Roman said. "Can you help us, it's our Grandfather?"

"How long has it been since he fell in?"

"It's been over an hour now."

"It's not likely that he's still alive."

"Please sir can we try? I am begging you."

"I apologize, but we have to keep moving."

"Man, I am a New Orleans police officer and I really would appreciate it if you would try."

All of us stood there on the roof, staring into the water still trying desperately to find Grandpa. Sergeant Minor went back up to the helicopter then came back with two orange flotation vests. They searched for twenty minutes and still, no Grandpa. They came up onto the roof and regrouped and went down again briefly. It was a lost cause, he was gone.

Lupanare cried out with a gut wrenching howl as an indescribable wetness streamed from her eyes as she fell to her knees calling out into the water for Grandpa.

"Daddy, Daddy."

She clapped her hands and reeled back in fourth as she cried out to God.

"God, please don't let this happen. I promise; I'ma act right from now on. I won't be any more trouble if you would just help me to find him Lord. Jesus! Oh my God y'all, Daddy is gone, he's gone!"

All of us stood on the rooftop of the house that we'd loved so much, crying over a man that we loved even more.

"I'm sorry, but we have to get out of here. The chopper has to move on and I need to take as many of you with us, starting with the baby." A basket was lowered from the chopper and Gabriel carefully put both babies in. He smelled the decaying baby and asked, "Are these babies dead?"

"Well sir, one is barely alive and the other expired over twenty four hours ago." Roman said.

"We can't take the dead baby onto the helicopter. It's a major health risk. I apologize for your loss. Are there any other dead bodies up here?"

"Yes, my wife died while giving birth to the twins." Gabriel said with remorse.

"I am sorry sir. We can only take those that are alive with us. Are you sure she is dead?"

Gabriel cringed and said with a grievous tone. "Yes sir."

The sergeant signaled for them to take the baby up.

"There's a paramedic on board; we'll do everything we can to save the baby. Who goes next?"

As Lupanare lunged forward, I threw up my arm in front of her, "Let Slone go, so they can take care of her leg."

She vehemently pushed my arm out of the way and stepped into the harness and wrapped her legs and arms around Sergeant Minor. Roman and I just looked at each other and shook our heads in awe of the ignorance that was before us. I looked at Slone and said, "You can go next."

Lupanare held on tight looking down on us as the Sergeant gave the thumbs up; she still had tears in her solemn fragile eyes. I guess it was well enough to let her go first. Just because we couldn't see her wounds didn't mean she didn't have any. The sorrow she had to be feeling, coupled with the guilt of her unrestrained behavior over the years was almost debilitating. Her wounds were deeply imbedded inside, and the stability she thought she was coming home to, was unraveling before her very eyes. But Lupanare always managed to conveniently play the victim. Her level of narcissism was always predictable. Grandpa was our father just as much as hers and probably even more. She had been perpetually absent for so many years, that she had disrupted the natural flow of relationship that a child should have with their parents. Her guilt had been compounded and she had clearly reached her quota.

Gabriel was with Sidney. It was a hard sight to watch him wrap her body in the blood and paint stained blanket. He wept bitterly over her as he held her in his arms one last time. There would be no burial, no funeral, and she and baby Gabriel would just become a random number in the body count. He picked her up and carried her and the baby back through the man made whole in the roof and placed them into the attic, with the hope that one day soon he could come back and retrieve them for a proper burial. It was unfortunate, but at the moment, that seemed extremely unlikely.

They managed to get all of us onto the helicopter. We were flown into Baton Rouge. The doctors met us on the helipad and took the baby. They cleaned her up and hooked her to an IV within seconds. We watched as they worked diligently to keep her alive. During the flight, the few tears we had left, fell from our eyes as we saw first hand the devastation that had taken place in our city. New Orleans was under water. My heart had been broken many times within the last seventy two hours. I had no idea what it would take to put it back together. Grandpa was supposed to be in the helicopter with us. How could we gather the strength to tell YaYa that the man she had loved since her youth was probably dead and unaccounted for?

We each observed, clothed in silence, the damage that the torrential hurricane called Katrina had caused. Lupanare broke down and wailed again, as she saw our city in ruins. A place that was once so alive and vibrant. New Orleans had been overtaken by unprecedented sorrow and tears that filled the streets of the historic and exuberant town that often only slept in order to prepare for the next celebration.

Mother Nature had grabbed our beloved city by the hair, twisted it really hard and brought it down to its knees. But no matter how fierce Katrina thought she was, the spirit of the Big Easy would one day live again. We survived slavery, prohibition, yellow fever, *Typhoid Mary* and numerous hurricanes. We would ultimately survive Katrina too. We will come back stronger, braver, and even more ebullient than before. The people of New Orleans will one day shine even more brightly than the flame carried by a carnival flambé masker.

Our hearts and arteries will continue to pump Creole and Cajun cuisine as well as our unique style of Zydeco, Jazz, Blues, and Funk music along with our African, French, Spanish, and Indian infused dialect and history. We will not allow our culture to die, but it will be resurrected out of the catastrophic ruins of only one small point in time in our vast history.

We had finally made it to the hotel. The baby was still at the hospital in critical condition. Gabriel stayed with her. We prayed fervently with him, before we'd left the hospital that Zoë Arabella would get through this. He couldn't take much more.

Lupanare was given a host of anxiety medications to suppress her state of torment. Slone and I had been put on antibiotics for ten days for the infections that had crept into our bodies and pills for pain. There was no remedy to extinguish the psychological pain and emotional suffering that we had endured. But we would live to see another day.

They had given each of us a clean pair of scrubs, bottled water, fruit and granola bars before we left the hospital.

I pined for my electronic communication devices. I had lost my laptop, my I-pod and my cell phone in the hurricane. I would try at some point to get to a Sprint store to get another phone. I needed to call all my credit card companies, so they could issue new cards. Thank God I lived in another city.

All the banks in New Orleans were under water and no one could access any money. Even when people were evacuating, they would only allow them to take out a hundred dollars. Hopefully, I'd be able to get money wired to Baton Rouge until we could get a flight back to Los Angeles.

We all took turns taking a shower. The air conditioning felt good as I lay across the bed, I wondered if YaYa had made it safely through the storm. My mind was racing a million miles per minute. We watched the news in horror throughout the night, until we fell asleep from pure exhaustion. That would be the last night, for months, that any of us would sleep soundly through the night.

The next day, I woke up with my eye jumping uncontrollably. I was still *dog* tired, although I had slept for nine hours. I was a nervous wreck. But I pretended in front of my family that I was calm and was holding myself together. Slone had slept with her arms tightly wrapped around Roman while he rested. She held onto him for as long as she could. She knew he would have to leave and go back to New Orleans soon. They needed all the police presence and as much help as they could get down there.

Roman had slept for two days. He only got up periodically to use the toilet and he deserved it. We all did. Slone and I were on the phone all day, contacting as many people as we could, letting them know that we were okay.

There was a lady that worked at the front desk of the hotel that promised us clothes and shoes when we first arrived. She knocked on the door and when we opened it, it was like we had won publishing clearing house, but with clothes, shoes, food, and personal items instead of money. She and two of her friends had brought so many nice things for us that it brought tears to our eyes; we were so grateful. There were some extra things that we were able to share with other hurricane victims that we'd seen in the hotel.

We spent time talking with other people that had evacuated from New Orleans as a result of the hurricane. Evacuees were everywhere and had taken over the city of Baton Rouge. All the hotels were packed, the grocery stores had run out of food and several gas stations had to shut down for a few hours, just to accommodate the mass exodus of people that had come to their city to hide from Katrina.

I had contacted Chase. When he arrived at the hotel, I jumped in his arms. I was so emotional; I just couldn't hold it in any longer. I broke down and cried like a baby, which triggered everyone else to cry. We all ended up in a huddle together on the floor of our hotel room. We went through an entire box of tissue and still didn't feel any better.

Chase walked over to Lupanare and said, "Mrs. Bordeaux, I am so sorry for your loss. Grandpa was like a father to me, he taught me how to be a man."

"Thank you so much young man. Is there any way that you can drive me back to New Orleans today? I need to go back and get my mother." Chase turned and looked at me. I stepped in front of him and took her hand.

"Lupanare, I'm sure she is fine. We can't go back right now; they're still not letting anyone back into the city just yet."

"Fine then, I'll ride in with Roman when he goes back in to work."

Lupanare stood to her feet and marched over to Roman and began to shake him vigorously.

"Roman, Roman wake up. We have to go now. Come on, let's go get YaYa."

Roman turned to her and said, "What, what's wrong now?"

"I need to go back and get YaYa. I'm going to ride with you alright."

"Okay, Lupanare what ever you say."

He rolled over and went back to sleep.

Slone said to her, "Come on and take a walk with me down to the lobby and get some fresh air. Let him sleep a little while longer, before he has to drive you home."

It was amazing to see her respond so positively to Slone. Lupanare, with her sad countenance and defeated posture, wearily followed her out the door.

Roman slept through the night. When morning came, he seemed refreshed and ready to get back to work. Slone started begging him not to go, right in front of us.

"Just quit the police force and move to California with me and Jenna. Roman, please come home with me. You can live with me. You don't ever have to work again if you don't want to. I can afford to take care of us. We can travel the world together or whatever you like." She said with her voice trembling.

"Slone, that sounds wonderful and all, but I made a vow to protect and serve my community. We are in the worst crisis we have ever experienced in the history of our city. I can't just abandon my post. I have to go back baby. I promise you when all of this is over, I might just take you up on that offer, but right now I have to get back to work."

"But where will you live?"

"Gabriel just got the house uptown remember. Lupanare and I can stay with him until we get things back in order down here. I need to check on my own place and see if *it's* under water or not. We have to find YaYa and I don't think it's a good time for Gabriel to be alone anyway. He's going to need a lot of help with Zoë Arabella."

Slone threw herself across the bed and cried like a five-year-old spoiled brat.

"I know you're disappointed, but believe me, it's for the best. You go home and get back to your life and forget about me."

Slone sat up with her eyes fixed on Roman; her face covered with tears. I will never be the same after this experience. I know without a shadow of a doubt that I want to be with you forever."

"Slone sweetie, how could you know that in such a short period of time?" Roman said.

"I love you Roman." Slone said to him humbly.

I rolled my eyes and pulled the covers over my head. She must have an extreme case of post-traumatic stress, she couldn't possibly be thinking clearly. Maybe we should have gotten her a prescription for some of those anti-anxiety drugs or something to help her think straight, because she must be losing her mind. She put her hands on Roman's face and kissed him tenderly and said, "I love you Roman. Please be safe, and call me as soon as possible. I need to know that you're all right."

He didn't even have her phone number. That's how ridiculous this scenario seemed.

Roman gave Slone a long hug and a kiss on her lips. Then he hugged Lupanare, told her that he would go and check on YaYa and call her soon as he'd gotten any information. He promised he would come back for her as soon as he could. He came and wrapped his arms around me and said, "Sister we should spend more time together in the future. I'm really glad you were here to help us through the storm." He walked toward the door, turned around, gave us an empty smile, and said, "Je t'aime beaucoup."

As Roman walked down the hallway to the elevator, he had so many thoughts running through his mind, as he tried to mentally prepare to go back to the devastated city that he loved so much. From the view that he had from the helicopter a few days ago, it would not be easy. But he was ready and willing to work for as long as it took. He took his vow seriously and went back with courage, into the height of devastation that surely awaited him.

Pandemonium

ncle Harold turned to Auntie Sharon and said, "Sharon we have to move away from this woman. I can't take it any more. She smells like an old carton of sour milk. Damn we shouldn't have messed around listening to Jacquet, talking about how we could ride this one out. Oh, I can't wait until I see him again, I'm gonna put my foot up his old ass. This is the worst shit that's ever happened in this city and I wish I wasn't here to witness it."

"Look at all these people. I got a damn car and damn it, I shoulda drove it the hell outta here before we waited too long to leave town and were forced to come down here in all this mess. Everything I ever worked for is gone Sharon. Gone, gone, gone!"

Uncle Harold complained constantly while Auntie Sharon was trying to do everything she could to keep him calm. "You don't know that for sure Harold." She said to him.

"Did you not see the news on that big screen they had inside? Just thank God that we are alive. But I'm hot as hell, thirsty, funky and hungry. I'm tired of sitting out here with all these folks. I want to go home and sit on my own toilet, in privacy with my dirty magazines and take a crap where it's clean. You know this kind of shit

183

is beneath a nigga like me. We're trapped outside in a hundred degree weather, the power is off in the Convention Center and have you been to the bathroom lately? It's cleaner out here on the damn street. This is a bad scene man. This is just foul." He said.

"You're only making things worse by complaining, they told us the buses would be coming any minute."

"Girl, you been talking to me about buses on the way for three days now. I ain't seen one yet."

"Oh Harold, just be patient." She said.

"Mommy, I want to go home." McKenzie said.

"We have to wait, just a little while longer baby."

"Why?"

"It's not safe right now sweetie."

"I'm hungry."

"I know honey, but you have to be strong for mommy and daddy right now okay."

McKenzie began to cry. Auntie Sharon wondered how she would comfort her own children during the fiasco. She couldn't even give her girls a drink of water. She felt like she had failed them all as a mother and a wife. She knew she should have talked Uncle Harold into leaving and taking their family out of there when she'd had the chance. They were miserable and so was everyone around them. They'd sat in the hot sun for hours on folding chairs, with pillows and comforters they had brought from the house, waiting for help to arrive.

"I can't continue to let my children suffer like this. We can't just sit here and do nothing. Maybe we should start walking." Auntie Sharon balked.

Uncle Harold was sweating uncontrollably, and when she looked at him she saw that his mouth was slightly twisted. Worry immediately leaped inside her mind. She knew he was used to sitting in an air conditioned office all day at the dealership.

Auntie Sharon looked frantically for water or anything liquid that he could drink to hydrate him.

"Please Harold don't get sick out here on me now."

She sat next to him and fanned him with a magazine she'd dug out of her purse. He had left his blood pressure medicine in a rush trying to get down there at the last minute.

Uncle Harold said, "Help me get on the ground, I need to lie down."

Auntie Sharon put the comforter down on the concrete sidewalk and she and the girls helped him onto the ground. He said his left arm was hurting him really badly. He thought he might be having a heat stroke or something. He rolled onto his right side and closed his eyes.

She shouted, "Oh my God, somebody please help me, I think my husband is having a stroke."

"That's too bad lady, 'cause he picked the wrong day to have a stroke. Look around you, there's dead bodies all over the place. You need to pray and ask God to help you, because he's the only one that can. If they don't send someone out here to help us soon, if he had a stroke for real, he gon' die right there on that concrete." One man yelled out.

A nice lady came over and handed her a bottle of water and said, "He's gonna be alright Miss. Just try not to stress yourself out. He just needs some rest that's all."

"Thank you so much. God bless you." Auntie Sharon said with a faint smile.

McKenzie and Shelby were so frightened and worried that they kept asking her, "Mama, what's wrong with Daddy?"

"He's not feeling well right now baby. But don't worry; your dad is going to be fine."

She told them what they needed to hear for the time being. For the next hour the girls sat with their eyes glued on Uncle Harold as they monitored his every move.

Lincoln had gone to Atlanta that weekend to play in a basketball tournament. Auntie Sharon was so glad he wasn't there to see his father in the condition he was in.

Lord please, help us, she prayed as she wiped Harold's face with the bottom of her t-shirt. She gave him the bottle of water, then perched her lips together and blew on him to try to cool him down. It seemed as if he was feeling a little better after that.

They heard a scream behind them and turned to see that someone else had died. She grabbed McKenzie and covered her eyes. The situation was getting worse by the hour. They were trapped, dehydrated and almost to the point of starvation.

"Mom" Shelby said. "Come here."

"I'm right here baby, what's wrong?"

"Mom please come closer, I need to tell you something." She went over to her and Shelby whispered in her ear.

"I think I'm bleeding."

"What? Oh my God!"

Auntie Sharon grabbed her and started checking to see if she had been stabbed or shot or something. All she could think was that she couldn't have been raped she was never out of her sight.

"No mom, I'm bleeding between my legs."

"Damn it, of all the times for this girl to get her period." Auntie Sharon murmured under her breath. Tears ran down Shelby's face and she was ashamed and embarrassed. Everyone around her could see the blood all over the back of her pale yellow shorts.

"Let's see if we can get you to the bathroom."

"I'll be right back. McKenzie, you sit right here with your dad and rub his arm okay. Mommy and Shelby need to go to the rest room."

"Nooo, I wanna go with you."

"No. You do as I say, and don't move. Do you understand me?"

"Yes ma'am."

"Go on Sharon, I'm feeling a little better now." Uncle Harold said.

Auntie Sharon rushed Shelby through the crowded side walk, then inside past several dead bodies along the wall, a few of them in wheel chairs and others left on the Convention Center floor, half covered with dingy blankets and comforters. When they reached the rest room, it was in complete disarray. The smell of urine and feces almost knocked them to their knees. Every stall was overflowing, the toilets didn't flush and there were no lights or running water. The tampon machine had been ripped from the wall and Auntie Sharon had no idea what to do. As she looked into the eyes of her teenage daughter standing in front of her bleeding, she dropped down to the floor and felt around the sides of the broken machine, running her fingers through every space she could.

"Oh my God, I found two tampons." She cried, "Thank you Jesus."

She saw the look on Shelby's face. She had never used a tampon before.

"You have to do it or it's going to get much worse." She talked her through it while trying to hold her breath at the same time, because the smell in the restroom was absolutely deplorable.

"You have to do this correctly, we can't waste it. I have no idea how much longer we'll be out here."

Shelby cried and said ouch ten times before she finally got the tampon in and then there was the problem of the enormous blood stain on the back of her shorts. Auntie Sharon pulled out a couple of *Wet Ones* from her purse and said "I know this is not much but, try to clean yourself up with these as best as you can." She looked in the mirror at herself while Shelby was in the stall. She looked like she had aged ten years in the last three days. She wanted a warm shower, a good night's sleep in her own bed and a big plate of liver and onions cooked in bacon grease. She wanted to scream. But she knew she had to stay focused on her family right now. Her pity party would have to wait.

Auntie Sharon reached for her cell phone. She only had one bar left after trying to call her son Lincoln and Grandpa's house five times to check on YaYa. The phone lines were still down. She even tried dialing nine, one, one several times and couldn't get through. She figured maybe the emergency operator had to evacuate too.

She rubbed her eyes, brushed her hair with her hand, took one more look in the mirror and shook her head. As Shelby was coming out of the stall, she ripped the bottom of her shirt horizontally and wrapped it around her daughter to cover her shame.

Uncle Harold spotted a police car coming in their direction. He said to McKenzie,

"Help me up Dawlin."

He seemed to be feeling a little better, since he'd drank the hot bottle of water. He told McKenzie to stay put because he was going to try and get some help. Uncle Harold confidently walked as briskly as he could toward the approaching police car. He was a little wobbly as he tried to flag down the policeman. He stepped in front of the car trying to get their attention so they would stop. He yelled, "Hey, could you stop the car and give us some help please?"

The car stopped and he aggressively moved toward the window, seemingly with one hand in his shirt. He rubbed his chest as he tried to get some relief from the throbbing pain he was feeling as a result of moving so abruptly to get help. The officer on the passenger side of the car yelled to him and said, "Please do not approach the vehicle. Step away from the car, sir."

Uncle Harold was so focused on the pain that reverberated in his chest and arm, that he didn't hear him and continued to walk towards the car. The officer turned and pulled a sawed off shot gun from the back seat, cocked it and pointed it at him.

When he saw the gun, he realized in an instant that maybe it was not such a good idea to approach the police. Uncle Harold turned in the opposite direction to run, with his hand still gripping his chest from inside his shirt. But it was too late. Before he completely turned away, he saw a look in the officer's eyes that let him know that maybe they felt threatened in some way. Two shots were fired.

His body hit the pavement with an unprecedented force. McKenzie watched in complete dismay while the policemen drove away. McKenzie's legs trembled as she ran to her father's side. She was only ten years old. No one was present to help her make sense of what she had just witnessed. She knelt down beside him, took his bloody hand in hers and observed through a stream of tears, the clotted blood that ran from the sides of his mouth. The gurgling sound of her father grasping for air made her cringe. Then he took his last breath.

She stood to her feet placed her hands on each side of her face, consumed by the stolen dignity of her father from an unlikely opposition. She unconsciously took a deep breath and released an almost operatic high pitched scream, from the deepest part of her tiny belly. Her head spun as she tried to process what had just taken place. McKenzie's adolescence was snatched away from her by an unseen force in that very moment. It would take her a lifetime to get over the senseless act of unprovoked violence from someone that was supposed to assist them in their time of need and vulnerability.

As Auntie Sharon and Shelby were coming out of the building, they heard gun shots. They both ran back into the smoldering hot building for cover. It was difficult to breath, but without a doubt they weren't going back outside, until the gunfire stopped. She knew her little McKenzie must have been afraid, but she was with her dad and Auntie Sharon knew he would take care of her, no matter how bad he felt. Auntie Sharon took Shelby's hand as they walked quickly to get back to McKenzie and Harold. The stress was almost indescribable, it was complete pandemonium. People were running and screaming trampling each other, tripping over chairs and empty ice coolers. Someone yelled, "The police are shooting people."

Panic took over Auntie Sharon's body and her adrenaline level was through the roof. She had to get to McKenzie and Harold as fast she could. They just started running, with no real pattern in mind. When the crowd cleared, there was McKenzie standing screaming and crying. Auntie Sharon was afraid to approach, fearful of what she might find. But she had to keep going. She ran and pushed McKenzie to the side. She looked down, only to see the love of her life lying on the pavement, surrounded by a thick dark pool, of the color crimson.

She dropped to her knees and let out a cry from the deepest parts of her soul. She was polarized. McKenzie and Shelby sat beside their father wailing with shrieks and cries unlike she had ever heard before.

This can't be our lives. We were good, hard-working, decent people. How could this be happening to us? Auntie Sharon thought as she frantically checked for his pulse. They had survived Katrina, but the after affects had become more intolerable than the winds and the rain.

A myriad of questions flooded her mind. *"How can we go on living without this man in our lives? It doesn't work without him. "Who will make us laugh when we are having a bad day? Who will carve the fried turkey on Thanksgiving and Christmas? No one could put a Cajun Easter egg hunt together, quite like him. Who will give our daughters away on their wedding day? Who would keep Lincoln on a respectable path to manhood, the way his father could?"*

How was she going to tell his only son, Lincoln, that his hero, his confidant whom he loved, that his father had been brutally murdered, shot in cold blood in front of thousands of people, executioner style by New Orleans police officers; and that he'd died on a concrete sidewalk in front of the Convention Center like an animal?

The buses pulled up and the people crowded outside the doors anxiously trying to get in. If only the bus had shown up twenty minutes earlier. If only Uncle Harold had been patient and not sought help from those policemen; then Lincoln, Shelby and McKenzie would have their father and she would still have her husband and best friend.

Compartmentalized Emotion

oman stumbled as he climbed across the mounds of trash and broken medical equipment that cluttered the hallways of what was left of the nursing home. There were no doors, no windows and the treacherous hurricane winds had turned the building into a semi convertible; the roof had been half torn off. The stench in the building was so strong it made his eyes burn. He spotted a man dressed in what looked like it used to be a white uniform. He wore gloves, a surgical mask and a bandana draped across his face. His hair was dusty and dirty and his shoes were covered in mud. "Can I help you officer?" The male nurse said.

"Listen man, my grandmother was here right before the hurricane, and I was wondering where the buses evacuated her to. I wanna get her home."

"I'm sorry officer, there was a van that came right before the hurricane hit, but it only picked up the nuns, one of the doctors and two of the nurses. They said a bus was comin for the patients and the rest of the staff, but it never came." Roman's eyes watered uncontrollably.

"So did anyone survive?" Roman asked.

"Yeah man. We had some survivors, but most of them were the workers and their family members that took shelter here from the hurricane. Most of the elderly people died from heart attacks, drowning, dehydration or heat stroke. They finally sent some ambulances to pick up the patients that survived and they took them to some hospital on the West Bank. It was only about eight of them though. But if you want to, I could help you look through the collection of bodies we have stacked up in the recreation room, if you want and we got a bunch in the hallway that we haven't figured out what to do with yet. The coroner still hasn't come through here."

He handed Roman a mask and a pair of gloves. Roman cringed and held his breath, not only from the foul smell, but from the almost debilitating ache that he felt in his gut, from the possibility of finding YaYa in this dreadful place. He hoped with everything in him that she was one of those who'd made it out alive. "Man, were you here when Katrina hit?" Roman asked.

"Yeah Bruh, unfortunately, it was a nightmare. We were only able to get only a few people up to the roof. The water burst through the doors and windows so fast and hard, we barely had time to swim for our own lives. After fighting our way up to the roof, it gave way and then we were really in hell. We lost a lot of folks.

I haven't slept much since then. Every time I close my eyes, I see dead bloated bodies floating all around me. I can't get the screams and cries out of my head. I've cried so much, I have migraine headaches all the time now. I swallow at least twenty Tylenol a day and drink myself into a stupor at night just to quiet down the flashbacks. But anyway, I feel like I owe it to these people to try and at least get them to the coroner's, so their family members can claim them. I wanna get this place cleaned up, before the nuns come back. They don't need to be seeing all this."

"Man, fuck them nuns. They left all these people here to die."

"They didn't know how bad it was going to be. This building has been through lots of hurricanes and has held up over the years."

"Yeah, that's the same bullshit they told my Grandfather, when he brought my Grandmother here."

"I'm sorry man. Hell, if I woulda known that bus wasn't coming, some kinda way I woulda tried to move them sick old people outta here myself. It's a damn shame what happened down here man. But anyway, let me take you ova to the rec room so you can look around in there, but check the ones in the hall on the way." Roman flipped over sopping wet mattresses, chairs, old medical equipment and trash searching for YaYa. As he turned over cold, hard, damp, decomposed body after body, he hoped and silently prayed that YaYa was not one of the unfortunate ones, that had succumb to the hurricane waters that had so violently flooded the nursing home.

"Brace yourself." The male nurse shouted. They turned down a grey dismal hallway that led to a room filled with death. Roman gasped out loud as they crossed the threshold of the large recreation room. He gritted his teeth while his eyes beheld the nauseating display of dead bodies scattered throughout the room. The detestable sight was a clear indication that these people had died abhorrent, terrible deaths and it looked as if a massacre had taken place. Swollen mud covered corpses with bulging eyeballs surrounded an ancient dirty white grand piano, that stood in three inches of stale water. As a fraction of light bounced across the multiple decomposing bodies from a small window, Roman spotted two large black garbage bags in the corner. He felt an unusual uneasiness as he reached down to open one of the bags. "Hey, do you happen to have a flashlight on you?" Roman called out to the male nurse. He pulled a black flashlight from his back pocket and handed it to Roman.

Roman turned on the flashlight, pulled back his mask and placed it between his teeth. He opened the bag with both hands. There were two bodies seemingly tangled together. One's face was clearly not his grandmother's and the other was unidentifiable. The agony of this uncomfortable exercise was *beyond* overwhelming but he had to continue his search for YaYa. He moved toward the second bag, carefully stepping between the elderly deceased bodies that were strewn throughout the area. He saw a silver crucifix that protruded from the other bag. He removed the flashlight from his mouth and took a deep breath. "God help me." He mumbled to himself. He took one hand and pulled open the bag and shined the light on the inside with the other. "Oh my God!" He fell to his knees as he cast his eyes on YaYa's crystal rosary beads, still securely around her neck. Her body was mangled, discolored, and her face swollen like she had been stung by a hundred bumble bees.

Roman was in shock. He knelt in the rancid water holding what was left of YaYa, staring at her as if his gaze could bring her back to life. He eventually sat with his body postured on top the other corpses in a daze wondering, "*How God could have let this happen to YaYa. She was a good person, she was a phenomenal mother and grandmother and most of all, a good Christian.*" He'd wished that it was him and not her.

"I'm so sorry man I'll give you some privacy." The sorrowful male nurse said.

He pulled her from the bag and straightened her arms and legs as best he could. Roman sat amongst the sea of dead bodies for almost an hour, holding and rocking YaYa in his arms. He talked to her as if she were listening to him intently, telling her all his secrets and apologizing for every bad thing he had done, that he thought caused she and Grandpa any grief when he was a kid. He thanked her for all the kind words she'd spoken to him over the years, all the meals she'd prepared for him with love and for all the nights she stayed up with him when he was sick or just having a bad day. He thanked her for the many jokes and delightful stories she'd told him to make him laugh and told her how it was her words that boosted his self esteem and gave him the courage to become a police officer. He ran his hand across her salt and pepper hair with a trembling smile. He remembered how she'd often chose him over the other kids, to lick the spoon after she'd finished icing one of her amazing cakes.

Finally he removed the *Swarovski* crystal rosary from her swollen neck and placed it around his own. The sight of YaYa in this condition sent his soul through a plethora of emotions. He was relieved that he'd found her, sad about having lost her, angry with that cruel bitch Katrina and pissed off with God. He gently wrapped her in a damp, mud stained sheet and placed her back in the bag. He carried her out to his squad car and placed her body carefully in the trunk.

Roman sped away from the nursing home at top speed. He cried tears of sadness, anger and great regret. The condition in which he'd found YaYa was more than alarming. It was a shame. He pulled the car over and struggled to keep his breakfast down. He quickly opened the door and vomited his Spanish omelet onto the sidewalk. He rinsed his mouth with a bottle of water he had hidden behind the seat. He attempted to wrap his mind around the thought of what life would be like without YaYa and Grandpa. Roman had no idea of how to deal with the magnitude of the pain he was feeling. He let out an enormous gurgling scream that bounced across the walls of the cabin of his squad car; he banged his hands hard on the steering wheel until they were red and bruised. Then, he realized he had to put his pain aside, find the strength to compartmentalize his grief and get back to work. He vowed that he would not allow himself the luxury of true sorrow until he figured out how he would tell the rest of his family. He forced his emotions into a state of numbness, started the car and headed to the makeshift office that was at the downtown Sheraton Hotel.

Lupanare and Slone were downstairs in the hotel parking lot, packing up the car. We had lived in that Baton Rouge hotel long enough to hate it and be grateful for it, at the same time. God knows how much we could bear, because we barely managed to tolerate each other without scratching each others eyes out. We had grown closer as a family, and spent countless nights at the hospital with Zoë praying that she would make it. She had finally been released a few days ago and Gabriel was ready to take her home.

Slone made the decision to stay with us. But I worried about her. I knew that this trip could have stretched way beyond any healthy person's boundaries and limitations. I'd hoped in my heart, that this chaos had not caused her so much stress, that her cancer would return. She was tired, drained and still emotional. We all were.

Thank God Gabriel had the uptown house for us to live in, especially since YaYa would need a comfortable place to recover, not only from the heart attack, but also whatever her experience had been with Katrina. I'd stayed awake most nights trying to find the best way to tell her how we lost Grandpa. How we didn't take care of him and watch over him the way he deserved. But my heart *ached* for her, I couldn't wait to give her a big hug and I was prepared to stay as long as it took to love her back to health.

I was in the room getting a few miscellaneous items together before our departure back home. There was a knock at the door. I figured it was my absentminded friend Slone, and she had forgotten something as usual. I opened the door and there was Chase. He was dressed in a pair of blue jeans that fit perfectly in all the right places, a white cotton shirt and a big smile.

"You didn't think I was just going to let you leave without a proper goodbye, did you?" I took two steps backward as Chase entered the room and closed the door behind him. I smiled as he came close to me and looked into my eyes. We stood with our eyes gazed upon each other, looking past the windows of our souls... beyond the years that were once between us and the recent distress we had both been under.

He lifted me off my feet and carefully placed me on the unmade queen sized bed. We began to kiss passionately. Tears slowly drizzled from our eyes, conveniently rolling between the crevices of our lips. We held each other tightly. Only the unspoken words of our tears communicated the depth of our feelings. His lips found the curve of my neck, just as I'd hoped. I closed my eyes and held onto him, longing for more of his unlimited affection, but time had run out for us once again. This time I wanted to stay, I wanted to feel the comfort of someone familiar, someone safe and I realized in that moment, that someone was Chase. I had taken him and his love for granted.

He placed his hands on my face and said, "Jenna Bordeaux, I love you. I always have and I always will."

I pulled him close to me and said without hesitation, "I love you too Chase." I was just as shocked as he appeared to be, when the words dropped out of my mouth. We laughed and kissed one more time. "Okay, now that we've gotten all that out of the way, I need to get outta here before Lupanare brings her crazy ass up here and ruins the moment." I said nervously as I pulled myself from his embrace.

"Jenna, this is not over. I want to come to LA and spend some time with you after I get things back in order down here." I didn't respond right away. I was trying to process what all of this meant, before I answered.

"Jenna, quit trying to figure everything out, just let it happen and stop trying to control how you feel. Allow yourself to be loved for once in your life. Let me love you, I promise I won't hurt you."

I quickly kissed him on the lips and said, "Look, I have to go, but I'll call you when I get back to California and we can plan for you to come out for a visit. Now, can you *please* help me take the rest of this stuff downstairs?"

"A visit Jenna, really? I was thinking we could get married, start a fam . . ."

"Shush" I said as I put my index finger over his mouth. I can't deal with this right now Chase, it's just too much, okay. Why can't you just leave it alone already? I don't have the capacity to deal with another thing right now." I said emotionally. He gently kissed the palm my hand and without another word, proceeded to help me bring my things down to the car. Slone, Gabriel, Lupanare and I hugged him and said our goodbyes. We were finally on our way back to what was left of our city, but at least we had each other and baby Zoë was alive and well.

Roman came to Gabriel's house later that night, quiet and aloof. He washed his hands at the kitchen sink, sat down at the table, ate the plate of food Lupanare had prepared for him in a chilling silence. He appeared to be extremely melancholy, but that was understandable considering all that had happened. "So, what's up with you man, did you get any information on where they evacuated YaYa to during the hurricane? When can we go pick her up? " Gabriel asked. Languishing tears streamed down Roman's face as he looked toward Lupanare, who was washing dishes.

"I need y'all to come and sit down." We each clung to a ball of anxiety that rolled around in our bellies, like an unborn fetus. An almost palatable silence permeated the room. Gabriel and I both got up from the table and stood over Roman with an unyielding anticipation. Roman reached into his pocket, took out a familiar strand of crystal rosary beads and placed them on the table. His voice cracked as he said, "YaYa died at the nursing home, they never sent the buses to evacuate them. I have her body in the trunk of the squad car. The coroners hadn't come yet and I figured they probably never will. I didn't want to just leave her there. I didn't know what else to do.

I felt like someone had stabbed me in my gut, over a trillion times. My body trembled as my knees buckled and I fell to my knees in unbridled sorrow. I wailed uncontrollably. Gabriel, who was holding the baby at the time, walked into the den and placed her in her bassinet. He sat down in a corner on the floor, his eyes were glazed but there were no tears, no words, and no sign of emotion. It was as if everything in him had completely shut down.

Lupanare was hysterical. "No, no, no!" She cried. "Mammmma!" As she threw herself onto the kitchen floor, "Oh my God, I killed my Mother! Jesus, help me." She repeated over and over.

Treasure Or Trash

We finally went back to the house. Some of the homes in the area were nothing more than a pile of rubble, with no sign that there was ever a house on the property at all. As far as we could see, there were houses with water lines up to the roof, trees toppled cars that had been submerged under water. There was an eerie silence as we walked through the neighbourhood. It was a ghost town. No sound or movement, no laughter or playful children. Not even the bark of a dog. Nothingness had converged upon our once beautiful subdivision and golf course. There was only the residue of destruction, pierced by the reflection of the windows of our eyes.

A stench that smelled of a hundred cartons of rotten eggs and rancid meat, burst through our nostrils as we entered the house. The aroma of death greeted us, giving a clear indication that the bodies of Sidney and Baby Gabriel had to still be lying decayed and abandoned in the attic. We quickly covered our faces with surgical masks, as we remorsefully surveyed what was left of our grandparent's home. We tried to find something we could salvage to remind us of the loving childhood that we shared growing up in their house. I found a set of pearl rosary beads that YaYa held dear to her. I needed them so badly now. It was going to be my job to become the prayer warrior of the family, now that she was gone. I could almost hear the sound of her voice as I stood in what was once her bedroom, her sanctuary.

You're strong Cher, don't give up. Never let life's tests anesthetize you to the point that it forces you to stop moving forward. Where there is life, there is hope.

Roman found a few of Grandpa's tools and a watch that had been handed down to the men in our family for decades. It was worn and the face was cracked, but on a day when his soul longed for a connection to his past, even a broken watch had become priceless. Gabriel saw one of the trophies he'd won when he'd ran track in college on the bathroom floor. He also found a gold chain and cross that Grandpa wore, that was smeared with dirt.

Despite the strong, repugnant stench of death that captured our attention as soon as we'd crossed the threshold of the house. Gabriel held the cross he'd found tightly and dreaded the idea of confirming that his dead wife and child were still in the attic.

As I continued to survey the house, I realized that anyone else would have thought that this pile of rubble was trash, but not us. It was three generations of our family history, which at that very moment seemed to have been blotted out. Our family photos, all of our clothes, furniture, a special Bible YaYa had that was given to her by her mother. Everything we held dear to us over the years had all been completely destroyed.

I walked down the hallway back into YaYa and Grandpa's bedroom. It was a mess. The floor was barely visible due to excessive amounts of mud, along with YaYa's pots, pans, forks, spoons and delicate china; that once belonged to my great grandmother, from the kitchen that lay beside the waterlogged books and the television with a broken screen. There were candles with pictures of saints, barely visible and a muddy plunger propped in the corner. As my eyes canvassed the room, I saw what was once a twenty-four roll package of toilet tissue that looked like it had already been used, still wrapped inside the plastic. YaYa's beautifully embroidered hand towels were now filthy from all the mud that came in with the water.

I looked down and in almost perfect condition was the beautiful perfume bottle that Daddy Bordeaux had given YaYa one year for her birthday. I bent down to pick up the delicate bottle. I could see the vibrant swirls of turquoise, blue and green ocean colors come alive as I wiped the dirt away from its surface. It was one thing that had seemingly been untouched by the predatory finger of Katrina.

Imagine leaving your home one day, coming back only to find all things precious to you gone. Every dish, cup, wine glass or vase; every family photo, computer, cell phone, iPod, television, piece of furniture, shoe, purse, award, favorite knickknack or piece of clothing, not to mention a home that you've worked every day to make payments on for twenty-five or thirty years, all disintegrated right before your eyes.

Thank God, at least we had rubble to scrounge through. Mr. Mac, our neighbor had nothing left of his home, but his front steps.

As I gazed at the tiny Egyptian perfume bottle, my heart was filled with a sense of hope that we would make it through the most difficult time of our life. That through all the calamity and devastation, by the grace of God, we would continue on our journey with a tenacity to live life to the fullest. Never to ever take our lives and the lives of our friends and families for granted again. To learn the lesson well, that our relationship with God, ourselves and others, are what's most important in this life. Life is fleeting and material things are replaceable, but the people we love can never be replaced. I would give all the money in the world to have YaYa and Grandpa back.

I stood in the kitchen, closed my eyes and for an instant, I could see YaYa stirring her pot of gumbo. I imagined Grandpa singing Christmas songs while we decorated the tree and hung candy-filled stockings from the mantle. It was strange, but even after all that had happened, I was able to still feel their presence in that house. I could hear Grandpa's voice saying to YaYa, "*Gurl, you know I would be absolutely nothing without you, my life ain't worth living unless I have you to share it with.*"

Amazing how things work out. Grandpa probably looked over the shoulder of the Angelic host as they checked for his name in the big book of life and saw that YaYa's name had been checked off right before his. God spared him the hurt and the pain of having to live on this earth without her. They would be together forever, just the way he'd always planned.

There was a massive configuration of mud in the middle of the bed. Grandpa's extra set of teeth sat right in the middle of the gritty mound of moist dirt. As I walked closer to the bed, I noticed protruding from of the mud pile, an unusual looking card. I pulled it out and wiped my hand across the top of it. The word 'DEATH' was sprawled across the front of the hard plastic card. A chill ran down my spine in a most aggressive way. At first it seemed that there was only one, but as I continued to inspect the mound, I found several more. I took them out one by one. There were six in all.

Suddenly, I heard Gabriel's guttural screams and cries, which was clearly the auditory evidence that death was still lurking in our attic. Sidney and Baby Gabriel were still tightly wrapped closely together in the tiny awkward space he had left them in. The bodies had yet to be removed.

Roman went outside and painted on the front of the house, 2 DEAD BODIES KILLED BY ARMY CORE OF ENGINEERS!

We found out that it was the gross negligence of the Army Corps of Engineers that caused the unnecessary death and destruction of our city and its inhabitants. Our house and everything in it had drowned. YaYa, Grandpa, Sidney and the baby died as a result of the breaking of the levees. It turned out that Grandpa was right. We had weathered the storm, but when the levees broke, our lives and the destiny of our family was changed forever. When the levees broke, our city broke, our heritage, music, culture and way of life were all scattered and sprinkled all across this nation.

The most difficult task for me was how to make peace with the finality of their deaths. Anxiety consumed me every time I thought of being separated from them forever. I tried to tell myself that one day we would all be together in the *Sweet By and By*, but that didn't comfort me in the least. I'll never be able to hug them again, laugh or chat about meaningless things. The idea of never hearing the sound of their voices or doing something as simple as rubbing

YaYa's tired feet whenever I came home, was a kind of void that I'd never experienced before. I would give anything to hear her call me "Cher" just one more time.

Gabriel came down from the attic. His face distraught, his eyes filled with tears of regret and disappointment in himself for not evacuating his new family. He walked toward us to the end of the hallway and collapsed onto the mud caked floor and bawled uncontrollably. We knelt beside him. Our tears joined with his and created a new dimension of sorrow.

We unanimously decided to bury them ourselves. Maybe no one would ever come to our once beautiful historic neighborhood to collect our dead loved ones. Why would we trust them after the level of reckless negligence and abandonment that had already claimed their lives in the first place? Maybe if the Army Corps of Engineers had kept the levee system up to their proper code, maybe if help would have come to us sooner, maybe if those ass holes George Bush, Ray Nagin and Kathleen Blanco had half a brain between them, maybe if we had evacuated, maybe if ....

Roman went outside and brought in the remains of our beloved YaYa. He had gotten a body bag for from the coroner's office, which somewhat helped to insulate the smell of her stiff fragile body and several huge sand bags with some rocks to keep the bodies underground. He also managed to find a shovel in one of the bathrooms. We had no idea how a shovel had gotten from outside in the garage into the bathroom, but nonetheless we were glad to have one at such a very solemn moment. Gabriel and Roman found a spot in the back yard and began to dig one big grave for Sidney, the baby and YaYa. The time came to bury our family members as best we could. Roman helped Gabriel get the badly decomposed bodies from the attic.

The smell was almost unbearable as Roman put YaYa's broken body nestled inside the dark body bag inside the grave first, then Gabriel regretfully placed Sidney in, then carefully laid what was left of Baby Gabriel on top of his mother. If there was ever a worse feeling of sadness, wrapped in unimaginable grief and torment, it was this moment. It was more than I could digest, watching my baby brother, bury his wife of three days, along with his son.

We all stood silently for a while, before Gabriel began to speak openly to Sidney and Baby Gabriel. It was such a private moment, that I didn't know if Roman and I should have gone back into the house. It was awkward, but we loved them and would miss them too. So we respectfully stood beside our younger brother as he poured out his heart to his deceased wife and child.

Tears rolled down his cheeks into the parting of his lips as he reminisced of private moments he and Sidney had shared.

"I awake in the middle of the night reaching out for you, wishing that I could feel the stroke of your hand running gently through my hair and your thigh blanketed across my body. I can almost hear the passionate sounds of the pure satisfaction that seeped through your clenched teeth as we made love and created our two beautiful children."

"Baby Gabriel, I loved you long before I had the brief opportunity to behold your tiny face. I wish so much that I could have had the power to save you. I wonder what your voice would have sounded like, or which one of us you would look like when you started to grow.

I wished I could have seen your face the first time you tasted some of YaYa's pralines. I looked forward to the day when I could have fed you your first spoonful of gumbo. I wanted to watch you tease your sister and make funny faces at you just so that I could see you get "tickled pink", as Grandpa Jaquet used to call it."

He dropped to his knees in front of the shallow grave and cried out with a loud voice.

"I love you both so much, I'm so sorry that I didn't take you guys away from here in time. I had no idea that it would turn out this way. Please forgive me Lord, for not taking better care of the blessings you gave me."

Through his sorrow we saw his strength, deep beyond the windows of his eyes. We saw a tiny glimmer of hope twinkling toward the future of his daughter Zoë Arabella, carrying the torch for a new generation. She would pass down the recipes, the stories of love and laughter and the traditions of our family.

I had picked up a spray of red and white roses at a quaint Baton Rouge flower shop, so we could say a proper goodbye to YaYa and

Grandpa. There would be no grave dug for Grandpa, only fond memories of the precious time we'd spent with him. Roman began, by saying with one single red rose in his hand, "Grandpa, I want to thank you for teaching me how to be a man. Thank you for all the long talks and the wisdom you shared with us, preparing us for life. I guess I should also thank you for all the whippings you gave me too, because I know they saved my life. I probably woulda ended up in jail or dead. Please forgive me for not being able to find you. I tried my best and I'm going to have to live with that for the rest of my life. I'm gonna miss you man. YaYa, I will always love you and I will never forget you."

Roman tried his hardest to hold back his tears. But he cried profusely, as he bent over and laid the single red rose down onto the pile of dirt that housed Sidney, the baby and YaYa.

I held a dozen white roses in one arm and ten red in the other. I stood numb between my brothers with a collection of tears coursing down my face.

"YaYa and Grandpa, you were the best thing that ever happened to us. We will never forget the unconditional love and sacrifice you gave to us. I'll always remember the enchanting stories, the laughter and the tears we shared through all of the good times and the bad. I promise to pass on the legacy of our family to our children. I love you both and it was a privilege to have you as grandparents. I will miss you all very much."

My voice cracked as I tried to talk through the tears. As I laid the flowers onto the shallow grave, I whispered, "Please tell Edmond we love him too, and that his presence has been missed these many years."

Gabriel was sitting on the dirty ground shaking his head—weeping with one of the red roses clenched in his hand, unable to form a sentence, that could express the depth of his sorrow. Finally after a long lingering painful moment, never letting go of the red rose, he managed to get up and go back into the house.

I turned to Roman and said, "Look, these must be the cards that Miss Dot threw in the doorway at YaYa's that day."

"I wonder why she kept them." Roman said. Just then Gabriel came out of the house carrying some pieces of wood to make a cross for the grave.

"What is that?" He asked with a profound sense of curiosity. Gabriel dropped the wood he was holding and grabbed the cards from my hand and asked, "Do you think this is why…"

"Naw man, that crap is just silly superstition. Don't nobody believe in that Black magic, voodoo, gris-gris shit no more man. What happened here, and to YaYa, was an act of God and nothing more. Roman said.

Gabriel looked at him and said, "The God I serve is a loving, caring and gentle God. He would never put this kind of suffering and pain on one family."

"Well, the God I serve allowed his own son to be thronged and nailed to a cross and die at the hands of some crazy radical fools. So I'm not sure how loving and gentle that is, but hey, who am I to mess with another man's religion?"

Tears welled up in Gabriel's eyes, but this time from anger.

"Why don't you shut the hell up Roman? You get on my damn nerves, with your constant sarcasm."

He turned and walked back into the house, taking the cards with him. He was clearly on edge and rightfully so. Out of all of us, I think he'd suffered the hardest blow from the catastrophic event that had contaminated our lives.

I'd slipped back into YaYa's bedroom one last time. I went into her closet and remembered the secret door. How could I have forgotten? YaYa had shown me a water and fire proof safe that she'd hidden behind a small door behind her clothes where she kept all the important papers. She said it was a secret and only she, Grandpa and I knew about the secret compartment and not to ever tell a soul. I pushed past what was left of her mildewed shoes, clothes and miscellaneous debris. There it was; the mysterious door where YaYa kept all the family documents. I held my breath with the hope that I would be able to get the door opened and retrieve the safe. Most of the doors in the house were swollen from the water that had sat for days after the levee's broke. I remembered the combination was first Grandpa's birthday, then Lupanare's, mine, Roman's and lastly Gabriel's. I pushed the small door with all my strength and it popped open. The safe seemed to be intact.

Amazingly everything inside was dry. I could hear Romans voice outside the door.

"Jenna, where are you? Come on girl, I'm hungry." He ranted.

I grabbed everything as quickly as I could from the safe and tucked it into my purse and ran out the door.

Seven Stages

*G*rief had become my companion. We walked together, we ate together, we cried and worried about the past, present and future together. When I tried to walk away from it, like a possessive, abusive boyfriend, it wrapped its arms and legs around me and forced me back into a consummate relationship. Grief and I had grown accustomed to one another. The more it hung around, the more we became one. We were married and about to give birth, to a realm I would not be able to come back from.

But I knew in a hidden place deep down inside, that I could not allow it to stay much longer. I knew that at any moment, if I didn't force it to leave, it would kill me. The evidence was clear, I grinded my teeth at night and my pressure was through the roof. The night sweats and the nightmares of vividly seeing Miss Dot's face with her hands around my neck, violently trying to drown me, were beginning to affect my ability to function normally. My thoughts were scattered, and sometimes I just wanted to die. I questioned myself daily as to whether I was strong enough to handle everything and move on with my life. It was a difficult process. What did I have to look forward to? My whole life was wrapped up in being a New Orleanian and coming home for holidays and being with those who understood me and where I came from. No matter how far I go, how much education or money I have or where I live, the Crescent City is my home. These are my people and there is no other place in America like New Orleans.

Flight Risk

We stood in line to check our bags. We were more than happy to be leaving the Big Easy. But because of Hurricane Katrina, nothing about it was 'easy' anymore. Our city would never be the same, and our lives were forever changed. Although we had our memories, the idea of never seeing YaYa again pained me deeply in the *pit* of my stomach. She was a phenomenal woman, mother, friend and grandmother. I'd made an eternal vow, to take on the tradition of cooking Creole dishes in the future in honour of YaYa. Having known her would always be a salient experience that my brothers and I would treasure for a lifetime. Since Roman was moving to Los Angeles, I thought it would be appropriate to keep him in the spirit of eating the rich, decadent, Creole foods that he was accustomed to.

As Slone, Roman and I boarded the aircraft, it was difficult to leave the city that we adored in such disarray. We wanted so much to help, yet we knew we were so broken, we needed to go home and put ourselves back together before we could be of any good use to anyone else.

Slone was able to get us in first class. She wanted us to be as comfortable as possible. She was too kind. We sat down and buckled our seat belts. Slone and I looked at each other, understanding without speaking a word that we were both two very different people from who we were when we arrived. We were grateful to God for allowing us the opportunity to continue our journey toward our destinies, when so many lives were taken abruptly.

As we flew above our city, remnants of destruction were still very visible. As we climbed above the clouds, the clear blue skies gave no indication that something horrible had taken place throughout the southern gulf region. Louisiana, Mississippi, Florida and every place in between, was filled with death, discouragement, homelessness, dreams rerouted, businesses foiled, and families ripped apart; all because one day, a hurricane named Katrina instinctively winked her eye and brought massive destruction in a short period of time. She will go down in history, as the worst hurricane these parts has ever seen. She is infamous, her wrath legendary and she will never be forgotten for her uncanny ability to terrorize and rob us of our unique culture which was forced to flee to other areas of the country. Katrina had turned us into what the new reporters called, "refugees" and it was as if, we weren't even American citizens.

"I am looking forward to starting over in California." Roman said. "You know, I'm thankful to y'all for taking me in like this. I promise you, I won't cause you any trouble. I'm a new man. I'm ready to make lots of new memories, get a fresh start, maybe even settle down and have me a family of my own. I'm looking forward to some sun and sand. Now I can go to the beach everyday if I want to. How cool is that?"

"I'm going to take you and show you everything that the Wild, Wild, West has to offer. We can take some trips together, anywhere you want to go." Slone said.

"Yeah, I can definitely wrap my mind around that, I should have considered moving to Los Angeles a long time ago."

"Roman, I am a firm believer that everything happens when it's supposed to." Slone said.

For the first time in weeks, I could finally relax. I was physically and emotionally bankrupt. My eyes became heavy as the air in the plane became thin and the wings of the plane leveled off. My window seat was comfortable as I slept, missing the cabin service of pre-packaged dinners, cheap wine, and the poor movie choices.

I awakened to the voice of the pilot over the loud speaker. "We've been cleared; flight attendants prepare for landing."

The plane began its decent and eventually touched down on the runway. As the plane taxied to the terminal, there was another announcement.

"Please keep your seat belts on until the pilot turns off the seat belt sign." We sat on the tarmac for three hours while the flight attendants served us alcoholic beverages and snacks to distract us.

I could usually gauge the level of threat, by the temperament of the flight attendants. If they were calm, I was calm. If they seemed anxious, I was worried and if I didn't see them for long periods of time, I freaked. They seemed calm enough, no indication of anything serious. As long as they were serving drinks, talking and moving around the cabin and we were on the ground, I was cool. But we all wondered with anticipation why we were being held on the aircraft. Suddenly, the cabin door opened. I could hear some movement from the crew and multiple voices speaking low. The captain got on the loud speaker and said, "We should be exiting the aircraft momentarily. Again we apologize for the delay."

I looked toward the cabin door and I saw two sheriffs, two airline agents and a tall thick man, with an olive complexion. He was wearing a cheap dark blue suit, black tie and a badge around his neck. They all stood near the door immersed in conversation for about fifteen minutes, then they slowly turned and walked toward first class. I sat up in my seat trying to see where they where going to end up. They stopped and stood near our row.

"Roman Bordeaux?"

Roman sat with his eyes closed listening to his iPod, tapping his foot and bobbing his head. He didn't respond to the sheriff. I reached over and tapped him on his leg.

"Roman, Roman!" I said.

He pulled the ear plugs from his ears and looked toward me.

"What's up sis?"

I pointed to the men in the aisle that now appeared to be giants, as they towered over us. Roman turned toward them.

"Are you Roman Bordeaux?"

"Yes, I am. What brings you gentlemen here might I ask?"

They pulled him really hard out of his seat.

"Roman Bordeaux, you are under the arrest for the murders of Rodger Kindler and Conrad Brown."

The one that was wearing the cheap suit whispered in Roman's ear.

"Please come with us sir, I advise you not to resist."

Slone jumped out of her seat and hit her head on the over head compartment. As she stood holding her head, she said, "What the hell is going on here sir?"

"I'm going to ask you to have a seat Miss, and keep quiet. This is police business." The officer said.

"I will not sit down until you tell me what's going on here."

"Slone, please sit down." I said as I pulled her arm.

She pulled away from me with an inappropriate attitude.

"Sit your ass down, right now Slone." I said to her through clenched teeth. "You are not helping the situation."

By the time I was done dealing with Slone, they had handcuffed Roman and had escorted him off the plane. I crossed over Slone, turned toward her and said, "You stay put and let me deal with this." She tried to speak, her face wet with tears. I put my hand up before she could get a word out.

As I attempted to exit the plane, I was stopped by one of the stewards. "You can't get off the aircraft just yet ma'am."

"That's my brother! Sir, just give me a moment, please."

They agreed to let me off the plane. I briskly walked off into the terminal, almost running to catch up to them. They were gathered right outside the door. I walked up and said to Mr. Cheap suit, "I'm Jenna Bordeaux, Esquire; I'm Mr. Bordeaux's sister. Would you please explain to me why my brother is being detained?"

"I'm sorry... I'm detective Gage Promise. Your brother was allegedly involved in a homicide before the hurricane. We have information from his partner about what may have taken place."

"Can I have a word with him please?"

"Of course, Miss Bordeaux." Mr. Cheap Suit said, as he gave me the once over.

I walked over to Roman. He looked at everything, but me.

"Listen, I know what happened, Logan told me everything. I want you to know, I love you and I'll do whatever I can to help you. What do you want me to do Roman?"

He hesitated, then looked up at me and said, "I want you to get your things off the plane and go home Jenna. I'll call you when I get some more detailed information. I need to have a conversation with Logan, I'm sure this is all just a misunderstanding. Tell Slone, I was really digging her and I'm sorry."

"I'm going with you. Just let me inform the agent."

Roman raised his voice, "No, I'm telling you Cher, go home now!"

His eyes were piercing and stern. He turned to Detective Promise and said, "Get me out of here boss."

I watched as the sheriffs too my brother away in handcuffs.

"Ma'am, it's time for you to go. Here's my card, call me with any questions you might have, anytime, day or night."

As I went back towards the plane, they were letting people exit. I pushed my way through the crowd of tired disoriented passengers, ambiguous and in tears.

Ribbons Of Paranoia

I was finally home. This was usually my place of refuge, but this time it felt empty and lonely. Every time I thought about how stupid we were to stay and ride out the worst hurricane in the history of this country, my heart ached. A merciless regret, whose tentacles had deeply imbedded itself within my soul, would surely follow me to my grave.

I poured myself a glass of merlot. I sat on the sofa in a daze, wishing that the last several weeks had been a dream. But it wasn't, it was real. I snapped out of it and began to sort through the ton of mail that had accumulated while I was away. I was glad to find that my lights and gas had not been turned off. So many things needed to be taken care of but all I wanted to do was crawl in my bed and sleep for another two weeks. Dealing with the menial chores that were once simple had become laborious. The thought of going back to work, paying bills, listening to phone messages and opening mail, all seemed so exhausting.

My cell phone rang and snapped me out of my trance. I didn't want to talk to anyone, but I was still waiting to hear from Roman or one of the attorney's from my firm that I had on standby in case Roman would need legal representation.

It was Auntie Sharon. She was trying to communicate something incoherent between screams and cries on the other side of the phone line. It was clearly more bad news.

Auntie Sharon explained to me what happened down at the convention center. How the police had gunned down my favorite uncle, her husband and father of her three children while destroying her family as she had know it for over twenty years.

"How in God's name do you come back from something like that? I thought to myself.

"Jenna, my husband is dead. My house is demolished, with everything in it and our cars are under water. I don't have a job to go back to. The damn hurricane blew away the kid's school and everything we worked hard for over all these years. That little bit of money and government vouchers they gave us ain't enough for me and my kids to live off of. How long you think they gonna foot the bill for us to live in this hotel room? There is not enough room in here for all of us. We still washing out some of the same nasty ass clothes we'd been in since the hurricane." Desperation hung on her every word.

"I have to decide whether to buy clothes and shoes or food and medicine. I can't afford to do both. You know McKenzie has to have her asthma medicine. I've been so drugged up on this generic version of anti-depressants that they gave me that I can't even get up out the bed to take care of my kids. They're just running wild all around the hotel. I'm overwhelmed Jenna. I don't know what to do. I swear if I had someone to take care of my children, I would take this entire bottle of pills and take my ass to sleep forever. Every day I hate to see the sun come up. I don't know if I can go on after all this, but I know I have to stay around and try to raise these kids the best way I can. This wasn't in my plan for my life. I don't know how to handle this shit. My husband took care of me and my kids. I was his queen, Lincoln was his little prince and the girls were his princesses. Oh, God! What am I going to do? Help me fix this, 'cause I have no idea how to begin to put our lives back together again."

"Listen Auntie Sharon, you guys can come live with me in California as long as you need to. I'm more than sure that Slone can get you some passes. You can get on the first flight leaving out into LAX in the morning. You and the kids need to be some place where you can grieve properly."

Auntie Sharon began to cry. "Oh my God Jenna, thank you so much. Are you sure this is something you can afford to do for us?"

"Of course, you're my family."

"How are we going to get the plane tickets? You know how slow the mail is these days. We wouldn't get them for at least a few weeks from now, if at all. Anyway, I'ma have to run and go look up the address for the hotel."

"No, Auntie Sharon, everything is electronically done nowadays. All you need to do is check to see if the hotel has a shuttle to the airport. Then when you get there, go to the counter and give them your names, the flight information, and show them your ID."

"Oh, is it that simple these days? I haven't traveled by plane since your Uncle Harold and I first got married." She said fighting through the tears.

"That was over twenty years ago. One year we went to Paradise Island in the Bahamas for his birthday. Oh, we had the time of our lives. God knows I'm gonna miss that man."

"I know we're all going to miss him. But I need you to let me finish giving you the details about your trip, so I can call Slone and get the flight time and confirmation numbers. Usually there is a strict dress code. But just let them know that y'all are some of dem refugees from New Orleans that they been talking 'bout on the news, and I'm sure you won't have a problem boarding the aircraft." We both did an uncomfortable chuckle and then said our goodbyes and hung up.

I was really angry with a God that I'd not served since my childhood. I was oblivious to the fact that my anger toward the ultimate deity was part of the seven stages of grief that usually manifested after great loss. I sat with my bottle of *merlot* yelling at a God that had disappointed me way too many times to count. "Why would you not protect us from the curse of death that Miss Dot put on our family?" I shouted into the air.

We had six tarot cards and now five deaths. Ribbons of paranoia wrapped themselves around my mind, revealing that maybe another death would take place in what was left of our family. I needed to call Gabriel and alert him to my newfound revelation and that he should destroy the death cards that he plunged into his pocket after we buried Sidney, the baby and YaYa.

I ran to the bedroom, threw myself onto my bed, kicked, screamed and spat out cataclysmic amounts of unholy verbiage toward God. Then amidst a fountain of tears, I drank obscene amounts of wine and began to pray to a God that I had just spent the last two hours reprimanding.

Promise

"This is detective Gage Promise. I have some good news concerning you brother, Roman. We have transported him back to New Orleans and will be releasing him soon. We found Logan Honore's gun in the swamp as well as a bloody knife and axe in his car. The clothing of both victims were found in his garage, as well as a black Jaguar parked two blocks from his house registered to one of the victims. We are led to believe that the bodies of the deceased were devoured by alligators at Honey Island. Therefore we have no real evidence that Mr. Bordeaux was present or privy to the murder of the two victims. All of our evidence supports the idea that Logan Honore' acted alone and attempted to frame your brother. We found no finger prints or DNA on any of our evidence. You should be receiving a call from your brother within the next forty-eight hours. He'll be going through the release process in the next several hours, and he should be back on his post before the week is out."

"Do you have any questions ma'am?"

"No, Detective Promise, but thank you again for all your hard work."

I called Slone and told her the news.

"Slone, the case against Roman was dropped."

"Oh, thank God. Have you talked to him?"

"No, Mr. Cheap Suit called and said there was no substantial evidence to support the charges against Roman for the murders. My goodness, how could Logan have done such a thing to Roman? He had been his best friend since childhood. Lord, have mercy. You think you know people and then they turn out to be murderers. What is this world coming to?"

But somewhere deep down inside, I knew that only Roman, Logan and God himself, would ever really know what happened that night at Honey Island.

Canon Law

*R*oman spotted a green Toyota Camry making an illegal turn. He turned on his siren and pulled the driver over.

"License and registration please?"

"Oh, thank God it's you Roman."

"Please refer to me as Officer Bordeaux."

"How are you today Officer Bordeaux? I apologize. I got a little turned around and made a wrong turn." Roman didn't respond as he wrote down his information onto the ticket.

"Surely you're not going to give me a ticket Officer. I've known you since you were a little boy." Father Timothy said.

"Yeah, you knew me alright." Roman said, as he checked the appropriate boxes.

"Why don't you come over to the rectory and have dinner with me tonight. I'd enjoy having a little company. Father Joseph and Brother Thibodeaux are out of town taking care of some of our other properties in Biloxi. You know that area was hit pretty hard by the hurricane too. They're going to be gone for at least three weeks. Was your home affected by the hurricane? Do you have a place to stay? You're welcome to stay at the rectory with me until they get back and then we can catch up on old times."

"You know what Father...I think I will take you up on that offer."

"Oh, wonderful Officer Bordeaux, I'll look forward to seeing you about seven o'clock this evening then."

Roman tore the ticket out of the book and handed it to him. Father Timothy opened his mouth and attempted to contest the ninety-five dollar inconvenience, but Roman stopped him and said, "Don't push your luck Father."

Roman arrived at the rectory at seven o'clock sharp. He rang the bell as he stood nervously holding a bottle of vintage wine and the only valuable thing his dad had ever given him was hiding safely in his pocket. Father Timothy opened the door with a big smile.

"Hello son, please come in."

Father Timothy escorted Roman to the dining area. They shared small talk and a hearty meatloaf, mashed potato and vegetable dinner together.

"Would you like a cup of tea?" He asked Roman as he cleared the dishes from the table.

"No thank you sir. Dinner was good though. I didn't realize you knew how to cook."

"Yes, we began to take turns cooking after Sister Francis was transferred to St. Tammany Parish. She would prepare dinner for us every evening before she returned to the convent. But change is good sometimes, you know."

Roman went into the cabinet and found the wine glasses. He held one up and said, "Will you be having wine Father?"

"No, thank you son, I'm going to have some tea. You go right ahead and I'll meet you in the library."

The library was modestly decorated with cherry wood book cases, a burgundy leather sofa, two high-backed chairs, a dark wooden coffee table and a big mahogany desk, strategically placed in the corner of the large room. Roman sat down in one of the chairs, while Father Timothy came in shortly thereafter. He was carrying a large cup of tea with steam swirling in the air, as he walked passed him to sit down on the sofa.

"So young man, how do you like being a police officer?"

"I like my job. I was trained very well and it certainly has its privileges. But I'm going to be relocating soon."

"Oh really, where are you moving to?"

"California. I'm looking forward to a fresh start. I'll be leaving just as soon as I take care of some unfinished business."

"Was YaYa's house damaged in the hurricane?"

"Yeah, it was about twenty feet under water. Just about everything was destroyed. I'm not sure if you heard, but YaYa died in a nursing home during the hurricane. They never evacuated the patients, but somehow every single nun was evacuated safely and lived to tell their version of what happened, while they let helpless sick and elderly people drown to death."

"That's really terrible." Father Timothy said.

"Some of the patients drowned trapped in their beds, some were still hooked up to heart monitors, and a few were paralyzed and unable to move. Others that survived the hurricane died as a result of lethal heat and unbearable conditions, while those that were supposed to take care of them were nowhere in sight. When I got there, YaYa was dead and stuffed in a plastic bag, thrown in the corner along with some other bodies of people that died unnecessarily. We had no idea that when we brought her there, that we would never see her again. After it was all said and done, they found an activity room filled with bed frames, destroyed medical equipment and almost too many dead bodies to count. There was a sign written in red paint outside the nursing home that read, 'MORGUE PLEASE PICK UP BODIES.' We were told by one of the survivors that the buses and rescue crews never came. By the time it was all over most of them had already expired. He described how the power of the water, burst through the doors and the building filled up like a punch bowl. He said the sound of the screams and cries for help would haunt him for the rest of his life."

"I am so sorry my son. YaYa was an honest hard-working woman. I considered her a friend. She will be missed. And Gabriel and Sidney; how are they since the wedding?"

Roman fought to keep his composure. This was the first time he had actually spoken to anyone other than his family and Slone about what happened to the members of his family during the hurricane. He had been so busy saving lives and comforting others, that he hadn't taken inventory of all that had taken place in his own life. He had worked seven days a week, keeping order and rescuing as many people as he could with a team of hard-working, selfless policemen, firemen and women. Many of them had sacrificed their own lives, as well as their mental and physical health to help victims that were in peril, as a result of Katrina. They were to be applauded or better yet they deserved a standing ovation for their courageous efforts. There were lots of good cops in NOLA; unfortunately the bad ones had gotten much of the media attention.

"Sidney didn't make it, one of the twins died, and Grandpa was swept away by the water from the levee."

Father Timothy stood and walked over to Roman and put his hand on his shoulder and said, "What can I do to make you feel better son?"

"Could you get me a glass of ice water?"

"Sure anything for you, I'll be right back."

Roman got up and went down the hall to the bathroom. He remembered walking down the very same hallways when he was a young boy. He and Father Timothy would sometimes read Aristotle, Socrates and Shakespeare together at the rectory after school. Father Timothy even shared stories with him about his own childhood. They became fast friends and Roman adored him. Father Timothy filled the void of abandonment that Roman's own father had created, when he had completely removed himself from the lives of his children.

It was like a little slice of heaven, the first time Father Timothy had taken him out on a swamp tour at Honey Island. Roman was fascinated with the sights and sounds of the pristine wildlife. The beauty of the moss hanging from the cypress trees and the smell of wild azaleas in the air would bring excitement to any young boy. He saw Red-wolf deer, exotic birds and fed marshmallows to the alligators. There were 'diamondback' water snakes, owls and huge turtles. They spent many weekends fishing there and it was truly a fisherman's paradise. There were largemouth bass, flathead catfish, bluegill, fresh water drum and buffalo fish, available to catch if you were lucky. But over time, these fun filled swamp and Pearl River trips turned into a convoluted glimpse into hell; filled with fear, pain, disillusionment and a perversion that he had no idea existed.

It started slowly at first; gestures that were inappropriate, but could be explained away if needed. Roman's first memory of something strange happening, was when Father Timothy gently wiped off his body one afternoon after they'd swam at the rivers edge. With each stroke of the towel, Father Timothy's hand seemed to brush against his private parts. On the surface it all seemed innocent enough but after several trips filled with fun and games, the man of God's actions became more overt in his advances toward Roman. Any questions or raised eye brows toward Father Timothy for anything that seemed unbefitting for a priest, was met with a response of merely teaching Roman the mechanics of his own body. He said it was just a course of instruction about things Roman would need to know as a man. Roman was very uncomfortable with the idea of a man touching him in the manner that Father Timothy had. He knew it was wrong from the first time it happened but he regretfully trusted him without reservation. After all, Father Timothy was a man of honor, a man of the cloth. He had been so good to Roman and his family. He had even given his older sister a job at the rectory and visited their grandmother when she was under the weather. How could Roman say 'no' to a man who was so well respected in their community? He was everything Roman wanted to be; influential, charismatic, powerful and beloved by everyone in the parish.

Roman loved Father Timothy, but also hated him at the same time. He was too young to realize the horrid dysfunction of the unusual activity, until it was too late. Father Timothy had used candy, toys and private field trips to seduce Roman, which eventually resulted in the change of the entire course of his life.

Most black folks from the southern region during that time were biologically programmed from slavery, to never attempt to stand up against a white man with an allegation of any magnitude. You could think about it, dream about it, pray about it, curse the heavens and the earth about what you had been through, but you could never speak about it. The soil in these parts had been cultivated from secrets that were supposed to die with you and taken to your grave.

"How was a ten year old black boy, going to bring an indictment against a white Irish catholic priest in a town where the Catholic church owned and controlled just about every television and media outlet, along with an obscene amount of real estate in the tri state area and not to mention the Vatican and the weight of all its power and wealth to back him up?" Roman thought to himself.

He imagined the feel of the sting of the hard wooden ruler across his knuckles coupled with the threats of damnation that Father Timothy had used, to enforce that he would never tell a soul. The only person that Roman had ever told was his best friend Logan Honore'.

He thought about the times he'd sat in the foyer of this very house waiting for Father Timothy to take him on field trips. Roman was driven to this same address biweekly by Grandpa, as he chewed on his freshly cut sugar cane, smiling with pride as he naively dropped off his grandson to spend the day in an underworld filled with lies.

Parents and grandparents blindly trusted the nuns and priests that unselfishly served God and their community with unbridled zeal. Yet somehow a deplorable counterfeit turned up amongst so many good ones. Twice a month Roman sat reluctantly waiting to ultimately receive the penalty for sins that he had unknowingly committed; with the threat of profound judgment from God for eternity, if he denied Father Timothy his filthy pleasures.

Distressing thoughts flowed with daunting rapidity, of the time he realized he was not the only one Father Timothy had taken advantage of. One day he ushered in five little black altar boys, ranging from eight to eleven years old into his private quarters, including Roman and Logan. He had them take off their clothes, made them run in place and do jumping jacks. Then after he was done humoring himself, he examined each one of their naked bodies, touching their penises under the guise of making sure they were clean and without blemish in order to serve God and assist him during the holy mass.

He used the Old Testament scripture of the priesthood of Aaron, as an example to assure them that this nontraditional behavior was from God. He walked back and forth as he read from *Leviticus 21:18.*

"For no man who has a defect shall not approach, a man blind or lame, who has a marred face or any limb too long, a man who has a broken foot or broken hand or is a hunchback or a dwarf, or a man who has a defect in his eye, or eczema or scab, or is a eunuch. ... *Leviticus 21:23,* Only he shall not go near the veil or approach the altar, because he has a defect, lest he profane My Sanctuaries."

Father Timothy convinced them, that he loved them more than anyone ever could. Their families and friends would never love them the way that he did. He told them that God was always watching to see if they were obedient and loyal to him, because not only did he speak on behalf of God, but that God spoke directly to him like he did with Moses. He reminded them that he was to never to be resisted for any of his requests, without dire consequences.

He told them with an unholy boldness, that everything that happened there was a secret and that they were a part of an *elite group* chosen by God. One boy started to cry and Father Timothy slapped him so hard, the spit from his mouth flew across the room, giving new meaning to slapping the spit out of someone. He said that if any of them disobeyed him or told anyone, that they would suffer torment in hell for eternity. He told them that God would punish them, bring judgment on their families and very bad things would happen to them. Father Timothy, their Shepherd, instilled in them that the Lord would bring plagues to their very doorstep the way that he did to the Egyptians in the bible, if they ever failed to follow his lead.

None of them wanted anything bad to happen to their loved ones, but most of all they feared hell. The threat of eternal flames and torment frightened them. They had no real indication that Father Timothy would turn out to be the devil himself, but over the next several years they would be in hell with him.

It was as if he dared them to rebel against him. He locked eyes with each one of them as he sealed his dastardly covenant, with a kiss that smelled of cheap communion wine and cigarettes. He giggled with delight as he kissed them one by one. He licked his lips, then darted his tongue in and out of their mouths. With this one abominable act, he contaminated their minds, wills and emotions and invalidated everything that they had been taught in the Catholic Church.

They all had something in common. None of the boys had a father present consistently in the home. One kid had never met his father. Another only saw his daddy on holidays, the other two every other weekend. Although Roman had Grandpa, Father Timothy must have sensed that he still longed for something more to fulfill the absence of his father, that he only saw two weeks of each year.

They went to school every day and played at recess together. They were so afraid, that none of them ever spoke a word to the others or anyone else, about what was happening to them at the hands of a servant of God. They blended in with the other kids without a hint, that they'd been manipulated into an arena of perversion, fear and disillusionment by a well respected authority figure. They laughed, played and did their school work while they continued the façade, even after they arrived home.

One day Roman saw Logan leaving the rectory, he walked with a strange limp, as if he couldn't close his legs. He ran up to him and asked him what was wrong. He smiled with the emptiness of a storefront mannequin and said he was fine and that they should go play kick ball before the bell rang. Logan sat on the side quietly, obviously pain, looking off into the distance with tear-filled eyes. When they returned to class, he acted as if nothing had ever happened. He remembered how Logan denied that Father Timothy had ever touched him inappropriately throughout the years. But

Roman knew better. The threat of what would happen if they ever told a soul was enough to keep him quiet for a lifetime.

Three months later, Roman and Logan both watched as Chucky Broussard came running out of the rectory, dazed and confused to the point that he mistakenly walked out into the street and was hit by a car. He was paralyzed and the doctors said that he would be wheelchair bound for the rest of his life. They never saw him again after that day.

Another one of the boys was found a year later by his little sister, who had gone out to look for her brother so that she could play a game with him. He was hanging from a tree in their back yard. He had committed suicide. She was never quite right after that. She became mentally deranged and hooked on heroin by the time she was sixteen.

Those in the *all boy's secret molestation club* were the only ones that suspected the suicide was the result of his desperate attempt, to find peace from the very man that conducted his funeral. Father Timothy stood tall and smug with confidence as he gave the eulogy at Roland La Blanc's funeral. That sad and rainy morning, the boys sat in awe of Father Timothy's unrepentant stature. They feared the day when the wicked demons of guilt, shame and judgment would take claim of their souls too.

When Roman reached the bathroom, he closed the door, stood in front of the mirror and attempted to see beyond the looking glass into his wounded soul. He turned on the water faucet, stood and watched the water run down the drain for a moment. He leaned over the porcelain sink and splashed cold water across his face. He sought for the lost, innocent, childlike version of himself but only saw the reflection of the adult he hated. He looked in his eyes to see if there were any signs that he was cleansed or refreshed but all he felt was a familiar frustration by the demons that haunted his psyche on a regular basis. Anger permeated him as the memories of betrayal and violation flooded his mind.

Roman drew back his arm, punched the mirror and broke it to pieces. He sat down on the toilet seat to check the damage to his hand but he only had a few scratches and a minimal amount of blood. He knew that Father Timothy would come knocking on the door soon. But he never did. He wiped the blood from his hand and returned to the library. There was a glass of water sitting on a wooden side table and Father Timothy was absent for the time being. Roman reached into his pocket and pulled out a small clear plastic tube. He briefly stared at Father Timothy's mug that was intricately etched with the Lord's Prayer on it.

Father Timothy appeared minutes later to the room with an ivory colored, marble chess board, balancing the pieces as he walked slowly into the library.

"Remember when you were a young boy, I taught you how to play chess? Do you still remember how to play?"

"Of course I do Father."

Tiny beads of blood appeared on Romans hand, almost mimicking the beads of sweat that rapidly began to form on his forehead.

"What happened to your hand?" Father asked as he coughed a bit, distracted by the taste of an unfamiliar essence that had crept onto his palate.

"Oh, I had a little accident in the bathroom. Not to worry." He said, as he reached for the napkin from beneath his wine glass.

They sat for hours strategically playing their intellectual, competitive game of chess. Father Timothy enjoyed having company. He had slowed down tremendously in the last few years, solely focusing on ministry to the poor and homeless. He had rededicated his life to Christ and had done his own cleansing ritual of the renewing of his vows to the Catholic priesthood, in the privacy of the rectory's chapel. He felt good about connecting with Roman that day. It was an opportunity for him to make amends for some of the wrongs he had committed in his younger days. He whispered, *Thank you* to God under his breath for his renewed sense that Roman showing up for dinner was a sign from God. He was grateful for a second chance to make things right with one of the kid's lives that he had damaged.

"So Roman, you said earlier that you had some unfinished business to attend to? Is there anything I can help you with?"

"Let me be honest with you Father Timothy, you are my unfinished business."

"How so young man?" Father Timothy asked, as he sipped on his tea while trying to ignore the foreign taste that had seeped between the crevices of his teeth. Oddly his tongue began to cling to the roof of his mouth.

"To answer your question, sure I remember lot's of things. I remember when you manipulated me into thinking you were an honorable man. I also remember when you took me to that dilapidated swamp house on the outskirts of Pearl River and raped me repeatedly. I remember when you forced me to suck on your nasty stinking ..." Roman took a deep breath and positioned his body so he could look directly into Father Timothy's eyes.

"That first few times you took me fishing and swimming, you made me feel special. It was just the two of us. Running around, playing and touching innocently. I was so happy to have a father again. I looked forward to those weekend trips. Then one day you touched me between my legs and I felt a sensation that I'd never felt before. My innocence and naivety were challenged, confused and disrupted. But, I ignored the voice inside of me that sounded an alarm, telling me that what was happening to me was wrong. I trusted you! I trusted in your words of authority that said it was 'okay'. That it was natural to have those feelings towards you because you were a man anointed by God. You were so subtle in your movements that it seemed dismissive at first. But by the time I realized that I was being violated, I felt as if I was somehow indebted to you for all the nice things you had done for me. Teaching me, spending time and money on me, you took what seemed to be an honest interest in me and who I was. I was a young black boy, and for most of my life, I'd felt invisible.

I ignorantly thought that the void I'd felt from my mother and father being absent from my life was somehow filled by your affirmation and attention. I had no idea that there was a completely different hole you were trying to fill. This went on for three years and then the way you abruptly dismissed me from your life, it was devastating although I was well aware of the dysfunction of our relationship. I guess I was getting too old and out of control for you.

I knew that I liked girls and never had a desire for boys, but you convinced me — for a season — that the sexual acts were preparing my sexual instincts for a time when I was old enough to start dating girls and that no man ever wanted to seem inexperienced with a woman. You said you were teaching me how to take the lead with confidence. But I assure you I hated the sexual part of what *I thought,* was a meaningful friendship. I missed the talks we had and the time we shared. The visits somehow began to define me and I foolishly continued to keep my mouth shut and obeyed your every command. I no longer felt special, I became *common* to you. You literally wiped your ass with me, like a brand of soft toilet tissue and then flushed my emotions down the toilet and moved on to your next victim.

Black families don't send you to counseling or have an intervention for you when problems arise. We are taught that you have to keep it stuffed down on the inside, just keep suffering and smiling; not to interrupt the equilibrium of an already dysfunctional home life. *Get over it,* they say, *whatever doesn't kill you makes you stronger.* But when you ejaculated inside me, you burned a whole into my soul. And 'no' it didn't kill me, I guess I am stronger in a sense, but I am a broken man because of it.

I have walked around for years collecting myself like pieces of a puzzle because *you* dismantled me. And I, like Humpty Dumpty, have spent years trying to put myself back together again. Well, I have successfully done that and destroying you is the last piece of the puzzle."

Father Timothy looked stunned and disappointed that the night was not going as smoothly as he'd planned. But he was determined to placate Roman while he rightfully displayed feelings that had been lying dormant inside him for years. *That was fair enough.* He thought. He'd let him get things off his chest, once and for all, so that they could move beyond their history.

"Look man, I found out about the safe that you keep in the chapel under the altar in the floor."

"There's no such thing." Father Timothy blurted out nervously.

"Oh really, let's find out."

"You can't make me do anything without a gun."

Roman laughed. "You think I need a gun to get you to do what I want you to do? Did you have a gun when you fucking sodomized me and God only knows how many other innocent children? "Would you say that Jesus has forgiven your sins?"

"Yes son, I believe He has." Father Timothy said.

"So then you believe that whatever a person does, if they ask God for forgiveness, He will forgive them no matter how bad it is?"

"Yes, that is what I believe my son."

"Well, thank you for confirming that for me."

Father Timothy interrupted the mind game that Roman had clearly rehearsed for years.

"Who told you about the safe?"

"Let's just say that you were not the only priest that tried to know me in the *biblical* sense. I persuaded Father John to tell me one of your most precious secrets, and that's the one he chose to tell. I managed to get valuable information from him, then I out ran his big fat, out of shape ass, before he could do to me what you had already done."

"Son, why are you doing this?"

"I am not your fucking *son* and you are not my father. If you call me *son* one more time, I am going to bust a cap in your throat. I'm about to lose my patience with you. Now get up and take me to the safe!"

Father Timothy was fully persuaded that Roman had the potential to do grave harm to him with or without a gun. He was younger, stronger and faster than he was and he figured that giving him the money might save him. But Father Timothy was completely unaware of the monster that he had created back in the swamps of Louisiana many years ago.

Father Timothy wondered, "*Where was the God that he had served so diligently all these years?*" He had conducted mass, listened to a multitude of confessions, administered penance and communion; he had married, baptized and performed funerals all in the name of the Father, Son and the Holy Ghost, for thousands of devout Catholics over the years. But most importantly, he had prayed and asked for forgiveness for his own sins, believing that he had been absolved from the indiscretions of his youth.

But Father Timothy had overlooked one thing for sure, that the type of atrocity that he had committed always comes with a consequence. There would be no protection for him from God, the Archdiocese, the Pope or the Vatican. He was alone in a house, with the full manifestation of the sins of his past.

"See Father, because of you, I made sure that I became a man of authority too, and I decided I would never allow myself to be in another situation that didn't have a clear exit. I've found out over the years, that if you find enough dirt on the right people in power positions, then you always have a way of escape. I vowed a long time ago that nobody would ever control me or make me feel helpless again.

You bastard, you owe me your life. You took mine and now I'm going to take your money, your reputation and your life; then we'll be even. After I'm done with you, you're going to thank the devil that you're dead when you see him in hell. Trust me Father, heaven has cancelled your reservation and removed your name from the guest list. God only knows how many other children's lives you've ruined. But not to worry, you are never going to have the opportunity to fulfill your sick, sadistic lust, with another innocent kid again. Do you realize that I was only nine years old when you started taking me on those little field trips; I can still smell the stench of your sweat in my nostrils."

"Roman, that's not fair."

"Maybe not, but it's damn sure accurate."

"I'm sorry. I'll give you the money."

"Alright then, let's get on with it."

Father Timothy got up from his chair, trembling with fear as he walked toward the tiny chapel, silently praying that the money would be enough to pay for his sins. He opened the door and walked toward the altar which was a large marble table with a white cloth covering it. Underneath it was a small trap door that had a rug across it which Father Timothy knelt down and removed, then pulled opened the old rusty, tightly shut door.

Roman was on his hands and knees watching closely as Father Timothy carefully took the money out. Roman stood to his feet as he handed him the stacks of cash and transferred the money onto the altar. Father Timothy stood up and said, "That's all of it, nine hundred and fifty thousand dollars."

"Why in the world do you keep this kind of money in the rectory?"

"Let's just say it's our petty cash, in case of an emergency."

"Oh, I get it. It's the money you use to buy off the families of the children that you molest. This pays for private schools, college tuitions and fancy cars right?"

Father Timothy was silent.

"Why don't we go and find something to put this in, shall we?" Roman said. They walked out into the foyer to a closet that had a set of old luggage in it. Father Timothy took out a rust colored suit case and walked back toward the chapel. Roman watched as he filled the suit case with the money. He rolled it into the library, sat down and nervously continued sipping his lukewarm tea.

"Father, you don't seem to have quite the same energy you used to." Roman said sarcastically.

"Listen, I have repented of my sin and done my penance. God has forgiven me. Please Roman, I don't want to die. Have mercy on me. I know you have a conscience, just take the money and leave. I won't say a word to anyone about this."

"That's like saying you had a conscience before you took advantage of me back up in those swamps. And I heard about how you violently raped Jenna and injected your poison into her purity, while that nasty bitch, Sister Francis watched."

"Let me explain!"

"Oh, you have an explanation? I don't think so Father. There is nothing you can say to me that will make what you did to us right. You can't explain your way out of your hubristic behavior. And for the record, I'm not God, so I don't have to forgive you for your sins. That's His job not mine."

"Better yet, let me explain it to you in a manner in which you can better understand. Remember the way you taught me after school? Aristotle defined hubris as shaming the victim, not because anything happened to you or might happen, but merely for your own gratification. The pleasure for you was that you thought that by ill treatment of others, in some sadistic, masochistic way, you thought it made you even more superior. Father you're familiar with Canon Law, correct?"

"Yes, I am."

"Then you know that under Canon Law, sodomy was considered a crime against nature."

"Uh, I'm not sure what you're getting at." Father Timothy said.

"During the Spanish Inquisition, nearly all cases of sodomy were between an older man and an adolescent, often by coercion or violent force. It was considered a crime against nature and punishable by execution."

Father Timothy became even more frightened and sensed that Roman was capable of just about anything.

"I should arrest you for the molestation and rape of at least two young children and take you to jail, spread the word about what you've done and then put your punk ass in with the general population. Or, I could just shoot you and it would be justifiable homicide, because I finally snapped when I drove by and saw you going into the rectory. But let me quote Socrates for a moment. I memorized it after you quoted it to me so many times while you violated me.

"The soul is polluted and is impure at the time of her departure, she is the companion and servant of the body, constantly in love with and bewitched by fleshly, desires and pleasures, until she is led to believe that the truth only exists in that which a man may touch, see, drink and eat, to use for the purposes of his lusts. His soul becomes accustomed to hate and fear, unable to avoid that which makes the bodily eye dark and invisible, but can the object of mind be attained by philosophy; do you suppose that such a soul will depart pure and unalloyed?"

Roman realized that he was once the benefactor of his lust. Father Timothy was unsympathetic to his cries and forbade him to "copulate", as he used to put it, with females. He preceded his reign of terror upon him with lies of professed virtue, but his actions were filled with a doctrine of an immoral discourse, that forced him to succumb to his illicit passions and appetites.

Father Timothy dropped the empty cup and grabbed his legs. "I can't feel my legs!"

"With all the pain and suffering you've caused; I've decided to do something a little more *creative*, something you can relate to. I placed a poisonous liquid called the 'Devils Porridge' into the tea that you've been drinking."

"What's the *Devils Porridge?*" Father Timothy asked, with a clear sense of panic in his voice.

"It's Hemlock. Remember, it's the same poison that killed Socrates for his impiety, it causes death; first by disrupting the workings of the central nervous system causing paralysis to the muscular system, then the respiratory muscles are unable to contract, resulting in asphyxiation due to the lack of oxygen to the brain and heart. Let me share with you Plato's description of Socrates death in the Phaedo, in the fashion that you taught me." Roman recited it in his best Shakespearean impression.

"The man...laid his hands on him and after a while, examined his feet and legs, then pinched his foot hard and asked if he felt it. He said, 'No', then after that his thighs; and passing upward in this way into his groin. He showed us that he was growing cold and ridged, and then again when he touched him, and said that when it reached his heart he would be gone."

And to think, you didn't think I was paying attention in class! But you were so wrong. Remember when you told me that Jesus used a cross to fulfill his mission? Well, I've chosen Hemlock to fulfill mine."

By the time Roman had finished showing off his intellectual prowess, the 'Devil's Porridge' was in full effect. Roman laid his head down on him and looked up into his darting fearful eyes.

239

Tears rolled from Roman's tired blue eyes, onto his wheezing chest. Father Timothy grabbed him tightly, before the feeling began to escape his arms.

He said in a whisper, "Son, I'm sorry for what I did to you, I was a sick man back then and I was wrong. I only did to you what had been done to me, many years ago from my own Priest when I was a young boy."

Roman responded in a low riveting tone, "I have been a slave to this secret most all of my life. Although I felt trapped by cynicism, anger, hate and corruption, I feel vindicated now. I once had great respect for you, admired you and wanted to be like you. You were my hero. I trusted you until you made me do things that no child should ever be exposed to. I often still wonder what my life would be like if this had never happened to me. What kind of man would I have grown up to be without the guilt.... without the shame? I wish things were different. But I met this really nice Italian woman recently. Her name is Slone and she makes me feel good when I'm around her. Before I met her, I felt empty, completely walled off emotionally and invisible. It's hard to explain it, but she sees me in a way that I'm comfortable with. I'm not paranoid with her. I don't feel like I'm being judged or scrutinized, you know. I'm gonna go and spend some time with her. I figure we could travel together, take some walks on the beach and make love to each other in a way that brings each other pleasure and not pain.

So do you understand Father that you must die, so that I can live? I guess this is my strange idea of closure."

Roman placed his arms beneath Father Timothy's body and picked him up from the sofa. His lifeless legs dangled as he carried him into the chapel and placed him on the altar. Father Timothy moved his eyes frantically while trying to breath, his body was completely paralyzed.

Roman prayed with a loud voice. "Lord, I'm asking you to forgive this man for his sin. I realize that he is only a man and not God. I also ask you, if you would forgive me for the bad things I have done in my life as well. I take full responsibility for my actions and I know that you are the only one that has the power to forgive sin.

Father Timothy, I forgive you and I release you today, so that I can move on with my life and begin a new one. I leave the disappointment that you, my father and my mother brought to my life, right here with you and God on this altar today."

Roman walked over to a delicate table filled with candles that rested beneath a statue of the Virgin Mary. Her head was slightly tilted toward the candles that represented the prayers of those that believed that their petitions would be solemnly granted by the baby Jesus, that she meticulously held in her arms. He pounded his fist violently upon the table and roared from the depths of his diaphragm, as he was about to commit the ultimate sin; murdering a man of the cloth, his spiritual father and one of God's priests. The brash sound of a regretful man, committing spiritual suicide, reverberated throughout the damp, cold chapel, as he took one of his arms of anger and swept every candle down onto the floor.

Roman sat down in one of the pews, lit a cigarette and inhaled. As the smoke bellowed from between his lips, he realized that he oddly still had a residue of respect for the part of Father Timothy that was of the Priesthood of God. He sat in silence, as he tried to remember some of the few good moments he'd had with him, before their relationship became shrouded by profanity.

Tears fell from his eyes, as he stood and kissed him gently on the forehead before pouring gasoline across his body. Father Timothy's eyes begged for help, with one last plea, he gasped for a breath that would never come. Roman emptied the large silver flask with his initials on it—RMB. Father Timothy had given him the flask as a gift on his tenth birthday. It was once filled with alcohol that he was coerced into drinking. As Roman threw the flask onto the altar, he glanced at the crucifix that was suspended high above Father Timothy's body and flicked the cigarette onto the sacred altar.

There he was on the altar of a God, that he claimed to have served. Engulfed in the flames of the consequence of his forgiven sin, Father Timothy's body was consumed as Jesus looked down on him from the cross. Roman stood still and watched as the fire devoured the man that had robbed him of his innocence. He had feelings of accomplishment and regret, solace and anxiety. The demons immediately attempted to wage psychological warfare on his mind, but the smell of Father Timothy's burning flesh, brought him a profound sense of comfort as he turned and walked away once and for all, from the spirits that had tormented him for years.

He stopped in the kitchen, turned on all the gas burners on the stove, grabbed the suitcase with the money used to purchase the purity of countless innocents, and walked right out the front door.

As he drove away, he felt the impact of the explosion and watched as the vast colors of burnt orange and yellow fire, coupled with black smoke through his rear view mirror. He hoped that it would burn away his dark painful past forever.

When he arrived home, he showered and had dinner with Gabriel and Lupanare. Soon afterwards, he went into his beautiful niece's bedroom and carefully removed her from her crib. He sat in a white rocking chair that was hand painted with colorful butterflies and held her in his arms rocking her gently. A metamorphosis had taken place in him and for the first time in years...he felt peace.

Lagniappe

*A*untie Bristol and I were meeting for lunch. As I drove to Santa Monica to meet her at *i. Cugini's Italian Restaurant*, I couldn't stop thinking of how much I missed YaYa and Grandpa. I wondered how they would handle the situation if they were still alive. I know things would be much different. I was not cut out for what my life had become. I knew that I had asked my family to come to California, but it was clear that I had bitten off more than I could chew. I was so happy when they first arrived, but once they did, my reality changed and I became completely overwhelmed. I couldn't even grieve properly. Cooking, cleaning, driving the kids to school, doing homework and trying desperately to find some peace in my own house, became my mundane existence. I needed help. How was I going to go back to work in this condition? Thank God they were lenient, but I knew I had to go back at some point. I had a car note, a gardener, bills and a mortgage to pay. My savings was getting low and my emotional state even lower.

"Hi Honey, how are you?" Auntie Bristol said as she sat down.

"Can you can write me a prescription for some *Prozac*? 'Cause I damn sure need something to deal with your family. They are really somethin extra these days."

"What's wrong Jenna? Has it been that bad?"

"Why don't you come over for about a week and find out, they're your family too. And anyway, what the hell are we going to do with Auntie Sharon? The honeymoon is over. She's driving me crazy. She won't even get out of the bed. All she does is watch TV, sleep, cry and complain."

"You have to be patient with her Jen; she's grieving the loss of her husband, her sister, her brother-in-law, her great nephew and Gabriel's wife. Not to mention, her home and her job as well as all that's familiar to her. She's a New Orleans' girl at her core. She doesn't know anything else."

"We lost them too and we're all trying to cope. She has to at least try and help me with her kids. It's a lot of work and I don't have a life anymore. They have taken over my house. Hell, I feel like a visitor in my own home. I know they're my family, but damn, they remind me of why I left home in the first place. The girls just want to lie around, watch TV and play video games. I have to threaten them to get their homework done, and let's not talk about how Lincoln is always on the phone, talking to them silly ass little girls. He's up all night messing around and then can hardly get up for school in the morning. What's wrong with these kids today? Every time to tell them to do something, you gotta have a damn conversation about how they feel about it. Well, I'm not *Dr. Fucking Phil* ladies and gentlemen. Just do what I say, is what I've told them."

"Jenna, baby, please calm down."

"I'm sorry Auntie Bristol, I'm just venting I guess. Waiter, can you please bring me a double *Godiva* White Chocolate Martini?"

"Wow, it's a little early for a Martini wouldn't you say."

"Girl, nowadays it's never too early for a drink, 'cause my nerves have been really on edge lately. I don't know who I am anymore. I look in the mirror wondering what happened to the Jenna I used to be."

The waiter brought the Martini and placed it on the table, then took our order.

"I'd like a bowl of Lobster bisque, the lamb chops with polenta and an order of crab cakes please."

"Yes, ma'am"

"Oh, and bring an order of Calamari for an appetizer would you. Thank you."

"I see Hurricane Katrina left you with a voracious appetite to go along with that drinking habit." Auntie Bristol said.

"Yeah, I know. It seems as if I'm not content unless I have something in my mouth at all times. Food, a drink, a cigarette or something, and most of the time I'm wound up on sugar from eating candy and salty snacks all day. I know it seems like I'm spiraling out of control, I'm just doing the best I can right now. But don't worry I'm slowly working my way toward the crack pipe and if your sister doesn't get her act together soon, I'll be smoking rocks before the week is out."

"Well, at least your sense of humor is still intact."

"I'm just delirious...that's all. But back to your sister, seriously... I'm worried about her. I can't get her out of the bed. She is so depressed that it's difficult to get her to eat. She's dropped more weight since she's been here in the last month, than I think is healthy for her. Although she needed to lose some weight, I don't think it's a good idea for her to keep functioning this way. It's like she's trying to starve herself to death. I make breakfast and bring it to her on a nice little tray. I even sometimes put flowers on it, to try and brighten her mood. But hours later, I'll go back and check on her and she hasn't touched anything on her plate and she takes the flowers and stuffs them underneath her pillow. I found that out one day, when I forced her to let me change the sheets and clean her room.

Finally she got up and let me take her to pick up her *FEMA* card and her food stamps. Then all of a sudden last week, she decided she wanted to go to the store. She went to *Ralph's* and bought two big bottles of *Courvoisier* and she's been drinking it at an alarming rate, along with popping those anti-depressants like candy. Auntie Bristol, I'm not sure what to do with her. I'm not going let her kill herself on my watch."

"Oh Jenna, I know I haven't been able to physically be there to help much with my schedule and all, but let me send someone to help you with the cooking and cleaning until we can figure something else out."

"Okay, I guess that would take some of the pressure off me for now. Thanks.

"So, how are things with you and my Uncle Preston these days? Didn't you guys have an anniversary last week?" Auntie Bristol's mood changed suddenly, from mellow and relaxed to uncomfortable, ridged and slightly pensive in a matter of seconds.

"Well, let's just say that he's like having a beautiful instrument and unable to play it. He's like a guitar whose strings won't allow itself to be plucked. A set of congas that resists being pounded, or a violin, carved with the finest maple and polished to perfection, with a bow that's not allowed to kiss its strings. Girl, he's a lyric without a cadence."

"What exactly are you trying to say?"

"I'm saying, I think I need a drink too. Get that waiter back over here please." "Auntie Bristol, are you still happily married or not?"

"I'm happy, I guess. I mean he is a successful doctor, we own our own home and he had three apartment buildings, bought and paid for when we met. He's smart, charming, tall, dark and handsome. He tends to most every one of my needs but one."

"Oh damn. Waiter, bring this woman a stiff one!"

"Jenna, that's not funny. I've been married for five years now and my husband has not touched me or kissed me passionately for at least four of those years. I'm tired of pretending that we have the perfect little life. Women swoon over him every place we go. I'm totally, unequivocally, sexually frustrated and I'm not sure how much longer before I do something I'll regret. My husband could very well be the poster child for ED."

"ED?"

"Erectile dysfunction"

"Girrrrl…that would most definitely be a deal breaker for me. I'm having a hard time wrapping my mind around the fact that your fine ass husband, that women covet every time you guys go out in public, can't give you a proper salute. Anyway, I thought that was an old white man's disease."

"No, on the contrary, it crosses all ethnic boundaries and is another thing that black men and women in our community don't openly talk about. Why do you think they've sold billions of dollars of *Viagra* in the last ten years? It's not just white men buying the product.

"So why doesn't he just take *Viagra?*"

"He won't take it. Says it makes him feel weird. He's very sensitive about the subject and gets upset when I try to talk to him about it. I just gave up on it. I've tried everything; dressing up in my doctor's coat with a stethoscope with my finest lingerie underneath, dirty movies, candles, gourmet dinners, soft music, even a can of whipped cream that I ended up eating alone one night after he went to sleep. It seems he is just not interested in sex or me anymore."

Auntie Bristol desperately wanted her feet in the air, with her knees to her ears. Instead, her husband turned his back toward her every night without a kiss, comforting touch, or ever showed any sign of desire for her. She went to bed most nights with a deep longing for intimacy, with a man that she adored. Instead of nights of passionate love making and cuddling, she slept on a tear-stained pillow with dreams of regret.

"I'm so sorry Auntie Bristol. I really don't know what to say. But one thing I know for sure, I'm not letting you get outta here without writing me that *Prozac* prescription. Cheers."

Double Barrel

ogan sat on the mildewed ottoman where his father had rested his tired feet every night for years. He looked around what was left of his parent's home with disappointment. He sat for hours smoking one menthol *Newport* cigarette after another. He sipped from a premium bottle of Scotch between each drag. He wished he had a blunt right about now but even the weed man had respect for Mother Nature and had skipped town before the fierce winds and rains of Katrina could imprison him.

He was glad his family had gotten out safely and Angela would still have their house on Constance Street to live in, whenever she decided to come home. He thought of all the sad, tormented, poor faces he'd seen since Katrina hit. He had done his best, but from the looks of things, his best still wasn't good enough.

Logan had rescued forty-five people. The sight of the city under water was bad enough, but witnessing the devastation first hand and pulling many of the unfortunate ones out of the bowels of Katrina, had taken its toll on him. It was great saving lives and helping people, but watching so many lives torn apart while they lost everything that they'd worked for carried with it an insurmountable burden. Families separated, dead bodies floating, some swollen up so badly that they'd exploded. The sound of gunfire at night was unnerving. Standing by watching other police officers looting and acting like common criminals was unbelievable. The police were present to bring order to chaos and comfort to those who were left homeless. They were not supposed to become a part of the disaster, but a healing agent during post Katrina.

Everyone was on edge. The police officers, firemen and paramedics had become so overwhelmed that it began to wear them down. Many had lost their homes and were separated from family and friends just like everyone else. *Yet they honored their creed to protect and serve.* They all attempted to work through it and tried to stay within the realm of protocol but none of this was in the training manual. The majority of them had not been trained to deal with a catastrophic situation of this magnitude. Nothing quite like Katrina had ever happened in the history of our nation before. Hell, even our government was at a loss as how to deal with the situation.

Logan had only a few hours sleep in the last four days. He was exhausted and delirious. There were still so many more to save, but he wondered if he even had the capacity to save himself. It was becoming more and more difficult to control the troublemakers. There were not enough policemen to get the city under control, while doing search and rescue at the same time. They needed boats and much more equipment to assist in doing the work of saving lives. The massive amount of help that was needed to complete the extraordinary job had yet to arrive.

That son of a bitch George Bush is going to rot in hell. It's amazing how they can fly equipment, food, water and medical supplies to the other side of the damn world, and yet can't get help to a city right here in our own country. It's pathetic. He thought to himself, as tears cascaded down his face and he began to pray.

Lord, please forgive me, but this is way too much for me to digest. I can't take it anymore. I can't bear to pull out another body, dead or alive, from another destroyed home. I cannot watch another family ripped apart. I'm not strong enough to endure this kind of heartache. I ask you to take care of my family and Angela. Please help them to understand my weakness. Forgive me for not being honest with Angela all these years. Forgive me for all the lies I've told and I pray that the lives I've saved, will make up for the lives that I've taken.

Logan put the bottle of scotch up to his mouth and emptied it. He raised the glass bottle high into the air and smashed it to the ground. It made a sound so loud that it carried an echo from the emptiness that shrouded the neighborhood. He threw his head back, looked up to the sky and screamed. But no one other than God could hear him.

"Fuck you Father Timothy for what you did to me! You dirty, foul, bastard. I became so emotionally undeveloped as a result of your perversion that I was forced to live a lie. I hope you burn in hell!"

Logan Honore' walked out into the middle of the barren street, holding two nine millimeter guns; one in each hand. He placed both barrels in his mouth, took a deep breath and pulled the triggers simultaneously. Although Hurricane Katrina was long gone, she still managed to take yet another soul from this planet.

They found Logan lying in the middle of France Street, in the lower ninth ward three weeks later with his head blown clean off.

Ocean Waves

t was magnificently beautiful that day. Slone and I had taken the kids to the beach. We laid out blankets, put up beach chairs and pushed our ice cooler down into the sand.

We thought we would just watch the kids play in the water. Shelby threw herself across the blanket and began to read her new adventure book. Lincoln was playing with his *Game Boy* that Auntie Bristol had brought for him when we picked them up from the airport. When they arrived, they were in T shirts and flip flops. They were a pathetic sight to see, with only two duffle bags between the four of them. Lennox was listening to her *iPod* while pilling up mounds of sand, building her version of a sand castle. McKenzie clung to me with an intensity that was bordering on abnormal.

"What's wrong with you guys? It's the perfect day to be at the beach." I said. Not one of them responded.

Slone stood up and took off her shorts and T shirt. We all had on our bathing suits, under our clothes.

"Come on you guys, let's get into the water. There's nothing more amazing than a nice dip in the ocean, right?"

McKenzie looked up at her and began to cry.

"What's the matter little one?" Slone said.

"We're afraid to die."

"What?" I said.

Shelby looked up from her book and said, "Can we *please* go some place else. She's afraid of the water.

"Yeah Auntie Slone and so are we. Let's go, before we all drown out here." Lincoln said.

"Oh my God, are you afraid because of the hurricane?" Slone said. "Baby, don't worry about that, we don't have hurricanes or floods here in LA; we only have earthquakes."

McKenzie started screaming, crying and gripped my leg so hard that I had to pry her hands off of me.

"I wanna go home." McKenzie yelled.

"Damn it Slone!"

"Oops. Sorry Jenna."

We decided to take them to the Santa Monica pier. We knew that if we took them home, we would never get them back to the beach again. Every kid should experience the refreshing feeling of ocean waves flowing over their bodies. But it was clear, that was not going to happen with them so soon after what they'd been through. Thank God they seemed to brighten up a bit when they saw the Ferris wheel, tea cups and arcade.

"Who wants cotton candy?" Slone declared.

McKenzie smiled and said with a soft animated voice, "I do."

Slone and I exhaled, and gladly adhered to her request, knowing that the small victory would after all, become a subtle breakthrough for them.

Lennox was so excited to spend time with her cousins. It was nice to see her enjoying family other than Auntie Bristol and me. She had been so loving and patient. She asked Lincoln if he would ride the Ferris wheel with her and he said 'yes'. She took off running to get them a ticket. I yelled to her to stop running and she slowed her pace down to a brisk walk.

"Shelby, don't you want to go on the rides?" Slone said.

"No thanks. But I would love to have a hot dog."

"Great." Slone exclaimed. We sat down at a table while Slone and McKenzie went to get the snacks.

"So Shelby, how do you like living in California so far?" I asked.

"It's okay, I guess. But I miss New Orleans."

"What do you miss about it?"

"I miss my room and my friends. But most of all, I just want to go back so we can find my dad."

I had no words for that response. Thank goodness Slone and McKenzie had come back to the table to wait for the food, before I had to get into the fact that her dad had died. She was clearly in denial. They still hadn't gotten any real closure because they had to leave their father lying dead on the street, when the buses came and took them away. It wasn't like they had a funeral or anything yet. We were still trying to locate his body.

Lennox and Lincoln came back giggling and hungry. We had lunch on the pier that day, but the kids ignored the water and kept their heads down while they ate their hot dogs and French fries. We went to the arcade and played games until the sun disappeared into the ocean.

When we arrived home, I noticed I had a package from New Orleans. It was a nice sized parcel. I grabbed a knife, cut the brown paper and enthusiastically ripped open the box; looking forward to the goodies that were sure to be inside. It would be nice for us to have some treats from home right about now. Auntie Sharon walked in just when I began to take some things out of the box.

'Hey girl, how was the beach?"

"It was good, we took the kids to the pier for lunch and they rode a few rides, seems like they had a pretty good time."

"So, I see Lupanare sent you something from home. What'd she send?"

"Let's see what we have here. Two boxes of Beignet mix, five big bags of *Camellia's*; two white and three red, two cans of *French Market* coffee and chicory; hot sausage, boudin balls, crawfish tails and some brand new prayer cards. Oh look, some pralines too."

"Here's a note." Auntie Sharon said.

Hey there, just thought you might be a little homesick, so I sent you a few items that might cheer y'all up. Jenna, check out the newspaper article. God sure has a way of taking care of things.
Love, Lupa

I thought the newspaper was just what she used to line the bottom of the box. I pulled out the paper and focused my eyes on the front page. I read the head line out loud.

Priest Dead, Body Found in Uptown Rectory. Father Timothy Fitzpatrick dies at the age of sixty-two.

"Isn't that the priest that married Gabriel and Sidney?" Auntie Sharon asked. "What else does it say?"

"As wailing fire trucks rushed to the scene, at the Holy Sacrament rectory, the entire house was ablaze. The fire chief stated that the fire was deemed an accident. The fire appeared to have been started by a gas leak in the kitchen. It says that he must have lit some candles in the Chapel, while preparing for a mass that he and several of the priest and nuns had every Friday morning. The case is still under investigation, because they found remnants of gasoline in the chapel, and a titanium flask that they released to the *Vatican,* for their forensic team to examine an inscription that was etched on it.

They also said that it was custom for the *Vatican* to do their own investigation, before the local authorities would be allowed to close the case."

I plopped down onto a kitchen chair. I sat staring at the black and white picture of Father Timothy. A wave of varied thoughts swept through my mind. The man that had haunted my dreams for years was finally dead. At first I'd hoped that the tormenting demons from hell, had consumed his soul. But then, I wished that he had gotten himself some help. He had to have been a sick individual to have done those horrible things to me and probably other people's kids without remorse.

What was I thinking? I must have been tripping. He deserved to die a violent and fearful death. God is a much bigger person than me, if He has the capacity to forgive that man and let him into heaven. If I were God, I would have pad locked the pearly gates, so he couldn't get in. I sighed with the hope that since he was dead, he would no longer have access to my dreams. Maybe the guilt and shame that I had lived with for so long, would somehow vomit me out of its acidic stomach, and the power of his actions that had me shackled, would be relinquished forever.

I shook myself, got up from the table and began to put the elements of our box of Creole treats away. Auntie Sharon began to unwrap one of the pralines.

"It's good to see you finally eating something." I said.

"Auntie Sharon, I thought we might go to church in the morning."

"Church?"

"Yes, church. You know the house of God."

"Now why would I wanna do that? God took my house, so why would I want to go to His? I mean really Jenna, for what? Where was God when they shot my Harold in cold blood right in front of our daughter; huh? Where was He when my sister drowned in that nursing home? You were there when Grandpa fell off the roof. Did you happen to see God up there helping y'all find him when he fell in that water? Where is He right now? What is the preacher gonna say to me to bring them back? What can he say to me that will fix all this mess? Hell, I need a job so I can feed my kids. And I'm tellin you now; I don't have no money to give, 'cause *I know* dat preacher got some prayers for sale and *I can't* afford it!"

"I'll tell you what...let's just wait and see how you feel in the morning?"

"Yeah, whatever."

Sorrowful Tulips

he day was hot and balmy; the city still damp with Katrina's residue as Angela and Juliann, cloaked in dark clothing, stood at the river's edge. Their hands clenched together in sorrow, during a moment of silence for the loss of Logan Honore'. Tears fell from Angela's eyes and infused themselves with the grey Mississippi water. Amidst a multicoloured bouquet of tulips, Angela held one white Magnolia and a large box under her arm. She took a long deep breath before she spoke into the air, as if Logan was standing in front of her. She carefully tugged each tulip, one by one, casting them into the water.

"Logan, the red tulips are for the perfect love that we shared. The yellow ones are a reminder of the brightness of your smile and the joy that you brought into my life. The pink ones are for all the hugs and kisses we shared, that I will so desperately miss. The white represents the forgiveness I wrestle with granting you in this very moment, for forcing me to live in this world without you. The purple is for the sympathy I carry in my heart for you, because things got so bad down here, that it made you take your own life. Baby, I'm so sorry I wasn't there for you. "

There was an assumption that with each tulip she released into the water, it would give her the ability to let go of him.

"I stand here with one more flower in my hand, a Magnolia, it's symbolic of perseverance. This one is mine to keep, to remind me that as long as I have life, I have hope and the ability to persevere beyond the pain and disappointment I have felt since I heard that you had abandoned me. But I am strong and I am determined to endure the sorrow and grief of your absence in my life. I choose to fight the pain, and unlike you, I choose to live on."

Angela held the Magnolia close to her heart with one hand and wiped her tears with the other. She adjusted her posture, held her head up high and walked away with an unrealistic sense of closure.

She got to the car and realized she had forgotten something. She turned and slowly walked back toward the box she had solemnly carried with her to the river. Angela knelt down, took the top off and gently ran her fingertips across the ivory sequins and pearls that adorned her wedding gown. She pulled the dress out of the box and surrendered it to the water. Her face was stern as she watched the future she had planned with the man she'd loved since high school, float down the muddy Mississippi River. They'd planned to wed on Christmas Eve that same year.

Soon after Angela arrived home, she spent hours dragging everything she and Logan had shopped for to make their wedding beautiful, into the back yard. Flower girl baskets, invitations, second line umbrellas, custom made handkerchiefs with their pictures on them and anything else she could find having to do with the wedding that would never happen.

Next she went into his closet, grabbed an armful of his clothes and imbedded her face deep into the fabric of his shirts, pants and suits. Angela inhaled deeply, realizing how much she would miss the fragrance of the love of her life. But she knew it was time to move on or she would not have the strength to resist repeating, the same deadly mistake that he had foolishly committed.

Angela piled all of his clothing, shoes, books, video games, jewelry, even his favorite red and white stripped bath towel on top of all the ivory wedding purchases. She dowsed the mound of memories, along with a few crumbled *Times Picayune* newspapers with kerosene and set it all on fire. She stood dazed, staring at the vast colors of gold, with hints of blue that grew bigger with each moment as the fire consumed her ideal future. She held her veil and *Swarovski* crystal tiara in her hand, along with the *Maurice Lacroix* watch she had recently bought as a wedding gift for her beloved Logan. She screamed from the depths of her sorrow, "How could you do this to me you selfish son of a bitch? Did you ever consider how much this would hurt me? Did you forget about the long talks we had about a bigger house, children and growing old together?"

She cried and cursed, cursed and cried, then cried some more.

Her body, drained by grief, made one last motion as she cavalierly tossed her veil and the expensive watch into the fire. Angela placed the tiara on her head, pulled up an iron rod chair that was part of a patio set they'd gotten as an early wedding gift from his parents and sat down. She slowly opened the bottle of *Remy Martin* that Logan had been saving for his bachelor party. She filled a large plastic Zulu Mardi Gras cup with the strong drink and sipped for hours, as she replayed so many of the good memories they'd shared during their ten year courtship, over and over in her head until the blazing fire burned itself out.

Finally she forced herself into the house and into what was once their bedroom. Angela cringed at the sight of their bed, rejecting the idea of sleeping in it without him. Not drunk enough to squelch her hunger, she went into the kitchen, pulled out the large red cookie jar from behind the mixer, hoping to find a few cookies that weren't too stale to eat. She reached her hand in and came out with three oatmeal raisin cookies that were perfect, and a tea bag that she assumed Logan had placed in there after she'd left before the hurricane.

"*Alrighty then, I'll have a few cookies and some tea.*" She said to herself.

Angela turned on the TV, propped herself up with pillows on the sofa, quickly gobbled up her cookies and chased it down with a cup of slightly bitter, unique tasting tea mixed with *Pet* milk and honey, then dozed off to sleep still wearing her shiny crystal wedding tiara.

The Power Of The Porridge

*L*upanare decided to take a ride and see if she could find out what happened to Miss Dot. She pulled in front of the house. It looked like it was still occupied. *How could this be?* She thought. Miss Dot peeked out the window and opened the door. She waved for her to come in.

Lupanare sat across from Miss Dot at a nasty little dinette set that looked as if they'd tried to clean it and was unsuccessful.

"So, I see you still alive." Miss Dot said. "Go pull me some French bread and get me some tea girl. Make yo 'self useful since you in my house."

Lupanare obeyed her command as usual.

"I heard about yo' family and all, that's too bad about YaYa and 'em. I tried to warn her, but she was too stubborn to listen."

"So how did *you* find out about my family?" Lupanare said.

"Oh, let's just say, Miss Dot just got a way of knowing things."

"My kids say you put some kinda curse on them and that's why they died in the storm. Did you have something to do with what happened to them?"

"Of course I did, you asinine child. Dem six cards I threw at YaYa that day, when she was acting like she so high and mighty wit me, got the job done real good. That wench got just what she deserved, with her stuck up ass. She had the nerve to shoo me off her porch, like I was some kinda cockroach. Yes indeed, I knew I shoulda took William from her behind a long time ago. She didn't deserve to have a good man like yo' daddy. He would still be alive if he had walked away from her and come home with me, when I offered him all a dis; now both dey dumb asses probably rottin' in hell as we speak."

Lupanare's face became contorted. She stood to her feet and screamed, "What did you say, you old bitch! Do you think I'm gonna let you sit here and talk about my family like that. I'll kick yo' raggedy ass into next week."

Lupanare lunged across the table at the half-blind, frail, old lady. She grabbed her by the back of her neck and began pounding her with her fist, then proceeded to choke her. Miss Dot's son ran into the room and pulled her off.

"What the hell are you doing" He shouted as he went to the side of his mother. She lay on the floor holding her face, dazed and confused.

"Don't you move; I'm going to call the police!"

Lupanare ran out the front door and into her car. She cried as she sped up the deserted street. She maneuvered through trash, trees and water-damaged cars. For the first time, she realized that YaYa had been right about Miss Dot for years. She was a dangerous woman and not to be played with. She wasn't really worried about the police, because she figured they couldn't have known where to find her, since she was living uptown with Gabriel since the hurricane.

She pulled in front of the house, then sat in the car long enough to catch her breath and calm herself down. She began to count; YaYa, Grandpa, Sidney, Baby Gabriel and Uncle Harold. These were five lives already taken by the curse of Dorothy Laveau. She remembered that there were six cards in all. She rubbed her eyes, ran her hands through her hair and exhaled. *I guess I must be next.* She thought to herself. She was not ready to die. She needed to figure out a way to dispose of Miss Dot for good. She had done a lot of crazy things in her life, but murdering someone was just not a part of her DNA. She sat outside in the car for forty-five minutes, trying to devise a plan to kill Miss Dot.

Gabriel was holding the baby on one hip and a spoon in the other.

"Hey Ma, how was your day?" Gabriel said.

He handed the baby to Lupanare as she walked slowly into the kitchen. Zoë Arabella laughed, smiled, and kicked her legs frantically at the site of her grandmother. The intense scowl Lupanare had on her face when she came in suddenly vanished, when she saw her beautiful granddaughter. There was no way she was going to let Miss Dot hurt her family again.

"So, what you cookin' on boy?" Lupanare said as she walked into Gabriel's new house.

"I stuffed some bell peppers, made some macaroni and cheese, I fried some okra too; and a pan of jalapeno corn bread is in the oven. Can you fix the *Kool-Aid?* There's a few packs of strawberry right there on the table. Dinner should be ready in about ten minutes."

Lupanare put the baby in her high chair and began to make the *Kool-Aid.* As she reached for the sugar, the door bell rang.

"Who could that be?" Gabriel said. "Were you expecting someone Ma?"

Lupanare didn't respond.

As Gabriel approached the front door, he could see a police car parked in front of the house, as he passed the bay window.

"Good evening sir. Does Lupanare Bordeaux live here?"

"Why, is there a problem officer?"

"It seems as if she was involved in an altercation with a Miss Dorothy Laveau at her home today. If she is here, could we come in and have a word with her?"

Gabriel let the officers in and asked them to have a seat in the living room. He marched into the kitchen and spoke to his mother with a stern voice.

"Lupanare, the police are here and would like to have a word with you."

Lupanare was spoon feeding Zoë Arabella, some *Blue Bell* ice cream. She never acknowledged his presence.

"Lupanare did you hear me?" Gabriel said.

"And down the hatch we go." She said as she continued to feed the baby and ignore Gabriel.

"Ma, what is going on? They said you got into an argument with that Lady, Miss Dot."

The police officers entered the kitchen.

"Lupanare Bordeaux?" One of the officers said. "Charges are being pressed against you for assault and battery. What happened today Miss Bordeaux?"

Lupanare stayed focused on the baby. She took her from the high chair, rocked her and patted her on the back and began singing.

The itzy bitzy spider went up the water spout...

Gabriel went to take the baby from her arms and she pulled away.

"Let me put the baby down and make myself presentable and I'll come in and give you my version of the story." She said.

"Ma'am, you need to come with us down to the station."

Gabriel knew that Lupanare was unstable and combative when pushed.

"How about we go back into the living room and give her a minute to get herself together officers."

They reluctantly obliged him. They stood anxiously in the living room when Gabriel asked, "Can you tell me what happened?"

"It seems she had a confrontation with this woman during an afternoon visit. They exchanged words and Lupanare attacked her. Look man, let me be honest with you, we don't have time for this right now. Her son made a bigger deal out of this than I think it is. She just had a few cuts and bruises nothing serious. She's probably home by now. Can you bring her down to the station in the morning, so we can get her side of the story and we'll proceed from there, we need to get out of here."

"You know, my brother is a cop. Roman Bordeaux, do you know him?"

"Oh yeah, that's my boy. How is she related?"

"She's our mom, man."

"No worries then. I'll take care of this one myself. Sorry to have disturbed you with this. Good night. Oh, and tell Roman, that David Le Geaux came through."

Gabriel went to check on the baby and to let Lupanare know that she didn't have to worry. He walked briskly through every room in the house and checked the back yard, but there were no signs of his mother or the baby. It was clear that Lupanare had run off with the baby. Gabriel got in his car and drove throughout the neighborhood for an hour. He was worried about Zoë Arabella. He pulled his cell phone from his pocket and called Roman.

"Speak." Roman said.

"Man, Lupanare has run off with Zoë Arabella. I've looked everywhere I could think of. I need some help."

"I'll start looking for them as soon as I get off, which should be in about twenty minutes. Don't worry we'll find 'em before Zoë Arabella's bedtime."

"Okay man, I'll keep you posted." Gabriel said before pressing the red button on his phone. He pursed his lips and thought about how he couldn't stand to lose Zoë Arabella. He had lost enough, and she was his only reason for waking up in the morning. She was all he had left of Sidney. He slammed on the breaks, almost running a red light—distracted by his thoughts. He nervously mumbled a prayer with the hopes of finding his daughter soon.

Miss Dot was in her sitting room watching television. Roman knocked on the door, then heard her yell that the door was open and to come in. Strange for an old lady at home alone to do, but not many people were back in the city after the hurricane yet, so he guessed she had a false sense of security. Roman entered the room and introduced himself. Her one good eye became wide with revelation as she stared at him. His eyes were the bluest she'd ever seen. Then it hit her, this was the blue-eyed boy that use to have violent tantrums as a child. But unbeknownst to her, he was now a man with more anger and fury than any young child could ever have during a tantrum.

"Yeah, I heard about how you used to cut up as a boy; so bad in fact that yo' Grandpa had to whip some sense into you.

Guess it musta worked since now you a big-time police officer. But anyway son, I ain't had nothing to do with what happened to yo' family. You can blame that wicked Katrina for that. But one thing is fo' sho', your precious YaYa crossed the line with me for the last time. Bet she ain't never gonna disrespect Miss Dot again. She thought she was better than me, but now she know betta who's the one with the real power. Damn sure not that God she wasted her time on all these years. Where was He when she was fightin' fo' her life in that nursing home? If He was so powerful like she say, den why didn't He save her and your fine ass Grandpa too? Can you answer me that blue eyes? And anyway, what choo want wit me now? You lookin' fo' yo' crazy ass mama? Well, she ain't here. And she betta watch out for herself, I know that. Can't believe she had the nerve to put her hands on Miss Dot like that. Crazy and bold that one is. Always has been. You a lot like her ain't you son? I got sum Gris-Gris I'm 'bout to make up just for Lupanare. Ma girl, she gonna wish dem police had found her and locked her away for what she did to me. She shoulda known better that to talk to me dat way. Let me tell you in advance, sorry for the loss of your mother. And if you see her before I do, tell her when she gets to hell, to let that *strumpet*, Lois YaYa Coubillon know, that it was me that sent her to hell. That old heifer—she got just what she deserved."

Roman didn't respond.

"How about I fix you a nice hot cup of tea Miss Dot? Lupanare tells me that's your favorite beverage, maybe even better with a shot of *Hennessy*, right?"

"Oh yeah Bay-Bay, that would be nice and not a moment too soon. I ain't had no hot toddy since I came home from the hospital. My son went and hid all the liquor. He said I couldn't have no mo 'cause I'm on pills from the doctor. But nothin' can get me down. I've lived through things that most folks would fold up under, and I got a *cast iron* stomach to boot." She laughed wickedly. "Go on and fix one for yo 'self and we can talk further ova tea. I can give you a reading too. I like you young man; you a good listener. You remind me of your Grandpa back in the day, good lookin as can be. Do you have a girlfriend?"

"No ma'am." Roman sat down across from Miss Dot and handed her a hot cup of tea, mixed with *Hennessy* and a slow painful death. She smiled at him with the absence of the majority of her teeth. She was all gums and her mouth looked like a vacant lot.

"So what happened to your eye?" Roman asked. She took a loud slurp of her hot toddy.

"Mmmm, this is so good! Well, YaYa and I used to walk the French Quarter all made up like fifteen-dollar whores when we were ready to make our money. That was about the going rate back den, for the mulatto girls, ya know. There was a man named Mr. Charlie, he was a white powerful politician that loved himself some black Creole puunani. I was his favorite girl but he was very domineering and possessive. He always gave me hundred dollar bills, pretty jewelry and fine clothes. A hundred dollars was a lot of money back in those days, you know. I could never say 'no' to him." Miss Dot went on to tell the story with much drama and animation.

She said that one particular night, she and YaYa were standing outside of one of the burlesque clubs and Mr. Charlie came out the door just as a young man had put his hands all over her. He was feeling on her perky breast with one hand and her voluptuous derriere with the other. Mr. Charlie jerked her away from him so hard, that her arm was black and blue for days. He screamed at the fellow so loudly, that the passersby stopped in their tracks.

"She's mine!" Mr. Charlie yelled. The fellow threw his hands up in the air, shook his head and said, "There are a lot of whores to go around man, calm down."

"Mr. Charlie punched him right in the face. By the time he hit the ground, Mr. Charlie had whisked her away down the street and into his car. She didn't want to upset him any more, so she just kept quiet. He drove with an uncomfortable urgency toward his house on Esplanade Avenue. It was strange because he'd never taken her there before. They usually went to some seedy cheap motel, ova on Claiborne Avenue.

He dragged her through the courtyard and pushed her into the beautifully decorated two-story Victorian house with high ceilings, shiny hardwood floors, and a chandelier in every room.

She was turned on by the fact that he liked her enough to bring her to his home. So she planned in her mind just how she was going to give it to him, after they'd gotten upstairs. He hadn't calmed down much after they got into the bedroom. He threw her down hard onto the bed.

"Take off your clothes and wash that crap off your face. I'll be back." He said.

"Okay, big boy, whatever you say." Miss Dot yelled after him. She had gotten herself all cleaned up, back in bed and waited patiently, while she enjoyed looking at the lavish vases, artwork, and furnishings. Every piece was gorgeous and the room was so nice, that she thought to fold her clothes and place them neatly on a fancy chair that sat next to the big mahogany four-poster bed. Hours had passed. She had fallen asleep, dreaming of one day living in a house just like that one, with a man that would love her unconditionally and take care of her for the rest of her life.

She awakened to the sound of angry footsteps coming up the stairs, then, they entered the room and walked toward the bed. Before she could roll over, she felt a rush of cool air all over her body. Mr. Charlie had snatched the covers off of her. She felt something hot and hard, then scorching. She screamed in agony, at the first burning sensation of excruciating pain and heat on her back and buttocks. The pain was unbearable, her body convulsed as he rolled her over and the burning pain was administered heavily to her thighs, stomach and across her right breast, while her body cringed and reeled uncontrollably.

Mr. Charlie stood over her. His lips quivered. He had a peculiar calmness mingled with rage in his voice when he spoke.

"When I told you that you belonged to me, I meant it! The way you touch my body, the way you make me feel when I'm deep inside you, it's like no other woman. You said what was between your legs was mine and I believed you. How could you let another man put his hands all over my property? Don't I take good care of you? Well?"

"Yes, Mr. Charlie." Miss Dot said in a child like whimper, through her clenched teeth that had begun to chatter as she tried to bare the pain. After that night, it was as if he became her Massa and she was his slave.

Miss Dot took a deep breath, then another sip of tea.

"I never realized how deranged Mr. Charlie was until…"

"Until what?" Roman said.

"Until he slammed the point of that hot iron into my eye and said, "I'll make sure that you will never look at another man with lust again. And I promise you that *no* man will ever set his gaze upon you with desire after tonight; you stinking whore. I ought to kill you. But I love you too much.""

Roman watched as Miss Dot exposed her horrid past without a tear. It was as if she was telling someone else's story. He sat listening quietly while counting every sip she took of the deadly concoction. He graciously poured another shot of *Hennessy* into her cup as she continued her story.

"Well, it turned out that Mr. Charlie did love me, but in a strange kinda way. He kept me dere in that house, nursed me back to health, and even had a doctor come in once every two weeks to check on me. When he went off to work, a nurse came by everyday, changed my wounds and fed me. I was Mr. Charlie's slave whore and I lived in that house for three and a half years. During that time I got pregnant with his son and stayed a prisoner in that house, until I gave birth to our baby. I guess he was ashamed, 'cause I wasn't allowed outside. We spent countless hours together as a family and I knew it was distorted, but oddly enough, my dream had come true. So I thought.

Little Charlie had his second birthday. We had cake and ice cream with lots of gifts, laughter and love. The next day when I woke up, he had packed all my things, called for a cab and said me and little Charlie had to leave immediately. His wife was a missionary and had been in Australia converting some Aborigines and would be coming home soon. 'Good bye my love', he said to me, then kissed the baby and pushed us out into the street.

Now have you ever heard a story that sad in your life boy?" Miss Dot took another sip of tea then gazed at Roman who sat staring back at her, void of any sign of emotion. She scurried to her feet, turned towards Roman and raised her housecoat up over her head and dropped it to the floor, exposing her bald vagina that looked like spoiled cauliflower. She peeled off her wig and tossed it across the room. She was working with about only six strands of her own hair.

"One thing Mr. Charlie was right about, no other man since then has ever laid eyes on this body and that was over forty years ago. But you look like you man enough to handle it." Miss Dot stood with her wrinkled shoulders, perched back proudly and moved her body as seductively as her arthritis would allow. She giggled and said, "Look at me, look at me! Aren't I pretty?"

Roman sat and stared as Miss Dot gave him a show of her suffering and shame. She laughed freely as she turned her prune like figure, doing a little jig, never realizing that it would be her last. She twirled and bounced her age old hips as best she could, round and round as not to fall down; her loose skin swaying amorously from side to side.

Roman was not amused. He was only thinking of the grandmother that had raised him with so much love, the grandfather that chastised him so that he could grow up with some semblance of character, the uncle that took him into his home on weekends and on occasional road trips; his sister-in-law and nephew that he would never get to see again because of the curse of Miss Dorothy Laveau.

Miss Dot moved her body directly in front of Roman.

"Touch me please. I long for the feel of a man's hands on my body, just one last time."

It was as if somehow she knew that Roman would be the last person she would ever lay that one good eye on. She took his hands and held them upon her pancake wrinkled breasts. She closed her eyes, gently tilted her head to the side and moaned. Tears trickled through the deep crevices of the years of regret that had left their tracks delicately across her face. They traced her face like a map, through an unforgettable journey of poor choices. The love she could have experienced, the friendships she'd lost, perpetual disappointments, one right behind the other; but most of all, the regret of the life she was never able to give to her son Charlie. She had wasted her life, tormenting good people to make herself feel better about the unfulfilled path she had taken.

She moved her hands to his face and said in a guttural, stoic voice.

"I know what you came here to do *Blue Eyes*. I'm in the twilight of my life now and I'm ready to leave this earth. It's time for me to go see my daddy, the devil. It's time to pay for all the dastardly deeds I've done, and I must say, I did them well."

She plopped down in her seat, reached for her housecoat and wig and slipped them back on.

"So, how you plan on killin' me Mr. Blue Eyes?"

She picked up her cup of tea and guzzled down every last drop.

"Wow, all that dancing made me thirsty. So what you gonna do, stab me or shoot me? Wish you would rape me, but I know that's probably too much to ask, since I lied to you about how I put the curse on yo' precious YaYa and yo' fine ass Grandpa, huh?" She laughed sinisterly. "Those pretty little baby twins and der mama. Oh, I can't forget about that sexy Uncle Harold, now he was a fine looking man. Do me a favor and tell yo mama, her sweet self don't have notin' to worry 'bout, 'cause guilt's gonna take care of her. So much, that it don't need no help from de ol gris-gris lady, Miss Dorothy Laveau."

Even Miss Dot's spiritual perspective was dim, as a result of the impending backlash of Hurricane Katrina. She could clearly see death coming in detail for others. But her own death came disguised as a charming, handsome, young man, and a simple cup of tea, spiked with *Hennessy* and Hemlock. The devil was getting a taste of his own medicine that he had dispensed to others for years. Even her one good eye couldn't see the subtle danger that lurked within her own cup.

"So what you waitin' for, let's get this over with den. What choo want, some money? You can have it, what do I care? It's under the mattress in my room. I raised my boy to take care of himself. He at work right now, working overtime, burning up dem bodies at the crematorium. He been real busy since Katrina swept through these parts."

"Bitch I already got money!" Roman lost his cool for a minute.

He wondered if the *Devil's Porridge* would work on the devil's daughter. It was taking much longer than it did on Father Timothy.

Then suddenly, Miss Dot sat straight up in her chair. Her one good eye rolled around obsessively in her head as she felt for her legs. She tried and tried to move them but she couldn't. Roman sat and observed as she attempted to speak, gasping for air.

"What de hell did you do to me, you....dirty bastard!"

She held her chest then leaned her head back hoping that would help her catch her breath. She shook her finger at him as if she were trying to curse him, but to no avail. Finally, she mustered up enough strength to speak. Her voice was strained as she said with a chilling voice, "I damn you to hell boy."

The deadly concoction was slowly stealing her ability to move, her body soon became completely paralyzed.

Roman lifted Miss Dot's limp, motionless body from the chair and carried her into her bedroom. He tucked her in, as if he was putting her to bed for a good night's sleep. Her darting eye cried for help, as Roman placed her onto the bed. Within minutes she took her last breath. She would never have the opportunity to curse another helpless soul. Roman felt a cold chill pass through his body, unlike he'd ever felt before. Evil had left Miss Dot and slipped inside of him, disguised as a cool breeze. He had no idea that by killing Miss Dot, he had opened a door for the demons that had held her captive for decades, would need a new place to live. Miss Dot was finally free, but he was now bound by a force much bigger than himself.

Roman felt invincible as he placed his hand over her eyes to shut them. The feeling of absolute power over those that assumed that he was powerless was stimulating; but he couldn't allow it to distract him, he had to cover his tracks. He took what was left of the *Hennessey* as well as the two tea cups that he and Miss Dot had drank from, wiped away the fingerprints of everything he had touched, including the door knob and went out the back door with a feeling of pride, for getting revenge for his family.

As he walked past the garage, he heard some rustling and the sound of a baby. Roman pulled up the door to the garage and there was Lupanare feeding Zoë Arabella a jar of *Gerber* baby food, with her fingers by flashlight. There was an old dusty chair and table. Old clothes that looked to have been in there since slavery times, along with a lawn mower, rakes, two rusted bikes and an old light blue Oldsmobile Delta 88, covered in mud. It was damp, moldy and down right filthy. No place for a baby, that's for sure.

"Lupanare what the hell are you doing in here? Lupanare never looked up to acknowledge his presence. She continued playing with and feeding the baby. Zoë Arabella turned and looked at Roman with a big smile flashing her gums. Roman walked slowly toward them and gently took Zoë Arabella from Lupanare's arms. He rocked her as he gazed at his mother, all the while prepared for a negative reaction. But Lupanare put her head down low and began to rock from side to side really hard. She started singing a Mardi Gras song.

Oh it's carnival time, and everybody's drinking wine, oh yeah, its carnival time...

She closed her eyes and tapped her foot. Zoë Arabella laughed and stretched out her arms reaching for her mentally-challenged grandmother.

"I'm taking her home. Your ass is crazier than I thought. How could you do this to Gabriel? You know damn well all the hell he's been through, and you go and do this to him? We should have never let you back into our lives. Why you always gotta go and fuck things up? Roman held the baby close to his chest and held her head delicately as he walked away closing the garage door behind him, leaving Lupanare rocking, swaying and humming. She sat there singing and rocking for two hours.

Lupanare remembered that Miss Dot's son Charlie worked the grave-yard shift. She made her way to the back door and found that it was opened. She knew that Miss Dot would be asleep. She went into the kitchen and found the biggest knife she could find. All she could think about was how Miss Dot had ruined her life, what little she had left of it. She was finally starting to feel like she had a purpose—helping Gabriel with the baby. She was happy to be back with her boys, on speaking terms with Jenna, and living a relatively normal life. Miss Dot had taken that all away from her, not to mention her parents, whom she never had the chance to tell how sorry she was for all that she had put them through over the years.

Lupanare slipped into Miss Dot's bedroom and into her bed. She was tired from all the commotion of the day. She laid her head down on the pillow, next to Miss Dot. She could see her face clearly with the moonlight that shined dimly through the window. She closed her eyes for a moment, thinking of how she could go about killing her quickly and get out of the house before sunrise. As she lay there making her plans, she was lucid enough to realize, that Miss Dot wasn't snoring as usual. She had spent countless hours at her house over the years, enough to know that she snored like a two hundred sixty-five pound, *NFL* linebacker. She placed her hand under her nose but felt no breath on her hand. Then she pressed firmly on her chest, but there was no movement.

Oh, my God. She thought. Lupanare placed two fingers on her neck to check for a pulse. There was none. Miss Dot had not only robbed her of the opportunity for another chance to cultivate her relationship with her kids, but she had even managed to rob her of the pleasure of personal vengeance.

Lupanare buried her face in the pillow and began to think of all the nasty things she had said and done to YaYa, how unfair she had treated Bordeaux, and how she was too selfish to raise her own kids. They deserved better. The thought of abandoning her own children began to suffocate her will to live. Lupanare took the large knife that she brought from the kitchen to kill Miss Dot and plunged it into her abdomen ferociously three times. The pain was daunting, but worth the freedom from the guilt that Miss Dot had promised would one day consume her.

She closed her eyes and bore the pain of her own self-destruction as the sheets, mattress and Miss Dot's housecoat, drank the blood of her guilt, until it sucked the very life from her.

Roman finally called.

"Oh my God Roman, how are you? Are you home yet?"

"Yeah, I'm ova here with Gabriel and the baby right now."

"How long have you been out?"

"Long enough for me to take care of some unfinished business; I turned in my resignation, my car, my gun and badge and then cleaned out my desk. They put me through hell down there with that dumb shit Logan told them about me."

"What happened with you and Logan? Give me some real details this time, please."

"Are you ready for some truth?"

"Yeah"

"Logan was bisexual Jenna."

"How can you say that, he and Angela had been together since high school?"

"He was on the DL. He would have caught all kinds of hell in the NOPD, showing up to work one day and making an announcement that he was kicking down the door of the homosexual closet, that he had been hiding in for years. They would've beaten him unrecognizable. He couldn't continue to live with the lies any more. I think the devastation of the hurricane, on top of the guilt, is what led him to kill himself."

"We weren't at *Snug Harbor* that night. We stopped at that gay spot, *Oz*. He caught his gay lover out with another dude and he brutally murdered both of them right in front of me. He made me swear, that I would never tell anybody about what he did that night. I freaked out really bad Jenna. I was having nightmares about it, he told me I should go and get some help from a counselor or someone to help me deal with it. It's too bad it had to come to this, you know. Then he had the audacity to come and flip the shit on me. Man, I loved that dude like my own brother."

"So what are you going to do? Are you still coming out here or what?

Oh My Gawd!

managed to get everyone, including Auntie Sharon, into the Sanctuary on Sunday morning. I prayed that Pastor Edward would have something to say that would uplift us all. Praise and worship was phenomenal. I could see tears running down Auntie Sharon's face as the choir sang. Pastor Edward walked into the pulpit and began his sermon.

"Please turn to second *Corinthians* chapter four and verse eight."

Just then, Slone walked in with Roman beside her. They sat next to us and Roman put his arm around Auntie Sharon. I could see it took everything in her not to lose it when she saw him. You could hear her let out a soft whimper as she continued to wipe the tears from her face. Roman acknowledged each one of us with a wink and a strong nod and then we turned our attention back to Pastor Edward.

"We are hard-pressed on every side… yet, not crushed; we are perplexed, but… not in *despair*; persecuted, but… not forsaken… *struck down… but not destroyed…*"

It's hard for us to understand where God is, when we're facing *insurmountable* circumstances, when it seems *He* is taking us down a path which is vastly different than the one *we* had planned. But we all are familiar with the cliché: *we make plans… and God laughs.*"

He chuckled and continued:

"I don't really know if He actually *laughs*, but it often seems as if He has an *interesting sense of humor*. Sometimes, it's like were going on with our everyday normal activities; we're *happy*, we're comfortable, then all of a sudden, a TSUNAMI of graphic proportions comes and hits us so hard that it feels impossible to recover. I don't know why God allows bad things to happen… it is a mystery; but what I do know is that in the midst of every storm, if you don't give up… *He will bring you through it.*

There is a still small voice that speaks to each of us, way down on the inside that gives us HOPE… HOPE to see the rainbow appear after the storm subsides, HOPE that leads us to recognize that, no matter how hard life gets, *God is always present* to bring comfort and peace, if we will allow HIM the opportunity to change our hearts… allow Him to take away the anger, the resentment, the guilt and the shame that sometimes feels like it will never go away. HE can, by HIS omnipotent power, heal us in the deepest, darkest places where we have been *hurt… abandoned… or betrayed…* sometimes even when it seems we have been hurt by *God himself.*

It is not God's intention to destroy you, *but to heal and deliver you* from the torment that life has brought upon you. Often times, we deal with sins of omission. Things that come against us, by others… or circumstances that are out of our control. *We beat ourselves up… over and over again,* rehearsing what we should have done or said that could have changed the outcome. Just know… that as bad as it might seem right now, that the bad and the good things are working together on your behalf, *to ultimately perfect and mature you into being more like Christ.*

Life is not always easy. Do you think it was easy for a loving God to sacrifice His only Son on the cross to die for your sins? Think for a moment of the worst thought that you've had, or the worst thing that you've ever done in your life… JESUS' BLOOD was shed for THAT VERY THING TO BE BLOTTED OUT. You are totally, completely, and unequivocally AQUITTED from your past, present and future sin. It's simple… just say that you are sorry and ask for forgiveness and don't do it again. And if you fall... *get up*! Repent! HE will FORGIVE you as many times *as YOU NEED HIM TO*. THERE IS NO LIMIT TO GOD'S FORGIVENESS. Why do we hold ourselves in a prison, where the cell doors are UNLOCKED AND WIDE OPEN! Forgive yourself and go FREE! God is not holding you hostage—YOU ARE!

The one thing that no one can take away from you is your personal relationship with God, your prayers, your conversations with Him, and your longings for Him to manifest Himself to you in a way that only you can recognize. This is not a religious exercise, but this is about your response to your creator. But as much as He loves you, He will never force you to love Him back. He loves you without condition.

God is always available to help you, if you ask, believe and move in the direction of change. He works in unison with us, not outside of us. Give Him an invitation to appear in the midst of your circumstance, allow Him the pleasure of doing what He does best, taking care of those who will call upon His name. I challenge you to invite Him into your life, your mess, your confusion, your state of depression and your inability to move forward in your life.

If there is anyone here that would like to come to the altar for prayer, or if you just want to commune with God, please come to the altar. No one will hurt you, harm you or take advantage of you. This is a safe place. You are welcome to come and stand, kneel or lay out on the floor if you like."

The presence of God was almost tangible. We were all in tears searching for tissue from any place we could find it. All of a sudden, Roman let out a *shrill* that brought the entire sanctuary to silence. You know the kind of cry that is so sad and guttural, that it makes *you cry* in response to it. I don't think there was a dry eye in the house. He was bent over with his head between his knees. It was the sound of a man that had been touched by the hand of God. It was evident that the flood of tears that streamed down his face, cleansed his soul. We were witnesses to a surgery being performed by the Spirit of God. He was cutting away all the heartache, anguish and emotional detriment he had experienced in his life. The anointing was mending the broken pieces of his heart that

281

had been ripped apart by the enemy of disillusionment, resentment, and bitterness. Yet, the sound was as if something far more serious was trying to get out, while God was trying to get in. He reeled and gagged then finally, he threw up. Although he had made a big mess, no one seemed to mind. They sent someone right away to clean him and whatever had escaped his body. He got up from his seat and ran into the rest room, while three men I assume were deacons followed after him.

Auntie Sharon got up from her seat and folded herself into a ball at the altar. She wept for so long, that Pastor Edward had given the benediction and the congregation had left the sanctuary. Pastor Edward and his wife Michelle kindly prayed and counseled with our family for over an hour. I believed that through our prayers and the prayers of Pastor Edward and his wife, that the curse of Miss Dorothy Laveau had been broken off of our family for good.

We headed out to Malibu for brunch, at *Paradise Cove.* We were all captivated by the spectacular view, while we rode along the winding Pacific Coast Highway. The sun kissed the white capped swells of the Pacific and the palm trees swayed in the light ocean breeze.

The kids ran out to the full-sized beds that sat right on the beach, just a stone's throw from the water. Roman's face was bright and cheery as he stood in the sand watching the waves, with his arms wrapped tightly around Slone. Auntie Sharon and I breathed in the fresh ocean air while we waited for our table.

"This is breathtaking. I've never been to a place like this before. And that's a nice touch with beds and chairs right here on the beach." Auntie Sharon said as she exhaled.

"They shoot lots of TV shows and commercials out here." Slone said.

"Really, like what?" Shelby asked.

"Like *Baywatch, The OC, Alias, Charlie's Angels* and one you might be familiar with McKenzie; The *Sponge Bob Square Pants* movie."

"That's really cool Auntie Slone." Lincoln said.

"Come on guys, our table is ready." I said.

Slone had called in advance and had a special table reserved for us. She was long time friends with the family that owned the restaurant. Our table was already filled with an assortment of food.

"Oh my Gawd, this is paradise!" McKenzie said with a smile that I had not seen since they'd been in LA.

We sat down and held hands as Roman prayed.

Lord, thank you for this glorious day. Despite all that we've gone through, we are truly blessed. Thank you for Jenna and Slone for their willingness to share there lives freely with us. Amen. Oh yeah, bless the food we are about to eat and bless the hands that prepared it. Amen.

"I ordered up lots of food for you guys. I figured since you all came from New Orleans, you'd love some seafood. It's a little different from what you're probably used to, but I think you'll enjoy it just the same." Slone knew the menu by heart. "This is shrimp balague, jumbo shrimp incrusted with parmesan cheese and onions. And here we have macadamia coconut shrimp, crispy calamari and Alaskan king crab legs. Oh, and let's not forget Papa Joe's fried fish po boy, along with my favorite, garlic mashed potatoes and crispy cheese fries, you see nicely placed inside the big martini glasses. *Bon appetit!*"

McKenzie looked at Auntie Sharon and said, "Mommy, there's so much food. I don't know where to start."

"Let me show you how it's done baby girl." Roman said as he reached for the fish po boy. We laughed, talked and ate until our bellies were beyond full. Then the waiter came out with the most unbelievable desserts we had ever laid our eyes on. A mile high chocolate cake and an enormous ball of vanilla ice cream, rolled in crushed *Oreo* cookies topped with hot fudge, as big as my head.

All of us immediately developed an extreme case of the Itis. You know, when you eat so much that all you can do is find a soft place to lay your head and sleep for about an hour, before you start thinking about what you gonna eat next.

We pulled up into Slone's driveway. Her house sat on a hill overlooking the beach.

"What is this place?" McKenzie asked.

"This is Auntie Slone's house honey." I said.

"This building is a house?"

"Yes sweetie, this is where I live, come on and get out of the car and I'll give you all a tour of the property."

Roman was really quiet. Not only was it his first time in California, but it was his first time seeing Slone's home. He had no real idea of the wealth the woman he had fallen in love with possessed. He stood outside the car looking at the house with his mouth opened in awe. I grabbed his hand and pulled him onto the walkway.

"Close your mouth fool, and don't act like you ain't never been no where."

As we entered the ultra-modern three-story house, I observed my family members demeanor, go from sluggish to complete exuberance. Slone took them on the deluxe tour. She enjoyed seeing the excitement in their faces too. It was good for them to see something fresh and new. Lennox had grown up out in LA, so she was used to the type of luxury that Slone possessed, but Lincoln, Shelby and McKenzie had not had much exposure. Roman was hard to read. I could tell that he was impressed but also slightly intimidated.

"Damn Auntie Slone, this is off the Richter scale." Lincoln said with pure delight. "Looks like somebody been working real hard or won the lottery. Hey, do you sell drugs like that white lady on *Weeds*?"

"You betta shut your mouth boy, or I'll pull that belt right off Roman's pants and whop yo' behind. You know better than that! I'm sorry Slone, he's just excitable, you know."

Slone had been awarded a trophy residence from her divorce. The house was three stories and fifteen thousand square feet. It had walls of glass, a bold contemporary art collection scattered throughout the house and a three hundred twenty-five bottle wine cellar. She had a top-of-the-line chef's kitchen, a sculptural staircase that graciously led to the second and third levels that included color injected flooring, surrounded by a salt water fish tank embedded in the floor of an enormous great room. There was also a library, an office, media room, game room, a gym, eight bedrooms and a luxurious master suite with a private deck, a spa bathroom, equipped with a steam room, sauna and a Jacuzzi tub that I personally envied, along with a closet that a small tribe from Africa could live in.

Slone escorted them onto the elevator with doors that opened onto the roof, exposing a breathtaking panoramic view of blue skies, ocean, and mountains; a pool and Jacuzzi with fiber optic lighting, an outdoor shower, cabanas, koi pond, full kitchen and BBQ, fireplace and a television with an eighty inch screen.

"What's that over there?" McKenzie said.

"That's the guest house and studio." Slone responded.

"Wow! Can we come and live here with you Auntie Slone, pretty please?"

Slone laughed and said, "Well sweetie, I'll tell you what...you guys can come over and hang out with me any time you like. Now let's go back down and watch a movie in the media room. I have a new popcorn and cotton candy machine I've been dying to use, but let me show you one more thing first."

We took the elevator down to the garage. When the doors of the elevator opened, the borders of the spotless personal show-case room lit up like a Christmas tree, illuminated by tiny white lights embedded in the floor and walls that looked like shining stars. Roman's blue eyes had a sparkle of their own. A look of pure delight manifested across his face and revealed a level of satisfaction any man would have, who suddenly had access to an array of premium vehicles to drive.

Roman examined each car, opening doors, observing gadgets while running his hands over the expensive custom leather seats. She had two *Aston Martin's*, one blood-red *Vanquish SS Coupe* and a British racing green *DB 9 Volante* convertible. A charcoal grey *Mercedes Benz* SI 55 AMG, two *Wiesmann's*, one pearl white *Stuttgart*, a piano black *Nord* and an indigo blue, *Fisker Karma*. There was also a peacock-colored *Bentley Azure* and my favorite, the one I'd had the privilege of driving several times, was the beautiful silver

Maserati Quattro Porte Sport GT. Each car was equipped with a premium sound system, remote keyless entry and all the conveniences that money could buy. Roman covered his chest with his hands when he spotted the vintage *Harley Davidson Softail Deluxe.* It was black, had custom yellow, orange trimmed flames, enough chrome to force you to put sunglasses on and a *Screamin Eagle Big Bore Kit* to make a grown man cry. I could have sworn I saw my brother's tear ducts moisten, as he stood in a garage that could very well become his new toy box.

We spent the rest of the night relaxing and hanging out at Slone's. I was teary eyed as I watched my family put aside their troubles and begin to relax. I hoped that the smiles I saw would last, hoping that the suffering they'd experienced wouldn't bleed through and snatch them away, with the memories of their past and the anxiety of their future. But at least for one day, we would all embrace the momentary solace that the ocean breeze brought with it. Within the next month, Auntie Sharon was working at the church and she and the kids were living in Culver City in a nice three-bedroom apartment, fully furnished with rent paid up for the next two years, all arranged by the church. I found a really good deal on a car for them. Slone took McKenzie to a dance class on Saturday mornings, Shelby had gotten a sympathy job working at *Bath and Body Works* in the Fox Hills Mall while Lincoln was playing basketball again and doing fairly decent in school.

Roman and Slone spent countless days and nights together; walks on the beach, sampling bottles of wine from her cellar, up all night getting to know each other better, while *Turner Classic* movies often played in the background. Several of those nights ended with love making that included them playing officer and assailant, with Slone gleefully allowing herself to be caught and ending up in handcuffs.

Early one morning Roman got up to make the sobering soup, that the New Orleans late night party locals often ate after a night of binge drinking, called *Yakamein.* It's a dish that could cure any hangover and the most of the local folks refer to it as *old sober.* It was one of YaYa and Grandpa's favorite late night eats.

Roman reached for the biggest pot he could find in the kitchen. He filled it with water, added a little oil, Bouillon beef base, seasoning salt, pepper and onion powder, then put in a beef roast he had picked up earlier that weekend when they had stopped at a *Ralph's Grocery Store*. While the roast cooked, he put on some eggs to boil and then some spaghetti.

The roast cooked until it was tender; he took it from the pot and pulled it apart and put it back into the broth and seasoned it to taste.

As Slone came down the stairs, she was greeted by a savory aroma. She found Roman naked, wearing sweat socks and house shoes, in the kitchen cooking breakfast. She was giddy with delight having him all to herself and loving the fact that he was actually cooking and it smelled fantastic.

"Okay, Cotton Ball, let's eat."

Roman took two bowls and began to assemble the '*Yock*'.

"Noodles first, then let's add some beef, then we're going to slice the eggs in half and put them in and now some broth and green onions on top with a little soy sauce, a dash of *Tabasco* and a shot of *Worcestershire* sauce and a little black pepper. Now taste."

Slone picked up her bowl and began to devour the spicy, flavorful soup that New Orleanians had adopted from Chinese immigrants that were brought in with the slaves to work the railroads more than a century ago. She moaned with satisfaction, after every bite "This is good Roman, I feel better already. Now let's go back to bed."

"Slone, I need to get back to New Orleans. I have someone I need to find; someone that impacted my life so much, that I just have to go check and see if they're still alive." Slone, of course, disagreed sharply with his decision to leave so soon. She begged him to at least allow her to accompany him on the trip.

"Listen Dawlin, this is something I need to do for myself, alone."

After an hour of debate, Slone gave in only after forcing him to promise he would return before the end of the month, which was in two weeks. They finally both agreed, but Slone was suspicious, wondering who the person could be that was so important, that Roman had to end their time together so abruptly.

"I'll be leaving tonight." He said as he kissed her on the forehead and headed back upstairs to pack his things.

The Fragrance Of Revenge

t was eight o'clock in the morning. The weather was overcast, damp and a bit chilly. Charlie was exhausted and glad to be home. The house was dark, all the shades were closed. He smelled the familiar fragrance of death, but seeing that he worked at a crematorium, he shrugged his shoulders, took off all his clothes and climbed into the shower. Afterward he wrapped himself in a thick, white, terrycloth robe and went to the kitchen to make breakfast. As the bacon fried and the toast popped up from the toaster, he wondered why his mother, Miss Dot, was not awake yet. She was usually an early bird, on deck, watching all the early morning new shows and *The Price is Right* until her stories came on. Normally, by the time he started breakfast, she would already have a basket of clean clothes sitting at her feet, while ironing everything from underwear to sheets.

Charlie sat at the dingy kitchen table and devoured his food. When he was done, he went straight to bed. When he awoke seven and a half hours later, with only a few hours left before he had to get back to work. He turned on his boom box and slid in a Kanye West, *Late Registration* CD, then turned the volume up loud enough for him to hear in the bathroom. He brushed his teeth, washed his face and put on his clothes. He plopped down on the bed and pulled out a tin box from underneath his bed. He separated seeds from leaves and rolled himself a joint. It made the deplorable job of handling dead bodies for a living, somewhat bearable.

He still hadn't heard Miss Dot moving around yet. He went to her room and pulled back the dark sheets that lined the windows since the hurricane.

"Ma" He called out. "What the fuck!" He shouted as his eyes came into focus. He saw the blood soaked sheets that covered his mother and Lupanare. He reached out and grabbed the cold hard body of his mother. He was in shock, but soon realized he needed to dial nine, one, one; immediately.

"Hello, hello. I have two dead bodies in my house and one of them is my mother. Please ma'am, send somebody ova here right now!"

He looked hysterically around the room with his marijuana-induced paranoia and wondered if the person that had done this was still in the house, as he gave the nine one, one operator his information.

The sound of blaring ambulance sirens and flashing red and blue lights from multiple police cars converged in front of the house. Policemen scattered throughout the block searching for clues, while paramedics lifted Miss Dot's cold hard body onto a gurney and placed it delicately into a black body bag. The pull of the zipper released the faint sound of complete closure and finality as they removed the body from the house. The others worked diligently on saving another's life.

"One, two, three..." The young medic said, as he placed the paddles of the defibrillator onto her chest. The jolts of electricity jerked her body upward.

"Nothing...but let's try it one more time."

"Naw man, this one's gone."

"No." He said with authority. "One more time, I said."

As the current flowed toward Lupanare's heart, there was a faint heartbeat. A syringe was opened and an IV immediately placed into her vein. The stab wounds that she had violently injected with the knife from Miss Dot's kitchen, where packed with gauze and taped up until they could get her to the nearest functioning hospital. Lupanare had miraculously survived the guilty curse of Miss Dorothy Laveau. But Miss Dot would never recover from Roman's revenge.

Doucette's Promise

*D*etective Promise was leisurely thumbing through the legion of reports that covered his desk. His thoughts were scattered as he tried to put the pieces together regarding several murders that had taken place in the last few months. It was bad enough that they were still dealing with an overflow of issues since the hurricane, but it seemed that someone had blown a gasket and gone on a killing rampage. He waited patiently for the final report from the *Vatican*. The death of Father Timothy had kept him up too many nights to count. Something about it just didn't seem right to him. *"A freak accident... his body found on the altar... what could he have been into? There had been rumors for years that he had fondled a few of the altar boys in his parish back in the day, but nothing ever came of it."* He thought to himself, as he exhaled with the satisfaction that he was finally going to get the closure he needed.

There was a knock at the door.

"Come in please."

A blonde haired, tall, full-bodied priest extended his hand and introduced himself.

"Hello, I'm Father Cameron Doucette. I was sent by the *Vatican,* or should I say; by the very Pontiff himself."

"Please come in and make yourself comfortable Father. Can I get you anything; water, coffee, whiskey?"

"I'll have a cup of coffee if you don't mind, I had a long flight. And from my analysis, it seems we have lots of work to do."

Detective Promise hesitated, he was faced with the moment he'd been waiting for, but suddenly he felt uneasy, which was highly unusual for him while he worked a case. He poured two cups of *Community Coffee,* added a shot of *Jack Daniels* to his and looked toward his guest, to see if he wanted a spike in his as well. Father Doucette motioned with his hand, clearly indicating that he was not interested in a dark bitter hot toddy.

"I like mine black and virgin, thank you."

Detective Promise sat down, but not before removing his suit jacket. He was burning with anticipation for the results of the autopsy report.

"Seems, as if we have some foul play involved here. Father Timothy's toxicology report revealed an unusual amount of a poison called Hemlock in his system. From where I stand, looks like he may have had a visitor. During our investigation of what was left of the rectory, some parts of the house were still intact. The downstairs restroom was virtually untouched by the fire; it only had smoke damage. We found broken glass from the mirror, which of course could have come from the blast, but several of the pieces had blood on them. O negative to be exact, which is a rare blood type. But I'll revisit that later. What I am most interested in is the titanium flask that was recovered. The initials on it were *RMB.* Would you have any idea who this item may have belonged to?"

Detective Promise sat quiet as a church mouse, conflicted and dazed, while his eyes blinked trying to hide the the fact that he may have already made some grave mistakes concerning the case. His mind raced with thoughts that he did not want to entertain.

"Anyhow, this substance is only found in certain parts of the world and it's difficult to trace the exact origin, but someone definitely murdered Father Timothy; whoever it was probably set him and the house on fire as well."

"Umm, I have some leads that I need to follow up on Father. Thank you for coming and ..." Father Doucette cleared his throat and interrupted him.

"Excuse me, but I didn't come here to dispense information, I'm here to catch a killer and I'm not leaving until I find the person who did this."

"Father you are way out of your jurisdiction. My team and I are well able to handle the rest of this investigation. We allowed you to come in and collect evidence and have the *Vatican* run some forensic tests, only because of the severity of what has happened down here with the hurricane and all; but now that evidence will need to be turned over to the local authorities and that would be me. It's out of your hands now."

"Listen, I and the *Vatican,* insist that you allow me to be a part of this investigation until we get to the bottom of what happened to Father Timothy. They sent me because I grew up here, so I'm quite familiar with how things are done down here, and whatever happened to him is ultimately our responsibility. I promise you, if you don't agree, then *we can and will,* make things very difficult for you sir. Do we have an understanding?"

Detective Promise reached into his desk drawer, pulled out a pack of *Juicy Fruit* gum, unwrapped a stick, popped it into his mouth and said sarcastically between chews, "Welcome aboard Father Doucette, I'm sure you and all your expertise, will prove to be an asset to the case."

Letters From Yaya

Slone and Auntie Sharon came over to help me with the gumbo. All the prep work had been done. It had become a new tradition for one person to read the recipe out loud, as the others cooked. It was my turn to read. As I turned the tattered pages of the tablet, my voice trembled through the salty tears that rolled down my cheeks and softly crept into my mouth, while I read from YaYa's cook book. Slone wiped the sorrowful wetness from my face as I struggled through it.

½ cup vegetable oil
½ cup flour
One cup chopped onion, diced
Two green peppers, diced
Three ribs of celery, finely chopped
Six cloves of garlic
Two bay leaves
½ oregano leaves
½ basil leaves
½ Tarragon leaves
One teaspoon of dried thyme leaves
Salt and freshly ground black pepper to taste
1/4 cup finely chopped parsley

Four quarts of shrimp stock
½ pound smoked sausage
½ pound smoked ham
Four blue crabs
Two dozen oysters
1/2 pound hot sausage
One pound peeled and deveined shrimp
½ pound chicken necks
One table spoon file'

Place all ingredients except shrimp, oysters, onions and crab in large gumbo pot, over medium heat. Cover and let cook for thirty minutes. Heat oil in skillet and add flour to make roux. Stir constantly until brown. Lower heat, add onions and cook over low heat until onions caramelize. Pour mixture over ingredients in pot, let simmer. Slowly ladle in shrimp stock that has been strained, stirring constantly. Bring to a boil. Add shrimp, crab, oysters with liquid and cook for 45 minutes then add file' to taste.

Auntie Sharon scooped up the ingredients with her hands and began to place them in a tall, silver gumbo pot. A quiet sadness came over us at the realization that we were making our first pot of Gumbo without YaYa barking orders at us, on how the shrimp had to be deveined properly and how to make the roux, so that it didn't burn and wasn't filled with lumps of flour. That evening Slone conveniently named our first pot, *Gumbo YaYa.*

After the gumbo was on the stove simmering, I quietly went to my room and closed the door. I'd decided it was time to read YaYa's letters. I emptied my purse onto the bed. There were five letters in all. One thick manila envelope with my name on it, the others written in perfect script had Grandpa Jacquet, Lupanare, Roman and Gabriel's names on them.

I picked up the beautifully hand written letter, that was written on laced trimmed paper and began to read.

My dearest Jenna,

If you are reading this letter it means that I have crossed over the threshold of heaven successfully. I know that this may not be an easy time for you, but wipe your tears and thank God for the good times we shared. You are a very special girl, and I have no doubt that you will accomplish more in the future than you already have.

I know this because your Grandfather and I did our very best in raising you to be an outstanding woman. I know that we made some mistakes along the way and we were not perfect by any means, but we only did what we thought was best for you at the time. I realize that life has not always treated you fairly, and it was sometimes even brutal. But use those times as a stepping stone toward greatness. Don't allow the negative voices that sometimes whisper in your ear in the quiet of the night to detour you from the goodness of God. Stay focused on Him and you will always persevere.

Remember to treat people the way you would want to be treated. Whenever you encounter foolish people, never forget that common sense ain't common. Smile often and thank the Lord for His mercy and grace, 'cause He don't owe nobody nothing.

I want you to make an effort to allow yourself the privilege of being loved child. Don't allow the violation of your childhood to stagnate your progress in life; emotionally, spiritually, creatively or even sexually. Try your hardest not to let what happened to you hinder your ability to give love or receive it. You deserve to experience the kind of love that me and your Grandfather had. Your past is not your present and your future is fueled by the words you speak and by the choices you make. Choose right Cher. When in doubt, ask God for wisdom and He will show you the path you should take. When sadness tries to overtake you, sing. When people speak ill of you, pray for them, and when things are going well, keep yourself humble. Learn to love those who love you, don't spend your time running behind folks that don't care enough about you to love you with the same measure that you give. That's what the Bible means when it says not to cast your pearls upon swine, less they trample you under their feet. So don't wrestle with a pig 'cause you'll get dirty and the pig will enjoy it. People can only do to you what you allow them to.

Jenna, your brother Edmond was not so strong. Yes, he did die in a car crash, but it was no accident. He too had been molested as a young boy by an Italian priest. The older he got the more conflicted he became about his sexuality. He was often bombarded with nightmares having the encounters run through his mind over and over so many times, that it eventually broke his spirit. Everything that was once important to him somehow became lost in the fog of him not being able to stop replaying the horrible experience in his mind.

Your father hated the idea that his son was beginning to show signs that he might be a little confused about his sexuality. One night Bordeaux put a gun to Edmond's head after a drinking binge and told him that if he ever found out that he decided to switch teams, that he would blow his brains out all over the kitchen floor; he didn't care what had happened to him when he was a kid. He said that he needed to be a man about it and put it behind him.

But Edmond just didn't have the strength to fight any more, so he saved Bordeaux the trouble and pulled the trigger himself. There were all sorts of speculations about him having been murdered, but we all knew better. I am so sorry to have kept this from you all these years, but I just couldn't find courage to tell you.

There should have been several bank books, the deed to the house, birth certificates and several pictures of your brother Edmond in the safe. I had accounts set up for you, your brothers and Lupanare. I was, by the grace of God, persuasive enough to have made a deal with the Archdiocese, that if they did not compensate you for the pain and suffering you endured from Father Timothy and Sister Francis, I would go to the television, radio, newspapers and any other media outlet available, PTA meetings included, and tell all the parents at the school what they had done to you. I promised them that I would have traveled all ova the region and started a campaign against the Catholic Church, exposing their dirty little secrets if I had to. This was surely a dangerous task for a black woman back then.

Jenna, I cannot express to you the sorrow I have had all these years, knowing that we didn't protect you and Edmond better. It broke my heart to know that this happened in our family again, but this time I was going to make damn sure that you would never want for anything. If you manage this money properly, you will never have to worry about money for the rest of your life. Now, don't go buying no expensive shoes girl, you know them designer shoes probably only cost them a nickel and a dime to make in the first place. Make some good investments and have some fun along the way.

Wickedness was no match for us. It tried to take us down, but we prevailed by living a decent life. Make sure that you are remembered for good deeds and not divisive actions. Your reputation will follow you to the grave. Discipline your mouth when it comes to secrets. Proverbs seventeen and nine says, "He who covers a transgression seeks love; but he that repeats a matter separates friends." Everybody thinks Samson lost his strength because he lost his hair, but I declare to you Cher, he lost his strength because he couldn't keep a secret. So take your secrets and the secrets of your friends to the grave with you.

Travel...see the world, the exposure will make you a more well-rounded, more interesting person. Never take for granted those little blessings that seem insignificant. Those same things turn out to be big things when you grow older.

There should be a pair of diamond earrings that I'd gotten for you, for your wedding day. I'm sorry I won't be able to make it, but remember me when you put them on, and that YaYa loves you the most. Also a gift for the man that loved you into marrying him, a 'Claddagh' cross pendant is in the small satin bag. This cross was designed by Richard Joyce who went fishing one day and was captured by pirates the week he was to have been married. He was forced to join their crew and ended up as a slave where he worked, melting gold plundered by the pirates. His task was to make the gold into jewelry and he became a goldsmith. He made the 'Claddagh' so he would never forget the girl he loved. The heart is for love, the crown is for loyalty and the hands for friendship. My prayer is that whomever you choose, that you will have these three things in your marriage. For these are what makes for a successful lifetime together as one.

The Italian crystal rosary with four medals that represent the most important Basilicas in Rome, blessed by the Holy Father, is for Lennox. I wanted her to have something special from her great grandma YaYa to pass on to her children one day.

There are two tablets filled with three generations of Creole recipes. Learn to cook them well. Pass the recipes, stories and traditions of New Orleans on to my great grandchildren. So that no matter where y'all go, our heritage and the spirit of our culture will live on for generations to come.

Please keep an eye on your Grandfather for me. Make sure that he don't take to drinkin' now that I'm gone. And don't let Lupanare get out of control, or do anything stupid. Keep in contact with your brothers and always try to spend the holidays together. Those times make for great memories.

Now, I've got to go, the angels have come to escort me to a meeting with the King of Kings and the Lord of Lords, so don't make me late Cher.

Je t'aime Beaucoup!

YaYa

I whispered, 'I love you too YaYa', while I breathed in deeply as my heart fluttered like a *Plum Judy* butterfly about to take flight. I ran my fingers gingerly across the lace-bordered stationary. YaYa always had the right combination of words to sooth my soul. My thoughts of her love and kindness were inconveniently interrupted by the doorbell.

Slone opened the beveled glass door. Standing on the door step was a tall man with an olive complexion, dark hair, thin lips, and a distinctive mole on the left side of his nose. He had almond shaped chestnut eyes, surrounded by crow's feet and wore a salmon colored shirt, black tie and a taupe colored jacket. The other man had blonde hair and his skin looked as if it had been rolled in porcelain, his eyes like two bright colored marbles and his clothing was dark like onyx.

I faintly heard sounds of articulate conversation. I went into the bathroom and with a warm cloth, wiped the dried tears from my face. I walked down the hallway and stepped down into the sunken living room.

"Hello Miss Bordeaux, it's good to see you again." I shook hands with the man that had arrested my brother wrongfully and escorted him off the plane. It was Mr. Cheap suit, standing in my living room. I looked at him puzzled, wondering how he knew where I lived and why the hell was he bothering me again. I guess being a detective has its privileges. You can just show up two thousand miles away from home and take the liberty to crawl up anyone's behind at a moment's notice, without a courtesy call.

"This is Father Cameron Doucette. It seems we have a serial killer on the loose in New Orleans ma'am."

"And you flew all the way to Los Angeles to tell me this…why? What does any of this have to do with me, Detective Promise?"

"Please, call me Gage."

"No thank you. Just please explain to me why you are here, sir."

"Well, I thought you might be able to tell me the whereabouts of your brother Roman. When was the last time you were in contact with him? We need to speak with him immediately. We found a flask at the rectory sight, with his initials on it and Logan Honore's fiancée, Angela, was found dead on their living room sofa with

green bile dripping from her mouth, with the residue of a simi-
lar poisonous substance that Father Timothy allegedly died from
in her coffee mug. We also found a *very informative* suicide letter,
in Mr. Honore's bedroom. Our investigation revealed that there
could possibly have been…"

Suddenly, I felt light headed, my left eye started to pulsate, my
heart pounded so loudly that it drowned out Detective Promise's
rambling excuse for being in my living room. A flash of heat soared
across my chest; the last thing I remembered was that I'd grabbed
a hold of Slone's T shirt, trying to keep my composure. But the
dizziness would not take 'no' for an answer. Then the room went
black.

Bronze & Blue

As Roman drove his rented Lincoln Town car from the airport, he had dozens of ideas swirling around in his head about his visit. He passed St. Stephens Catholic Church, turned the corner on Napoleon Avenue onto Magazine Street and parked the car a few feet away from the park. He walked down the narrow sidewalk that led him to a well-preserved convent. He was dressed in a dark grey suit, an eggplant coloured tie and a crisp white shirt. He was clean shaven, bright eyed and well rested. He rang the doorbell and waited patiently for the door to open, hoping that the next recipient of his vengeance would answer. Roman smiled pleasantly at the middle-aged woman dressed in a cotton short-sleeved, cobalt blue blouse, a black knee length skirt and flat comfortable looking shoes.

"Hello young man, how can I help you?"

"Hello ma'am, my name is Logan Honore' and I'm looking for a nun by the name of Sister Loraine Francis. You see, she played an instrumental part in making me the man that I am today, and with the hurricane and all; I just wondered if she was okay. I'd love to speak with her if at all possible."

"Oh, by all means, let me see if I can find her for you, wait here for a moment."

Roman had become good at pretending. For his latest mission, he would pretend to be Logan and confront Sister Francis with the sins of her past.

"Hello, I'm Sister Francis, how can I help you? Sister Paulette informed me that a Logan Honore' was at the door, but I clearly remember that he was found dead, according to the news. So exactly, who might you really be sir?" Roman stood frozen, as his eyes locked with hers. He nervously lowered his eyes in shame. Not for pretending to be his dead friend, but because she had caught him in a lie. But the reality was that he had become so mentally and emotionally bankrupt since the passing of YaYa and Grandpa that his usual arsenal of full proof plans was empty.

"Excuse me, but I distinctly remember a young black boy with the most spectacular blues eyes that went to a school I taught at many years ago. His name was Roman Bordeaux. Would that be you?" Roman nodded his head yes.

"I would recognize those striking blue eyes next to that bronze colored skin anywhere. Please come in son and have a seat. I'll get us some coffee and dessert." Roman followed Sister Francis beyond the threshold of the enormous convent, into the foyer, then into a quaint living room area. The room was filled with the ugliest flowered upholstered furniture he'd ever seen.

"Have a seat young man, I'll be right back. Seems we have a lot to talk about and if I must say, it's long overdue. I knew one day you would come knocking at my door." Roman sat down, his buttocks were immediately swallowed up by the multicolored, flowered sofa that should have been re-stuffed or replaced more than a decade ago. His mind was racing as he tried to figure out what he should do next. He was in such a trance that he began to hear bells ringing. After a long irritating moment, he realized it was his cell phone.

"Roman, this is Gabriel. Where the hell are you man? Listen, Lupanare is in the hospital. They found her at Miss Dot's house with multiple stab wounds to the torso. I called California and Slone said you where already here in New Orleans. I need you to get over to Ochsner Hospital as soon as possible man. She's on life support and I'm not sure if she's gonna make it."

"I'm in the middle of something, but give me twenty minutes and I'll call you when I get on that side of town." Roman hung up the phone and stood to his feet. Sister Francis walked in carrying a silver tray with a pink porcelain tea pot with tea cups to match; a white antique plate trimmed in silver, that held blueberry scones and petifores with white icing. "I'm sorry Sister Francis; I just got a call that my mother has been hospitalized. We'll have to do this another time."

"I'm sorry, I pray she recovers quickly. Please let me walk you to the door." Sister Francis carefully placed her tray of sugary goodies on the coffee table. As they reached the door, Sister Francis gently placed her hand on Roman's shoulder and said, "I know the pain you've suffered over the years could not have been easy. Father Timothy was a brutal dysfunctional man with a lot of issues. I know he hurt you and manipulated you and so many others, including myself. But he's dead now and hopefully God will give us all the grace and strength to let the awful things he did, die with him. Move on with your life son, go find some happiness while you're still young."

She somehow had the uncanny ability to tap into the dark dismal place that Roman had kept himself locked in for eons. Salty tears ran down his bronze cheeks, seeped through his white shirt and onto his chest. They were safely absorbed by his broken heart, slowly mending the shattered pieces back together. Sister Francis took hold of his hand and held it tightly as she wept quietly along with him.

Roman tried to compose himself as he looked into the eyes of a woman that he'd thought was an enemy, only to realize that she had been a victim too. He wiped the tears from his face, never taking his eyes from hers while squeezing Sister Francis' hand; he gave her a slight smile, then turned and walked away as a leering glare of deceit, darted wickedly across his sapphire eyes.

TO BE CONTINUED